Praise for *Ye.*

MW00709914

"A lovely, intelligent novel. *Yellow Sky, Emerald Sea* possesses timeless and universal appeal and will give pleasure to any reader who appreciates good literature." -Mark Spencer, Author of *Ghost Walking* and winner of the Omaha Prize for the Novel

Also by Sally Ann Sims

Halt at X: A North of Boston Novel

Publisher: Sally Ann Sims

www.sallyannsims.com

Yellow Sky, Emerald Sea

Sally Ann Sims

Dedication

To all those taken by hurricanes.

"Time stalls in pockets and backwaters, ticks in seconds and epochs, sweeps past us with indifference, pulls us into its irresistible current, hooks back on itself, sucks us through portals that connect all points of time with eternity, spills on."

—Oden Vacca to Jack West

PART 1

Wednesday, September 21, 1938
23 Atlantic Drive, Ponkipaug, Rhode Island

Albert Boothroyd found his fiancée at 6:45 pm. Running toward the demolished beach house over the sandy lawn, he'd stopped abruptly when he saw her arm. It extended beyond a piece of wall still attached to a corner of the roof. Diana Coggeshall's body lay face down, head pointing in the direction of the receding tide.

His grandmother's sapphire-and-diamond engagement ring caught the evening sunlight. He'd slipped it onto her hand three weeks ago as they strolled Ponki Beach under hazy August stars.

He knelt next to Diana's body. Her right wrist was twisted and jammed under a board. After tossing the board aside, he gently turned Diana's limp body over to rest on her back. The gash across her jugular appalled him, the sight of it a fresh stab to his heart.

Albert shut his eyes. Three hours earlier, thousands of windows were shattering all along the Weekapaug Coast. *Like hurled axes just missing my head*, Albert thought. That wind and flying glass forced him to stop, duck, and dash three times before he reached his Ford truck. But then he had to retreat to the boatyard office. His windshield was cracked like two massive spider webs, and the fourth wave that breached the seawall poured over the hood.

As he struggled across the parking lot in waist-high water, Albert heard what sounded like the father-of-wind tearing the sky apart. He'd just grabbed the stair railing as the last wave topped out at the base of his neck. The worst combination possible, he realized, the highest high tide of the year magnifying the height of tidal surge.

Now, Albert opened his eyes and peered across the road. The blow had refinished the few remaining white houses in a green churn of masticated maple and elm leaves. All along Atlantic Avenue smashed boats, slack power lines, crevassed pavement, unhinged doors, unmatched shoes, shards of dishes, splintered lobster pots, and heaps of battered lumber lay entangled in mounds of debris. Turning away from the road, he peered southwest toward Ponkipaug Point. Unlike the mounded wreckage of Atlantic Avenue, the point was stripped clean of houses, docks, and dunes.

Albert's gaze returned to Diana, to the lavender dress she loved to wear for him. *She must have been so cold, so scared*, he thought. Only 22. Did her God help Diana at the end? The one she offered to him for solace after his mother's death last March? Despite her condition and against all hope, he pressed his ear to her chest and listened for a heartbeat. All he heard was the edge of the ocean. It was now just three inches high, gently scuttling pebbles and shells a couple dozen yards away. Suddenly, the thumping outboard motor of his own racing heart startled Albert. As if *anything* could outpace the events of this unimaginable afternoon.

Albert gently removed the engagement ring from Diana's swelling finger. It was tight. Then he eased the slim expansion watch from her wrist and stared into its face. 4:29. He slipped them into the pocket of his rain slicker.

Albert slumped forward, as if boneless, onto Diana's chest. After a time—*minutes, hours?*—cold, thick-fingered hands on his shoulders gently pulled Albert onto his feet. They were collecting people at the high school, now serving as a morgue, a voice said. *Yes*, Albert thought. He would bring Diana there. Somehow it gave him heart to think there was something to do next.

CHAPTER 1

The gnarliest bank of clouds Vieve Clough Beale had seen in years consolidated over Ponkipaug Village. The tumble of roiling violet-black puffery began rumbling its displeasure as she hurried toward the Salt Breeze House main entrance.

It's too warm for April, Vieve thought, admiring the cloudscape's lovely purple hue despite its threatening overtures. Bracing herself against a glacial blast of air conditioning, she pulled open the heavy oak door inlaid with a stained-glass clamshell design. Her phone burbled from inside her cross-body bag. Pulling it out and glancing at the caller ID, Vieve frowned. *Picard*—the portrait client turned pest and potential stalker. She pushed away the thought of him and headed toward the grand dining room.

The empty table surprised her. Her uncle was never late to their dinners. In fact, Carl always beat her to their reserved table with its miniature cityscape of crystal glassware, porcelain china, and heavy silver on thick navy linen. He'd be eager with their two fresh drinks to toast the occasion. Vieve was going to explain why that wouldn't work this time.

Well, Vieve *could* toast with virgin iced tea or one of those fancy lemonade-based mocktails they offered, an option that pinged her with longing for a lovely glass of something white and dry. She was one month totally sober and, well, she hadn't been *that* bad with the booze *really*, just too many wine-smeared evenings alone after Kyle died. But, of course, the canoeing accident that claimed her husband was eight years ago now.

Vieve and her uncle made a point of visiting at least once a season. At his insistence, the meeting place was invariably the most extravagant hotel and restaurant in the state outside of Newport. A cozy, boozy multi-hour dinner packed with the telling of new and old exploits. Carl Roger Beale had made a few million dollars in his forties and fifties in Providence for patenting a process of combining crystals and faux gems to resemble a modern curvy approach to Zuni inlay and then went on to do dazzling things with rare sea glass. He was enjoying those millions in "retirement" in Ponkipaug Village, a low-key, but moneyed, beach town just east of the Connecticut border.

Vieve stood next to the head waiter, Evan Button, as they peered through the expansive window overlooking the private beach with the Atlantic Ocean beyond. Balding and disgruntled, Evan hadn't seen Carl that afternoon and was no doubt mourning the loss of the largest tip of the week. Vieve, looking south toward the two-mile-long sand arm of Ponkipaug Point, noticed what looked like a raven hang-gliding inshore over the bay. It landed on a garbage can by the new bathing cabanas, letting out a *croank*—asserting that it wasn't, in fact, an overgrown crow. *Ravens in Rhode Island?*

She was sure ravens weren't the only thing that had changed in this town since childhood summer stays with her uncle and aunt and her sister Joss. For one thing, Carl had announced over the phone last week that he'd taken in boarders. He'd brought the subject up casually as if he just decided to change out the rugs and window treatments.

On these dinner-evening days with Vieve, Carl usually spent a chunk of the afternoon on the hotel's private beach flattering the old moneyed ladies—fit from grass-court tennis and ocean swimming—who'd been his clients for years. Or else he'd float his small yacht out on the salt pond for cocktails with a few friends. He'd developed this routine in the wake of Bonnie's death a year and a half ago after her long decline, but Vieve knew none of those women could take Bonnie's place.

Twenty minutes on, Vieve called Carl's phone but it flipped immediately into voice mail. Although that was not unusual, Vieve felt queasy. She texted *Where r u?* with little hope of an answer. Carl was not a big texter.

After a half hour, Vieve returned to her small sport utility vehicle parked in the shade with the windows cracked. Jack West, napping in the passenger seat, roused himself at her approach. The adolescent terricr mix bounded over to the driver side door. With paws on the window edge, he barked his hearty welcome as if she'd been away for four days instead of a half hour. Her prior dog companion, an elderly and dignified Gordon Setter named Gainsby, after the venerable painter Gainsborough, died of cancer the day after Thanksgiving last year. Vieve wasn't quite sure why this particular bundle of high-decibel excitement had come into her life to take his place. But somehow, there he was one day. A missing family member she didn't know she had until a happy coincidence united them.

Vieve accepted Jack West's wet affections, started the car, and shifted into reverse. Heading toward Carl's house took them north across the rocky headland on which perched the Salt Breeze House, its understated name belying its exclusivity, and, farther out, the Coast Guard station and lighthouse. They passed the down-to-earth eatery JohnnyCakes and the delightful Flying Horse Carousel. A scant two miles later, Vieve pulled to a stop in front of Carl's storage shed.

A remnant from the property's pre-renovation days, the shed was the semi-secret location of the spare house key, a decades-old can once containing crushed tomatoes. He'd started leaving secret messages and bits of treasure maps for Vieve there as a lark when she was five. She opened the unlocked door and grabbed the tomato can with the faded label. What she found underneath made her even more queasy than the fact of Carl's unanswered phone. A note.

You always loved this pile of boards at Ponki Point. Now it's a renovated pile of boards freshly painted. You'll take better care of the place than me, Vieve. -C

A suicide note masquerading as a bequest?

As Vieve stepped out of the shed, dazed, the storm let loose. Registering the slaps of cold fat raindrops on her forehead and cheeks, she dashed to the latticework porch. A briny gust of wind shoved her into the cobalt turquoise front door of 17 Salt Pond Drive. It always smelled stronger at day's end, she remembered. The sea. She flashed on a girl running down a sandy beach, just eluding a taller boy holding, at arm's length, a person-long section of cold, slimy seaweed.

Vieve shifted her weight onto her heels and shoved Carl's note into her right hip pocket. The rain pelted her back and filled the air with its signature scent of sea iodine and shell chalk. The pop-up spring thunderstorm was now in full throttle. Lightning forked the sky over Fort Devlin. Another lightning bolt, closer, flashed above and behind her, and then, almost simultaneously, thunder boomed from the direction of the cabanas. She felt the power of the strike along some ancient nerve line in her spine.

It would be just like her father's younger brother to fake his death to get out of some kind of jam or play a practical joke. Joke on whom though? Was mourning called for, or reprimanding? Did he just take off for Bermuda?

A bark from the car, a more immediate reprimand.

No, Carl couldn't be gone really. Should she just let herself in?

Jack West let out two sharp barks. Vieve slammed the door with her right palm. "Shit, Carl! Where *are* you?"

Tears fell, mixing with the salty rainwater on her face. Of course, Carl might just now step around the corner laughing that full-bellied laugh that ended in a wheeze. Then they could go in, order takeout fried clams—forget the pretentious restaurant!—and catch up. She smiled, through rain and tears, long curly wisps of strawberry-blonde hair plastered to her forehead and cheeks.

Three more barks, louder, now with a growling prelude.

"I know! I'm coming! Let's get in, get dry. Both of us. Dish of kibble. Glass of wine," she added under her breath. "No. No! No glass of wine! You're not doing that now. Remember?"

Vieve opened the passenger side door and scooped up Jack West. He let out one more bark, more of excitement than irritation, then licked her cheek when she leaned over him, pulsing with puppy love. Jack Russell mother and West Highland White father was her best guess. A double-trouble terrier stray.

"We're too late, Jack West. He's gone.... No! He can't be!"

The rain came down as if poured from a giant bucket. Vieve scooted into the car beside her dog. As she watched the water fall, memories of summers at Ponkipaug Point pulled her to the past—long beach days, dodging waves with Joss and the other summer kids, body surfing lessons from Uncle Carl, narrow wooden dressing stalls painted light blue, lobster rolls, sunburned shoulders and thighs, sand in bathing suit bottoms, and happy exhaustion at day's end.

When the rain let up a mite, Vieve sprang from the car, the terrier tucked under her arm like a large clutch purse, and hurried back to the porch where she set him down. Jack West cocked his head and inspected Vieve's face. He stepped up on the door rim to be let in, looking as confident as if he owned the place although this was his first visit. When Vieve opened the door Jack West entered, shook his compact body front to back, barked once as if calling "Hello?," and then bounded toward a stairway where a light had just popped on. She smelled...something, *brownies? Mud? Fish baking and rubber boots?*

Seconds later, a man descended the stairs. *Early thirties, thirty-four?* Vieve wondered. Wavy, deep brown hair, too thin, like addicted-to-something thin, closely clipped beard. Eyes that stopped Vieve, distracting her from noticing at first the tiny, brightly colored particles of something in his hair. But those eyes. They were simultaneously soft and penetrating.

"You must be Vieve Beale," he said, reaching down to stroke Jack West, whose right front paw pressed insistently on Marley's sneaker. "Carl said you were visiting this weekend."

After the man had straightened up, Jack West looked up at his face, a long way up. *The man must be six-two*, Vieve thought. She still couldn't quite accept the reality of Carl taking in boarders.

"I'm Marley Kinnell," he said. As the terrier's paw continued to press on his left shoe, Marley looked down. Jack West's glossy black eyes and wet nose gleamed in his pure white face. One ear black and the tip of his tail caramel, and everything in between bright white coated.

"An earnest young pup," Marley said, smiling, which greatly lessened the severe impression lent by his height and dark, clipped beard.

"This is Jack West," Vieve said, smiling at her canine buddy.

"That's what I like," Marley replied. "A dog with a surname." He reached way down to scratch behind Jack West's ears.

"Join me for a drink? Tea? Or something more brutal? Whiskey? To match the weather?" Marley added, arching his eyebrows.

"Does *anyone* know where my uncle is?" Vieve blurted out. "He was supposed to meet me at the Salt Breeze at five."

"Come in and sit down. You too, ah, Mr. West."

Marley pivoted left and led them through the living room in the corner of which was a bouzouki on a stand—"my housemate's," Marley said in passing, "everyone asks"—and on into a newly remodeled kitchen, done in peach and sage. When he held up a tea kettle, she said crisply, "Coffee please," with the steely resolve of new sobriety.

Vieve sat on an island counter stool, her five-two frame leaving her legs dangling above the floor. There was a pan of brownies on the counter, chocked with miniature islands of nuts.

"Take your coat off. Have one of Asia's famous hazelnut brownies. Make yourself at home."

"Ironic, given the note."

"Note?" Marley stood still, holding a scoop poised above the coffee canister.

"Suicide note. Leaving me the house."

She handed it to him. "In the spot where he keeps the spare key."

Marley scanned the note quickly and set it back down on the counter. He turned his back and filled the kettle with water from the filtered tap. Vieve noticed the colored particles in Marley's curls. Teeny-tiny balls—dots really—of ultramarine blue, permanent light green, cadmium yellow only much brighter, an orange she wasn't familiar with, and she knew oil pigments.

"Suicide? That's bull. Why would he do that?" Marley put the kettle on the gas burner and lit it. "He had just about everything to live for. No way that's a suicide note."

"How can you be sure?"

"He'll be back. I just saw him a few hours ago. He mentioned you were coming tonight. 'Meet-the-boarders night,' he joked, as if we were in-laws." Marley chuckled.

Vieve did not smile. "It's just not like him. He always calls when he's late. Maybe if he's done something...." Her voice caught, so she took a breath and swiped wet hair off her face to compose herself. She hiccupped. She would not lose it in front of this Marley Kinnell, *whoever the hell he is.*

They stared at each other for a good minute. Marley looked away, out the window at the rain crossing the lawn in blowing sheets. He opened a drawer and pulled out a tea towel with an embroidered Celtic harp on it and handed to her. She wiped a bit of rainwater off her cheek and hair. Marley looked at her with an expression she couldn't decipher.

"What did you mean when you said he had *just about* everything to live for?"

"Nothing exactly, but everyone's got issues," Marley said, pouring himself a whiskey and tending to the whistling kettle. "But not suicide, not Carl." After a pause, he continued. "But...he may want to break up with Deena, the latest girlfriend. Start a business in Bermuda under a different name. A bit bored he is, I think."

Or he can't stand Bonnie being gone, thought Vieve. "So why not just call me up, say he's moving to Bermuda and is giving me the house?"

Vieve looked at Marley's glass for a long beat. *The lovely burnt umber caramel hue and insouciant way it would burn down your throat....* Although wine is—*was!*—her drink of choice, she did—*used to!*—enjoy the occasional whiskey neat with her uncle, especially in his high-flown jewelry empire days.

"Want one? Carl's best," Marley said, holding the tumbler up, wiggling it a bit. "Night like this—" A crash of lightning in the backyard made them both jump and then clutch the counter to steady themselves. Jack West let out a volley of insults at the storm. *Hurts my ears!*

"No thanks. Don't drink." Vieve pulled her gaze away from the glass. She passed a hand over Jack West's back, and he settled back in at the base of the bar stool.

"Really," she added, more to leave her options open if it all got unbearable. "More of a wine person. Was."

Vieve's arm rested on the counter, her left hand still clutching her phone. She swiveled her watch upright on her wrist, a slender timepiece set with aqua sea glass in an elegant net of sterling silver that Carl designed and presented to her when she turned eighteen. "With the anti-littering laws we've got now," Carl told her after she first fastened it around her wrist, "sea glass, the really good stuff, is getting a tad pricey. Hold onto it!" *As if he had to add that*, Vieve thought. She would treasure this gift from her closest uncle forever.

Marley smiled at the continually qualified answer. "Alcohol issue, eh?"

Vieve looked down at Jack West, hesitated a few seconds, and then wiped his wet coat with the fine Irish linen tea towel in retaliation.

"Sorry. None of my business." He moved the whiskey bottle back to a wall cabinet.

Vieve resisted the urge to elaborate on her drinking, her flimsy solace after Kyle's death. Marley peered into the whiskey glass. "Yes, powerful stuff. Don't mess with it." He took a seat next to her at the end of the counter.

"My guess is Carl just took off on some unplanned business errand. He does that. More than likely he got stuck in that insane I95 traffic coming back from Providence. I've had my share of that on Friday nights."

"It just doesn't feel right. It's not like him not to let me know. I'm calling the Ponkipaug police. They can at least look out for his car."

She searched the internet for the police number, called, and explained what happened. Dash Bliven, the officer on duty, knew Carl, thought Vieve was overreacting given the content of the note, but would have a patrol officer look for his car. It was too early to file a missing-person report. Bliven also said he would check airlines at Providence, Boston, and Hartford to see whether he'd flown recently. Vieve reported this news back to Marley.

"Well, if it makes you feel better, then great." Marley looked over at Vieve's wrist as she lowered her phone to the counter. Jack West settled again after the last thunder crash, but Vieve noticed when she glanced down at him that he seemed to be vibrating.

"You know," Marley said, as if the thought had just occurred to him, "Carl could be signaling something to you about who he wants this house to go to *eventually*. There are at least three people I know with their eyes on the place. Cool watch by the way."

"Thanks. A Beale original," Vieve said, examining Marley's head close up as he peered at her watch. "What are those particles in your hair?"

"Acrylic if they're colored," Marley said, looking back up into her face. "I'm an artist. The *painter* type of artist." He smiled.

Vieve laughed. "So am I! I do portrait commissions in oil. People mostly. Rich people with their horses. Children and dogs for folks of more regular means."

"Ahhh. Yes. So Carl said." Marley took a sip of whiskey, an enigmatic smile on his lips after he swallowed. Vieve considered the implications of Marley's expression. *Diplomatic, patronizing, superior, twisted envy?*

"What do you paint?" Vieve asked, almost a verbal jab.

Marley looked at Vieve for another long minute. She felt as if he could see right into her soul. Vieve met his gaze firmly, raising her chin.

She must have passed some test. "I'll show you," he said.

Marley downed his whiskey dregs and headed for the stairs. Vieve slid off the stool and Jack West bounded forward, his open-mouthed face giving the impression of a dog smile.

"Senate! Are you serious?" David Hallowell said. "*U.S.* Senate?!"

Richard smiled. It sounded sweet. *U.S. Senate. Senator Coggeshall.*

"Don't you think you ought to try for mayor first?" David said, draining his rocks glass of bourbon. He peered down onto the marina dock from the enclosed terrace that flanked his second-floor office on two sides. There'd been a surge in slip rentals this year, and the marina bustled with activity on Friday nights. Smiling, he turned toward Richard, leaned against the window sill, and crossed his arms over his chest.

"Not now," Richard answered. "Now that Bear Hill's doing well, and we're expanding operations at the quarry. Two megacontracts just inked. I've got enough clout to go for something *much* bigger."

Richard paused to toss back his second bourbon. "Guinta and Coburn have promised to open doors and send me donors. We see eye to eye on a lot of things. Like bringing more business to the western side of the state."

"Go slow with Guinta. He's gone slippery in the past."

"He understands his priorities now," Richard said. "All those distractions are over."

"I find that hard to believe," David said, chuckling.

"Then why'd you go and get me on the quarry board if you thought Guinta wasn't solid?" Richard smiled again, signaling his lack of concern.

"Well, he seemed really serious about the quarry at the get-go. Anyway, it was just a few stray perks and that thing with his assistant. God, I hope you're right!" David sat down and leaned back in his swivel chair, planting his three-toned Docksiders on his massive oak desk.

"He did bring in those contracts before he got elected," Richard said, glancing through the window at the bay. "That little thunderburst cleared out nicely."

"So you think Mason will take over at Bear Hill? I thought he was headed to Boston."

"Not till August. I hope Mason will take over after college." Richard frowned. His son Mason hardly talked to him these days. "If not, I'll hire someone. I can run Bear Hill during the campaign if I have to. Tilly could run it too, but—"

Someone knocked on the office door. "It's open," David yelled.

Kent Hallowell entered. A good forgery of his father, 30 years younger, slightly narrower face but same cleft chin, sunburned cheeks, and unruly hair.

"Dad, one of the rowboats is gone." Kent flipped his long bangs off his slate blue eyes. "Nobody rents that thing."

Probably gets any of the high school girls he wants, Richard thought.

David frowned. "Which one?"

"One behind the engine shop."

"That piece of crap? Who would bother?"

Kent shrugged.

"You don't think Oden would—"

"No, Dad. He wouldn't." Kent glared at this father and then left, slamming the door.

"Touchy," said Richard.

"That thing barely floats," said David. "Who would—"

"Let's head over to Ponki Beach and scope the spot. We can get chowda at JohnnyCakes on the way back."

"I thought you were banned from the place?" David teased.

Richard smiled. "If she's still holding a grudge about the liquor license, I'll send you in for takeout. Nina's got the best damn chowda around here."

They took Richard's sedan over to Ponkipaug Point and parked in the cabana parking lot. Following the path along the narrow beach on the western side of the peninsula, Richard said, "Got a doozy of a sunset building." The sun melted tangerine on the sooty blue horizon.

David ignored the sunset and scanned the cobble beach ahead of them where it transitioned into low dunes. "Look, even if you do get to be Senator, you can't make it so you can build out here. So what did you have in mind?"

"There's got to be something we can do out here with our

parcels," Richard said. "There's the history of the fort and that hurricane. Sunset evenings, with food service? Hell, this beach lost a whole mile to the storm and forty-four houses. I'm sure we can whip up the historical angle with the commemoration coming up."

David gazed over Little Narragansett Bay. "Nothing's going up out here. It's all ancient history; folks just want to get on with things. Rebuild closer to where there's parking. Besides, the conservancy people will block you every step of the way if you try to do anything constructive out here."

Not if we can tie it into…. Oh, jeeez, look what the cat dragged in?!"

A man sporting a tawny-gray beard approached them down a poison-ivy-lined trail leading out of the dunes a few yards away. Oden Vacca reminded Richard of an Appalachian trapper from the 1800s and was just as out of place in Ponkipaug Village. Wearing a faded yellow tee shirt, with a tear below the front pocket, and even older beige cargo pants, he had commandeered a three-foot-long piece of driftwood for a walking stick. Around his neck hung a pair of Nikon binoculars. The wind shifted to the east, and Richard caught a blast of Oden's rank and salty body odor, with an overlay of rum.

"You missin' a rowboat?" Oden asked David, snubbing eye contact with Richard.

"I might be," said David. "How'd you know?"

Oden pointed to the southwest. "There," he said. "Headed toward Fisher's. Had a bead on it for a half hour now. No crew."

"Really?" David said, grabbing for the binoculars. "How could it row itself?" Oden unhooked the binoculars from around his neck and handed them to David.

"Maybe you rowed it," Richard said. He wouldn't put it past Oden to try to get ransom for an ancient rowboat.

"Where'd you say? I don't see it," David said, scanning the mouth of Little Narragansett Bay.

"Between Fisher's and Wiscasissett." Oden pointed between the two islands. Fisher's was large, but Wiscassisett couldn't be seen without the binoculars.

"I don't see anything," David said. "Like I said, it's a piece of crap. Glad to have it off my hands."

"But how did it leave your marina?" Oden asked. "Aren't you curious?"

"He would be if there was actually a rowboat out there," Richard interjected.

Oden glared at Richard and stepped toward him. "This is between him and me."

Richard took a few steps back. Oden's odor was acrid, and there was nothing to be gained from riling him up. At best, Oden would regale them with a fantastical prediction or a veiled threat and they could go about the rest of their evening. At worst, fists would fly. Richard wasn't going to get pulled in this time. He pondered telling Bliven to haul Oden in for trespassing again but decided to let things lie.

"There's something needs settling here," Oden said, looking between the two men. Then he disappeared down the trail, letting out a low whistle.

"Well," said David, "we escaped without any blows or accusations."

"And just as well since he's hit the rum again," Richard said. "Makes it easier to see phantom rowboats."

David nodded. They both laughed.

Richard said, "We're going to have to clear him out if we're going to do anything out here with tourists."

Oden watched Richard and David from the top of the nearest dune. He let out another whistle and scanned the sky to the north. Thirty seconds later, a raven landed on the osprey-nesting platform a few dozen yards from the fort. Oden scanned the ocean with the binoculars and nodded. "It's out there!" he yelled to the two men, pointing southwest.

"Agreed," said David. "He needs to go. Didn't you get him off the beach for a few months last year?"

"Yeah, before Carl Beale and Gordon Boothroyd butted in," Richard said. "We're not going to let them ruin this point project, whatever we decide to do." Frowning, he slapped at an insect on his neck. Behind Richard, the sky swirled with flaming orange and cobalt purple.

"Don't let it get to you, Bud," David said. He slapped Richard on the shoulder. "Hey, let's head back. The chowda's on me!"

CHAPTER 2

Marley led Vieve and Jack West up a staircase that turned twice and then through a door on the left when they reached the third-floor landing. The studio spanned a good two-thirds of the entire top floor of the house, except for whatever was behind that far door. The east-west light exposure was good, but the work space didn't get north light, Vieve noted, comparing it to her own studio.

Jack West peered under a taboret and sniffed his way around the room. The rain stopped, and Vieve could hear dripping in the eaves.

Leaning against the studio walls on three sides were wooden panels—four-by-four-foot square—thick with multicolored striations, hills, and valleys of three-dimensional color. Braided strands of texture. Veins and highlights of sharp contrasting color. Each playing off a color structure of triads or tetrads, or so Vieve thought that was how they were structured on first viewing.

"Oh, abstracts," Vieve said, walking toward a predominantly blue panel. She wasn't able to totally cover the tone in her voice that implied, *Oh, second-class art by people who can't master perspective.*

She looked up from the panel, meeting Marley's gaze. He raised his eyebrows again. *Dancing hieroglyphs*, Vieve thought. And just as indecipherable.

Vieve touched the panel's smoothly braided surface. It felt thick and cool. Surface fascination and mysterious depth. Like Marley's eyes, copper-brown, she'd just noticed, like Carl's dark whiskey, with flecks of pale jade green. She shook away the thought.

She searched Marley's face, with a question not articulated. "These are...." Vieve hesitated and inspected another one, a symphonized braided wall-knot of orange, gold, and green, with shards of metallic blue-violet. Despite her first thought that he would be indifferent to the opinion of a commercially successful portrait artist, Marley watched her face intently, waiting for a reaction.

"Compelling," Vieve proclaimed, letting out her breath. *Irritating,* she thought, as if she had wanted them to be hokey but was instead presented with something that shifted her whole concept of art. A swift kick to her solar plexus. Jolting a deep-seated certitude that she traced back to her great-to-the-sixth grandmother Mary Beale, a distinguished portrait painter in Devonshire, England. The gut-felt truth that portraiture was her calling and that her current dissatisfaction with her work was only because of her overbearing clients' demands and egos. Especially Picard, the tech company CEO who expected a relationship to accompany his portrait.

Vieve's hands, she'd made fists evidently, rested on her waist. She leaned forward toward another predominantly silvery one and squinted. *How did he do this? These are not brush strokes!—*

"They sell, actually," Marley said, obviously enjoying himself, leaning one hip against the wooden taboret. "And, just recently, for quite a bit." He held his body loosely, but with care. "After Nina hung a few on the walls at JohnnyCakes."

Another man entered the studio, saying to Marley, "Gordon's out on his 'copter with the Bassets—"

Marley interrupted. "Jud Cahoone, this is Vieve Beale, Carl's niece. Now you've met all the housemates except Asia."

"The brownie maker?" Vieve asked.

"Marley's highly intelligent daughter and upcoming star of my next production," Jud answered. Marley rolled his eyes.

Jud bowed slightly. "Pleasure to meet you. Carl talks of

you...quite a bit."

Jud was bearlike compared to Marley, who resembled a very tall and underfed soccer player. Jud's sun-faded red hair glinted with bits of silver, his eyes a light blue-green, his fleshy face sported a graying chin beard.

Vieve asked, "Have you seen him today? He's gone missing."

Jud peered straight into Vieve's eyes. "Missing? How can you know? He's always off here...there." He waved a hand in the direction of the ocean.

"He left a note. Could be a suicide note," Vieve said. She pulled the folded note, still damp, out of her pocket and handed it to Jud.

Jud scanned it and then snorted. "With everything Carl had on, why would he do the deed? He's been talking about relaunching his jewelry empire in Hamilton to sell a new line on the shopping channels in the US and UK. And then, of course, there is beguiling Beryl to lure him away from the, eh, fair and devoted Deanna Vaughan."

"Hold it!" interrupted Vieve. "Slow down! Who's Beryl? Who are the Bassets? And why fake a death in order to relocate to Bermuda?"

"Debts, secrets?" Jud said, teasing. "Deceptions? The possibilities are fascinating." He smiled wide, enjoying himself and irritating Marley, who shook his head in disapproval. "Frankly, I think he's just trying to give Deena the brushoff."

"Bullshit," said Marley. "Jud's full of crap eighty percent of the time, Vieve. You should be aware of that. In fact, you'll be tempted to smack him fifteen times a day once you get to know him. Look, we don't know anything yet about where Carl went. He could have gone over to Fisher's Island again. He and Gordon are like kids in a candy shop about finding some moldering U-boat in Block Island Sound. A big-kid treasure hunt. Harmless fun for rich boys."

Vieve turned to Jud. "What's this about a 'copter and the Bassets? Are they a couple?"

"Gordon Boothroyd is famous for his three Basset hounds, left to him as puppies from his former superior officer and devoted friend who died in a car crash," Jud said. "They were in the Navy together, in Tetlow's unit, another local. Gordon also flies a helicopter in his quest to locate an alleged sunken German U-boat from World War Two. Occasionally Carl joins him in these amusing jaunts, which are often spur-of-the-moment and, I think, more like an excuse to pal and poke around while appearing to have a noble goal."

Vieve was beginning to wonder about everything she didn't know about her uncle's life. "Could that be where Carl is now?'"

Marley shrugged.

"I don't know," said Jud. "Gordon headed out before the storm broke. I saw him over at the marina earlier at about four."

"How did you all end up living with Carl?" She looked at the two men in turn. They seemed like polar opposites.

Marley leaned back against the taboret and said, "Carl got lonely after Bonnie died. You know that, I'm sure. He decided to freshen the place up—i.e., major renovation—and take in tenants for company. Artsy tenants, it seems. Jud's attempting to commit regional theatre, and you see what I do. I also adjunct at Rhode Island School of Design."

Jud looked at Marely's face. Marley shook his head almost imperceptibly.

"Why don't you two head over to JohnnyCakes for dinner? Marley can fill you in about all the latest skeletons in our closet here at Ponki Village. You know a bit about Gordon, but there's always Richard Coggeshall's obsessions, the haunted fort, and Oden." Jud chuckled. "He's been acting weird lately."

"How can you tell?" Marley said, smiling.

Vieve looked down at Jack West, his tilted head gazing up at Jud.

"They will love your little friend at 'Cakes." Jud smiled broadly, tipped an imaginary hat at the attentive terrier, and sauntered out of the studio.

"I could do nicely without seeing Richard Coggeshall," Vieve said after Jud left. Marley looked expectantly at Vieve but she didn't elaborate. She turned away to examine another one of Marley's panels.

"Tell me why at dinner," Marley said. "And I'll fill you in on all the rest."

Vieve and Marley walked down Salt Pond Drive to the main tourist drag and turned left along the row of shops, Jack West keeping up at a trot. The Atlantic Avenue shops offered lemonade, sun catchers, sunglasses, sunscreen, fudge, $45 tee shirts, hand-dipped ice cream, and fried clams.

"They're ready for summer," Marley said. "Who could possibly enjoy this town without sun catchers and fudge?"

JohnnyCakes was situated at the east end of the clapboard row next to the famous Flying Horse Carousel. The restaurant was formerly two shops—an indie bookstore and a fried clam shack—before the current owners bought it, eliminated the wall, and transformed it into the funky local eatery with the bag of Johnny Cake meal painted on the front door. The next shop over was Candy Crush—a new candy shop where Vieve's niece Lucie had secured a summer job a couple weeks ago.

The restaurant's interior was yellow, a soft cadmium yellow light, Vieve noted silently. There were still set-in bookshelves and reading nooks that fit one small table for two, lending the place an intimate charm. Nina Pucci, one of the owners, greeted them enthusiastically. Heads turned to the pair and the dog.

"Nina, this is Carl's niece, Vieve. An artist too," Marley said.

"Hello," Vieve said. "And meet Jack West. Is he ok in here?"

Jack West sat with tilted head, gazing up into Nina's face. Nina was dressed in a deep-purple pintuck shirt and gray linen slacks and wore small silver seahorse earrings. She returned Jack West's inquiring glance with one of her own. Her hazel eyes sparkled with delight.

"He certainly is ok," Nina said. "Anyone allergic?" she turned and asked the room. The response was a four-year-old girl with a head of tumbling black curls who broke free of her table. She ran over to grab Jack West's tail, but she didn't pull it. Two 7-year-old twin boys advanced. Jack West stood tall, accepting all forms of admiration. His tail gyrated like a pinwheel in the breeze after the girl let it go.

Vieve gently extracted Jack West from his newly formed fan club, and Nina led them to a front corner booth with a view of the carousel. She handed them menus.

"This place is great," Vieve said. "I don't know why Carl and I don't meet here for dinner."

"Yes! Best place to eat within fifty miles. Richard tried to buy this place too, stirring up trouble to get the liquor license revoked," Marley said, accompanied by a wry smile.

Vieve looked into Marley's eyes. She felt herself being pulled toward a strong force, the very edge of the wake of a train, the hem of a riptide, the teasing slaps of a still-far-off tempest, a puff of warm wind—the seed of a hurricane—on the desert sands, off the Cape Verde Islands, east of the Atlantic hurricane alley. If she didn't watch herself, she could fall for this young guy, what seventeen, twenty years younger? That was not the plan. *Or is it pure lust?* She smiled.

"Why would he want to do that?" Vieve asked, releasing eye contact reluctantly and glancing at the menu, not registering any of the words on the laminated page.

"Why? Well, ostensibly, someone got drunk here, broke a windshield out front, and then started a fight out on Ponki Beach during which two people had their faces smashed and ribs broken.

Shit like that just doesn't happen that often in this town," Marley said. He looked out onto the street, now busy with families returning from the beach and from fishing off the docks.

Vieve stole another glance at him. No doubt a beautiful man, no doubt trouble. An artist. *We know about them, don't we, Vieve! I'm not looking for that anyway. How about some wine? No!* Frustrated, she mauled her sea glass bracelet watch and looked down at Jack West.

Marley continued. "Nina said she didn't know the guy had been drinking before he got to JohnnyCakes, but she cut him off after one round when he and a buddy started getting loud. Then he insulted her and Maeve Pelletier—she's the chef—before going to the beach to cause more trouble."

Vieve looked out the window and started. "Was that a raven I just saw flying over that telephone pole?"

"Most likely. Oden has a semi-pet raven," Marley said, pointing to her menu. "I suggest ordering light to save room for dessert. Blueberry cobbler to cry for."

Marley winked at Nina as she returned to the table with a tray. She set down a wicker basket of hot rolls with pats of butter tucked around them, filled their water glasses, reached under the table to place a bowl of water on the floor for Jack West, and then took their orders for clam chowder and salad. Two orders of cobbler were placed on reserve.

"But the real reason is not the liquor license thing. It's that Richard wants this spot for a restaurant, after he's bought your uncle's house to open an inn. My guess is he also doesn't like seeing Nina and Maeve be successful, especially on a turf he's got his eye on."

"Because they are Nina and Maeve. Together?" Vieve guessed.

Marley shrugged. "Who am I to judge?"

"You sound like Pope Francis."

Marley laughed. "First, and I bet last, time anyone will compare me to a pope. Hey, see that red horse?" He pointed out the window toward the carousel. "The one with blue and gold embellishments? My handiwork. I helped the town repair and refinish the carousel in the last year. Great fun."

Marley stabbed a cucumber in his salad. "Of course, it was too lowbrow for the college crowd, my RISD colleagues, but who cares?"

Their chowders arrived, water-based, not creamy, steaming and smelling fantastic.

"Ok," said Vieve. "Back to those skeletons? I know about the fort. I know it had a fatal flaw. Uncle Carl told me the story when I was a kid. Its design. That it could be fired on by ship from the water on the other side of the lighthouse without being able to see its attackers. But I didn't know it was haunted."

Marley blew on his chowder, sending a flotilla of crackers afloat across its surface. Vieve smiled. Her uncle Carl approached his chowder the same way.

Marley said, "Allegedly haunted. A young couple and two clammers survived there during the Hurricane of '38. Only survivors on the point. Back about five years ago, according to Nina, people started claiming to hear the wailing of a ghost, sounded like a young woman screaming for help, some nights. You know how these things go. Then it stopped, then it started again about six months ago. Some say it's the wind blowing through the concrete hallways of the fort. Others that it has something to do with the noise of the waves when they hit the end of the point at high tide, at that bluff with the swallow nesting holes. Some are convinced it's a ghost."

"So which camp are you in?" Vieve asked.

"I'm for mystery," Marley said. His direct gaze made Vieve look away, turn toward the window. Seeing that carousel took her back in time again to Ponkipaug Beach. The final summer she stayed with her uncle before she got swept up in life drawing classes in Boston. When the discord between her father and Carl, who'd butted heads since Vieve's childhood, became more than her mother could bear. Vieve had subsequently come to rely on Carl for the kind of moral support, indeed courage, needed to become an artist, something her father could never offer her.

They finished their chowder and salads, the hubbub of the restaurant providing a comfortable backdrop. After tucking reverently into his blueberry cobbler, Marley said, "We could check out the carousel, maybe head down to the beach."

Nina appeared. She gave Jack West a large stew bone for takeout before she placed their check on the table next to their empty cobbler plates.

"We finalized the funding for this gig. Bit of a hiccup, but it's definitely on," Nina said, handing Marley a flyer. "You two should enter. I know you're already plotting to, Marley." She raised her eyebrows and looked between the two of them, as if ready to staunch any objections.

Marley read aloud from the flyer:

Notice of art competition!
The Weekapaug Chamber of Commerce and the Ponkipaug Village
Fire District announce a competition to design and install a mural
in memory of the victims of the Hurricane of 1938. This will be the
first permanent public memorial in all of New England to those who
lost their lives in the hurricane.
All interested artists may submit entries
for the mural design by May 11, 2018
The winning artist(s) will be announced on May 25, 2018
The mural will be installed for the 80th Anniversary
of the storm by September 21, 2018
Visit the Chamber's website for more details.

"Yeah," Marley said, "I saw the notice when it first came out in

February. So you all finally nailed the money for this, eh?"

Nina nodded and beamed. "We're not amateurs, and we don't give up! There was a bit of a hiccup with one sponsor, but we're back on track," she said, winking at Marley. "Lost a great aunt in that blow. She used to swim every day off Ponki Point with a thermometer in her mouth and record the temperature. First one around here to get a waterproof watch." Nina frowned and the sparkle in her eyes dimmed. "She had the last house before the fort. First one to go."

Marley put a hand over Nina's on the table. She sniffed and turned away quickly and headed back to the kitchen.

Marley got up. "Take your doggy bag, Jack West! Shall we inspect the carousel and then hit the beach, Vieve?"

"Sure, but I'm going to check in again." Vieve tried Carl's cell and his landline again. Jud answered the later and reported Carl hadn't called in yet.

CHAPTER 3

O nce they were out on the sidewalk, Vieve took the flyer from Marley and read it silently. As they walked toward the carousel, Jack West matched their stride at a trot with the bone crosswise in his mouth.

"Interesting," Vieve said. "Really interesting that there hasn't been some kind of memorial in all this time."

"New Englanders," Marley said. "Stoic bunch. Anyway, there is one memorial, technically speaking, but not really public *per se*. It's a stone engraved with the names of the Christ Church women who were picnicking at a house on Atlantic Avenue when the hurricane hit and—Ahhh, speak of the devil!"

"Genny Beale!"

Vieve looked up from the flyer. Richard Coggeshall and David Hallowell approached them from the sidewalk ahead. Vieve stopped walking, her eyes narrowing on the advancing men. Jack West stopped too and crossed in front of Vieve, his eyes trained on Richard.

"Shit!" Vieve said to Marley, out of earshot of Richard. "I hoped we wouldn't run into each other."

"Genny!" Richard said again, advancing toward them quickly. "I didn't know you were in town! Long time." She was Genevieve to her parents or Genny to the other kids as a child. *The Artist Vieve!* in her own mind.

She hadn't seen the adult Richard in about eight years and found comfort in the fact that he was aging rapidly, his nose more prominent and his formerly light brown hair turning colorless. His skin was suntanned and toughened by drink; Vieve remembered he loved to sail. Richard's gaunt cheeks were undergirded by the same high, chiseled cheekbones.

The sight of him this close up raised Vieve's neck hair like hackles. Sensing this, Jack West dropped his bone, growling. He leaned forward against the restraint of his leash. If Jack West had owned a proper glove, he would have slapped Richard on the shin. *A duel, you fiend!*

"Think that uncle of yours is ready to sell 17 Salt Pond? I hear he's spending more time in Bermuda. Lucky stiff," Richard said, delivering the slight with a broad smile. *As if it were luck that made Carl so successful,* thought Vieve. *As if it weren't talent and nonstop work.*

Richard did not acknowledge Marley, whose expression continued to sour. David Hallowell nodded in greeting at Marley and Vieve and then slipped into the restaurant to order takeout.

"Oh, he's always buying and selling," said Vieve. "But I doubt 17 will be on the market anytime soon."

Jack West made a lunge for Richard's bare ankle. "Hey!" Richard said. "Rein him in!"

Vieve smiled. "He rarely breaks skin."

Richard and Vieve exchanged glances. Richard frowned and took a step back.

Vieve started to walk, pulling Jack West away from Richard. The terrier snatched up his bone and let himself be pulled along. Marley fell into step with Vieve.

"What was up with all that?" Marley asked.

"I'll tell you later," Vieve said, moving away quickly. They drew up to the merry-go-round known as the Flying Horse Carousel. The horses, suspended from chains, swung out when "flying." Jack West dropped his bone and lay down with a leg over it.

"Damn proud of this silly thing," Marley said. "The center pole enclosure structure is an octagon with scenes from the theatre troupe that donated it way back in the day, like late 1800s. See? All retouched and brightened up."

Vieve looked briefly at the carousel. She'd seen it dozens of times, although not in this good of condition. Her gaze lingered on Marley's profile, and she felt an overpowering urge to touch him, as powerful as the urge for a drink. She turned away from him, feeling the evening sun on her face. She shut her eyes and focused on her breath. She stepped toward the path that led away from the carousel toward Ponkipaug Beach.

Then her feelings surged again, agitating her. This lust for Marley. *No! How about just sex and art. Could that be enough?*

She couldn't bear letting anyone get as close to her heart as she had let Kyle get. *Having a drink right now would put that whole heart damage pain back under a lid for a time, back in temporary storage. But uggh! The tradeoff?* She scooped up Jack West and held him close to her chest, like a living balm over the place throbbing with a visceral sear of memory, of throbbing pain. Jack West relaxed in her arms. He looked into her face and licked her nose. *Mom! Love you too!*

Searing sexual attraction, Bacchanalian lust for wine, jagged broken heart pain salved with puppy-love comfort all in a couple minutes. These were her days now.

"Hey, are you ok?" Marley asked, stepping toward her.

Vieve set Jack West back down on the dune path. As she straightened up, a tattered German shepherd barreled past her, almost plowing into Jack West, who stood on his bone and barked his displeasure.

"What the...?!" Vieve said. She clipped Jack West's leash back on his collar.

"Meet Frek," Marley said. "Well, you could meet him if he would stand still. Must be on a scent."

The shepherd didn't break stride, turning down Ocean Front

Avenue toward Salt Pond Drive.

"Frek?"

"Oden's companion animal. Along with that raven we saw tonight, who hangs out on the cabana trash cans. Munin."

Oden, Vieve thought. *Ah, yes, the one who's been acting weirder than usual.*

Marley led the way through the gate from which Frek appeared at full throttle. They walked beyond the cabanas, up the short, steep dune trail, and past a sign welcoming them to enjoy the area's natural beauty and then warning them to stay out of the roped off nesting habitat of the federally threatened piping plover and least tern. The sign also admonished them to leash their dogs and not to litter. They continued down the path to the beach, making their way through the fine, deep sand.

"I guess Frek can't read," Vieve said, nodding back toward the sign. "Who's Oden?"

"He's actually Ted Silva but don't call him that to his face. And he's not big on leashes, of any kind."

Marley paused and then spoke again. "Schizophrenic, PTSD, ADHD, just wacko, misunderstood? No one knows. Frankly, Jud thinks he's a Shakespearean fool who wandered off stage. He's actually an ex-lobsterman. Carves driftwood. Some kind of trauma in his past."

They started down the ocean side of Ponkipaug Point with its wide, almost flat, off-white sandy beach. A gull glided by and dropped a live crab, pillaged from a few yards offshore, onto a rock. Dinner. Soon another gull eyed his catch, and a raucous ownership argument ensued.

Dropping his bone again, Jack West joined in the argument, straining against his leash. A third gull, noticing the stew bone, still padded with meat in the middle, dove for the dog's prize. Jack West lunged at the thieving bird, barking furiously. Vieve scooped the terrier up and away from the bird's dagger-like bill. The gull was bigger than Jack West and flaunted an impressive black back. Vieve flashed on her previous dog, Gainsby, who would have never compromised his dignity to enter into the fray of a gull argument. She smiled at her feisty friend, scrapping for a street fight to defend what was his.

"Easy come, easy go," Marley observed, watching the gull race along the water's edge with its prize.

"Not so easy go," Vieve replied. She carried Jack West, furious and wriggling to break loose, away up the beach toward the roped off nesting area. She did not breach the rope and continued walking a few feet below the high tide wrack line.

"So tell me what's up with you and Richard Coggeshall. I thought you might deck him back there," Marley said when he caught up with Vieve. They were heading south along the beach toward the fort. Vieve set Jack West down on the sand.

"Richard Coggeshall *the Fourth.* Hah! He's grandson to the seventh power of one of the town's founders, which he felt gave him the right to bully me when we were kids. He used to chase me with that long slimy seaweed that the tide throws up. And four times, he'd tried to hold me underwater, just off that jetty there—" Vieve pointed to the end of Ponkipaug Beach near Fort Devlin. "Kind of like waterboarding. But in those days it was boys being boys."

"Probably had a crush on you," Marley said, scanning the shells at their feet as they walked.

Vieve considered saying more, but held back. She'd gotten her sweet revenge at the time. In the days after the fourth dunking, Vieve had worked out an elaborate retaliation plan involving photographing Richard and his girlfriend skinny dipping, drinking, and drugging at the Weekapaug National Wildlife Refuge. She'd threatened to expose him at the senior prom, with a spread of photo enlargements, and to his father, then head of the local chamber of commerce. The reverse blackmail scheme worked, and Richard backed down.

Since the last of the dunking incidents and her whitemailing, there had been an uneasy truce between them. Vieve continued to visit her uncle in Ponkipaug Point over the years, while Richard got his MBA and opened an auction business that had morphed into a modestly impressive coastal real estate fiefdom. But the sight of him still set something off in her.

"That's just sick," Vieve said. Jack West glanced behind himself every fifteen feet and hurled another insult in the direction of the gulls. It took about a half mile to draw his attention forward again. "Tell me your ghost theory."

"Actually Oden was the one who started talking the ghost thing up about five years ago and especially in the last six months. Claims he hears voices in Fort Devlin and at the end of the point. He sleeps in the fort some nights, which is technically trespassing. In the winter, he stays with a girlfriend from Providence who inherited a small house at the edge of the Beach Plum Development. Some unusual soul who accommodates his, err, his eccentricities." Marley turned toward Vieve but she kept her gaze on the sand in front of her where Jack West trotted along like a sled dog in harness.

We could all use one of those," she said. They were nearing the jetty of Vieve's childhood nightmares.

"Oden sold his stake in the lobster boat back in 2013. Fishery's dying down here anyway, water's getting too warm, too acidic. But before that, a decade ago, he started drinking too much. That's why his partner eventually bought him out. I heard Oden even got a Purple Heart from the army for saving three guys from a roadside bomb in Iraq that he *gave back*. Then, well, he snapped. Something terrible happened with his twin sister."

Vieve listened, her gaze still on Jack West's back, avoiding thoughts of pouncing on Marley or memories of nearly being drowned by the jetty. She inhaled deeply and tried to relax.

Marley continued. "Oden tinkers with engines for a few bucks over at the Stonington Marina, but mostly he turns Ponki Point driftwood into touristy items. Between what led to the Purple Heart and the sister dying, he just came unstrung."

"Any family history around here?" Vieve asked. "I don't remember a Silva family growing up."

"Not sure. But he claims he's related by marriage a generation back to that Bray fellow on Newell Point who sheltered hurricane refugees in 1938."

Marley stopped walking. "Right here, along this strip of sand. A whole little neighborhood wiped out. You must of heard that tale a lot as a kid. The storm also ripped a mile-long sand arm off Ponki Point and set it down in Little Narragansett Bay halfway to Connecticut. Two hundred fifty townsfolk and end-of-summer revelers died due to wind, wave, flying object, or heart attack. And that was just in Ponkipaug."

Vieve ventured a look at Marley's face. "Too awful," she said. Vieve peered east across the darkening ocean at the Sentinel Point Lighthouse. "It's a really exposed piece of land." She'd heard stories as a kid, but it had all seemed so unreal and disconnected from her.

"My parents didn't talk about it, although they lived in the Point Judith area until I was about twelve. Then we moved to Massachusetts. Carl would talk though. Many of his jewelry clients were the children and grandchildren of those families who lived on Ponkipaug Point and along Salt Pond Drive and Atlantic Drive or summered down here back in the 60s and 70s. Some of those families go back to when there were houses on Ponkipaug Point."

Vieve turned to the west, the dune now blocking their view of Little Narragansett Bay. "Imagine not knowing where you're going— back to mainland Rhode Island or Connecticut or out into the Atlantic? Clinging on for dear life to a hunk of wall or a door.

Negotiating with God, or begging for mercy."

Marley glanced at Vieve, walking alongside him on the dune side of the beach, Jack West clipping along a few feet ahead. "That's why we should do the mural! Could we get any of that feeling into a picture on a wall? Or the relief when you touched the earth again and still had your family? Your children? Your neighbors? Or that you woke up on Thursday morning, after a night of biblical-scale natural disaster, with nothing but your life? Family, spouse, dwelling, place of business, gone."

They walked past an osprey-nesting platform, resembling an antenna for the dunes, and enjoyed the breeze now shifting offshore. The sun arced lower in the west, and the industrious shorebirds, who had plied their trades in the gravelly intertidal area near the jetty, settled back down in the dunes for the evening.

Vieve scanned the ocean. A black skimmer, its exaggeratedly long lower bill just touching the ocean surface, flew by heading north.

Marley smiled. "Well, think about it. Anyway, back to the ghost." Marley stepped forward, glanced down, and did a sidestep jig. "Branislau!" he said. "You made it another year!"

Vieve looked down to see whom he was addressing. "You know this, this....?"

"Horseshoe crab. Yes! We go back to 2014 when I first noticed him. He's tagged, see?" Marley pointed to a yellow plastic tag with a number attached to the great brown dome of a shell, sculpted like an ancient military shield. "I didn't know what he was at first either, but I called the phone number on the tag to report him to Fish & Wildlife. They sent me a horseshoe crab pin, which I gave to Asia, and a little brochure about horseshoe crabs and their research. Asia's got three pins now. This will be four!"

Vieve looked toward the end of the peninsula where a tiny islet, Poki Dot, poked just barely above the sea surface. "Let's head back," Vieve said. "I want to see about Carl. Perhaps he left his cell phone at the house."

As they were turning around, Oden popped up in the dune a few yards away. Jack West strained forward but didn't bark. The terrier whined softly and folded his legs underneath himself, still facing Oden. Then he sprang back up, tugged on his leash, and whined again. Oden advanced down the trail toward Vieve and Marley.

"Hey, Oden!" Marley said. "This is Vieve Beale, Carl's niece."

Oden bowed slightly toward Vieve and spoke to Marley. "There's a rowboat on the loose on the other side of Ponki!"

"Really?" said Marley.

"I wouldn't lie!"

"No, no. I know that. Just unusual, isn't it?" Marley and Vieve exchanged glances. They could both smell the rum.

"No one's in it."

"Runaway rowboat," Marley said lightly. "You staying over?" Marley pointed back to the fort.

"I might be," Oden said. "I bet it's from Hallowell's Marina. But he don't seem to care.

Jack West leaned forward and sniffed Oden's shoe.

"Hey, little guy!" Oden said.

Jack West wagged his whole hind end and sat down.

"This is Jack West." Vieve smiled. "He likes you better than he does Richard Coggeshall."

"Animals can tell what's in your soul," Oden said, looking into Vieve's eyes. His gaze was intense and his breath reeked of rum. She stepped back.

"We've got to head back," Marley said. "Looking for Vieve's uncle. You haven't seen him today, have you?"

"No," Oden said. "I've been huntin' driftwood most of the afternoon."

"Well, have a good evening, then," Marley said. Vieve nodded and pulled a reluctant Jack West away. Oden walked toward the tip of the peninsula, and Vieve and Marley headed back toward town.

"Welcome back to Ponki Point," Marley said, "and the beach of battered souls."

"He looks like he's been through the wringer." Vieve glanced back in the direction where Oden was headed.

The sun began to spread itself in brilliant cadmium orange over the horizon to the west. After a long silence Marley said, "We should do that mural together. I've got color and I bet you've got drawing. What do you think? I've already worked up some preliminary ideas."

"You sound like Matisse baiting Picasso," Vieve shot back. Then looking over the dune toward Connecticut at the sunset, she added softly, "I can't answer now. I need to find Uncle Carl first. Ask me after that. Like you said, he's probably fine, but...."

Her voice trailed off as she felt a surge of intimacy with this man she'd really just met. It was what they were saying to each other underneath all the words, the whole evening. Intriguing in a way, but she didn't want this...*this what?* This connection, *this attraction* to a man who wasn't Kyle?

CHAPTER 4

Saturday, April 7, 2018

Vieve woke to barking from somewhere down the hall, and she immediately threw on yesterday's clothes. She'd packed for an overnight on this Carl visit as she did back in the days when the two of them drank a lot at dinner. Vieve had planned to stay over sober this time and enjoy the beach for a day. But now with her uncle still missing, she wasn't ready to head home so soon.

Following the barking down the hall led her to Marley's studio. She pushed on the partly open door and walked in.

Marley switched off his power drill and stepped away from the silver-dominated four-by-four-foot panel. An air purifier purred to his right.

Lifting his facemask up to speak, Marley said, "If you're going to stay, you'll both need masks."

"Do they make them for dogs?" Vieve asked, scooping Jack West up and pulling him away from the suspended acrylic dust. *You're not a painter, you're a driller.*

"Yes, search-and-rescue dogs," Marley replied.

He lowered the drill down onto a chair and adjusted a fan to clear the air near the panel. After rummaging through the taboret, he pulled out another mask and a clean rag and tossed them to Vieve. Turning back to the panel, Marley examined the silverscape in front of him. There were now patches of peach, black, turquoise, and deep fuchsia peeking out from the braids of silver. He flipped it "upside down"—*How did he know?*—and inspected it again. Then he took two steps back and narrowed his eyebrows at the panel.

After donning the mask and covering Jack West's muzzle with the rag, Vieve approached the silver panel.

"Ok. My big secret is this: I paint with a brush, layers and layers and layers—I'm talking *many* layers—takes weeks, in between I pour layers of acrylic. Thick and thin. There are tinted gels involved. It dries. Way more quickly than oil by the way. Then I drill. Exposing the different color layers at different depths. It's all intuition and color vibration." He laughed. "It's all colored glue."

"Do you always drill at 7 am?" Vieve said. It looked bizarre, but fun. Her oil portrait work had become a smelly chore, or maybe it was because many of her recent clients were unpleasant. She had just about reached her capacity to tolerate the pitfalls of her profession, the straightjacket of commission work—glorifying narcissists. Not all of them, but too many, like Picard, who requested tweaks to this or that in his finished portrait when she knew that was not what he was really after.

Marley smiled. "Everyone in this house gets up at dawn. Well, me and Asia. Usually Carl. Jud, not so much. He stayed out somewhere last night, as he often does," Marley said, hinting at possible promiscuity. "Were you sleeping?"

"Until the drilling and barking started, yes," she said. "But no big deal. I usually get up around now. Carry on." She walked out of the studio still holding her dog. The drilling started up immediately after she shut the door. "Drill Baby Drill!" Vieve said to Jack West.

Vieve sat at Carl's bedroom desk without consciously deciding to, the panel Marley was drilling still in her mind's eye. Incredible, the impressions that the texture and color made. When she looked down at the desktop, she noticed a contract related to a Bermuda jewelry launch that Carl, most likely, had marked up heavily with a pen, a printout of a flirty email from a Beryl Martin (signature box:

Hamilton, Bermuda) discussing a visit this month at some unnamed date on which Carl wrote *Next weekend?*, and his laptop.

There also was a manila folder containing beautiful pen-and-ink and watercolor renditions of jewelry model mockups that he'd had commissioned based on some sketchy drawings he made, which were in the back of the folder. So he hadn't really retired. Vieve smiled; she knew retirement wasn't going to stick. She'd spend time with the laptop today to try to figure out where he'd gone to.

A landline phone rang on the night table, and Vieve picked it up. "Hello?"

"Who's this?" A female voice.

Surprised at the caller's tone, Vieve collected herself. "I think that's my question."

"Where's Carl?" A southern New England softened "r" accent, full of anger.

"Look. Who are you? I don't have to take your—" Vieve stood up.

"Is this Asia's mother?

"I'm going to cut this off if you don't tell me who you are," Vieve said, more calmly than she felt.

"Deena Vaughan. Carl's fiancée. Who are you?"

Fiancée!

"Vieve, Carl's niece."

Silence.

"Where the hell is he?"

"Good question," Vieve said, relaxing a bit. She was tempted to bail on this rude call. Hell, she hadn't even had coffee yet, but at this point, everyone was a potential source of information about Carl. "We were supposed to meet last night, and I still don't know where he is. When did you last see him?"

"Thursday night. He was in a foul mood. Said a lot of things he didn't mean."

Oh interesting.

"Do you know what he did on Friday? We were supposed to meet for dinner."

A ten-second pause.

"No," Deena said, the anger fading a bit along with the volume of her voice. "He mentioned going to Bermuda. If he—" The anger flared again.

"Look," Vieve said. "When you've calmed down, get back in touch." Vieve hung up the landline and turned the ringer volume down. She breathed in deeply and walked over to the window. Carl's huge master bedroom was the only room on the second floor with a full, unobstructed view of the bay, sparkling now in the morning's full brilliance, baby blue-gray with glints of white wave crests. Calmer, Vieve turned back to the desk.

As determined as Vieve was to tackle Carl's laptop next, Jack West was equally determined to go for a walk. He communicated this by retrieving his nylon leash and depositing it on Vieve's shoe. Such different behavior than Gainsby. His method was to work her with his soulful eyes, ready to spring out of his bed if she walked toward the front door. Jack West didn't believe in such subtle innuendo. Vieve smiled, snatched up the leash, and clipped it onto his collar.

She paused on the porch and watched the wind ripple Little Narragansett Bay into orderly waves advancing on the beach and docks. A view a post card would frame. Back in the day of post cards.

Jack West led Vieve down the steps with purpose. She thought to walk the quarter mile to the dock area, but the terrier apparently had other plans and veered left toward the storage shed. Some interloper animal had burrowed by the left front corner, and Jack West appeared intent to get to the bottom of it. His unspoken motto: *Locate and evict!*

Jack West dug and Vieve's mind wandered as she watched sailboats and motor boats crisscross the bay and a pair of scuba divers muck around the dock sorting through their equipment. She noticed two plastic chairs under the three-trunked gray birch on the left side of the shed and sat down in the closest one. It was the first snatch of time recently when she felt she could begin to relax, try to figure out what happened—with Carl, with her portrait business, or even with Kyle and her life. Sobriety brought everything a bit too close, making it a little too real. She hadn't counted on that. She thought sobriety would unfurl gently into an oasis of calm clarity, not advance like whitewater rapids with bursts of opinion, fantasy, fear, and memory lying in her path like a tumultuous jumble of boulders.

There was one evening she remembered. She flashed on it as Jack West alternately dug and growled with rising irritability at the large rock he'd encountered, blocking his forward progress. That evening, two years ago, when she'd drank four-fifths of a bottle of wine and ended up on the heart-pine kitchen floor leaning against Gainsby.

She'd recently captured that dignified head in what she considered to be her best portrait painting, people or animal. Paws down. She'd challenged herself to paint a Garden Setter without using black. After finishing it, she realized the energy in the painting came from her feeling that the dog connected her forever with Kyle. She remembered the first time she saw Kyle on the Old North Bridge photographing an egret flushed orange in the late afternoon light on the shore of the Concord River. He turned in her direction and saw her watching him. She felt a sudden rush through her body, like a crystal flash of rainwater through a dry gully. That path of sparkling joy ran the same channel as the groove of prickling pain that Peter had carved so deep.

Peter Tilden. Her first husband. *What a disaster.* They'd married, a bit rashly, at twenty-two. Peter, from a lineage of eastern Massachusetts engineers and lawyers, was determined to be an artisanal heritage orchardist in the apple belt northwest of Boston. At that point, as Genevieve Tilden, she was working to make it as a fine artist while scrambling to make money as a commercial illustrator, which she hated, and getting increasingly sucked into the labor-intensive work of the orchard. Three harvests in, and during the cider-pressing season, Vieve miscarried her first child. By the Memorial Day weekend, she'd found out Peter was having an affair with a coffee shop owner in town, whom he left Vieve to marry.

Vieve looked over at Jack West. He'd pulled something from the hole and plopped down to rest, panting in a dog smile, his tongue out. The sun glinted off his left front canine.

That was Vieve's dark time, but not as black as what was to come. She immediately changed her name back to Beale after Peter left and before her art had really taken off. She tried to run the orchard, which she had grown to love, by herself, an impossible proposition, and then tried to find a business partner and work on her art. The business partner, it turned out, wanted more than just a business partnership. When she quickly severed that arrangement, a couple of financially rough years followed, trying to run the orchard, do illustration work so she could eat, and get up early to work on her own art. And drinking to tuck away all the anxiety and grief. That's when the drinking really got bad. Then she stopped drinking for six weeks out of sheer grit, and in that small window of brutal clarity resolved to simplify—sell the orchard—and then threw herself into her art. Which then flourished under all the attention.

Fifteen years later she found her soul mate on the Old North Bridge amid a mosaic of fall foliage and tourists stalking Revolutionary War history and family photos. Kyle Clough was an outdoor photographer and journalist. She and Kyle—partners, soulmates, friends, lovers—faced the world together with a refreshingly direct and generous love, burnishing each other's souls. They had five years together before he died in that freak canoeing accident while on assignment for a national outdoor publication. He hit his head on a sleeper rock that pinned him underwater, nine months after he'd presented her with puppy Gainsby.

After the funeral, she added Clough as a middle name for comfort. She felt hollow after Kyle's untimely death, the news delivered in person at midnight by the wife of his bowman, who survived the accident. Her drinking flared again while her portrait work became recognized in Massachusetts and, soon after, throughout New England. More resolve followed. She readjusted her name once more, streamlining, like stacking up a cairn against the vagaries of the world, the flood of time and happenstance. She became Vieve, signing her work *VC Beale.*

Then she got the commission to paint the governor and his black-and-white springer spaniel. She threw everything into her now lucrative profession, obsessed with shoring up her living. She spent eight more years continuing to perfect the technical challenges of realistic portraiture, fighting the grief over her lost marriage, child, and soulmate. Her heart was reduced to a low burn in pain, under a never-healing scab. The magic gone from art making.

Her sister Joss became alarmed at the changes in Vieve's life. The drinking was winning. "Does life just dissipate away like this, amid a scrim of disappointments?" Vieve asked Joss one day when they were drinking coffee at an Amherst coffee shop overrun with students and their attending e-devices. She thought, *Hell, no! But how do you get yourself back?*

So when Gainsby, at age eight, was diagnosed with cancer, something changed in Vieve. She painted that transcendent portrait, dumped out all the wine and liquor in the house, even the Kahlua she poured over her ice cream. She nursed Gainsby through that time with eyes open, heart raw, and full of gratitude that they'd had eight years together. She resolved to witness each remaining day of the dog's life and not dull it or wrap it in wool with drink or hide from it. A vow to honor Gainsby and Kyle's memory with her sobriety. To her, Gainsby was order, faith, choice, calm, beauty, service. Something that she *still* had that Kyle had touched and loved also and wanted her to have.

No one since Kyle, Vieve reflected. *And now, suddenly and out of nowhere, this Marley person—*

Jack West let out a sharp yip and bounded forward, stopped, and raised his right front paw. Vieve looked in that direction and saw a teenager wearing lime green cargo shorts and a fitted black tee shirt.

She stopped in front of Vieve and said into her phone, "Ponkagannsett—Where he roasts oysters. They think there are more sites. Hey! I gotta run, Wes. I'll call you later." Without missing a beat, the girl reached down to pat Jack West.

The girl's left wrist was encircled with six bracelets made of some kind of large polished seeds ranging from pale yellow ocher to a purpley brown. A one-inch-long sterling silver feather dangled from a silver chain around her neck. She'd applied walnut brown liner with a heavy hand to the lash line of her almost violet eyes. Multiple piercings with amethyst and moonstone studs outlined her ears like a line of bulbs on an actor's lighted mirror.

"You must be Asia," Vieve said, smiling.

Asia plopped down into an empty plastic chair, seed bracelets clinking. "Great to meet you," she said. "Dad filled me in. Any news of your uncle?" Asia showed her gap-toothed smile.

"No," Vieve said. Jack West lay down in the small space between the chairs. "Nothing. Oh, meet Jack West!"

"Cool dog," Asia said, patting the terrier's head again. Jack West stood to be fully appreciated by his new friend. "I've tried to talk Dad into a dog but no dice. My aunt's got three, but they're spazzy. And they're *hers.*"

"Jack West just kind of moved in with me. It really wasn't a choice," Vieve said. The dog sat now, between his friends, eyeing his excavation.

"It's always a choice," Asia said. "It's only not a choice for people with big hearts."

Vieve looked at Asia, who was stroking Jack West's back. *Interesting girl.*

"I hear Jud's planning to make you a star. What are your rehearsals for? If you don't mind saying."

Asia groaned. "An Ibsen play that Jud twisted my arm to join. *The Master Builder.* I don't know if I'm really doing it. There's so much time spent standing around waiting. Most of the people are vain."

Vieve chuckled. "That can happen in a theatre." They heard scurrying under the storage shed. Jack West sprang up and circled the base of the wall.

Asia laughed. "That hole's new. What is it?" she asked, pointing to the corner where Jack West had dug.

"Jack West's excavation. He knows there's an animal down there. Is there a cellar space below this shed?"

"I don't think so. Hey, I'm getting involved in a dig over at the Pawcatuck River! It's starting next week. A professor at the University of Rhode Island is leading it. My history teacher knows him and knows I'm into archaeology. URI has got a lot going on in local digs."

"What kind of archaeology? What period?"

"Native peoples around here. Late Woodland Period. Pequot, Narragansett, Niantic. I'm Niantic through my mother. Well, we think so. Of course, so do half the people in the state." Asia laughed her infectious tinkle of notes.

Vieve examined Asia's expression. She had that kind of adolescent face that its owner wishes would belie nothing, remain inscrutable, but instead broadcasts fear, curiosity, and defiance clear as a radio station.

"Cool," Vieve said. "How far back?

Asia peered into Vieve's face. "Pretty far. Wish I knew."

Asia watched Jack West bound toward the corner of the shed and resume the excavation. "You're the only adult I've told who thinks it's cool. Everyone's obsessed with their own things these days. Dad and his plastic-coated panels that now are hot shit. Ah, excuse me. He...."

Asia trailed off, but not before Vieve could tell she wanted to say more but stopped herself. Vieve wanted to know more but didn't want to pry. *Like, why was Marley not with Asia's mother?* Instead, she said, "I've got a niece your age. Lucie Rollins. Coming to town next week. Got a summer job at Candy Crush."

Asia swiveled the seed bracelets around her wrist. "Been-there-done-that!" She glanced at Jack West and smiled. "I worked there last summer to help them open. One summer was enough to put me off a candy career."

Vieve lifted her face to the fresh southerly breeze blowing in from the ocean. "This house has such a great location."

Asia nodded. "Which is why half the town is after it. You got Richard, Carl's Bermuda girlfriend, and Deena."

Vieve closed her eyes and let the breeze pour over her face. Warm sunlight and cool air, salt, freshly turned soil, and a hint of fossil fuel from the marina. When Vieve opened them she saw Munin, in the distance, perched on his cabana trash can. At least, she assumed it was Munin. Asia was gone and Jack West was snarling at the rock blocking progress in his hole.

A helicopter buzzed over the bay heading toward the wildlife refuge. She jolted upright with an unwelcome thought from what Oden said yesterday. *Would Uncle Carl, a yacht owner, row to his death in a dilapidated rowboat? Would he have just rowed away toward Fisher's in the night?*

She blinked and pondered what she could of Carl's state-of-mind. *No. Not his style.*

She resolved to stay in Ponkipaug Village until Carl returned. Standing up, she noticed Jack West had deposited his newest find at her feet—a weathered object with a curved end that looked a little like an old animal bone with horizontal notches halfway down the shaft. Probably from a deer. She placed it on the narrow window sill of the shed. Maybe Asia would be interested. Then she forgot about it.

Back in Carl's room, Vieve noticed a blinking light on Carl's landline and checked for messages. There was only one, from ten minutes ago: *Lay off Hamilton. Big Shark.*

CHAPTER 5

Tuesday, April 17, 2018

J ust beyond the resolute bunker of Fort Devlin, Ponkipaug Point ends in a short cobble beach and a jumble of rocks and boulders. As Oden approached from the fort, he heard Gordon's helicopter buzzing in the west across the bay near Newell Point.

One by one, cliff swallows dive-bombed Oden as he stood on the sand bluff over the beach. "Nesting time again, my friends!" he said, bobbing up and down to avoid their low reconnaissance flights meant to discourage his trespass.

Oden quickly moved down the bluff onto the cobble. He checked the rocky toe of the point at least weekly for driftwood—his artistic medium—but this spot often tossed up sea paraphernalia of the manmade kind.

He looked to the southwest at the rotting dock posts emerging from the receding tide, lending an air of forgotten time to the point. The original dock, of which these posts were the last remnant, was built when there was a restaurant on the point in the 1800s. Then Fort Devlin, built in the early twentieth century, used it as a restocking access point. He'd love to get his hands on those posts that were slowly eroding, almost melting, into the sea just a few yards from where he stood.

He'd hacked away at them last summer at low tide. Despite their dilapidated looks, they were still firmly set into whatever anchored them, and he'd been ratted on by some beachgoers to Hal Raybacker of the town council, who railed at him about "defacing" them. He'd also gotten an earful from Dash Bliven. *Some folks*, Oden thought, *are overly touchy about the posts' historical significance. Life, in all its glory and debris, is meant to be recycled.*

Today, he found a piece of a broken oar, a fine, curved hunk of driftwood, and, oddly, a pair of newish men's leather boat shoes. He left the oar and took the piece of driftwood—he could make into salad tongs—and the shoes. He glanced over at Munin on his osprey perch and wondered where Frek had gotten to. Raybacker also harassed Oden for letting Frek run off leash. Frek always turns back up and, undoubtedly, would this time too.

Gordon's helicopter buzzed louder now, closer to town. As Oden turned to follow the sound, he noticed that one of the swallow burrow holes had a ragged bottom, rough jabs gouged out of it. Munin, he suspected, harassing swallows. Below the gouged burrow was a piece of paper. "Litter!" Oden cried in disgust.

He picked up the scrap of paper. A string of numbers handwritten in ink—*dates?* Suddenly, Oden heard a boat motor. A Bay Boat-style powerboat approached the point from the southeast, and he jumped behind a boulder to keep out of sight. Fifteen seconds later the motorboat veered toward the west and picked up speed. Oden watched its wake wash over the dock posts. He slipped the paper in his back pocket. The swallows vanished abruptly.

"Something's going on!" Oden informed Munin, who'd just landed on a boulder to his left. "Right here! At this fort, ignored by everyone for decades. Except by us!"

Munin croanked.

"Yes! We are at the hub of the universe, my friend!"

Oden headed back to the fort with his finds along the path lined with briars, poison ivy, sweet pea, beach rose, and the occasional clump of beach plum. His daily commute. He hurried down a moss-carpeted stairway and along a dank concrete passageway, stumbling over a four-by-four. He righted himself, preventing a fall onto the muddy floor, and then pondered the cluttered hallway in which he stood. *What can I do with all this lumber strewn about? Is there enough to build a dock? A dock of one's own? A dock to sit on with Carl when he returns and catch up on all his adventures?*

He stashed the boat shoes in his room, the one furnished with a dilapidated bench and a rusty iron ring near the ceiling. *Be it ever so humble*, he mused.

Originally a jetty/breakwater combination, it was the only solid spot above sea level within the low-lying marshy expanse. Gordon brought the helicopter down at sunrise. It was open water at King Tide, but at all other times a 'copter could land on this hunk of dirt road just off the coast. *Had Frek swum from Newell Point, forty yards away?* Gordon had missed this speck of earth—easy enough to do—on his flyby yesterday.

Gordon cut the motor, and the loud whirring of blades ceased, the marshland absorbing the sound. He didn't get out right away; he knew what was there. Carl had been missing for more than a week, and they never went that long without checking in briefly by phone or at least email.

And then there was Carl changing his will late last month. He'd seemed happy enough at the time, relieved in some way, and went on for an hour about his new jewelry line. Odd. Did he think starting this jewelry line would threaten his life in some way? Stir up enemies? Gordon listened to the dry swish of salt grass in the breeze and the whiskey-throated croak of a green heron on the point.

Frek loped over to the helicopter as if to corral Gordon and lead him back to his find. Gordon spotted what was left of Carl partially wedged under one of the old jetty rocks. By the looks of the exposed green-black skin, he'd been in the water awhile. Frek barked and pawed at Carl's left leg, which was out of the water. Gordon pulled him away, remembering how Carl had indulged Oden and his menagerie of two, even paid for Oden to take Frek to the vet once a year. Carl never said a judgmental or critical word about this man who defied the town's conventions. The man most of the town prided themselves on feeling superior to.

Gordon looked back over Little Narragansett Bay toward Ponkipaug Point. Between this minute island and the point arose an intricate swirling dance of currents in the bay. The shorelines were irregularly fringed with small estuaries and feeder streams. *You wouldn't choose to visit this particular spot voluntarily,* Gordon thought. *If Carl had been on Ponki Point or Poki Dot, fell, been pushed into the water, perhaps from a boat, would he have ended up here somehow? An accident? A staged accident? An inebriated misstep? A deliberate dive?*

Frek sat and stared at Carl's body, letting out a short, anxious whimper.

So, wondered Gordon. *Suicide or murder?*

Gordon had noticed after the agony of Bonnie's death two years ago that when Carl emerged from his initial phase of debilitating grief, he'd adopted a kind of hypercharged optimism. He'd plunged into the remodeling of 17 Salt Pond and eagerly joined Gordon on his buzzes over the sea to scout for that elusive U-boat.

Those trips had trailed off lately as Gordon began employing scuba divers to continue the search in one particular area to the southeast off the tip of Ponkipaug Point. He was hoping to find some preliminary evidence of a sunken U-boat in Block Island Sound—another one. Of course, if he did find one, it would constitute a German war grave that they could not disturb, but the implications of what another boat would mean for history intrigued him. Anyway,

Gordon knew it was all his own indulgence. Carl didn't care one way or the other about a more nuanced view of World War Two history, but he loved the hunt for buried treasure.

So did the hyperoptimism only partially tamp down growing despair over Bonnie? Carl's new jewelry line, was that enough for him?

"Did you do it or was it done to you?" Gordon asked out loud. Nothing, except a fainter croak of a heron.

Frek, head tilted, listened to Gordon ask questions of the universe in the guise of talking to himself.

Three gulls mewled and wheeled above. Biding their time. Gordon peered again at the body of his friend, frowned, and then radioed the Coast Guard. They would pick up the body. They would tell the police, they would confirm the ID with Carl's dental records, and they would determine whether this was a crime scene. Gordon photographed Carl's position in the water multiple times with his cell phone. Then he pulled Carl out from under the rock onto solid ground and covered him with a tarp he stowed in the helicopter, weighted down by rocks to keep the gulls away.

What he *could do* is tell Vieve, whom he knew was still in town waiting for her uncle to return home. Himself, in person. Frek hopped in the helicopter after Gordon. The sun shone with a cheery intensity, oblivious to Gordon's personal grief that would soon spread throughout the village of the man they all cherished in a way as their uncle.

Vieve passed through the living room on the way to Carl's bedroom. She noticed Marley at the dining room table working out something in charcoal on a pad of newsprint. Outside, someone hesitantly plucked the bouzouki. Its buzzy yet full-sounding notes reverberated through the first floor, loud through the open window. Suddenly, Vieve saw the metallic blue-violet of one of Marley's panels.

Marley looked up as Vieve approached the stairs, with Jack West close at hand. After Vieve had spent a fruitless week searching and waiting for word of her uncle, the two artists returned to the point to discuss possibilities for the mural. Where, last night, Vieve and Marley had kissed. That development had surprised both of them, and they hadn't made eye contact since then.

"I got an idea for the mural I'd like you to see," Marley said.

"Later," Vieve replied, climbing the stairs. She was intent on continuing with Carl's laptop. It seems he was really into this new line of jewelry, and it was very promising looking as a business proposition. And if he were gone, then.... She didn't want to think about it.

Vieve was just opening the email program when she heard a knock on the door. *I'm not doing that mural now.*

"Yes?"

Jud opened the door and leaned his head in. "We're heading out to Ponki Beach with a picnic lunch this afternoon. The three of us. Want to make it a fourth? There's going to be a concert too. I'm in a tiny band called The Rip Tides. If you can call two people a band." He smiled.

Vieve looked at Jud, wondering how close he was to Carl.

"Do you have a minute, Jud? Can you fill me in on something?"

The door opened wider and Jud entered the room. He shut the door behind him.

"Sure. What's up?" He looked for somewhere to sit. There wasn't anywhere so he half sat, half leaned against the window sill. Vieve rose and offered him the desk chair. Jud refused the chair, and Vieve began to pace.

"Were you and Carl close?" Vieve asked.

Jud smiled. "Close how?"

"Well, this is weird but..." Vieve looked out the window and thought at bit. "Were you close enough that you ever had discussions about his attitude, his plans, whether...." She couldn't say it.

"Whether he disappeared on purpose or not?" Jud's voice was deep but soft now, his theatrical tarnish momentarily discarded.

"Well, yes. I mean, what I can figure from all this"—Vieve motioned toward the laptop and folders on Carl's desk—"is that he had a great new business venture ready to launch. *Rainbow Elite*, based on this find of rainbow hematite in one big mine in Ecuador. And, according to an email string with a mysterious contact in that country, it seems he had business competitors who weren't happy about the prospect of an intriguing new Carl Beale line of jewelry in a new market at the moment. The line he wanted to open in Bermuda. But I keep asking myself, was he happy? What the hell was he up to? Could he have really done something to himself?"

Jud shrugged. "I don't know. At first, when he went missing, I didn't think so. But I've been going over and over this too, and I remember a talk we had soon after I moved in. Bonnie had been dead over a year by then. We drank too much whiskey. It got a bit maudlin, even for me." He chuckled and stroked his chin beard. "Anyway, I asked him if he was ok, down deep. If he would...reach out if it got really bad."

Vieve stopped pacing and sat on the bed where Jack West was sleeping, his left hind leg jerking in his dreams. "And?" She almost didn't want to hear anymore.

"He said he didn't think he could do it. Suicide, he implied. He didn't say the word. That despite the loss and disappointment there was still too much to do. That he had a lot of people he didn't want to let down."

Jud looked out the window and then turned around, taking the chair that Vieve had abandoned for the bed.

"The whole town leaned on him in a way to give him spirit to move forward. That irritated the hell out of Richard—who longs for that kind of respect. You gotta know Carl was almost a patron saint in this town. Supporting this and that. Not just with money too. He mentored people. The folks who revived the carousel business for one. He paid for five local kids' tuition at URI in the last year."

Vieve wondered, *Is it any worse that he was maybe murdered? Dead is dead. But not knowing is agonizing.*

"But..." Jud said. He looked at Vieve, then out the window at the bay, and then back at Vieve.

"But?" Vieve said. She was hanging on to each word for something to justify her hope, anything to make sense of this newly opened hole in her life.

"I don't think he really believed what he was saying. About having so much to do that the pain didn't beat the hell out of him."

"Why do you say that?"

"I can't really put in into words. You see, when you've been an actor, you get this bodily sense of when—"

Two knuckle raps on the door interrupted Jud. Marley's head appeared around the opened door. "Vieve, Gordon's downstairs. He found...Carl." Marley looked down. When he looked back up, his soft gaze told her what he didn't utter. But he also offered a bit of hope and comfort as he met her eyes directly.

In fact, the look that passed between them then was the third time Vieve felt intimate with Marley, but more than the kiss last night that she was not sure how it happened. They'd debated doing the mural while walking on the beach, and it veered into an argument somehow. But on the dune path up to the cabanas, Marley reached out and touched Vieve's waist, and the next thing she knew they were in a full-body embrace. But just as quickly as it happened, Marley pulled himself away.

When they reached the living room, Gordon was peering out the back bay window to the storage shed. He turned when Vieve entered,

Marley and Jud close behind. Jack West stayed at Vieve's heels.

"Vieve, this is Gordon Boothroyd," Marley said. "One of Carl's oldest friends."

Gordon advanced to meet Vieve. She took in a man in his mid-fifties, younger than Carl by a decade and a half, wavy, dark blond hair, slightly bulbous nose in a face with only minor crow's feet. He was slightly shorter than Marley, a purposeful man who seemed now somewhat lost.

"Vieve," he said. "I...found Carl. I'm so sorry to tell you this. He's...he's been dead for a while. Frek led me to him at the old jetty off Newell Point."

Vieve could not open her mouth. Tears began streaming down her cheeks and she reached down to pick up Jack West.

"The Coast Guard has been alerted. They will bring him back here. I'll take you to meet them."

Vieve stroked Jack West and struggled to form words. She didn't care about the tears, although she snatched up the tissue that Jud offered.

"Was he....? How..?"

Gordon lightly touched Vieve's upper arm. "I don't know. I can't tell anything about how he died. There will be an autopsy to help us figure it out." Anger rose in his voice. "But you don't just wade out to that island on a whim, trip and fall and drown." He stepped away from Vieve and turned toward the window to compose himself.

Jud retreated to the kitchen to make coffee while the others sank into sofa cushions and the wing chair around the fireplace. Vieve held on to Jack West. He seemed to know when to be still, when that was absolutely the best thing; otherwise, he found it hard to contain his enthusiasm. There was silence for several minutes, the news sinking in all around.

Jud returned with a tray of steaming coffee mugs.

"Carl was my friend for fifteen years," Gordon said. "And I was his lawyer for the last eight. I'll help you in any way I can with the estate, Vieve. Gratis."

Marley watched Vieve closely. Vieve's face, already very fair, drained of color. She clutched her terrier for some kind of handle on reality; she struggled just to breathe evenly. She said softly, "Carl was my uncle for fifty-one years and way closer to me than my dad."

More silence. Marley glanced at Vieve as did Gordon. "It's always great when someone believes in you," Marley said. "For however long you have them."

Vieve turned toward Marley, his words a rare gift. "Yes," she said. "I...I—"

Three loud bangs on the front door interrupted Vieve and startled everyone. Jud looked out the window. "Deena," he said. "All we need!"

Marley groaned. "I'll handle her," said Gordon, heading for the front door. "Everything's too raw."

Jack West settled deeply into Vieve's lap, her tears sliding off his wiry white fur. *Would Carl have just rowed off?*

CHAPTER 6

Friday, April 20, 2018

"So, who is Big Shark?" Vieve asked Gordon.

They sat in Gordon's law office. Boothroyd, Ledyard & Tetlow was located in a former church, minus the steeple top, at the beachfront intersection where a recently widened access road led up to the Salt Breeze House. Vieve had left Jack West with Asia, who wanted to walk him on Ponkipaug Beach with Lucie and see whether he'd catch a Frisbee if she threw one.

"Traced the call?" Gordon asked. He moved a legal-sized Geographic Information System map of the South Coast Granite property from the center of his desk to the left side and pulled out a document from a manila folder and laid it where the map had been.

"A cell phone no longer in use. Number based in Texas," Vieve said. "How close was Carl to launching the jewelry line? Did he tell you?"

Gordon's office with its dark walnut furniture and navy and burgundy accents sported a nautical theme—an oil painting of a U-boat, a lithograph of a cod-fishing scene from the 1700s, when the cod fish were bigger than teenagers, and a real ship's wheel. Gordon could view the coast and ocean east of Ponkipaug Point from his desk, and he glanced at the Sentinel Point lighthouse after turning on his laptop. An iron cross a foot long, left over from the church office, hung over his printer. A similarly sized iron anchor hung over the coffee maker behind where Vieve sat in an upholstered chair with padded armrests.

"The last he told me, he was having some issue with the hematite ore supply. Someone somewhere along the line wanted a bigger cut than they first agreed to. Don't know if that thug has any connection to this Big Shark character."

The last he told me, Vieve thought, lingering on Gordon's phrase. She was trying to remember her last conversation with Carl Beale in person. It seemed really important now. Vieve peered out the window behind Gordon's desk. It was another sparkling summer beach day, yet talking about Carl in the past tense drained the beauty from the view.

Gordon handed Vieve the copy of Carl's will from his desktop and reeled off the contents. After debts to the estate were paid, 17 Salt Pond and Carl's new and past jewelry lines went to Vieve. Fifty percent of his remaining financial assets were to be split between Vieve and her sister Joss. The Town of Paukipaug Village was to receive the other fifty percent—for college scholarships and high school renovations. Gordon got Carl's small yacht and his cars. Beryl Martin got some emerald estate jewelry that she mentioned she liked and $250,000 for a tennis charity she ran for kids in Bermuda. Ted Silva (aka Oden Vacca) got $75,000 held in trust. Richard Coggeshall, Carl's adult stepson, nothing. Deena Vaughan, ditto. There also was a sentence requesting that Vieve allow the current tenants of 17 Salt Pond to rent for as long as possible given her plans for the property.

"It's a bit embarrassing really," Vieve said. "Why I should get…all this…stuff?" She looked at the document Gordon gave her but could not bear to read the words.

"He must have loved you more than anyone. That's not a bad thing." Gordon scanned her face while Vieve measured the pain in his light gray eyes. Deep. There were way more souls than her suffering at this moment.

"Not as much as he was loved. By many." She looked out the

window at a sailboat just crossing behind Sentinel Point before the sun pulled a shadow curtain around its shoulders, darkening that patch of sea.

"I bet he also knew, what with all you've been through, that you'd be able to handle it without frittering it all away," Gordon said.

"Fritter what?" Vieve asked, coming back into the room after momentarily following the sailboat in her mind around the point.

"The money?"

Vieve laughed. "I'm too much of a damn Puritan at heart to fritter that kind of money away."

"I'm sure there will be many to help you do just that. Don't let them."

Vieve frowned. She stood and walked over to the window, Gordon swiveling in his chair to follow her.

"Hey, look. I'll help with this. There are lots of options. Start a trust or foundation. Hell, take his jewelry line and run with it. But...."

"But?" she glanced back at Gordon, who examined his clenched fists on his thighs. He looked up into Vieve's face.

"We still don't know whether we've got a murder on our hands." He shoved his chair back and stood up.

"I know. I know. The whole thing is surreal. I just want my uncle back. Paint my silly pictures. Throw sticks to Jack West on the beach. What do you think?"

"I've got a lot of questions. No answers." He glanced at the quarry map and frowned.

Vieve crossed the room and leaned back against the short counter where the coffee maker squatted under the anchor. "I think I could start to tuck this whole horrid thing away, deal with it as a suicide, if it weren't for this Big Shark message. And this feeling I have that there's something he's going to tell us. When he's ready. But that's absurd."

"Maybe not," said Gordon. "Big man, big soul."

Jack West took to Frisbee catching with the same passion with which he approached everything. Fling yourself at it, body and soul.

Asia threw the pink Frisbee farther and farther down the beach each time, Jack West leaping and catching it, landing on the hard wet sand. Asia laughed and reveled in the sunshine on her face, arms, and legs. She missed Carl, a lot, thinking of him seared her heart, but she knew he'd want her to enjoy this day. She saved the crying for the nighttime, early morning really, 3 am, the hour when you think nothing in your life will resolve.

Lucie followed behind, ear to phone. She hit End to terminate her call, slipped the purple device in her hip pocket, and caught up to Asia. "This place is cool. Day two and I met this hot guy whose parents own the marina. And he likes me!"

Asia smiled. *Eager kid,* she thought, although Lucie was only a year and a half younger than she was. Most of the guys in this town were obsessed with sports and binge drinking, a waste of time as far as Asia was concerned. Maybe college would offer more interesting possibilities. She was really looking forward to the Pawcatuck dig— the URI crew—and maybe there would be the added bonus of more mature guys? But not too mature—like the guys in Jud's play. It could be hoped. If not, she didn't care. The hell with guys. She was taking the first step in her dream of uncovering an undiscovered Niantic site. Somewhere between Providence and Mystic, she would find one. She knew it. She felt it. *Maybe I'll even get a PhD!*

Lucie looked at Asia. "Don't you want to know who?"

"I know whose parents own the marina. So I assume you're talking about Kent because his brother Ryan is too young for you."

"Yes, Kent! We're hanging out tonight with some of his friends. Getting pizza and then who knows?" Lucie said, peering at Asia, gauging her audience. "He's working the gas pumps at the marina this summer. Meets people from all over. He gets to ferry the gas out to the bigger yachts that can't dock."

The Big Boat People, thought Asia. *How tiresome.*

Jack West had retrieved the last throw, and the three of them walked up the dunes to higher drier sand.

"So how's Candy Crush?" Asia asked.

"It's ok. Bryce's gonna let me do social media, so that's cool. The tourists are friendly. Well, so far. Bryce is a bit *too* friendly though."

"He was too friendly last year too," said Asia. "I stayed away from him as much as I could when we were setting the place up, ordering supplies and the ready-mades, making the candy, and stocking. It helped that his wife was there a lot."

"Anyway, he's old. Gotta be like thirty. Creeps me out!"

"If he touches you, smack him. Otherwise, ignore him as much as you can. It's his wife who really runs the place."

"Well, it's just a job. And now that I've met Kent, things are looking up this summer. What about you? Any cool guy?"

Asia laughed. "No. There was a guy last summer but he moved away. Didn't answer texts after a couple of months. Typical." She reached down to inspect a tiny shell, whole and pink blushed. "Let's go to the tip. Have you seen Poki Dot?"

"That little island? Yeah, no big deal. It's too far to walk."

"I heard you used to be able to walk out to Poki Dot during really low tide once a month."

Suddenly, Oden popped up ahead in the dunes. He stood with Frek near the northernmost disappearing-gun installation, of which there were four associated with the fort, mostly briar covered.

"There's that psycho," said Lucie. "I hear he stalked a girl."

Asia spun around. "Who told you that?"

"Richard Coggeshall told Kent's father. We saw him yesterday."

"Figures."

"Figures what?"

"He's a liar. Oden's got more heart than Richard could ever dream of." Asia watched Oden reach down to pick up a piece of driftwood in the dunes. And then he stood up and saluted a passing swallow with his left hand.

"He's weird. Look at those rags he wears."

Asia began walking back to the cabanas.

"Wait up! Where are you going?"

"You said the walk was too far. Let's go back. You can go hang with Kent."

Asia turned away and walked faster.

"Look, Asia, it doesn't matter about that weir...that guy. What do you care?"

Asia slowed. "You don't know anything about him. Anything about this town. Why don't you go play with your rich boyfriend? He's not what you think he is either."

On a snatch of wind they heard the tail end of a voice screaming, although it could have just been wind blowing through a gun turret. Or a gull.

"What was that?" asked Lucie, hurrying to pull even with Asia.

"I don't know. Some ghost. A lot of people died here you know." Asia was aware that she could easily lapse into cruelty if she didn't watch herself. Not good. So Lucie was boy mad, there was no law that said they had to be friends.

"What?!" Lucie asked. "Who?"

"Ask Kent, he'll know. I heard he was caught tagging the fort last summer."

"He's not doing that anymore. He's got a job now."

"Good for him," Asia said. With that Asia clipped Jack West's lead on and slipped away through an almost hidden trail to the western side of Ponkipaug Point, with its narrower cobble beach and shellfish pools. It was named The Kitchen a century ago for its vast shellfish offerings there for the digging.

Lucie stood and watched her go. "What did I say?" she called out to Asia's receding back. Her phone cha-cha-ed, and she answered it while heading back to the cabanas.

Asia looked northwest toward 17 Salt Pond. Where she stood was the only point on the peninsula from which you could look northeast and see the salt pond after which the road was named. She shivered as a cool breeze found her, and she wished she could hug Carl one more time. Jack West, paw on her left sneaker, leaned against her shin. She looked up and saw Munin in his perch, packing a piece of metal.

PART 2

Saturday, April 21, 2018

W es Tetlow, stunned by Albert and Diana's plight, was eager to read more. He flipped to the front of the three-ring notebook of typed pages where his great-grandfather had drafted a short prelude sprinkled with his own editorial comments and proofreading symbols.

August 5, 1988

It rained near every other day that summer of '38. And if it didn't, the sky was clogged with clouds and the air sticky. But that Wednesday was the first bright sunny day since late June. Everyone flocked to the bay, the beaches, the rivers, and the golf courses. All of them were looking to squeeze a final drop of summer out of the first day of autumn. Except for a few seasoned fishermen I knew then. They each told me how the scarlet tint in the dawn sky made them hunker down in ports along the Weekapaug Coast that morning. By mid-afternoon, the sky turned a sickly yellow-green with a reddish overglaze. The crows and gulls disappeared. Then it hit. After a couple hours' wind and wave chaos, the town I knew vanished.

Wes flipped to the entry after Albert found Diana behind her parents' wrecked cottage. An old postcard, a colorized photo leached by time to Easter pastels, fell to

his lap. It showed the Coast Guard Station and, farther
out, the lighthouse surrounded by a tangerine sea. Wes sunk
deeper into the couch, and time spilled out in front of
him.

September 22, 1938
Sentinel Point Lighthouse and Coast Guard Station
Ponkipaug, Rhode Island

"It was a gray-white oblivion," Boatswain Coleman Miller
told me. He pointed to the upper floor of the Coast Guard
Station tower. "I was waiting up there for the view toward
Ponki to clear." Scratching his gray cheek stubble as if
to draw blood, he said, "Too late. Never cleared."

Thursday dawned bright and sunny, like nothing happened
yesterday. But it did. The south coast was a junkyard of
mangled house, docks, boats, and cars. So I bushwhacked
through hillocks of assorted lumber and house chunks out
to the lighthouse to find out what the Coast Guard knew.
My sneakers were sliced to ribbons by broken glass.

Coleman planted a foot on an upturned rowboat and
leaned his weight onto his thigh, crossing his hands over
his knee.

"All those Fort Drive summer folks. Forty-four houses."
Coleman shook his head. "They know I'm coming for them when
we get a blow." He smacked his thigh with an open palm,
jerked his leg off the boat, and straightened up. I saw
something pass over his face before he tamped down whatever
emotion he'd churned up.

"Then I realized I hadn't seen Foster return from
juicing the foghorn." Coleman swung an arm out toward the
lighthouse only one-tenth mile away. "The next time I could

see to the lighthouse, there was a swath of ocean separating us."

Coleman peered at Daniel Foster as if surprised he was still upright on this Earth.

The boatswain continued, while James Perry, the lighthouse keeper, joined us as we stood on the rock cliff-face above the seawall on Sentinel Point. "The waves tore off hunks of earth and loads of sand, one big bite after another. Then they smashed the launching tracks and demolished the cutter. By the time the boys were able to string a rescue line between the two buildings, we were each islands."

Daniel piped up, "Perry and I saw that yawl and thought there was still time to warn it off. After stepping off the porch toward the foghorn, I learned otherwise."

I suppressed a smile. Foster, assistant lighthouse keeper, was renowned for his arid wit. That he kept it dry through a hurricane seemed an achievement of note. "A gust threw me against the foghorn." He smoothed the edge of the bandage covering the deep gash on his cheek. "And then it seemed the whole Atlantic Ocean was gunning for me."

Coleman weighed back in. He knew the assistant lighthouse keeper to be too modest to elaborate. "Daniel spent two hours lashed to a water pipe to keep from being tossed into the bay toward Ponki along with everything else that wasn't nailed to solid rock."

Daniel shrugged. "I counted the waves. Got up to thirty before I passed out, I guess. Next thing I know, I'm being pumped like a well."

James Perry chimed in next. "Had to thump the water outta his lungs. Daniel's part seahorse. I don't see how else he survived. Never did see that yawl again."

Perry indicated the grievously battered seawall below us. "Without these rocks, no doubt the lighthouse and the life-saving station would have ended up in the bay." Perry was stout, a former college heavy-weight boxer. If he were a dog, he'd be a bull mastiff. He also grew African violets but no one teased him about it.

Perry turned west and we all followed suit. "Ponkipaug Point had no such rocky footstool. All that's left? Two docks and a few feet of seawall."

The men and I bowed our heads, each alone with our own particular pain. Coleman looked, still with disbelief, at the gap where Annette White's cottage had stood for 30 years. She'd been town librarian since my father was a kid. In the village, there were so many bodies to recover. Hastily formed teams were finding and burying the dead, cleaning up debris, and comforting those who survived but lost everything. The broken and bruised. The defiant and the despairing. Anyone who could move was doing something: restoring power, clearing roads, hauling in supplies, and nursing the injured. I knew what I had to do: Tell the world. There were no communication lines operating all along the coast. On that day after though, all I knew was that there was no way to get word out of Ponkipaug Point.

I pocketed my notes, left by car for New Haven with the news. It would take me eighteen hours to get there over roads that usually allowed the journey in under two hours. Trees lay across the road like jumbo pickup sticks. I almost lost my Ford five times in gaping pits in the pavement like bombs exploded, and I slalomed the car around streams still overrunning their banks. When I reached the offices of the *New Haven Register*, I saw on the editor's desk why no one was focused on the coastal mayhem. Hitler had tightened the noose on Czechoslovakia.

When I returned to Ponki Point on Sunday, Perry told me he'd spent the rest of Thursday afternoon with the Coast Guard crew clearing sodden furniture, rugs, and timber from the lighthouse living quarters. He found two crabs scuttling in the bathtub. He threw them back into the sound. Anyone who survived that blow, he figured, deserved not to be eaten.

Wes flipped to the next section of the notebook, which was also laden with copyediting marks and notes. The storylines and viewpoint were jumbled, and the time disjointed. Some entries featured interviews in which Wendell appeared to be interviewing townsfolk to record the events of the day, and some were written as if he were the one who'd gone through the calamity. The last note read: *Try for the sixtieth anniversary—1998.*

Yeah, thought Wes, *1998. That was four years after Wendell died of that heart attack. He never finished the rewriting and editing.*

"Well!" Wendell's great-grandson said to himself, brightening. "The eightieth anniversary will have to do!" He laid the notebook back on the coffee table and rubbed his palms together, savoring the challenge.

"What did you say, Wes?" his mother called from the porch.

CHAPTER 7

Friday, April 27, 2018

The flyers were plastered on storefront windows all over town like arrows, like stepping stones: **Carl's Memorial Service** *and Clam Bake!* someone had added in slanted handwriting before it was printed. Part two was to take place on the private beach of the Salt Breeze House, which was bracing for basically the whole town showing up. Part one, the more or less private family service, took place at the United Congregational Church of Ponkipaug, with Joss's family, Vieve and Joss's mother, and other close family guests filling three-quarters of the pews.

Carl's brother, Vieve and Joss's father, had been estranged from Carl for reasons that still weren't clear to Vieve and despite repeated peacemaking attempts by Vieve's mother, Claire. Well, the reasons were clear, but, frankly, juvenile, Claire always said. The arguments were tiresome, and Vieve had tuned out from them well before the final split between the brothers when she was in college. Now it was too late for a reconciliation.

Claire returned from the ladies' room and seated herself with dignity next to her daughters in the front left pew. Vieve knew that Claire would not let her stubborn spouse, Professor Stephen Beale, rob her of the opportunity to pay last respects to her brother-in-law, whom her mother loved and respected.

Gordon walked to the podium to say a few words about his

closest friend.

As Gordon began to speak, Vieve felt unmoored, like she were rushing down a river to the sea. Her hands gripped the front edge of the pew and she closed her eyes, listening to Gordon's voice but not the words. She remembered her uncle, probably only early twenties at the time, holding her tiny hand and leading her to the edge of the ocean. Her first solid memory of this shore town. Screeching and giggling, she stomped and kicked the waves that swirled around her little bowed calves. Then he swung her high on his shoulders. He pointed to the lighthouse and told her about how Neptune fashioned Ponkipaug Point from a broken necklace of rocks and pebbles and then sprinkled it with sand from Africa. She tugged on his ears and kicked her feet against the front of his shoulders. He cantered like a pony.

Claire laid a hand on her youngest daughter's skirted thigh. Vieve looked up to the stained glass behind the alter, through a mesh of memory unrolling and spilling forward like the fingers of tide to land her back in the pew next to her mother. Gordon had returned to his place in the pews, his face glistening.

The real action took place at the Salt Breeze House private beach. Everyone came and then some. Richard Coggeshall glommed onto the rotund Congressman Tony Guinta, who arrived with his entourage and offered what Vieve felt were rather rote condolences to herself and her mother and sister. Vieve spent the next twenty minutes tending to a distraught Evan Button. He was supposed to be working the event, but every time he looked at Vieve he burst into tears. She wasn't sure it wasn't from the logistics of offering an open bar to half the population of Rhode Island.

After the church service, Vieve had gone back to the house to retrieve Jack West. The crowd reminded her of the day she first saw Jack West. He'd dashed up to her, a stray at a three-day event, a demanding equestrian sport in which competitors gallop cross-country jumping massive, solid obstacles, dash up and down hills and steep banks, and fly over water bodies. In the midst of the crowd lining the course, Jack West looked up in the sea of legs to find...someone who would listen to the story his eyes told. *Vieve!* Today, she held him tight, and he carried himself with a somber dignity worthy of Gainsby himself. Then he noticed kids at the ocean's edge with a Frisbee. He wriggled free of Vieve's arms and raced out to join them.

Deena was there by the clam-roasting pit, her head held high with an air of the wronged wife. She'd refused to come to the church, said Carl wouldn't have wanted a church service. Marley was downing Long Island ice teas at an alarming rate. Even Jud raised an eyebrow. Half the town was crying or drinking or both at this unlikely mixture of wake and block party. Carl would have loved it.

Vieve wondered, *Is Big Shark in attendance?* She scanned the crowd from the terrace. She noticed an African-American woman walking from the parking lot to the Salt Breeze House in a light gray linen sheath dress with a large bright coral-pink necklace. She was six feet tall and not without substantial forearms. She was stopped and bear hugged by the restaurant manager.

Claire approached Vieve. They hugged. After they separated, Claire said, "I knew a month in I had married the wrong brother." They watched each other's expression in the wake of Claire's confession. Vieve nodded.

Vieve wasn't surprised at her mother's pronouncement, or that she'd waited until after Carl's death to admit it. They stood in silence next to each other by the terrace stairs overlooking the clam pit. Vieve laid a hand on her mother's forearm and then scanned the crowd on the beach.

"Carl would have wanted a party," Vieve said, linking her left arm through her mother's right one. "Except he would have wanted to be here to enjoy everyone's company."

Vieve noticed Richard Coggeshall, near the clam pit, lean in and whisper something to the congressman, while Gordon slunk in a low-slung beach chair staring at the receding tide, nursing something in a rocks glass. The urge to have wine, have a margarita, have a double-whatever was strong. Jud came up behind her and handed her a seltzer with lime. Claire walked toward the restaurant to greet a cousin.

Thanks," she said. "You seem to have a knack of knowing when I'm about to fall off the wagon."

"I can read the signs," Jud said.

"Any way you can slow Marley down?" She nodded toward him on the beach. "He scares me how fast he's putting those away."

Jud nodded. "I try. He doesn't listen. He drinks more since you moved in. He used to think he'd be monk forever."

"Have I moved in?" Vieve asked.

Jud smiled. They both looked over the railing at the crowd expanding around the clam pit. The scent of pine reached them as the white wood smoke swirled off into invisibility in the sunlight.

"You're not going to kick us out now, are you? Now that you've this lovely beach house." Jud raised his eyebrows playfully.

Vieve smiled back and shook her head. Jud hadn't seen the will, and, of course, Carl wouldn't have dropped word of his intent to let the tenants stay on. She had no desire to rid her new house of tenants. In fact, she seemed to have stumbled on some of the best folks in town. Vieve realized she actually liked Asia more than her niece Lucie, not that Joss had to know. When Vieve asked how the Frisbee throw went, Asia had mentioned that Lucie had a new boyfriend and she doubted whether she and Lucie would be palling around much this summer.

Vieve and Jud moved down to the clam pit and helped themselves to corn-on-the-cob, garden salad, and roasted quahogs and oysters. Joss joined Claire on the deck near where the Salt Breeze House manager, Reed Matterly, and the sheath-dressed woman stood.

Vieve wanted to let Marley know how much his kindness meant to her this last week. And that their kiss needn't mean...*needn't mean what?* She spotted Marley in the middle of a group of kids overseeing the construction of an elaborate sand castle, complete with a moat, dinosaurs, space aliens, and the fox and rabbit from *Zootopia*. A young girl, Mia Coggeshall, had buried most of Marley's right calf under the fine white-beige sand, with its dazzling white quartz crystals sparkling in the sunshine. Vieve approached, and Marley glanced up.

"You ok?" he asked.

"No. But I'm still functioning. Can we walk down the beach a bit? There's something...."

"Sure," Marley said. "Carry on, guys," he said to the children after extricating himself from his sand castle and standing up. Jack West dashed past with the Frisbee in his mouth, and the girl who buried Marley's leg gave chase.

Vieve smiled. "That is the best companion I could have found." Until she met Jack West, she'd always had a bit of a thing against terriers. Too noisy, too assertive, too much. Now she saw that terrier vibe as affectionate, active, spontaneous, engaged. A big, wet, happy balm after too many disappointments.

"Your dog is a natural-born leader," Marley said.

Jack West veered up into the dunes, children strung out behind like a snap-the-whip game from a Winslow Homer painting. Then he stopped, turned around, and raced through the ragged line of children, barreling back down the beach the other way. The children screamed and laughed and wheeled round to chase after him.

Vieve and Marley walked toward Sentinel Point. There were

many steps in silence on the hard, dry sand with gulls overhead and sandpipers working the tideline. Vieve inhaled the scent of hot sand and dried seaweed. A wave spilled turquoise-green close to shore and then pulled and rattled shells and stones as it disappeared colorless down the beach face. Vieve scanned the upper dunes fronting a row of elaborate beach houses.

They reached the hardened inlet separating the Salt Breeze House beach from the continuation of the beach extending another three-quarter mile to Ponkipaug Point. Marley lowered himself on the flat top of the rock wall, facing away from the clam bake crowd. Vieve glanced one more time into the dunes before sitting down next to Marley.

"What are you looking for?" Marely asked.

Vieve checked Marley's face, deciding how much to say. "Someone named Big Shark."

"Big Shark? Shouldn't you be looking out over the ocean?" he joked. Vieve didn't smile.

"Some bully who's been calling Carl. Left a cryptic, innuendo-ish message. I wonder if it's someone around here. I wonder if it's Richard?"

Marley narrowed his eyes against the dipping sun. They were facing directly west.

"I doubt it. Richard will threaten to buy you out, to get your permit revoked, or to steal your competition. But he won't physically hurt you."

Vieve considered whether Richard might have changed since the jetty dunking episodes. She didn't really think Richard was Big Shark. As he'd aged he appeared to have taken on a more shrewd approach to crushing the competition.

"Change subject," Vieve said. "Tell me about this mural idea."

Marley brightened at the turn in the conversation. "We do it in sections, alternating, so that the abstract and the representational reinforce each other—the sight and the feeling. Six sections." He swept out his arm toward Ponkipaug Point.

"This really was the epicenter of the hurricane for Rhode Island. Hell! For all New England. Here west to New London," he said. "Hey! Why not put the mural right on the point?!"

Vieve laughed. "How much LI tea have you had?" The mechanics of it were ridiculous. "How would that work? There is nothing, well, no buildings on the point. You can't put it on the beach."

"Well, I know there are two private properties next to the fort. Coggeshall and Hallowell properties. It was Hallowell who suggested Richard get on the board of the reopened quarry back a few years ago to rekindle their high school camaraderie. There must have been something else in it too. Something with Guinta maybe? But their families go way back to before the storm, together on Ponkipaug Point. Nina told me all this when Richard was seriously trying to close JohnnyCakes a couple years ago."

Jack West sat down next to Vieve on the jetty, and Marley continued. "But, no, I mean on the fort. Put it along the top level of the fort. Wipe off the tags."

"On the concrete? You'd have to have it weatherproofed too. How much of a budget can the committee afford?" Vieve joked. "How would you stop it from being re-tagged? Who's going to actually *see* it? It's an Indiana Jones expedition just to get out there."

Marley shrugged. "A couple details to work out." They watched a gull soar on the other side of the inlet searching the surf line for goodies.

Marley smiled. "We could hire Oden to guard it. And do the interpretation. A museum curator of the dunes! Widen and improve the trail from the dunes, clear a half acre of poison ivy—"

Vieve laughed. "Yeah, a couple of minor details. Like the red tape to break through to put anything on that property. Isn't it still Fed property?"

"I think the town bought the whole point except for the two private parcels. The fort was a folly the Feds wanted to forget. The fatal flaw."

Marley peered into the water of the inlet. Perch swam by in the transparent green-brown water.

"Well, you have to admit it would make for a good challenge." Vieve considered for a moment. "What would be the theme?"

"Certainly nothing that could be put into words, otherwise why bother with a mural?" Marley turned to look at Vieve. "I'm not a big believer of putting art into words."

There was some change in Marley's face she couldn't name. An expectancy about him perhaps. The intensity she'd seen when he made art. Suddenly Vieve felt embarrassed. Exposed.

"Hey," Marley said, laying a hand on her upper arm. "What happens on Ponki Point, stays on—"

"...is most likely all over town by morning," Vieve said. She couldn't help smiling.

"Look," they both said at once. Then they broke eye contact to peer into the inlet water, the tide rising.

"You go," said Vieve.

"Look. It just happened. Oh, hell, I'm attracted to you, Vieve." Marley picked up a fragment of quahog shell and hurled it into the inlet.

Vieve watched the circles enlarge themselves from the point where the shell disappeared. She pulled up her knees and wrapped her arms around her shins.

"I...well, you throw me, Marley Kinnell. You really do. I mean, you're, what, almost twenty years younger than me? Eighteen?"

"Only sixteen," Marley said. "Since you so conveniently told us you're fifty-one. Who the hell cares anyway?"

"I'm not looking for that kind of thing now."

Marley laughed. "What kind of thing? All I said was I'm attracted to you. Ok, so I kissed you. I apologize if it was awful." He tilted his head to the left, the sun glinted off his hair, and she felt a rush of something she didn't want to feel.

"Hardly."

They looked at each other. Vieve's head said she was not looking for a guy, a romance. Casual sex was simply not possible. It always entangles. That was why we should care about the people we do it with.

But Vieve's heart was working another side of the street. A street that did not want to let itself be open to...losing someone else. She found Marley's art mesmerizing, seductive in itself, and Marley's presence, his physicality, excited her. She was a mishmash of conflicting desires amid a fresh round of grief from losing her uncle.

Marley stood up. "Ok, at least we agree on that. And I don't have to apologize."

Vieve unfolded herself and rose too. They watched each other, as one would watch the sea during a sudden color change, looking for some clue as to its next move.

At that moment, they heard yelling from the beach just down from the clam pit.

"What's that?" Vieve asked, turning just in time to see Marley take off toward the commotion. Vieve followed.

In between the clam pit and the edge of the sea, Richard confronted Oden, trying to stop him from moving up the beach to join the circle of folks surrounding the clam pit.

Oden raised his fists and declared, "He was my friend. Just the same as all of you!"

"You've been drinking," Richard said. He grabbed one of Oden's wrists and tried to pull his arm back down. Oden resisted and stepped closer to Richard.

Marley whispered to Vieve, "What he really wants to say is, 'You haven't washed in a month.'"

"Hah!" Oden replied. "As has half of Rhode Island!" Oden swept his right arm toward the crowd around the pit and swayed unsteadily on his feet. He widened the distance between his feet and glared at Richard, leaning toward him.

Richard rocked back on his heels and then stepped forward toward Oden. At 5'9", he was shorter than Oden, but he was a Coggeshall. He would not lower himself to name calling like a middle schooler.

They glared at each other.

"How do you sleep at night, Richard Coggeshall? The Fourth! For what you did? You killed my sister!"

Jud told Vieve a few days ago that it was true you never knew what was going to come out of Oden's mouth. Bitter truths, startling accusations, phantasmagorical tales, snippets of lyric poetry, or elaborate weather forecasts.

Vieve poked Marley's waist and raised her eyebrows. Marley asided to Vieve, "Richard was proven innocent in an inquest, but not in the court of basic decency."

People nearby turned to watch Richard's response and then Oden's reaction.

"I'm not even going to acknowledge that. Ted." The last word hurled as an insult.

When Oden heard the offending syllable, he took a swing at Richard that glanced off his cheek. As Richard turned to evade another blow, he tripped over a piece of driftwood and fell awkwardly onto the sand.

"'Twas a fatal flaw that took him down, alas that day at sea," Oden said, then tipped an imaginary hat at the crowd. "Tuck yourself in well tonight, oh town, and remember those whom you've forgotten. Who have died before their time. Behind the bitter dragon's breath of grief, you'll—"

Gordon interrupted the monologue, grabbing Oden by the elbow.

In his other hand he carried a plastic plate of food. He pulled Oden down the beach a bit to the east and sat with him on a desiccated fallen tree up on the dune where the dry reddish grass grew. Oden helped himself to clams, dipping them into a little metal tub of melted butter. After licking his fingertips, he said, loudly—"Oh, the noble quahog, oldest living beast"—and then released one into his mouth.

"He's wasted," said Marley. "Of course, the same could be said for me." He considered the group around the clam pit. "Us."

Vieve scanned the crowd again. "Who's the lady on the terrace? Gray sheath dress?"

Marley looked over. "I don't know. Never seen her before."

"Excuse me, I'm going to introduce myself." Vieve started for the terrace. She passed Richard, in an argument with his wife, Tilly, on the edge of the parking lot. Vieve heard Richard say, "Don't defend him, Til, you have no idea..." before Vieve veered right and climbed the wooden steps to the terrace.

"Ah, Genevieve," said Reed Matterly, whom everyone called The Colonel. "I'd like you to meet Beryl Martin of Hamilton, Bermuda. A dear friend of your uncle's."

Beryl held out a hand to Vieve, who took it. Beryl's grip was strong, and she peered straight into Vieve's eyes.

"It's great to meet you finally," Beryl said. "Carl thought the world of you. We all thought the world of him." British accent, Vieve noted. "Hell of a doubles partner." *Was she trying to keep it light to keep herself together?*

"I'm glad you could come all this way," Vieve said.

"I've only just come from Newport where I consult at the Tennis Hall of Fame. But I would have flown around the world to be here."

"Did you make it in time for the church service?"

"Just slipped in the back right before it started."

The Colonel was pulled away by Nina Pucci, and Vieve moved in to stand closer to Beryl. She looked to be a good decade younger than

Vieve and still in shape to play competitive tennis. *If she had married Carl,* Vieve thought, *she'd be my aunt.*

"Beryl, I'd like to talk to you about Carl," Vieve said. "But. Not here. There are things that...aren't making sense."

"I'm not surprised," Beryl said. "It's the same with me. I think Carl was one of those people for whom everyone had a different piece of the story and—"

Deena Vaughan approached Vieve on the terrace, glaring at Beryl, who stopped midsentence. Deena walked by both of them and headed to the ladies' room, in passing sloshing some of her red wine on the back of Beryl's sheath dress.

Beryl gasped. "What!"

"Pardon me," Deena said without a shred of sincerity and kept walking. "Caught my heel."

"Who was that?" Beryl said.

Vieve tried to wipe red wine off Beryl's dress. "Looks like you've a bit of a spot."

Beryl pulled herself up to her full six-foot height. "Don't fuss," she said. "Who is she?"

"According to her, Carl's fiancée."

"Oh, that Vaughan woman." Beryl let out a low laugh. "Yes, we really must talk. I can see that."

"If you're staying over, let's meet tomorrow, at the Salt Breeze breakfast room. We'll have a bit of privacy there. Tell The Colonel what happened. He'll have Deena pay your dry cleaning bill."

"Oh, she'll pay all right. Don't worry about that," Beryl said. "I've got a meeting in Providence tomorrow, but I'll be back and we can breakfast on Sunday."

More noise from the beach, whose action Vieve had ignored until then, engaged as she was with Beryl. Vieve hurried over to where Gordon advanced on Richard. Before anyone could intervene, Gordon clobbered Richard in the chest with his thrown shoe and Richard threatened Gordon with a piece of driftwood. All pretense of Richard maintaining dignity was gone. Tilly pulled on Richard's left arm, and Jud grabbed Gordon around the waist.

Vieve noticed a look pass between Gordon and Tilly that did not reflect their positions on opposite sides of the fight. Vieve looked at Marley, who shrugged. Jack West sidled up to Vieve's feet with the Frisbee, dropped it and began panting. Then he flopped down on the sand. He was soaked with seawater to his hips, a thin ribbon of dark brown seaweed curled around the base of his tail, and his eyes gleamed mischievously. Munin flew overhead, comparing the delectability of food items on the abandoned plastic plates and half-eaten ears of corn in the sand. People began walking to their cars in twos and fours.

Vieve expected to see Carl walk out of the Salt Breeze House then, wanting to share just one more story with her before dark. Reveling in the success of his memorial party.

CHAPTER 8

Vieve felt a light evening breeze play through her hair and a hand on her shoulder. When she turned, Vieve could see the tell-tale soft pinkness around Tilly's eyes and her splotchy cheeks. She'd been crying too. Richard was moving off toward the deck, face averted from Vieve.

"Your uncle was one-of-a-kind, and we'll all miss him terribly," Tilly said softly.

Vieve nodded. "Thank you. He would have been pleased to see this crowd."

"That's about all the solace there is now." Tilly shrugged and looked out over the ocean.

"Even the little beach scuffle would have amused him." Vieve didn't feel she could say more without losing it, but she did manage a halfhearted smile.

She felt confused about Tilly, married to a man Vieve couldn't stand, yet nice to a fault. Tilly had been in Vieve's biology class in high school, before they drifted off into different worlds. Tilly didn't take up with Richard until they met in South Kingstown at the university.

"Let me know if there's anything I can do," Tilly said. "People always say that, but I really mean it. Even if you just want to talk." She gave Vieve an unexpected hug and slipped away toward the deck where Richard stood talking to The Colonel. Marley and Asia left to walk back to 17 Salt Pond together. Most of the other guests had vanished.

On Vieve's right a few remaining restaurant staff members peered into the dying embers, holding, she imagined, their private memories of Carl like smoothly weathered stones in their hands.

"Walk with me," Gordon said, stepping next to Vieve and interrupting her thoughts. "I've got to clear my head. I usually have it more under control. My apologies to you....and Carl." He shook his head as if to erase the fact of the embarrassing brawl with Richard.

"Carl would have gotten a kick out of it," Vieve said, laying a hand on Gordon's arm to acknowledge the apology. They moved off in silence while behind them the staff began clearing up the clam bake remains.

"Will you be staying around?" Gordon asked after they walked a few dozen yards down the beach. "It would help with the estate if you could. Things will be pending for a good while, but there's lots to do with handling the bequest to the town. That was a new one he added last month."

Vieve had been avoiding her portrait clients since she'd come to Ponkipaug Village three weeks ago to have dinner with Carl. *Three weeks ago?* There were two commissions due in mid-July that she hadn't even started yet.

"You're the executor, I forgot to mention the other day. You probably guessed."

"Yes, I'll stay. Of course," Vieve said. "I still need to know why he's gone. I can't just go back home and move on until I know. And even then...." *No*, she thought, *don't*.

She watched Jack West, revived after eating leftover stew meat that one of the restaurant staff served him, galloping along the surf line, phosphorescence bubbling into the dark in the surf. Her heart felt a tiny bit lighter.

"Good," he said. Vieve wondered whether to Gordon her staying was like he could still hold on to a piece of Carl.

Gordon scanned over the sea to the south. "Right offshore here, 'bout four miles out." He pointed. "That's where we're looking for the German U-boat. One was sunk east of Block Island in May 1945, the one under Heinrich's command. I've been scouring maps for years, and now they have these cool submerged vehicles that can do really fine-grained mapping and, by my calculations, there is likely another one southwest of Block Island in a straight line due south of Poki Dot."

Vieve watched as Gordon's expression brightened with the subject change. "Imagine," he said, "how close the Germans were to the mainland! Those guys were sent to mess with our cargo shipping. But it could have led to an invasion."

The sun had set, and the moon shone over the lighthouse to the east. Jack West trotted along at Vieve's side. Gordon's Basset hounds bounced along on Gordon's right, their ears scrunching up and then unfurling with their strides. They'd been sleeping in his office during the clam bake: MacArthur, Winston, and Clementine.

"These underwater vehicles? They take something like pictures of the ocean floor by bouncing laser beams off it. They have enough resolution to show whether there is some big object projecting up." Gordon looked at Vieve. She was frowning at the sand, lost in thought. "I usually lose most folks by this point. Anyway, it's techy and you're an artist."

Vieve looked over at Gordon and said, "Actually, good artists are techy too. But we often narrow our focus to chemical and physical properties of paint and supports. And what light does, if that's a priority. Carry on. I want to hear." She really didn't care about the subs, but it served to get Gordon's mind off Carl.

"Well, we're deploying these things! URI has a great oceanography department, and I helped talk them into experimenting on refining the tool right here off Poki Dot."

Gordon continued, taking such joy in the topic that Vieve felt a bit happier sharing in it. "A lot of this technology stuff is becoming more accessible, cheaper. More useful. Hell! Even rocket science isn't really rocket science anymore. It's all connected."

Gordon fell silent and the moon rose higher. The sea was murmuring, a large comforting weight off to their left, hording, yet whispering, its underwater secrets.

Finally, Vieve asked, "Why'd you let Richard get to you tonight? Not really your style from what I know of you."

Gordon looked over at Vieve, his mouth tight. "It wasn't just tonight. It's been building."

"What has?"

They reached the jetty, turned around, and began walking back. Once they traversed the hotel beach to the east, they would enter a state natural resource management area. From there to the hardened inlet on which the lighthouse stood was patch pocketed with beaches and tidal flats, hotels and summer houses, grand beach estates, parking lots, golf courses, crumbling remnants of 1950s clam shacks and ice cream stands, marshes, salt ponds, and hard-packed sand roads that changed shape with tide and storm surge and bulldozer. The few cottages on this stretch of beach that were left standing on September 22, 1938 were gone now.

"Richard's obsessions," Gordon said as they passed the remains of a sand castle, melting with each receding wave."

"Which are?" Vieve asked.

"One, to take as much as he can," Gordon said. He threw a stick for MacArthur.

"Can you tell me, once and for all, what it is with the Boothroyds and the Coggeshalls in this town? It was always a vague mystery when I was a kid, and I thought it would have faded away and been forgotten by now."

"Hah!" said Gordon. "Forgotten!"

When MacArthur returned with the stick, Clementine grabbed one end of it and shook her head. MacArthur tightened his jaws around the stick and weighted his hind end. Gordon threw another stick and the two took off after it. Winston looked after his siblings as if he thought they were daft. Jack West tugged playfully on one of Winston's great ears and then plopped down, letting out a bark.

Gordon and Vieve stood still. Facing the ocean, they watched the moon's reflection bathe itself in the shimmering water offshore.

"My great-great uncle Albert Boothroyd was supposed to marry Diana Coggeshall. Let's see, that would be Richard's great-grandfather's cousin, I think. Albert had presented to Diana this elaborate sapphire-and-diamond engagement ring that his grandfather gave to his grandmother. Albert's family owned a lobstering fleet and boat servicing area—the beginning of the marina—it really took off after the war—and the Coggeshalls had been in quarrying. Granite. Sand. Before they took up real estate. Of course, Richard's back in quarrying with the reopening of the old West County Mine six years ago. Well, maybe not in it hands on, but on the board. I was on it too...." Gordon looked out over the darkening sea. Choosing words, Vieve speculated.

"Until six months ago." Gordon smiled wryly. "Actually the Cogges were in real estate acquisition even before quarrying, if you count pushing the Pequots off their land in the late sixteen hundreds. There was a famous Coggeshall in the first batch of Europeans that settled here in Misquamicutt—meaning red fish—salmon—in the language of those who were already here."

"So what happened with the marriage?" Vieve asked, thinking Asia would love this stuff. Or might actually already know it. She'd have to ask.

"Nothing," Gordon said. "It never happened. Diana was killed by flying glass and the tidal surge from the hurricane. Right over there." He pointed to the first parcel of land between the Salt Breeze House property and the jetty, the former 23 Atlantic Drive.

"Oh," said Vieve. "How ghastly!"

"Yes, it was ghastly all right. So many died here. Most of them all within a couple hours."

"Then what? What started the animosity that never seems to die?" Vieve asked. Gordon's words brought back all the loss in this town. Vieve wondered, *When will these memories disappear? Who will tell them when Gordon's—our—generation is gone? We really do need this mural.*

"It seems Diana's parents never really forgave Albert for letting her be alone in the house during the storm. But there was no warning! That was the thing about this hurricane. First, it wasn't supposed to be a big deal. Early in the afternoon, there were vague warnings about a gale heading toward Long Island Sound. Line storms are common in September, so folks just thought it would be a pesky little storm, maybe a bit bigger than normal, certainly not a major blow. When the magnitude of it became clear—after it had leveled whole towns on Long Island—the communication lines were all down. The Connecticut and Rhode Island coasts were doomed."

Gordon glanced briefly at the location of the former 23 Atlantic Avenue, closed his eyes, opened them, and then continued. "By the time Albert tried to leave the boatyard to reach Diana by car, he couldn't make headway against the storm surge and wind. And it was too late by the time he'd walked there. The roads were full of rubble, in some places twelve feet high, and downed power lines, some still sizzling."

He took a breath and turned to his left in the exact direction from which the storm had approached the coast almost eighty years ago.

"Quarter of seven he found her. She'd been dead for about two hours by then, according to family legend and the broken watch on her wrist."

Vieve listened and then sunk down onto the sand as if under the weight of what she was hearing. Jack West rolled up in sled dog sleeping position in her lap and made for a nap. From Jack West's perspective, *a most satisfactory day!*

Gordon lowered himself onto the sand next to Vieve. MacArthur and Clementine returned, each with their own sticks, and joined Winston, already lying down, facing the ocean next to Gordon, Vieve, and Jack West. The moon rose higher and cast short shadows behind the little group of kindred souls.

"Then what happened?" Vieve asked, although she wasn't sure she wanted to know.

"Albert said Diana was supposed to be on the other side of town with her sister Violet that day, but, for some reason, she changed her mind and decided to work on the wedding invitation list in the morning at the beach house. The wedding was set for New Year's Day 1939 in Newport. Then she would read and watch the high surf for the rest of the afternoon."

Gordon shuddered. Clementine rolled over onto her back against MacArthur and closed her eyes to nap, pudgy paws aloft.

"Anyway, Albert, probably messed up by grief, and after three months of semi-courting, decides he and Violet should marry. They'd turned to each other for consolation after Diana's death. He mistook that for love."

Gordon rested a hand on Winston, who sighed.

"Violet was only eighteen and very different from Diana, although they looked alike. Violet was the more social and volatile of the sisters. The hurricane brought destruction, panicked land sales, and opportunity for those shrewd, steely veined souls the hurricane didn't take. In the wake of the storm, Albert bought the Atlantic Drive lot for almost nothing from Diana's parents. After all, he was to become their son-in-law."

Gordon leaned back, propping himself up with his forearms in the sand. The moon shadows reached closer to the dunes.

"The new couple was miserable within six months, but it takes them until the early fifties to divorce. Albert needed a confidant and Violet wanted excitement. She wasn't interested in settling down in sleepy Ponkipaug Village to raise a family."

"If I were eighteen and just lost a sister, I might marry the wrong guy too," Vieve said. *Of course, I did marry the wrong guy even without losing a sister and being older than eighteen....* Then she considered the storm survivors and how things were never the same for anyone after so much destruction.

Gordon frowned. "Well, it was more complicated than that. After Albert realizes their mistake, he just works harder and starts drinking. Violet tries to get into the theatre but isn't successful. She meets actors in Providence, in New Haven, in Provincetown. It was a mess. And then she has an abortion."

Vieve glanced over at Gordon.

"It wasn't Albert's child," he said. "I think Albert's spirit broke after the abortion and divorce. Violet took off for Providence, had no interest in the house of her painful past. Albert never remarried and had no heirs."

Winston stood up, turned around, and flopped down again, his muzzle resting on Gordon's thigh.

"Kenneth and Lily Bea Coggeshall never forgave him for the divorce. Diana had been their favorite, but Violet could do no wrong in their eyes. But to me it seems like they blamed the whole damn hurricane on him. Sometimes things turn out nothing like we expect and we just want to blame someone."

Vieve let out a sound like a stifled hiccup. "I know." Out of the corner of her eye she saw movement in the sand. Or did she?

"So that property came into my branch of the Boothroyds after Albert died. He did well for himself, although I doubt he was ever happy. By the time I sold it to the Salt Breeze House, the current Cogges—Richard and his cousins—were livid at the value gain that they had thought would stay in the family. Another reason why Richard wants your uncle's, well, *your* house. Richard thought it was on track to go to his mother, but we all know she died before Carl."

The waves hitting the beach sounded louder now in the fading light. A creature called sharply from the other side of the inlet. Then faintly. And the ocean ran darker. Like sparkling onyx threaded with veins of flashing silver.

"What about Richard's other obsessions?" Vieve asked, looking up at the stars as they stretched and twinkled across the black sky canvas.

"Hah! They go further back. In the late 1700s, there was the first infamous land squabble between the Booths and the Cogges—as my dad put it. He joked that that's why the Booths went into law and the Cogges real estate. It was over that strip of land on the shore side of Salt Pond Drive, across from Carl's, eh, your house. The commercial potential of that area has been huge since the days of the Niantics. But then came The Gale of 1815 to add another twist to that story. Killed the Boothroyd in question that time. Stripped the trees off Ponki Point. Another time...." Gordon said, raising his hand as if to stop the unfurling of the story. "It all seems so pointless now."

"You expect me to believe that these silly land squabbles would precipitate such an epoch family grudge? Like your fight on the beach tonight?" Vieve asked, watching Gordon's profile. In the bright moonlight spilling on the beach, she saw his jaw muscles tighten.

"Believe it or not. It's true."

Another movement on her right toward the dune. A ghost crab scurried into a burrow just in time to miss the sweep of a Basset hound tail.

"Richard's other obsessions? He wants more land, more say in this town. Mingled with a minor urge to do good in some way, in the kind of way that will get him attention. But mostly, he wants to get the best of me."

Gordon turned toward her. "Were you ever married, Vieve?"

Vieve's mouth twisted into a frown. "Twice. One left me. And the good one died in a canoeing accident."

Gordon winced.

"How about you?"

"There was someone once," Gordon confessed. "But she married someone else before I got to propose." He jabbed his right heel into the sand. "I try hard to keep a rational perspective when it comes to Richard. To control myself. We got to break this cycle sometime," Gordon said, his face darkening again. *Another sharp-edged memory?*

"But it isn't easy. If only... No! Enough, eh kids?" he said, fondling the ears of the closest two Basset buddies.

Gordon pointed to Ponkipaug Point, shaking off gloom. "Did you know General MacArthur visited Fort Devlin in 1902?"

Vieve smiled at Gordon's evasion, wondering what he had gotten close to telling her.

Saturday, April 28, 2018

The morning after the memorial service, Marley didn't appear until nine-thirty. Very rare for him and also that he consented to Asia making him pancakes for breakfast. Jud appeared as the scent of maple syrup reached the living room.

Vieve knew what kind of hangover Long Island ice tea would punch with its potent blend of multiple liquors. She felt a sense of accomplishment in fighting off the alcohol cravings even through the pain of this last month. Losing Carl. She also realized that these gifts of clear evenings and productive mornings could have been hers all along.

She'd risen at seven, walked Jack West, and breakfasted on coffee, berries, and yogurt. Then it was time to attack her next project. There was an office that Carl had kitted out on the first floor that

Vieve decided to convert to a studio. She was way behind on those two commissions she'd gotten before moving to Ponkipaug Point. Vieve considered asking Marley to share his studio space, but then thought the close proximity during work would be distracting. She wanted to just cancel his lease, but she couldn't go against Carl's wishes and she didn't want Asia's world upended by having to move, especially during the school year. Vieve found herself liking Asia more and more. She had a strong sense of who she was and what she liked. She obviously liked approval, like most teenagers, but she wasn't willing to tie herself into a pretzel to get it. And she wasn't afraid to think independently.

Asia carried a plate of steaming blueberry pancakes toward the dining room table when Vieve passed through the kitchen.

"Join us?" Asia asked. She was wearing freshly laundered dig clothes and her signature gap-toothed grin.

Vieve considered the invitation, inhaling the scent of hot blueberries and vanilla extract. "Ok, just one," she said heading for the dining room table. "I did eat already."

Jud, overhearing in the dining room, declared, "If you can eat just one of Asia's pancakes, your will power will be unquestioned. Coffee, everyone?"

Jud poured mugs of coffee from a carafe. Asia preferred Rooibos tea from South Africa.

Marley didn't look much like chatting. He leaned his ladder-back chair toward the wall, the chair's front legs off the floor, and cautiously sipped his black coffee.

"So," Jud said. "What did you think of the service and the—"

"Block party?" finished Asia. Jud nodded. "Quite."

Vieve helped herself to one pancake, but slathered it with butter and maple syrup. Jud smiled.

"The church service went by in a blur," Vieve admitted. "The clam bake was...raucous. Amusing."

"Especially the Richard-and-Gordon show," said Jud. "When I was in the restroom, I overheard Richard saying at least he's a Fourth and Gordon's only a Third. He must have had quite a few by then. That tinder box is going to flash any time now, especially now that Carl isn't around to distract Gordon." He fingered a crumb of pancake out of his chin beard. Marley helped himself to a tiny pancake, his expression full of trepidation.

Vieve found herself feeling both superior to Marley and wanting to console him for his lack of restraint.

"After everyone left, Gordon and I took the dogs up and back along the beach. He needed to talk," Vieve said, noticing Marley's eyes narrow on the orange juice glass he lifted from the table.

"I asked about the Booths and Cogges' rivalry. Got a tale of storms and real-estate clashes going back 300 years. But there seems to be something more fueling this thing. Like today, between Richard and Gordon? More personal? It seems odd to dwell on ancient real-estate transactions."

Jud and Marley exchanged glances, but Asia spilled the beans. "Perhaps Gordon forgot to mention that Richard stole his girl."

"Tilly?" Vieve asked. The look that passed between the two yesterday popped into her head.

"It goes back to college." Jud continued the story. "Wires got crossed between Gordon and Tilly, and Richard moved in like a shark, convincing Tilly that Gordon had several girls on the string. By the time the dust settled, Richard and Tilly were engaged and Gordon enlisted in the Marines."

"I still don't get why she'd go with Richard," Asia asked. "She's way too nice for him."

"Gordon had a bit of a temper back then. He could be scary. Richard wasn't as egomaniacal, well at least not in front of women. That took time for him to cultivate." Jud lifted a forkful of blueberry pancake and eyed it with reverence before putting it into his mouth.

"Richard was nasty in high school," Vieve said.

Jud and Asia turned to look at Vieve. "Go on," she said.

After swallowing, Jud said, "The military drove that impatience out of Gordon, especially since he kept getting promoted. He got way more controlled. Then law school. When he realized he could verbally lash people for better results, his whole life changed."

"Carl told you all this?" Vieve asked. Jud nodded.

"So Richard's got Tilly," Jud said, offering Vieve another pancake. She shook her head and he put it on his own plate. "Much better than a piece of beachfront property already sold. But that still burns Richard."

Asia finished her two pancakes and rose to carry her plate to the counter. "You guys are on cleanup. I've been invited to the dig site over by the river. They found a lot this summer."

"Any of your ancestors?" Jud teased.

"No. Mostly stamped pottery. But an interesting kind of stamped pottery." Asia said, ignoring Jud's teasing.

"What about rehearsal? This afternoon," Jud said. "You've been doing really well. You could—"

Marley looked at Asia. "Do you want to be in that play, A?"

"Yes, but...."

Marley glanced at his plate, missing the look that passed between Asia and Jud. *A secretive defiance*, Vieve thought.

"No," Vieve said. "You don't really, do you?"

Asia looked at Vieve, surprised. And then a smile spread across the teenager's face.

"Vieve's right," Asia said. "I really hate it." She grabbed her plate and bolted from the room.

Jud glared at Vieve. "How would you know what she thinks? You haven't known her a month!"

"She talks to me, I guess." Jack West came trotting into the kitchen, leash in his mouth, and sat by Vieve's chair. "I listen."

"You got a stand-in," Marley said to Jud, peering at the small puddle of syrup on his plate. "Fire her up." He left the table without making eye contact with Vieve.

After a quick spin around the yard with Jack West, Vieve spent the rest of the morning arranging the office to serve as her studio. She'd need to head home to get her easel and supplies. Meanwhile, Marley had taken over the kitchen table for some project after he and Jud had—wordlessly—cleaned up the breakfast things.

Curiosity got to her on her third trip by to freshen her coffee from the pot in the kitchen. By that point Marley had the kitchen table covered in newsprint and was drawing gesturally with a sanguine Conté crayon.

"What are you doing?" Vieve asked. "Have you abandoned your panels?" She thought—*Hey! You can draw!*—but restrained from fanning the flames.

Marley worked on, ignoring Vieve. *Or pretending to?*

"They're preliminary sketches for the mural."

"Show me," Vieve said pulling up a chair.

"Haven't you got portraits to finish? Clients to please?" Marley's first dig at her. Maybe she deserved it, interfering with Asia, although he seemed to be on her side. It was a bit of a stab, but Vieve didn't care. Let him be annoyed.

Marley went through the drawings, explaining how it would work. Vieve took it all in. In the last couple of days she'd considered—despite her doubts about working with Marley—that this mural was really important for the town. *All those lives. Gone. And how many left remembered?* It also seemed like an overwhelming artistic and logistical nightmare. But not if you weren't alone, like for many challenges, well maybe, just maybe doable. She continued to study his sketches. They were powerful and stylized and almost frightened her with the ungodly power of the storm.

"Look," he said. "I'm going to enter this blasted mural contest either way! Are you with me?"

Vieve calmly lifted another sketch to examine it more closely. "Of course," she said.

Marley, who was leaning against the table, sat down in a chair. "I have no idea who you are."

"That could be good," she replied. "Let's help the town remember. Bring the memory to life for those who weren't there, hadn't been born yet, of all the brave and resilient souls. Dead and alive."

She looked into his eyes, and he didn't look away.

CHAPTER 9

Sunday, April 29, 2018

S unday dawned misty. They met in the dining room set elegantly
for breakfast. Beryl arrived in a fuchsia-and-white tennis dress,
the fuchsia curves emphasizing Beryl's own. "I'm playing with
The Colonel at ten. We're taking on a couple of chaps from
Connecticut." She winked at Vieve. *Yeah,* Vieve thought, *probably
like Ivan Lendl.*

Vieve was dressed in white slacks and a jade green silk top with
three-quarter-length sleeves. She noticed the really rich people who
felt comfortable here tended to dress down, while outsiders dressed
up.

As Vieve raised her orange juice glass to her lips and eyed the
menu card, Beryl said, "What's worse to her: that he preferred me to
Deena or that I'm black? Not that it matters anymore." The low laugh
of yesterday was gone, and Vieve watched Beryl peer out the window
toward Ponkipaug Point, her ready smile subdued. *Was Beryl
struggling to keep grief in check behind the confident exterior?*

Vieve noticed the edge of the ocean blur in the mist. "Who
knows? All I know is she's not getting the house."

Their orders taken, Vieve said, "How long have you known Carl?
How did you meet?"

"We met in oh nine at Newport, the Hall of Fame induction
ceremony. Played a pickup doubles game later on opposite sides, me

and The Colonel, Carl and Gordon. Then we saw each other occasionally on Carl's trips to Bermuda—he was laying the groundwork at the big hotel gift shops for his jewelry line. Seeing socially, mind you. Bonnie was still alive then, she used to travel with him, and Carl was devoted to her. Then about six months ago it started getting serious. He wanted me in on the jewelry deal, but I've got too much on my plate. He was a genius." She looked out the window and smiled. "A genius who loved a good time."

When breakfast arrived, it looked divine. Omelets et fin herbs, homemade rye bread toast, and blueberry and peach compote with maple-flavored yogurt garnish were presented exquisitely.

After a few bites, Vieve said, "What I don't understand is what happened? I mean, all I've pieced together so far is—Carl was absolutely devastated when Bonnie died, he and Gordon liked to lark around looking for phantom U-boats, he had some two-bit gangster named Big Shark making trouble about the jewelry thing in Hamilton, or something else I have no clue about, and then—he washes up dead. I can't believe he just jumped into the ocean."

The mention of Big Shark did not apparently raise any kind of alarm in Beryl's expression. She nodded before dipping a spoon into the compote.

Beryl poked her spoon in Vieve's direction. "Well, I've got one more thread for you to weave with." She looked across the room and lowered her full voice. "He was very sick, your uncle."

Vieve swallowed her bit of toast, dry and scratchy in her throat. "What?"

The Colonel chose that moment to appear suddenly behind Beryl and inquire how everything was. Beryl responded with friendly grace, while Vieve wanted to shoo him away. She looked out the window again and toyed with her sea glass bracelet watch under the table.

"Sick how?" she asked as The Colonel moved off to the front of the restaurant to greet David Hallowell who'd brought a guest Vieve didn't recognize.

"Carl had a rapidly growing brain tumor at the end. Actually, several. He was beginning to make a few err...erratic choices. Like Deanna."

"Like not really ending with Deanna before he started with you?" Vieve stopped eating and leaned back in her chair. She felt dizzy, and the sun, which had broken suddenly through the mist, dazzling off the ocean, hurt her eyes. Beryl sat up straighter.

"He made me promise not to tell anyone. Anyone. Inside your family or out. But I suppose his death annuls—"

"Why?" Vieve said.

"He didn't want anyone to change the way they treated him. He didn't want sympathy. He didn't want 'help.' He simply *loathed* sad people. I tried to get him to tell you and Gordon at least, but he refused."

"Then why did he tell you?"

Beryl shrugged. "That I can't tell you. Really. Only he knew."

"So, you think this disease might have pushed him toward taking his life?"

Beryl shifted in her chair. She opened her mouth and closed it. The Colonel returned.

"Is anything wrong with the food?" he said. They both had stopped eating.

"Everything is superb," assured Beryl. "We just need some time...." She nodded slightly toward Vieve. A look passed between Beryl and The Colonel.

"Yes, yes, I understand completely. I am so sorry for your loss, both of you. All of us," The Colonel added softly. He backed away from the table slowly, his gaze on Ponkipaug Beach through the bay window.

After The Colonel was out of earshot, Beryl said, "I don't think that would have done it for Carl. He was so optimistic. But maybe his judgment was affected by it in ways he wasn't even aware of."

"So we still don't know," Vieve said. She smoothed a wrinkle out of the tablecloth and then swiveled her watch face upright, her lips twisting into a lopsided frown.

"He didn't talk to me the whole week before," Beryl said. "We'd been planning a Hamilton visit, and then he just stopped calling and emailing."

"And he revised his will the month before he disappeared. Putting you in it, among other changes."

Beryl's eyes widened slightly. "He didn't tell me." She smiled. "He was always trying to give me things that I refused. It was a silly little game we played."

Their coffee cups refreshed, Vieve took a sip and then a spoonful of compote, hardly noticing the perfectly ripe fruit and pungent cinnamon. "He left me a note that made me think it was suicide, but it's rather opaque." She handed the note she'd found in the storage shed to Beryl.

She read it quickly and gave the slip of paper back to Vieve. "I don't think he was murdered," Beryl said.

"But what about Big Shark?" Vieve said, remembering the message. She'd meant to bring it up and almost forgot.

Beryl laughed. "Carl joked about Big Shark. He gave Big Shark his moniker. It was Ferdinand Aquellas-Chapitas before that. Ecuadorian wholesaler of rare hematite. Co-owner of the only known pocket of rainbow hematite on the entire globe. Charm the needles off a cactus, that hombre."

Beryl took a rather large sip of one of the two mimosas that Evan had surprised them with. "On the house," he'd said, when he placed them on the table after their entrees arrived, nodding toward The Colonel. When Evan moved off, Vieve had moved the potent drink toward the middle of the table, out of easy reach. Beryl raised her eyebrows and smiled, but made no comment.

Vieve knew from her dinners with Carl at the Salt Breeze about the rare gem. Rainbow hematite, that artist palette of the gem world. A joyful florescent rainbow rock that shimmers and shifts hues with the changing light. But the gem is also soft and flakey and extremely elusive. Making a line of jewelry out of it is not for the faint of business heart.

Beryl leaned in close to Vieve, her voice a whisper. "Mind you, I think Ferdinand was keeping the drug dealers away from the mine and from Ponki Point. There seems to be some connection with Richard Coggeshall's quarry—"

"More coffee?" Evan asked, circulating with the carafe and washing up suddenly at their table. Vieve, startled by Evan, sat back in her chair.

"Not for me," Beryl said, straightening up and glancing at a highly polished grandfather clock on the wall behind Evan. "I must get to the courts. Vieve?"

"None for me," Vieve said. "Too much already. We'll float out of here."

At the top of the front entrance, Vieve embraced Beryl. "Thank you," Vieve said. "It's got to be so hard for you too."

"It is," said Beryl. "But I was at least able to brace for Carl's death in advance. Not in this way, mind you." Beryl's somber expression brightened. "Still. Carl was an unforgettable confidant and friend. What a run we had! I wouldn't have traded that for any of the Queen's palaces or even the Hamilton Princess Hotel!"

Vieve hugged Beryl again. When they separated, Vieve said, "Carl was lucky to have found you."

"I think it's the other way round," Beryl said, winking.

They parted. Vieve walked slowly down the terrace steps and set off along the Salt Breeze House beach to ponder what Beryl had told her. Her uncle's advanced cancer.

Guests lounged by the sea on beach chairs or expensive-looking blankets, with drinks on short tray tables. Vieve remembered those childhood vacations, spent one beach over, with much less fancy paraphernalia but loads of fun. The hot, mineraly scent of sand, thin brown seaweed mixed in, chalk-white seashells, gulls like kites in the wind, the lovely breeze from the vast ocean unfurled to the south. It all rushed back to her with the scent of hot beach sand. Uncle Carl teaching her how to body surf when the waves piled up a bit.

"Make yourself into a surf board," he'd said, demonstrating in his short, snug nouveau graphic swimsuit. The height of sixties beach fashion.

And then Beryl's words popped back into her mind, *drug guys and Richard's quarry?*

~~~

Monday, April 30, 2018

Professor Dayton McClintock assigned Asia to the sifter along with the undergrads. The pace of excavation had picked up considerably in the last two weeks after the pottery chard finds so, with half the URI archaeology department already on board for the duration, McClintock's grad students hastily recruited highly motivated Ponkipaug High School students.

The state environmental management agency was wrapping up the Black Rock Dam removal near the spot of the dig, and McClintock was hovering around the backhoes and trucks to ensure that nothing was lost or touched that could be of archaeological interest or value. McClintock's postdoc protégé Jeffrey Glackins—whose recently minted PhD on intertribal cultural exchange between the Pequots and Narragansets had bestowed upon him celebrity status that went right to his head—liaised with the low-level field crew, the ones who sifted mounds of excavated material and painstakingly brushed away dirt, practically grain by grain, from artifacts or suspected artifacts already uncovered.

And they were mostly shells. Shell dumps excite archaeologists. With this dig, Professor McClintock had, in fact, uncovered the easternmost shell middens in Connecticut that also appeared to continue onto the Rhode Island bank of the river just adjacent to the downstream side of the condemned Black Rock Dam. McClintock was full into revolutionary theories of Middle Woodland Period occupation of the site when, in the grid that Asia worked, a master's student had uncovered a curved piece of stamped pottery that brought excavation to a halt and McClintock running. It was too early to tell whether this was Pequot, Narragansett, or, most unlikely but most tantalizing, Niantic origin.

Asia sifted her dirt. A few days ago she'd found a piece of bone that might be part of a fishhook point in a pile of remains that a graduate student had already combed through. The piece was set aside for further study, but McClintock first really noticed Asia that day, which was almost as good, Asia thought, as finding the bit of bone tool. At the micro-level of discerning natural from hand fashioned, one must have a careful and patient eye.

Asia and the undergrads were given breaks in rotation to watch the geolocating process for the shell middens. She was returning from a quick trip to the porta potty, when Jeff Glackins called to her from one of the recording tents set up to keep things going in heavy rain.

Asia lifted the canvas flap and went inside, frowning. She didn't like Glackins.

Jeff put a hand on Asia's shoulder and looked her directly in the eye. "Good job, kid," he said. Asia backed out of his arm reach. He stepped forward and laid a hand on the curve of her waist. "Really great," he said. Asia stood her ground and shoved his hand off.

"I heard you," she said. "You don't need to touch me."

One of Jeff's dark bushy eyebrows curved up over a gray eye.

"Would you like to be doing this for credit?" he asked. "We could arrange that. You could help more with the documentation. Stay after the dig a few nights a week." Asia picked up on the falsely casual tone that had crept into his voice.

She also noticed he tried to pull back a bit, took a slight step backward even, although he verbally ploughed on. Surprised by her response, she knew. She'd heard he usually got what he wanted. Asia considered this offer in light of Glackins's behavior. She took a step farther away from him and pulled herself up to her full height. She would not be intimidated.

"McClintock has plans for you. He could arrange a nice little four-year scholarship. Maybe more."

Asia eyes narrowed on Jeff's expression. He gazed back at her, then pretended, she thought, to consult something on a laptop on a tiny table by the tent flap.

"I've also got some follow-up work on my doctoral research and could put you right on it, even as an undergrad. You're a standout, Asia."

"Doing what, exactly?" asked Asia, folding her arms in front of her chest. It would be interesting to see how he spun it. Men: childish, clueless, or predatory? But then again, there was Wes. Wesley Tetlow. The only exception to the rule Asia had bumped into in 17 years. Well, besides her dad and the other guys at 17 Salt Pond. Wes had been in her class since freshman year, but they hadn't really talked much until a few weeks ago when he approached her about doing a newspaper article about the dig.

Jeff purred on self-confidently. "There's a good bet that there is more of this pottery to the east. Ten to one it *is* Niantic. We're going to need ground-truthed maps, advanced GIS. That's a skillset you can take to the bank. I'll teach you."

She glanced at the laptop. There was a GIS map of the dig site on the screen. She'd love to know how to work that software.

"As I said, McClintock thinks you've got something special and is offering more opportunities for helping with this dig." He walked behind her and lowered the tent flap, standing between Asia and the exit.

Asia was sure that what her gut was telling her was the truth. He was not to be trusted—yet she would not cede ground.

"I'll talk to him then," Asia said, walking around Jeff and out of the tent.

Wes Tetlow rounded the corner of the tent, just missing tripping over a stake while looking into the viewfinder of his SLR camera. Asia had originally given him the scoop about this dig for their high school paper, but he was trying to make it into the *Ponkipaug News Post*. He was reporting on the excitement about the new artifacts uncovered and information coming to light on the Native American tribes that had lived for millennia in this productive coastal woodland place. So little was definitively known that could actually be geolocated to specific towns other than scarce pottery chards archived 40 years ago; research that was published and promptly forgotten. Asia knew that McClintock was the one to change that if anyone was.

"This stuff is great, Asia! Thanks for the tipoff," Wes said.

"It's just really going to a whole 'nother level with the pottery chard and if the thing I found pans out as a piece of fish hook. But I've got to get out from under him." Asia pointed, thumb over shoulder, back to the tent.

"What's up?" asked Wes.

"Glackins. Too touchy. Happened in Candy Crush last year with Bryce Lester. Touchy-feely. Happens there and here." Jeff had laid a hand on her back when Asia was bent over her quadrat earlier this morning. When she turned to respond, heart racing, anger building, to shove his hand off, he had moved over and engaged in conversation with a grad student and she went back to her work. A graduate student—Julia—had given her a look of comradeship and made a fist.

They both ended up laughing with relief.

"Tell McClintock?" Wes looked concerned.

"Not yet. I can handle it," Asia said, although she doubted he'd change his tactics.

"I don't really know him. But, yeah, kick up a stink. Sexual harassment with academic pressure. Glackins is outta line. Nip it in the bud. Could make a story...." Wes ran an index finger and thumb along both sides of his jawline, considering. Then he looked at Asia and, as if suddenly realizing how that sounded, said, "Hey! Sorry! Just thinking out loud. I wouldn't.... No story is worth that." Wes shook his head.

"Are guys this clueless forever?" Asia teased. She swiveled her bead bracelets with her right hand, flashing the tattoo of a tiny dolphin a few inches up her inner left forearm.

"Not me," Wes said, looking into her face and then down at the tattoo. Asia looked out over the river. Over the middle there was a distinct shimmering with a subtle white glow, pulsing. This had happened yesterday when she looked, but then it vanished after about twenty seconds.

"That's true," Asia said, turning back to Wes. "You're a keeper. We won't throw you on the sifted debris heap. Not yet, anyway." Asia began walking back to her quadrat.

"Best thing I've heard today," Wes shouted after her.

Asia sat on her favorite ledge-like rock and lifted her sifter. A cool breeze flowed around her shoulders alternating with a warm one. She looked over the Pawcatuck River below where the water from the dam finally ran free. Her eyes blurred and she shook her head.

The young woman was back. She hovered over the water in a sitting position, wearing a slit deerskin skirt out of which her knees and the lower portion of her thighs showed. A necklace of shells lay against her bare skin. She paused in her work incising a wet clay pot and peered downriver. The tide was draining back out to Quahog Bay and beyond to the sea. She looked straight at Asia before shifting her gaze to the east, transfixed perhaps by the sun's sudden emergence from the clouds.

Asia shook away the illusion—or visitation—she saw shimmering over the river, focusing on what was right in front of her. Dr. McClintock's blue-jeaned thighs viewed from her sitting position on the ledge.

"Asia Kinnell!" McClintock said, his voice booming but not without warmth. "I must thank you for your excellent find! I like a good eye. Thoroughness. Tenacity. Not seeing much of that in kids these days."

Asia brought herself back from the shimmering world of the young woman to where she sat on a granite ledge on the bank of the Pawcatuck River. "Thanks, Dr. McClintock."

"Oh, dispense with that academic folderol! It's Dayton."

"Dayton," she repeated. It sounded so strange to call him that. But somehow right. Just shy of fifty, Dr. McClintock was known among his students to be intense while simultaneously laid back, loyal, a work horse, and an intellectual powerhouse.

Asia regained her archaeological train of thought. "What are the chances this *is* a Niantic site?"

McClintock scrutinized Asia's expression. "You tell me," he said, smiling.

"I'd say good, if not excellent. And why not? Nobody's really been serious about looking around here."

"I agree," McClintock said. "And with all this flack by the fish folks to pull the dams down, the timing's perfect."

Asia nodded. They exchanged a glance of professional conviviality.

"Carry on," McClintock said as a state hydrologist called out to him from a dozen yards north on the river bank. "Oh. And let me know if you'd like to borrow any literature from my modest library.

I've got ancient thumb drives full of Narragansett culture, but I'm painfully lacking in Niantic documentation." He ran a hand through his lanky hair, pulling out a curl of birch bark and tossing it over his shoulder.

Not bad for two weeks' work, thought Asia, watching the professor dash away. She would definitely end her acting career. She would be The Master Digger.

CHAPTER 10

Thursday, May 3, 2018

"They call it the Stairway to Hell," he said.

Marley got there first, the briars clinging and then ripping from his shins, pulling out dots of blood. Vieve, sensibly, wore pants. Behind them a dozen yards, the tide was high at the tip of Ponkipaug Point, with the old dock posts barely breaking the surface. The sun poised itself three hands above the horizon.

Vieve stopped next to Marley and looked down.

"Looks like dried blood. But dark green," Vieve said. *Like the desiccated blood of some ocean serpent who spilled its life force down these stairs.* She shivered, telling herself it was because of the chilled air blasting them from below.

On the edge of old Fort Devlin, Vieve and Marley looked down from atop the southern wall twenty-five feet to the opening of a century-old stairway festooned with stunted plant life and dark moss, looking indeed like dried serpent blood. Swallows, sporting light dusky brown caps and capes, popped out of the stairway, some on a transit loop that would bring them back around to zip up the stair flyway again, others to catch insects over the shrubbery and perch on the wires protecting curious visitors from falling into the window wells and gun turrets.

"How do we get down there?" Vieve asked. "There's not that much light left."

Vieve briefly shut her eyes and rested her right hand over her heart. She took a breath. A flutter of wingbeats. Another breath.

"Think there are bats?" Vieve asked, opening her eyes to examine the stairway again. She wasn't all that fond of bats. She wasn't all that fond of tunnels and darkness and confined spaces so bats made a good out in some situations.

Marley checked the sky over Little Narragansett Bay where the sun settled onto a fiery orange cloud that blanketed the ocean at the horizon line. "Let's go around to the left here, down the bank. There isn't really a trail but it's not far."

They worked their way downhill around the side of the concrete bunker. The back of the fort was open 125 feet wide, whatever back wall was there in its heyday now long gone. They beat their way through the thick underbrush and up a set of crumbling cement and stone steps.

Vieve stopped and took it in. The tagging—reds, blues, ballonish letters spelling out names and private messages, including the admonition "Phone Home"—was weathered but still gaudy against the fort and all the silver-dull green vegetation surrounding it. The remaining overlay of handiwork of humans of generations divergent in time—the men who built the fort in the 1890s and the boys who tagged it in the 1990s. They walked up another partially crumbling stairway to the topmost level, the level of the Stairway to Hell.

"I don't know, Marley. It's really too remote for any kind of memorial. Who would come out here, except Oden and a few bored teenagers?"

"We're just scoping the place. Don't be so literal. That's the problem with you portrait painters." Marley scanned the walls, considering.

"Touché," Vieve said.

Marley and Vieve headed toward the sinister cement stairs they'd peered into from above, scattering swallows with each step.

Closer now, when Vieve glanced down the Stairway to Hell, she noticed the dried-blood look was tempered by lineaments of lichen in an orangey gold along the edges of a couple of stairs. Water dripped from somewhere and there was another flutter of wingbeats. A cold echo of sound, as if some memory were trying to get out, reverberated deep within both Vieve and this hollow heart of a former stout military fortress.

As they descended the stairway, Vieve felt the cold air on her arms, raising goosebumps. At the bottom of the steps, the hallway ran to the left. They passed a small room on the left and beyond that a larger hallway perpendicular to the first one, running the length of the fort. All the hallways were strewn with lumber lying at random angles and studded with chunks of jagged cement and rocks.

"Kind of creepy," Vieve said, "I hope we don't stumble on something...unpleasant," as she rounded a corner and noticed Marley in a room that held a large, rectangular cement block in front of a slit-like opening in the wall. She stepped sideways, turned her ankle on the edge of a brick-size stone, and went down.

"These slits used to be open in the direction of the ocean. For big guns," said Marley. "This is where one of the eight disappearing guns was placed, I bet." He turned to Vieve, "Hey! You ok?" He hurried over to help her up.

They heard voices, getting louder. Marley motioned to the large rectangular block. Vieve limped while Marley supported her elbow to bear some of her weight, and then they squatted down behind the block to conceal themselves.

"Why are we hiding?" Vieve whispered. She was glad she left Jack West with Asia. This place was booby trapped. God knows where he would have gotten to. Lumber, rocks, wet moss, slippery silt-covered patches of concrete. She looked to her left in a tunnel opening. Desiccated bones. *Bones!* thought Vieve. She leaned into the tunnel. The mostly intact skeleton of a midsize mammal lay on the rock floor.

She elbowed Marley, who was listening to the interlopers, and pointed to the skeleton in the trench.

He considered the skeleton and then mouthed, "Fox."

Vieve leaned in toward the skeleton. Marley held a finger to his lips. "Poor soul," she whispered, looking at what remained of the fox. "To die alone in this fort." Then she leaned over a bit more, hearing a faint moaning sound deep in the tunnel behind the fox skeleton.

Someone walked in front of the rectangular structure they were crouching behind. Marley heard the chink of metal hitting metal, but whoever it was didn't speak.

Marley waited a full ten minutes after the footfalls trailed off to the east before helping Vieve out onto into the hallway and back up the stairs to the open area of the fort.

"Why are we hiding?"

"Jud mentioned hearing about something going on here last year other than tagging and the occasional pot smoking."

"Something like what?" Vieve said, shivering again. This time it really was the cold as the sun sunk nearer to the sea.

"No one ever found out exactly. There were some boats at anchor west of Poki Dot really late in the afternoon some days. Boats no one in the marina was familiar with according to Nina."

"Could it have been Gordon and his U-boat searchers?"

"Too soon for that. He didn't start the water part of that search till early this spring."

Marley scanned the beach, now empty of tourists.

"Anyway, it's probably not a big deal, but no need for folks to know we're out here. You're right; it is a bit of a harebrained scheme. But, man, can you imagine clearing out this brush, building a trail from the beach? Throwing up some historical signs?"

"A mural or two?"

Marley smiled.

"How would you even do it?"

Marley scratched at his clipped beard. "You ever see Diego Rivera's *Liberation of the Peon*?" he said, helping Vieve up the hill to the top level of the fort. Her ankle had recovered somewhat, and she was relieved it wasn't a full sprain.

"I don't think so," Vieve said. "Was it a mural?"

They stood back on the top level of the fort. Marley looked north toward The Kitchen. Vieve followed his gaze and saw a collection of red knots settling into the dunes behind the mostly enclosed lagoon.

"It's a fresco he did. It's in the Philly Art Museum now to the right of the grand staircase. But it's mounted and movable. I mean, could you do something like that? Doesn't have to be here, but somehow all this concrete and a fresco would seem to have something to say to each other." He motioned to the walls below them. "Could you set it in the wall without...?" Marley frowned and rubbed his beard. A swallow dived at his head, swerving away with only six inches of clearance.

Vieve considered but made no response. As they headed off toward the overgrown Ponkipaug Beach trail, they came upon another stairway leading down to the right. Narrower, darker. Marley started down the stairs. "Stay up there if your ankle hurts."

Vieve followed Marley. She just didn't like the vibe of this place and didn't care to be left alone. *Chicken*, she thought, *but still.*

There was another doorless room at the base of the stairs, also strewn with lumber and rocks. One room over from where they had hidden from the other fort trespassers.

"What is it with all this lumber?" Vieve asked.

Marley smiled. "Richard financed an attempted renovation of this place a few years ago, but his partner in the deal backed out and Richard moved on to something else. I expect our tagger friends disassembled as much as the renovators started to build. It seems—"

"Hey," Vieve said, "look at these shoes!" She pointed to a pair of men's boat shoes in the corner by a dilapidated bench. "They look new."

Marley glanced down. 'They look like something I've seen Carl wearing." Vieve and Marley locked gazes.

Vieve scanned the room, examining all the driftwood. "How did all this stuff get in here?" Vieve took in the remains of a bench and above it a rusted iron ring on the ceiling. A hunk of rock was missing from a line of stones that had once been cemented together. They all looked loose now.

Suddenly, Oden loomed in the door opening.

"You're in my room," he said.

"Oden," said Marley. "You surprised us."

"Get out of my room," Oden said. He stepped toward them, eyes red rimmed, wielding a three-foot piece of driftwood like a club.

"Whose shoes are those?" Marley said steadily, his eyes tracking Oden's eyes. "They're nice."

"Found 'em," Oden said, just as Frek pushed past Oden into the room.

Oden's eyes softened as he peered at the shoes, rendering him less menacing, Vieve thought. *Was this rough-edged-sage bit just an act?* She noticed he always seemed close to a laugh or smile when he tried to appear intimidating.

Frek lay down next to the shoes. His tail brushed slowly back-and-forth across the dirt as he tried to capture Oden's gaze.

"They're Carl's, aren't they?" said Marley.

Oden threw the driftwood onto the accumulating pile. "They were in the rocks, at the point tip. I've never seen Carl out there."

Vieve's eyes settled on Oden's beard. The long grayish straggles aged him, and she wondered what he would look like clean shaven. Throw a clean shirt and shorts on him. No, he still wouldn't look like a Ponki tourist. There was an unusual intensity in his gaze, as if pain were sharper and pleasure more sweet for him than for mere mortals.

"We're leaving, Oden. We didn't disturb anything."

"Good thing. There's a lot of disturbed things here." Oden looked into Marely's face and then at Vieve. "Ghosts and battered souls. Abandoned shoes."

They stood, all of them silent, no sound of tide penetrated the fort. Vieve watched Frek chew a bone that he'd pulled out from under the broken bench and held between his front paws. *Fox?*

Marley and Vieve left Oden to his room, his dog, his driftwood, and Carl's shoes. His battered souls.

Munin was perched on the concrete slab at the top of the stairwell, giving Vieve the eye when she reached the top stair. As they emerged from the fort, they heard a boat motor engage over in the area of the sunken dock. They hurried to the point to try to identify it, but the boat had already made much headway toward Connecticut by the time they had navigated the brush-tangled path.

Vieve and Marley picked their way gingerly around the point in the dusk, past the jetty where Richard dunked Vieve long ago, and back to the sandy beach. Vieve felt her throat constrict and then coughed. She breathed deeply and looked away from the jetty.

"We should have taken the shoes," Vieve said. "We should give them to the police. I'll call and tell them."

"They'll harass Oden, again," Marley said. "He doesn't have a savior like he did when Carl was alive. In fact, I don't know for how long they'll let him live in the fort."

"Maybe this is his vacation home," Vieve said.

Marley laughed. He moved to touch her on the waist but stopped himself. A blue light flashed over Poki Dot. "You see that?" Marley said. "Sometimes you see a light from there."

Vieve looked in that direction and saw nothing. "Anyone ever see it while on Poki Dot?"

Marley's grin grew slowly.

"Forget I mentioned it," said Vieve. "We don't need any more distractions. We should have made it out here earlier when there was more light."

Vieve heard a whoosh of air. Close. Munin flew over their heads with only a foot clearance.

"That's what I like," said Marley. "A raven with a sense of humor."

Richard steered his black sedan left onto the narrow two-laner and glanced briefly at David Hallowell before returning his gaze to the road ahead. "We've been buddies awhile, right?"

"Watch out, with that kind of opener," said David smiling, lowering his phone to his lap.

"What's your take on Guinta?"

"Bites off more than he can chew. Makes more enemies than friends. Gets stuff done."

They drove past another *For Sale* sign near the mailbox of a three-bedroom house before the entrance to the quarry. "That place has been up for five months. You think the quarry really is pissing the real estate around here?"

"I think that's bunk," David said. "That place needs alotta work, and they're dreamin' if they think they can get $350k for it."

"What about Fitzi? Do you think Guinta and Fitzi are—" Richard swerved away from a white pickup hogging the center lane at 15 mph above the speed limit. He honked, but the truck had already turned a curve out of sight. "Asshole," Richard said to the rearview mirror. He pulled out from the narrow shoulder and resumed driving.

David said, "That's the thing, huh? Are what?"

Just then, a head-splitting blast shook the car, and Richard pulled over again to the forest edge. He noticed a fine white sheen glittering in the sun on the maple leaves in front of the bumper. There was an eerie stillness after the blast as if the air had contracted and then flowed back into its former space. Thirty seconds later, Richard, back on the road, turned left into the quarry lot.

They stopped at a locked gate with a guard station at which Richard, as board member, was waved through. They drove past an area of cone-shaped piles of sand and shapeless heaps of broken rock, continued between two pale candy green pools of water opaque as milk, and stopped at a double-wide trailer serving as the field office of South Coast Granite. Fitzwilliam wasn't there. The office manager said he hadn't come in that day. And yes, that was the last of the blasts for the week.

"No Fitzi," Richard told David, who'd waited outside, watching the backhoe activity by the high wall across the excavation site. "He asked for this appointment so what gives?

David shrugged. "What was it for?"

"He said they were going to have to take a loan out to pay for an unexpected operating expense and he thought me or Guinta might help. Guinta can't really touch it directly anymore now that he's in the House. But he's a master of doing things through other people as you know."

Richard glanced over David's shoulder as a tall, helmeted man approached them.

"Can I help you men?" he asked, his smile tight.

Richard looked into the man's sun-leathered face. "I had a meeting with Fitzwilliam. On the board." He held out a hand. "Richard Coggeshall. You're new?"

The man nodded. "New to this position. Jay Groves. Operations Manager." He looked straight into Richard's face, his expression less strained. "I'd been overseeing work on the high wall."

Richard frowned. "What happened to Peterson?"

"Accident. Fire in the equipment shed. Everything's back in order. He was planning to retire this summer, so he's takin' it a bit early." Groves smiled, this time showing at lot of teeth, while his eyes closely tracked Richard's response.

"Have you all resumed the watering operations?" David asked. "Some folks at the marina complained to me about the dust in their neighborhoods, other side of Route 12. But I assured them it was being handled properly."

"Yes," Groves said. "Well, I need—"

"What about the fence around the high wall?" Richard said.

"Going up next week," Groves said, looking back over his shoulder and then toward Richard.

"Tell Fitzwilliam to call me ASAP," Richard said. "I'll let you get back to it."

"Will do," Groves said. He turned and walked toward the trailer. Richard and David turned back toward the sedan. Someone yelled over by the excavation. Groves veered from the trailer, pulled out his phone, and beelined for his pickup.

"Man's lying," Richard said as he drove back out through the gate. "There's shit going on here, David."

"You're just suspicious by nature," David said. "Calm down. I told you Fitzi would straighten things out."

"Or that's what you hope," Richard stated firmly. "They promised a moderate scale of operations when we reopened, and I'm not seeing that. I'm also sensing a lot of musical chairs and maybe worse. Coupled with the sudden need for more money? Come on!"

David looked straight ahead.

"And those financials certainly weren't all they were billed to be," said Richard.

"What?" David sat up straighter in the passenger seat, his head swiveled to check Richard's profile.

"Something's going on, and I bet Fitzi can enlighten us. After he comes back from the regulatory agency or his lawyer's office. Or wherever the hell he went." Richard smacked the dashboard with his right hand.

For the rest of the drive, Richard remained silent and David sent texts to his employees. After Richard pulled into the marina parking lot, David got out quickly, slammed the door, and headed for his office.

Richard leaned back in the driver's seat. Things were getting way too weird at the quarry. He guessed David was finally starting to feel that way too, after practically begging him to join the board seven years ago amid the excitement of economic prospects for the town, the shareholders, and, of course, his own bottom line. But the promise of fifty more local jobs was slow in materializing, and then there were operational fines by EPA and the state that the company lawyer was trying to fight. Fitzi had better come clean.

Richard shut his eyes and leaned forward to stretch his back, thinking that it was time to make a move. *But what?* He opened his eyes to the view of the marina dock, and his mind filled with the memory of his first sail from this exact spot. The first time his father let him go out alone. Age eleven. Speeding across the bay on a perfect tack, he owned the world that day. Richard looked up over his steering wheel and watched a boat, tiny at this distance, sail out of sight behind Poki Dot.

CHAPTER 11

Friday, May 4, 2018

Vieve considered the hinged wooden screen in front of Gordon's billiards table. A blank triptych. *Stress the vertical with these most horizontal of dogs?*

She frowned at the empty panels and then smiled as the layout came to her in a flash. After—of course—she'd pondered it for two weeks before the portrait photo appointment. It would be a horizontal beach scene with dunes and waves and sky—set across the three vertically oriented panels. Winston, Clementine, and MacArthur, freshly bathed, sat looking up at Vieve and Gordon, three tails sliding across the carpet like windshield wipers.

"Now that they're all washed and proper, let's take them out on the beach and get them sandy!" Vieve said, putting the camera strap around her neck.

Eyebrows raised, eyes sparkling, Gordon said, "Yes!"

Carl had gloated to Gordon last winter over Vieve's reputation after the governor-and-his-spaniel painting first appeared on the governor's Facebook page. And Gordon thought, *Why not?* He'd get a portrait of his brace of Bassets done by the best portrait painter in New England. Would she do dogs alone?

Vieve mostly painted people alone or people and their animals. But now that she'd moved away from suburban Boston to quiet beach resort Rhode Island, she'd been wondering why she'd put herself through it. Those pretentious clients. Like the patrician pharmaceutical magnate who wanted his private plane prominently placed in a portrait background and insisted on telling her at each sitting how much it cost. And reeling off all of his other toys and residences and their price tags as Vieve cajoled him to keep his head still.

Or the state senator, a mother with twin daughters, who wanted them to look nothing like their pleasant but not ravishingly attractive faces. Their fine open expressions and green eyes enchanted Vieve, and she painted what she saw, including their slightly large noses and endearingly crooked smiles. The senator refused to pay for the piece, and Vieve, stung but not out, entered and sold the piece—titled *Twins for Life*—through a juried exhibition.

The final straw was Trent Picard. The tech company president who was thrilled—too thrilled—with his portrait, done in a mountain-climbing setting in the Dolomites. He'd pestered Vieve until the day she last came to Ponkipaug Village for dinner with Carl. Since then he'd been in Mumbai on business.

She longed for less emotionally challenged subjects. The idea of switching solely to animals and pets had its appeal, well aware as she was of the status she'd lose in the status-conscious art tribe in which she found herself. And animal people are, it turns out, and well she knew, very emotional. But, as in many things after Carl's death, she knew it was more important what she thought of her profession, not what anyone else thought. How had she gotten where she was anyway? Not by following the pack. It didn't hurt that Gordon was offering twice her regular fee—more status to him that he could boast about, just for fun.

"I'm game," Gordon said. "Got a town council meeting at 3 pm though, more quarry talk."

"Plenty of time," Vieve said.

They headed out in Gordon's Lexus with the dogs, their heads out the window, ears horizontal in the backdraft. A first-grader, delighted at the sight, waved from the edge of his yard at an intersection. Vieve smiled and waved back. There is something about three Bassets in a car, off on an adventure, all open-mouthed smiles and flying ears.

"What about the quarry?" Vieve asked. There had been talk here and there around town about the quarry, and didn't Asia just mention something about it? Something to do with her dig?

"South Coast Granite," said Gordon, turning onto Atlantic Drive. "Used to be West County Granite & Sand. One of the first quarries in the state. Reopened a few years ago. Prospects look good, both for profit and town, except...."

Clementine barked out a cat sighting. The other two joined in on the alarm.

"Hush, guys!" ordered Gordon. The Bassets obeyed the direct order.

"Except?" Vieve asked, intrigued.

"Except, Richard Coggeshall is now a key board player. His family actually started the business, but it was taken over by a larger mining company before it closed up shop in the 1970s. Now he's back. I was a dissenting vote on his reelection back when I was on that board but—Here we are!" Gordon said.

They pulled into the yacht club parking lot associated with the Salt Breeze House. "We can run the dogs here without bothering folks. And no plover nests to invade. Keep the plover rangers happy."

Vieve turned her mind from granite quarry to reference photos, and within an hour and a half, she'd snapped dozens of shots of frolicking Bassets—in both sand and surf—that she could mash up and combine and extrapolate and distill to construct the basic composition of the painting. The color palette would be key, and she noted how the Bassets' coats changed color in sunlight and shade, how the blue of the sky differed from the greener blue of the sea, the range of cloud shapes and hues, the multiple colors of grains that made up the beach sand, that particular lovely bronze-reddish tint to the dune grass. She saw Gordon reach down to pat Winston and snapped a few more shots. She also got Gordon to sit among the three of them for a group shot and snapped him throwing sticks. *Wouldn't it be sneaky,* she thought, *to toss Gordon into the piece?*

"I hear you guys are entering the hurricane mural competition?"

Vieve nodded. "How the hell we'll pull it off is beyond me. *If* we get picked. A big if."

"It's so long overdue—something to honor those folks with. The folks who lived through it are almost all gone, except those who were tiny babies. Some of whom survived strapped to floating mattresses."

Vieve tried to picture a baby on a mattress riding on the ocean. It was too absurd.

"So do you focus on the devastation or the life-goes-on part?" Gordon asked.

"Good question. What's your take?"

"Life-goes-on part," he said, looking over to Ponkipaug Point. "Yeah. Maybe the rescue and rebuilding. Starting over. Hanging together. All the folks who worked endlessly to help the injured and put the town back together."

Vieve considered. Was Gordon referring to Albert Boothroyd, among many others? That was not where Marley's sketches were headed; they were full of the high teeth of the storm. But it was early yet. If this project were like anything else worth doing, they had a lot of fuzzy concepts, good but impractical ideas, and false starts to work through. Even though the application deadline was rapidly approaching.

As a girl growing up in Rhode Island, Vieve hadn't thought much about what local people had gone through. It was more like some hung on, some went to higher ground, and some didn't. She never had considered what it had meant to the survivors. As she'd worked with

Marley these last few weeks on a mural design, though, she'd dwelled on questions she'd never considered. *How do you keep body and soul together after that much loss? Why do some find courage and some lose heart? What would happen if another big storm pounded the town? After eighty years, have we really learned anything new about living next to the sea?*

She turned back to Gordon. "Good point," she said. His attention was fixed on the access trail on which a figure dressed in a mint green linen sundress and a wide straw sunhat advanced toward them.

"Tilly Coggeshall!" Gordon said out loud with obvious glee. Tilly was still too far away to hear. "Very pale skin, very tough soul," he murmured to himself, but Vieve overheard. When Tilly arrived in front of them, Gordon grasped her two hands in his own.

"I'll apologize for Richard's behavior at the clam bake, if he won't," Tilly said, nodding at Vieve. Her sunhat dipped over her eyes and she set it back up her head. Silhouettes of forest green spaniels paraded across the marigold yellow hatband.

"I think we bring that out in each other, Tilly. No apology needed. I should apologize to you." Gordon reluctantly let go of Tilly's hands.

Tilly looked at Vieve, her mouth tightened.

"Are you ok?" Vieve asked.

Tilly glanced between the two of them. "I'm worried about Richard. I know you two hate each other, but—"

Vieve laughed. "Which two? Richard and Gordon, or Richard and me?"

"Yes?" Gordon encouraged. Tilly looked again at Vieve and then over Gordon's shoulder at the ocean.

"Look," said Vieve. "I'll leave you two to your discussion."

Vieve wandered off and the Bassets followed. Getting involved in this triangle, still smoldering after all these years, was something she'd avoid. She threw sticks and watched MacArthur and

Clementine race for them. Winston preferred to dig in the sand. He barked at a gull, just alighting near the high tide line.

"Fightin' 'em on the beaches, eh Winston?" He cocked his head to look at her, and she snapped another photo. Then he returned to his trench.

Gordon caught up with Vieve. "I need to go out to the quarry. There's some kind of dispute going on with the foreman and the state inspector. Or so it sounds. I can't talk now. Don't mention it to anyone. I really shouldn't even be talking about it."

"I wondered why you were telling me," said Vieve.

Their eyes met.

"Hell, I trust you. You're not a fan of Richard's either."

"Hardly," Vieve said.

"Seems Richard's been accused of bribing the state environmental inspector, or at the very least knowing about it. Tilly just found out."

"And she is telling you this, why?"

"She thinks he may be in some kind of danger and wants help." Gordon was visibly agitated, his face muscles tightening, his eyes avoiding Vieve's. *His need to help Tilly something he couldn't put aside even with his animosity toward Richard?* she wondered.

"Look, I have to—"

"You go," Vieve said. "I can walk from here. It's a nice day."

"For some," Gordon said. He turned and sprinted down the beach, a wake of Bassets cantering at his heels.

The moon shone like lemon honey in the sky as the three figures, accompanied by their three shadows, advanced along the dirt road toward the low stone wall bordering the cemetery. Jack West paused at the open entrance, a gap in the roundish field stones, sniffing the soft breeze. Crickets ticked away the seconds amid the fragrance of white pine, pungent fern, and sweet damp earth.

"You scratch down an inch of sand in Rhode Island and you get Celtic, Italian, and French-Canadian backgrounds, civic pride, political corruption, native place names, Johnny Cakes, and clams," Asia said. She led Vieve and Jack West to Theresa Silva's grave marker. "It's a hodge-podge. Like anywhere else, I expect."

Vieve had to smile at Asia's perspective, unlike that of a typical seventeen-year-old.

"She's not really here," Asia said. "Oden won't part with her ashes. It's just a place marker for her memory."

They stood before a polished pink Ponkipaug granite slab, paid for by Carl on behalf of Oden. The moon obliged, illuminating a slanted portion of the stone face reading:

Theresa Marie Silva

Beloved Sister of Oden Vacca

1963–2013

Sail Before the Wind

Toward the center of the cemetery compound, grainy limestone grave markers titled, their eroding angel wings and dissolving sheep bringing to mind the forgotten of earlier centuries. Lichen smudged out the names.

What about Theresa and Ted's parents? wondered Vieve. As Vieve was about to inquire, Asia spoke again. "I could use one of these for my mother. A place marker for her memory." She fondled a tiny urn with elaborate handles carved atop the tombstone next to Theresa's.

Vieve put her hand on top of Asia's hand and squeezed gently. "You haven't talked about your mother. I assume she and Marley were...were...." What could Vieve really assume about them? Sometimes, best to just shut up and wait.

Asia inspected the tombstone and then peered up into the canopy of the trees. Her bead bracelets clinked around each other in the still night. She turned to Vieve.

"Actually, I was a baby of a one-night stand."

Asia laughed, like a quick exhalation of air. "Sounds like a bad country song title. Doesn't it? My parents were never a couple. I lived with my mom till I was three, and then she was killed during a robbery of our house. She fought the guy over a stupid TV."

Vieve heard a splash of water to the north where Guilford Pond and its outlet stream, Everrun Brook, began.

"Dad tried hard for joint custody from the beginning, but Mom said no way." Asia let out a harsh bleat of a laugh. "She didn't think he'd amount to much. That's what she told him," she said, peering in the direction from which they'd heard the splash.

"Do you remember her?" Vieve asked. A nighthawk called in the woods to the east, as if questioning the deepening dark velvet overhead. Vieve inhaled the spicy scent of fern.

"No. I've seen some photos. I dream around those photos—but I don't really remember anything. Except...."

"Yes?" Vieve asked.

"I remember lullabies. She used to sing in this beautiful deep voice." Asia looked back toward the row of gravestones from the 1700s. "I don't know; maybe I dreamed that too."

Asia looked at Vieve and her voice grew softer. "Lately I've been dreaming of a prehistoric village by the sea, by a river. Like the one we're digging on the Pawcatuck. There's a young woman there, who's trying to tell me something, but she keeps...fading out." Asia stepped away from Vieve and ran her index finger in the groove of the letter T in Theresa's carved name.

"What does she look like, this woman in your dream?" asked Vieve.

Before Asia could answer they heard a branch snap off to their left and the resulting scramble of tiny mammals scattering underneath the fallen birch bark, curved ferns, and tiny maple saplings. Oden appeared and stepped over the north wall of stones. A sudden whoosh of wings above them out of sight. Munin.

Standing between them and a massive white pine tree, Oden inspected the graveyard as if assessing an attentive crowd before he was to address them. "My sister's murderer remains free, while here she sleeps beneath crumbling angel wings and melting lambs," he said, stopping a few feet from Asia and leaning on a driftwood staff.

Jack West searched for Munin's location in the canopy of the wolf tree, his front paws against the trunk of the great tree grown old and thick while nudging against the north wall of the cemetery compound. He barked and then he began digging at the tree's base.

"Crumbling angel wings and melting lambs," said Oden, gesturing to the eroding limestone slabs. "You too seek to hear their stories," said Oden, peering at Asia. "There is many a tale of folly and pride and caution to be heard among these souls."

Vieve registered the fierce scent of body odor with a lingering note of rum in the vicinity of Oden. She now felt Oden really wasn't a threat, despite picking that fistfight with Richard. He'd calmed down quickly when she and Marley crossed him in the fort. Perhaps he was just a sentimental drunk among friends or the roving Shakespearean fool-prophet Jud claimed him to be. On the other hand, Vieve considered, he could be wiser than the rest of us put together, or kinder hearted. She didn't know whether any of her conjectures were true, but she felt less on edge around him than she had the first day she saw him on Ponkipaug Beach.

Oden pointed to the tombstone. "My sister, as well as murdered by Richard Coggeshall, The Fourth, and has he paid for his crime?" Oden turned his attention to the gravesite, combing out orange pine needles from the surrounding grass with his fingers by the light of the lemony moon. "And now he eyes my home. Ah! No matter, he will stumble over his own ambition before the storm."

Vieve noticed that Asia watched Oden with interest, concern almost. Did she feel a connection to him? Vieve turned to Oden. "I'm so sorry you lost your sister."

"The last of the clan," Oden said. "She had the eye, too."

Oden's gaze narrowed on Asia. "Your mother was another wise soul. I could feel, as I walked the last few yards to this place, that you still await word from her. Word that brings the quickness of long ago to today. Which is why you dig with such heart."

Vieve rolled her eyes. Asia peered up into the pine branches toward Munin, who was tossing plucked pine cone seed triangles down onto them. Jack West kept digging.

CHAPTER 12

S unlight streamed into the living room from the bay window as the three housemates finished their third cups of coffee.

Jud, pulling a new string taunt on his bouzouki, was next in line to offer his two cents on the mural. He envisioned a diorama—like the one at Gettysburg National Historic Park—to take in the vast scene. "A whole civic space." He spooled out in words his extravagant vision. "Echoing in its own circularity the hurricane shape or the carousel, which of course was a key meta—"

"Bullshit, Jud." Marley dismissed that idea with a wave of his hand. "There's no way the chamber of commerce will cover something on that scale. If anything we need simpler, not more complicated, ideas than that."

Vieve thought the sketches that Marley had started and they both had collaborated on intensively over the last week looked promising. They were focusing on Ponkipaug Village as a whole—from the golf course on the east to the Weekapaug National Wildlife Refuge on the west—the fishing fleet and the lighthouse—told in a horizontal format of sea and shore. The center image would highlight the devastation at Ponkipaug Point.

Marley's techniques of manipulating acrylic were offering exciting possibilities for sea and sky; he'd been working up samples. And Vieve was obsessed with how to portray the human drama—

keeping it anonymous, universal, not a particular person, but the townspeople in general, and respectful of the dead—while at the same time translating it to a medium without the flexibility of her beloved oil paint. She'd started gnawing her fingernails and glancing at Carl's whiskey decanter a little too often. She fought that urge to drink it straight from bottle by taking frequent breaks, walking Jack West on the beach just north of The Kitchen.

How they would translate these ideas to a fresco format by the end of the week was the elephant in the room. Well, one of them.

Wednesday, May 9, 2018

"Second page, top left," said Jud, handing Vieve the paper. "Would have made front page, no doubt, if there hadn't been that hideous car accident in front of the carousel."

Vieve flipped over the front page of today's *Ponkipaug News Post,* skipping the horrible car crash, a tourist and a local fisherman's son.

"Distracted driver and faulty airbag. Not a great combo." Jud poured himself another mug of coffee and snagged the last piece of cranberry coffeecake that Asia had pulled out of the oven just an hour ago. "The day tripper was texting when he suddenly caught sight of the carousel after ignoring the red light. The tourist, a bruised forehead; the local, in the hospital suffering a concussion and broken ribs." Jud shook his head.

Asia passed through the kitchen on her way out, listening to someone on her phone. Jud caught her eye and made a motion with his hands as if he were digging and tossing dirt with a toy beach shovel.

"Lay off her, Jud," Vieve said. She'd lowered the paper, preparing to swat him with it.

"She knows it's all in good fun. Besides, the understudy is glowing in the Hilde role that Asia cast aside to dig in the dirt."

Vieve finished reading the story, while Jud raked his chin beard for coffeecake crumbs.

"It's a good thing the idiot was only going twenty-five at the time, could have been much worse. Anyway, you see now. They are suing the quarry board. Well, trying to. I'm not sure they can legally." Jud snatched up the arts calendar off the dining room table. "Six weeks until opening night, my friends!"

"Gordon will know," Vieve said, lowering the paper. "He's on the town council."

"Ah," said Jud. "Indeed. Helpful, that. I know Richard had a very good buddy on the quarry board, Tony Guinta, who's now our not-so-well-loved congressman. And Richard got on first thing when they decided to revive the old rock pile. What? Six, seven years ago?

"Two thousand eleven," Vieve said, reading from the article.

"Let's see," Jud put down his fork and picked up the coffee carafe. "Guinta got elected, or rather, *bought* the House election in....it was...2014, I believe. So in theory he's off the board, but in practice, perhaps not so much."

Vieve did not notice Jud's self-satisfied grin as she read more from the article. "Wow!" she said. "Lots of complaints about granite dust. Something about silica. And people and pets getting sick!"

"Anyway, Gordon doesn't think Guinta's pulled back all that much, despite the conflict of interest," Jud said, lifting his refreshed coffee mug.

"How do you know this?" Vieve asked, looking up from the newspaper.

"Gordon mentioned it at the clam bake. It's no secret he's against anything Richard and Guinta try to do that benefits mostly themselves. Or so that's his take." Jud looked regretfully at the empty coffeecake plate.

Jack West entered the dining room, making a beeline for the green-plaid dog bed that Marley had bought for him. He plopped down with a sigh.

Marley descended the stairs carrying a wide roll of gritty pastel paper. Wordless, he hurried through to the living room. Vieve and Jud exchanged glances and shoved their seats back to rise. When Marley unfurled the rolled paper across the living room floor, it stretched from the fireplace, all along the length of the bay window, to the kitchen doorway. Marley stepped back to take a broad view of the piece, backing into Vieve. Jud stood transfixed off to Vieve's left, mug in hand, jaw lowered.

"Holy shit, Marley! Is this what you've been doing this last week?" Jud asked.

The three of them stared at the mockup on the floor. Vieve felt so much all at once but couldn't, for some reason, unlike Jud, open her mouth.

The power of the emerald ocean, the wind, the whole vast yellow sky—beyond, it seemed, what you could see from one viewpoint—the incessant spin of the globe. Marley used pastel in a way she'd never seen before. Stabbed and swirled and lush—yet meshed and welded like a glowing tapestry of sand, water, wind—a bit like his acrylic panels but more obviously ordered and at least minimally representational.

Vieve could visualize suddenly where the people could go, their scale; they would be in it and above it at the same time, on two physical planes, and two times—1938 and eternity. They would be sanguine, like the Conté crayon of the same name—they would be outlines and edges, within which glowing souls would pulse life, spinning in a tempest, a transitional world in which nothing would ever be the same again, even as the last of the waves drained through the sand and back to the bays and ocean.

She'd enlarge the two black T-shapes—the fear of what you don't know below—that is probably not as bad as your imagination—those two hammerhead sharks reported sighted in Little Narragansett Bay that afternoon—everything out of place, blown in from God-knows-where. She felt the blood rush into her fingers and her head lighten. There was a sparkling deep emerald wave—it might have been going over the lighthouse point—there had been people trapped out there. It was just that second before the worst was going to hit. That was it—she felt she was inside the storm. Vieve stepped over the gritty paper and collapsed onto the couch.

"Well?" Marley asked.

Time ticked by, according to the see-through clock mechanism on the stand by the overstuffed armchair, a token the theatre folks had given to Jud in honor of his unflagging service. Jud looked between Marley and Vieve and hastily left the room.

Marley sat next to Vieve on the couch.

"Damn you!" she said. Low and hissing. "How on earth?" A tear slid from her eye on the side away from Marley's view.

Marley smiled. He stood up and stepped away just as she reached out to place a hand on his chest. To gauge the warmth of his heart through his tee shirt.

Damn you, Marley Kinnell, for touching that place in my soul. Was it that he kept shredding the notions she had of what art could do, what bounds it couldn't go beyond, or that he might have been inching closer to the place where Kyle still lingered in her heart? Lust is just so much easier to relieve, but that was not, she knew this moment, what she was feeling. A wall of water raced toward her heart.

PART 3

The doctor confirmed her condition just that morning. After many months of trying, Caroline Babcock was pregnant with their first child. She felt such bliss. The sun shone invitingly for the first time in months, and she was finally going to be a mother. But in the early afternoon, the sun disappeared and the wind blew harder than Carrie ever remembered it blowing. A few yards from the cottage, the sea kicked up an angry green.

Her husband, Paul, had let the workers go home early from the West County Granite & Sand quarry he managed. When he arrived back home at Crandall Pond, he felt more amused than fearful of the storm. But a sudden flash of caution prompted him to nail boards over a few windows after shutting their Pierce Arrow into the garage.

He told Carrie about the fallen elms and maples he'd seen driving the five miles south from the quarry to the cottage. These September line storms were annoying, but never got really bad. This one seemed a little more angry than usual, but Paul predicted they would ride it out fine. So they settled in to wait out the storm, and Carrie poured them both tea. Her face animated by her unshared news.

Carrie met Paul's gaze. "I'm finally, finally pregnant!" she said. Paul rose abruptly, knocking over his chair. They embraced. For twenty-five seconds, their whole world was holding each other in joy. Then the ocean bashed over the seawall, and a wave reached within three feet of their front steps.

When they sat down to their tea, the wind slammed the side of the house, like a slap to the ear and cheek. Carrie set her china teacup down a little more firmly than she had anticipated. The remaining four ounces of Earl Grey lightened with milk sloshed within her teacup.

Paul had left the side window uncovered, doubting that the strong onshore or offshore winds from a line storm would bother it. As Carrie opened her mouth to bite a molasses cookie, she peered out the window over Paul's shoulder. The wind blasted them suddenly like a hundred bullhorns. The whole garage, with the Pierce Arrow, lurched to the south. As Carrie screeched and pointed, the wind lifted the second floor of the cottage off the first floor, despite steel reinforcements and granite wedges. The top half of cottage settled on the Atlantic Ocean like a launched boat. She heard the wind keen with a burning fury that accelerated and veered off the ocean surface. The entire Babcock property was under the sea.

An overwhelming pulse of nausea gripped Carrie, and she slipped off her chair to the floor. Paul lifted her as a massive wall of emerald water shoved the top of the cottage back toward the mainland and out over Crandall Pond. Carrie's stomach lurched and her head spun, as if the storm had invaded her body and swirled on within. When she raised her head again, she noticed the roof of their garage lurch past the cottage in the water. Everything was in the water.

As the land became ocean, Carrie and Paul crawled over

to the dining room window to see where they were headed. Through the window toward the west Carrie saw her neighbor Karen Belton clinging to a mattress with her baby daughter strapped to the headboard. Carrie fainted, and Paul pulled her away from the window.

The second floor of the cottage rode relatively smoothly on the high crest of a swell across the salt pond. Ahead was the backyard of their bridge partners, the Sweeneys. The small patch of lawn fringed with salt grass and surrounded by stunted cedar rushed toward them, or they toward it. It was hard to tell what was happening as Paul enveloped Carrie in his arms. He tucked her head against his chest while she regained consciousness. A thirty-foot fishing boat, oriented sideways, swept ahead of them on the left. Its path was set to converge with the cottage.

Their trip stopped abruptly after the fishing boat passed.

The Babcocks and their second floor landed on the Sweeney's backyard, a trip of less than a mile. On the lawn to their left, the wayward fishing boat tilted to port. Their garage roof hunkered on their right. It was as if the ocean were a hand with palm and fingers spread, settling their house like a plate of cake on a table of grass. There was still half a cup of tea in Carrie's teacup.

Carrie shut her eyes and laid a hand over the place where her baby would continue to grow.

CHAPTER 13

Wednesday, May 23, 2018

"It only has to withstand wind, blasting sand, teenage taggers, the occasional Cat 4 hurricane." Marley scanned the east wall. "And this highly developed defense force." He indicated, with a nod at one bird passing, the cliff swallows circling the artists like agitated electrons ovaling their nuclei. "I've been mixing industrial resin into my acrylics and getting some interesting textures."

"And Richard," Vieve said. "It has to survive whatever Richard is up to out here. Oden's convinced he's poking around the point for some nefarious reason."

Vieve had steered clear of Marley for a few days after he unveiled that pastel mockup of the mural cartoon. His art incited such strong responses in her, she felt unable to face him. Vieve's next few days became consumed with Gordon's triptych project and a few other locals who wanted to discuss commission ideas. And then they pulled two all-nighters to finish the mural application and design cartoon to meet the Hurricane Memorial Design Committee's May 11 deadline.

On May 16, the committee had contacted the three artist teams that were in contention asking for tweaks to their designs related to reproducing the winning mural in other venues around town. Marley and Vieve had made the final-round cut. But the mural announcement date was looming on Friday and they still had changes to make and submit to the committee by Thursday.

In the time she worked so closely with Marley over the past six weeks, Vieve's fascination and terror of Marley crossed her growing interest in honoring the town's memory. She wanted to keep Marley and the mural separate in her world, but that was impossible now, especially after the all-nighters. They needed each other to pull this off. So back out to the fort they went to work through the final design challenges.

Marley turned to Vieve. "Nina told me that Richard's trying to agitate the town council to let him fund another renovation of the fort. And put in a dock. Will he be for or against a mural on the fort?"

Vieve said, "I'm surprised he's considering that with the quarry thing in the paper now. There was another article yesterday in the *News Post* about abandoned properties near the quarry that won't sell and all the health concerns that have popped up. Nina and Maeve are concerned, and they live three miles from the quarry."

"It's probably *because* of the quarry debacle that he wants to distract them with something intriguing at Ponkipaug Point. Do some civic good." Marley smiled. "That could actually be good. Really." He turned to inspect the vast wall in front of them behind the Stairway to Hell.

"Get him to pay to clean all this off!" He gestured at the wall. "You know, that dream we have, clear some poison ivy, make a real trail, make it so—"

"I don't trust him. I bet he'll find some way to make money off it for himself." Vieve shaded her eyes from the overhead sun.

Marley smiled. "You just plain loathe him, don't you?"

Vieve shot back, "Yes, as a matter of fact. We started off on the wrong foot way back in the day." She flashed on that cold gelatinous seaweed on her back, the sensation of lungs about to burst—then quickly shook those memories away.

More swallows shot by. Testing them. Marley leaned left, while Vieve ducked.

"I just don't believe this faux civic pride thing he's on about," Vieve said. "He'll reap in profits somehow and may limit access to this place. And the dock. Will it somehow be *his* dock?"

Marley said, "They've proposed docks in years past, but that did not make the conservation folks happy."

"Somehow, I think he's up to a lot more than trying to push me out of Carl's...my house." The thought of Uncle Carl gone made Vieve pause in her wrath against Richard.

"Yeah," Marley said, picking up on the conjecture. "Richard could, say, dig offshore from The Kitchen, pillage the buried debris that we all know is still there, and sell salvaged household goods from the hurricane through his auction house? Wind chimes made of silverware?"

"God! I would hope that would be too tacky even for him." Vieve shook her head.

"Look, let's focus on a concept the chamber can't refuse. Then we'll deal with whatever Richard throws at us. Ok?"

Vieve wondered what that might be. An easier thing to guess than how the heck they were going to pull this mural off. Yes, they were in the top three, but Marley was still tinkering with the design and there were aspects of it Vieve wasn't quite happy with either. Jack West broke her reverie. He'd pulled a femur bone from the fox skeleton in the fort and laid it at Vieve's feet. He thumped his tail against the cement, pride in this bearing. *Sit and smile. Graciously acknowledge praise.*

Oden's head popped up out of the Stairway to Hell. "If you want my opinion," he started.

"Looks like we're getting it," Marley said to Vieve.

"You should focus this whole thing on the fort! No one considers what this fort meant in the storm. This point, within feet of where I live, has seen a panorama of history that you wouldn't believe! Did you know there was a forest out here? People actually used to go turkey hunting? And at the time, gold nuggets and flakes were churned up by the surf on the bayside beach."

Oden emerged whole out of the stairway, warming to his topic. "The turkeys used to forage for stones for their gizzards, eat gold pebbles and specks. And the proprietors of the Olympic Tea Room, as the restaurant out here was called—yes, there used to be a restaurant here!—used to offer to clean the shot turkeys for free. The hunters thought it was most generous of them, while the restaurant owners sacked the gold." Oden belly laughed, ending in a wet coughing fit.

Vieve's mind wandered while Oden spoke; she inspected the cylindrical gun turrets, thinking they would make a great visual story surface in themselves. Jack West climbed a crumbling cement and stone staircase that led to nowhere and sat in the sun next to his femur bone prize, sniffing the sea breeze while Oden talked of turkey innards and gold and 200 years of civilization on Ponkipaug Point.

Munin landed next to the stairway, opened his mouth, and dropped an old bent spoon on the cement next to another piece of metal. Oden responded with delight. "Another find! Thank you, my noir friend! There is no end to your collection!"

As Oden continued his historical saga, Marley began applying a gritty sort of primer that he'd concocted in his studio to the fort wall to test it.

"And we come to...us. Me. Munin and Frek. Our point now. But for how long? The trees are gone, the Feds are gone, the point is eroding away," Oden said, as he turned to wander off down the trail toward the end of the point. Munin flapped along behind, leaving the old spoon to shine dully in the sun.

Marley said, "Let's head to The Kitchen for our picnic lunch and go over the designs again. Make a final cull."

Vieve nodded. She knew they needed something simpler, less intricate in design. But something strong to reflect the raw power of fear and hope, to conjure memories both forgotten and untarnished by time. To make it even more powerfully universal. And they had two days to do that.

They sat on the driftwood in the dunes near The Kitchen, with empty takeout clam roll and coleslaw containers from JohnnyCakes next to them on a blanket. To their left, five sketchbooks lay open on the dune, with Jack West digging underneath the fifth one. The one that showed one wave about to hit...you. The water coming right down on the viewer, the wave a menacing hand.

"Jack West is about the only one who hasn't weighed in on the design," Marley said. "But now that's about to change."

"His input is just as valid as all the unsolicited advice we've gotten so far. Too many cooks in the kitchen."

"No pun intended."

"What? Jeeez Marley! Lowest form of humor, the pun!"

She shoved him over the back of the log. She hadn't touched him since that day on the dunes when they kissed, when she'd been resisting, avoiding, sashaying around her feelings. She'd tried to touch him, well, his heart somehow, on the couch the day he showed her the pastel mockup of the mural. That design was gorgeous but way too complicated to be a cartooned into a mural without losing everything that made it work. But Vieve hadn't made contact with Marley before he moved off, and he hadn't noticed her attempt. Later that day she was seized with a fear that in getting close to that place inside Marley that scared and enthralled her, she would lose all that she had left. All that connected her to Kyle.

It was really silly, but perhaps, she'd thought then, that she should find a new place to live. It was *way* too intense living with Marley. She certainly could find another place, say she needed more room for her art. She was getting into large screens and needed a room as large as Marley's studio on the second floor. Or she could just take over Marley's studio. But she didn't want to turn them out, especially Asia....

Yeah, she was running away from herself. And not getting far.

Laughing and shaking sand from his hair, Marley grabbed Vieve's waist from behind to pull her backwards off the log. Jack West left off digging and ran to Vieve's defense, nipping playfully at Marley's ankle.

"You've riled the likes of the scourge of Ponki Point!" Vieve laughed.

She stopped resisting Marley's playful tugs, and they all three fell over in a heap behind the log. Turning over to rise, Vieve ended up lying on Marley's chest, her face inches from those intriguing whiskey-colored eyes. His right eyebrow lifted. There was a suspended second in time, one when she just stopped putting things in categories. Ordering it all. Being afraid. They kissed a second time, tongues intermingling, and Marley pressed his hands around Vieve's short, strong back.

The sun was just past overhead to the west. Farther up into the dunes, there was a bit more privacy among the tall grasses. They pulled the blanket along behind them, Jack West attempting to thwart its disappearance by pulling the blanket in the opposite direction. It was on a gentle slope in the back dunes, canopied by marsh grass, where they tossed their clothes and saw each other's bodies full on in the brilliant sunshine.

There was no more thinking, negotiating, parsing. Vieve enjoyed Marley's soccer player body, the smell of him, the essence of him. The sun strong on her breasts, her eager rising desire. After kissing her everywhere he could reach, Marley entered Vieve with a delighted urgency. As Vieve's excitement built, rushing through her like a wave of fire set to ignite, she matched Marley's love dance, short limbs entwined with long ones. Waves pounded the shore, faint in their ears. Gulls wheeled above them, while the beach, their sandy mattress, shifted under their swells of pleasure. They rolled unaware to the toe of a small dune before they separated.

The tall and short of it, thought Oden, looking through the binoculars that Gordon had given him two Christmases ago, standing on the top level of Fort Devlin. He'd seen the tumbling around the log, and although they were screened from view in the long caramel-colored marsh grass and the swell of a dune, he could imagine quite vividly what he couldn't see.

Meanwhile, Jack West raced up and back along the shoreline of the bayside of the beach, trashing the leash law, terrorizing the shorebirds, especially the great black-backed gulls, as if seeking revenge for his pilfered stew bone from weeks ago. When that enterprise yielded nothing, he wandered south toward the end of the point, sniffing the wind, worrying whatever moved at the tideline, until he saw an indentation in the sand just down from a dune covered in poison ivy. *An invitation to dig*!

Eighteen inches down he encountered the top of a four-by-four-inch granite post that would not budge. He excavated around it, in a manner that would make Dr. McClintock proud, but he couldn't nudge it or get his mouth around it. He left off and returned to the log, where he dug again, this time under the picnic blanket, unearthing the broken-off corner of a lobster pot circa 1930 at one foot down. *Triumph!*

Satisfied, Jack West curled up in the lee of the log for a nap, waiting for Vieve to return.

A few minutes later, Vieve stood over Jack West, still sleeping, Marley behind her. They sat back down on the log, and were silent together for a long interlude as the dog slept. The tide lapped the cobblestones a few yards away—this side of the peninsula was much more stony—large pebbles and small rocks—than the other side of the point.

With no warning, Vieve spoke, as if from a faraway place. "Nobody thinks Carl would commit suicide except the only person, the woman, he told his deepest secrets to."

Marley laid a hand over Vieve's and said nothing, watching the sun dazzle the choppy bay water. He turned to her. She was gazing in the direction of Newell Point.

Tilly worked in her garden, weeding and watering her dwarf bayberry bushes just a skip-jump from a cliff overlooking the ocean's edge. She hadn't thought much of Richard and Theresa going over to Wiscasissett Island that Thursday. They were going to inventory an estate for the auction house of a longtime homeowner and the town's favorite physician, Dr. Kendellwood, now deceased. But even now, five years on, there were still pieces of the story that Tilly couldn't reason out.

It gnawed at her like a virus that blooms into a rash that flares and recedes and then sleeps for months only to return, worse. Something was happening to Richard, something that was eroding the whole foundation on which their marriage was built. But she couldn't put her finger on it. Richard was tense, ambitious... *desperate? Had he been unfaithful too?*

Delta, Tilly's Brittany spaniel, joined her in the garden. Tilly took a break, sitting on an elegant resin bench that exactly resembled teakwood, and gazed out over Little Narragansett Bay. Settling in at her feet, Delta sniffed the salty onshore breeze. Tilly's mind wandered back to Theresa's return to Ponkipaug Village from Wells, Maine, where she'd moved after dropping out of the University of Rhode Island after freshman year. She'd gone into antiques. Gone in big. With her business partner, she'd run a successful antiques trade in the well-trod vacation destination on mid-coast Maine.

Theresa was a couple of years behind Tilly in high school, where Tilly knew her as Ted Silva's kid sister, beautiful, artistic, and with a head for business and an entrepreneurial bent. Their parents—the

Silvas—were erratic, partiers and spenders not into parenting, and Ted and Theresa, already close, being twins, leaned into each other to survive. When business dropped off in the Maine town, Theresa put feelers out back home, hoping to build on a still-growing tourist spot, especially with the rebuilding after Superstorm Sandy. And to return to her brother, who hadn't adjusted well since the water in southern New England grew too warm for lobsters and he'd lost his stake.

Theresa phoned Richard when she arrived back in town eight years ago. Would he be interested in a partnership between her antique business and his auction and real estate concerns? They met at the Salt Spray Bistro—the outdoor, informal café run May through September on the Salt Breeze House terrace. At the end of a friendly business lunch, Richard answered no. But he would like to hire her to expand and grow the antiques auction side of Bear Hill Ltd.

Theresa took the bait, never having embraced the inevitable headaches of keeping a small business going and dreaming of mingling in that elusive upper social strata of the Weekapaug Coast. The same clique from which she and Ted felt excluded in the wake of their parents' death and after the truth came out that their parents were never really in those circles but functioned more like professional partygoers. Their father, a small-time lawyer, and their mother, a wannabe interior decorator. The Silvas plied these trades only in desperate circumstances when there were no business deals or bribes or embarrassing favors they could do discreetly or offers of marriages they could broker for prominent families with unpleasantries to hide. It was a bizarre lifestyle that both Theresa and Ted were confused about, fascinated with, and excluded from.

Tilly had hoped that Richard was hiring Theresa in part to help with the business side of Bear Hill since she had experience running a small firm—there were so many changes in technology that the book-keeper and the office manager were not keeping up on. Tilly her-self had tried to stitch these parts of the business together, but it just seemed to get more and more complicated. In other words, worse and worse.

Then Tilly started seeing things in the item inventory records that alarmed her. Antique estate jewelry pieces, one emerald set in particular, on a referral from Carl Beale, that had been left out of the ledger for that client. Tilly remembered a conversation she'd overheard one day, just coming into the office. Richard, on the phone, the only employee there—evidently not hearing Tilly enter the waiting area—said, "How many clients just after an untimely death are really interested in checking piece for piece against a list they only wish they had written?"

And another time when Theresa got a commission in addition to her already, what Tilly thought, too-high salary. The bookkeeper had brought it to Tilly's attention to make sure it had been approved. Richard had not discussed it with Tilly first. And with Richard and Tilly's son Mason Dean to put through that ungodly expensive prep school, they couldn't be that careless with their good fortune. And now, Tilly mused, there was this board business diversion with the quarry that seemed to preoccupy Richard.

Tilly straightened up and stretched her back, enjoying the cool onshore breeze. Delta stood too, watching a pair of kayakers just off the Coggeshall property. Tilly was planning to pull back from Bear Hill soon, funnel her energy into her own business, building on her growing reputation in coastal garden design and outdoor furniture.

Five years ago, when she'd told Richard he needed to lower Theresa's salary or find some other pocket of money to pay a business manager because she was going to cut back on her time working for Bear Hill, Richard went silent for three days. This was right before the boat trip in which Richard and Theresa sailed to Wiscasissett Island and only Richard returned.

CHAPTER 14

Thursday, May 24, 2018

I t rained heavily Wednesday night, but the dawn broke clear and the day warm. Vieve woke up on Thursday disoriented, back at the beach, under the dune grass fronds. Where she'd gone in her dreams. She'd never made love with someone so tall. Hell, she hadn't made love with any man since Kyle drowned.

She felt like a river flowing back on itself with an incoming tide. She *did not* want to get involved with Marley, but she was pulled to him, fascinated by him. And somehow, he gave her more energy to be herself. There was something inside him that was like the reverse of a black hole, spewing out energy in all directions. She wondered whether—

"Ughh! Jack West! You dog you!" He'd landed on her chest. "Yes, I'm getting up!" Vieve kissed the pinkish skin on the bridge of his nose, where the white fur parted, and then she sat up.

Marley was out when she came down for breakfast at 7 am. Jud hadn't risen yet, and Asia was getting ready for school.

"Mornin'," said Asia. "Good time at the fort yesterday?" She eyed Vieve from over her mug of Rooibos tea, her seed bracelets tinkling out their song. Asia's face was already made up, although she hardly needed it at her age. Vieve smiled, remembering her own eagerness to experiment with makeup in her early teens.

But then Vieve wondered, *Does Asia know? Should she know?*

"We did...hmmm...some testing on the concrete, and may have stumbled onto a way to simplify the picture to keep the committee happy. Actually Jack West cast the deciding vote by digging under the best of the revised sketches. Marley's emailing the committee the design revision." Vieve tried to keep it light but she was talking too fast. She filled Jack West's bowl with kibble, avoiding eye contact with Asia.

"Great. I hope you guys get this gig. Dad will be inconsolable if you don't." Another knowing smile from Asia.

Damn! I hope she doesn't know. Vieve put the dogfood scoop away. "Hardly, I think. "He's got his panels and a show coming up in November. And a new class to teach next winter."

Asia finished her tea and put her mug in the dishwasher. She saddled up with a bulging backpack. So much for everything being online these days. Of course, with Asia, the pack could be filled with bones and rocks and shells.

"But those things don't involve working with you." Asia winked at Vieve and shoved her phone into her back hip pocket. "I'm off, back late. There's an all-hands-on-deck meeting at the dig at five."

From the mouths of babes, Vieve thought. She hoped it wasn't that obvious. *Is Jud on to it too?* Anyway, she needed to get on with the Bassets portrait.

She opened the door to her new ground-floor studio in which she'd hung a framed photograph of Carl, age forty, at the start of his biggest jewelry success. She missed him so much. Had she known their last dinner was their *last dinner,* she would have told him...well, it didn't matter now. She silently thanked him for bringing her back to Ponkipaug Point. She loved this studio and had arranged the work space based on lessons learned over the past three decades of what needs to go where. Lights, mirrors, mediums, brushes, oil paint tubes—all there for the playing. It hadn't seemed like playing for a long while, and she looked forward to this change in subject, or really, change in attitude about her work.

Now—composition! Clementine had *to be in the middle*, thought Vieve. *She played the instigator, easily luring MacArthur into adventure...or trouble! Winston would sit on high, looking over the scene, almost leaning on Gordon, perhaps.* She'd put part of him in on the left panel—and a low horizon with a sea and cloudscape behind, as if on Ponkipaug Point rather than the yacht club beach. Most of the works she set in landscapes were composites of places and snatches of things she'd noticed—that glowed enough for her to tuck them away in her mind's eye only to pull them out later. Some admirers of her paintings confessed that they searched for the exact spots she worked at but couldn't locate them.

She leaned over her work table, drawing with the soft German woodless graphite pencils she loved to use for preliminary sketches. *Or no, Clementine in the middle, yes, but almost all the way toward Winston, mouthing a piece of driftwood to tease him with. Or no, perhaps Clementine would chase MacArthur around in the surf?* She wasn't sure what to do with those two rambunctious Bassets, but she had a fairly clear idea about how to start the left side of the triptych.

She auditioned several sketches of Gordon and Winston sitting in the dunes, playing with dune, horizon line, and—*yes—there would be a curl of wave coming into the lower part of the foreground that Clementine, in the middle panel, had just dodged. Mouth full open, ears flapping.* She knew she had a shot similar to that from the photo shoot. She sorted through the shots, and, of course, when she did find it, Clementine was going from left to right, not right to left, as she wanted. She'd find a way to transpose it. *Now, what to do with MacArthur?*

Jack West scratched at the studio door with a Frisbee in his mouth. Sometimes Jud threw it to him in the yard while he savored his second cup of coffee, said it helped him decompress from the prior night's rehearsal. As she opened the door to let Jack West dash out, she flashed on it: *The Frisbee!*

MacArthur could be retrieving it from the last throw that Gordon had made from the left side of the scene. Or it could be sailing through the air near the top of the panel—adding another directional element. She could play with the color of the Frisbee based on the dominant color palette she settled on. Given the subject matter, she was considering an orange-blue dominated color scheme. *There would be verticals, horizontals, and diagonals to balance since Gordon would be throwing the disc from the dune in an arc and—*

Two knocks at the door. "Vi?" Marley said.

He'd never called her that before. She kind of liked the sound of it. It was not something that Kyle ever called her.

"Come in," she said. She still faced the panel—she'd removable-taped tracing paper to it with her initial sketches. Marley open the door and entered the room. She'd just lifted a color wheel and looked up when their gazes met.

"Wow," Marley said softly. "I didn't realize your eyes were really...just about... aquamarine. I thought they were green. In this light..." He trailed off and started walking toward her but stopped halfway. "Really though, I didn't think I'd feel like this, like something I've wanted for a while and then...well. I didn't expect I'd feel this...this. Warmth."

Vieve put the color wheel down on the table. Her heart pounded painfully. She watched this beautiful man, whom she would have never tried to look for, steal closer to her soul. It was like a very hot sun entering your room; you could never shut the door against it. It would dissolve the door. Dissolve everything.

"Anyway," Marley said, exhaling and closing his eyes for a few seconds. "I just got the call." He looked at Vieve's face, smiling broadly. "We got the hurricane mural! They loved the design revision."

"Marley, really?!" She wanted to rush to him and celebrate in his embrace, but something stopped her. She wasn't sure if she could separate quite so easily from him if she did. Would you ever return from the place where that sun burns so hot?

She walked to the window to distract herself, paused, and then walked back to her easel. *I have work to do. I'll have to move out. I have to...*her mind racing to outpace her heartbeat. Instead, she turned and fist-bumped Marley. The hug happened anyway, with Vieve pulling away quickly. Then she turned to the window to regroup from the immensity of what Marley brought into the room.

She saw through the window, in the yard, Jack West leap and twist his hind end to catch the Frisbee Jud threw. Jud wore a cranberry red cotton bathrobe with white cranes on it and gestured with this arm like he was trying out a line of dialogue. It didn't seem like it had taken all that long to make an odd sort of family out of this group of artistic souls whose only connection was Carl Roger Beale.

When she turned back toward the easel, Marley was examining the preliminary sketch taped to the panel. "Gordon will love this," he said. "You could even show a tiny U-boat surfacing beyond the point. Just for fun. Throw Branislau in." He laughed. *Nerves?*

How can you not love this man?

When Marley left the room—a crisis phone call from RISD, Jud said, letting Jack West back into the studio—Vieve had the strongest desire in months for just a glass of wine. *Please!* A large glass of wine. An endless glass of wine. A lousy mimosa since it was still morning. *Hell, just hand me a bottle of vodka!*

She looked down at Jack West, his head tilted. *Yes, Gainsby. Kyle.* Her promise. *Clarity. Yes clarity! But damn, all the time? Can't you ever have a break?*

Jack West nudged her shin. The wisdom of no escape. Where had she heard that phrase? She opened the front window and listened to the soft shallow boom of the ocean.

"Thanks, Bud," Vieve said to Jack West. "Who exactly sent you to me anyway?" Kyle, she imagined.

She looked at the sketch in Marley's wake. *Yes, a little U-boat would be a perfect touch for Gordon. In the upper right corner. There.* Vieve frowned. *Is Marley jealous of Gordon? Is that why he'd acted so reticent? If jealousy were entering into this, Marley was taking it all way too seriously. First, Gordon was a friend and that was it. And too, any fool could see that Gordon was still totally taken with Tilly.*

And besides, *Marley and I are...? Are what?* She pulled the sketch from the screen. It needed more work before she squared it up for transfer. She liked to hand transfer rather than use a projector. She always wanted to be able to adjust the sketch—revise the story—along the way depending on what her heart told her about the choices her head and hands had made.

She and Marley were...were something. Housemates, lovers, friends, more? And now, they had to do this mural together. Coworkers. She would need to nip this sex stuff in the bud. It could hurt Marley by getting him too hopeful; it could hurt Asia. What did she want?

Vieve returned to the window. Folks were already unloading their cars near the cabana for the upcoming Memorial Day weekend, their children rushing to the dock to look at the water. It was almost as if she were looking at him from some distant future. Crossing in, close to the shore of Little Narragansett Bay in his red kayak. Kyle. Wasn't that what she saw? It felt like he was carrying her with him across the bay to land on Ponkipaug Point. It had been months since he'd come back to her so vividly. Would she find him somewhere again? Would it not be until her death?

Vieve looked down. Jack West was right next to her, his paws placed on the window sill. Looking through the window, craning his head to the left...toward...*the storage shed!*

Asia made another find only an hour into her sifting shift, a bit of unmistakably drilled shell, a piece of a bead most likely, similar to one that had been found a couple years ago on the Connecticut side of the river. Probably Ceramic-Woodland timeframe, hundreds of years ago. She was finding things that, though minor in a sense, had never been uncovered on the Rhode Island side of the riverbank. For some reason, Dayton had pulled the crew back from the areas close to the almost totally demolished dam this afternoon, so there were many at hand when she called out her find.

After Dayton inspected the shell bit, Asia asked him if she could tag along for a little while with the map makers, she was eager to learn GIS. He smiled and said he thought he could arrange it for next week. She mentioned that if it were with someone besides Jeff Glackins she would appreciate it.

"Has there been some issue?" Dayton asked, hands on hips, frowning.

Asia gauged Dayton's expression. She didn't feel like telling him about it, just would rather it go away on its own.

"Ok. Look," he said. "If something, or someone, is out of line on my dig, I want to hear about it first. No kidding. Nip it in the bud. So? Speak! Don't pussy foot!"

"I would prefer to not work with him. He's too touchy," Asia said. There, it's out. Period.

"Yes, yes. I've warned him about that. Will do it again, only this time—" He made eye contact with Asia. "Anything more?" he asked.

Asia looked into the earnest eyes of Dr. Dayton McClintock, and she didn't flinch. She felt a wave of strength. "No, I will tell you if he tries "

At that moment, the hydrologist barged into the conversation. "McClintock! A word please."

Before he turned to leave, Dayton said, "Don't hesitate, talk to me anytime if the...situation crops up."

The two men walked down the north bank trail away from the dig workers. Asia watched them huddle under a birch tree that, as the late afternoon sun struck it, transformed into a stained glass window of golden leaves. She was beginning to think she had stumbled onto a powerful ally.

Wes drew up to Asia's quadrat. "Hey, you know what this five o'clock thing is?"

"No," said Asia. "No clue."

She looked at Wes. "What?" she said. "You look like you're going to burst."

"I got something to show you. I found it in April. I'll bring it over tomorrow if you're home."

"Sure," she said. "Morning's good."

Jeff walked by the site. "Heard you found another one today," he said, laying a hand on her shoulder.

"She doesn't like that," Wes said, moving in between them.

"Like what?" Jeff said.

Asia stepped out of Jeff's reach.

"The hand thing on the shoulder." Wes stood square, legs wide, arms crossed over his chest. Jeff pulled himself up taller.

Asia flashed on a vision of two mountain rams about to have at it.

"Doesn't mean anything, kids," Jeff said. "Chill. Looks like it's almost time for this announcement. This has been a long time in the works." He moved off.

There was no vision hovering again over the river, but Asia did feel a distinctly chill breeze and then a warm one before everyone put their tools down at five for the meeting.

Dayton returned from his pow-wow with the hydrologist and took a spot on a glacier-dropped boulder five feet tall. Everyone gathered round to listen.

"I'm going to start with the good news first," Dayton said. "I thought that was going to be it, but we have a safety update we need to make too." He waved some latecomers into the crowd around the boulder.

"So, drumroll, please! We were notified yesterday that we got the Grantham grant and National Archaeological Association grant! One million, seven hundred sixty thousand dollars—the whole damn wad!"

Clapping and whoops erupted from the crowd.

"Thanks to all your hard work and perseverance through all these delays and the business with the dam kerfuffle. As a result of our combined effort, there is going to be a comprehensive native coastal and woodland cultural exploration over the next five years— in tandem with local tribes. We are still trying to locate interested Niantics or Niantic descendants, but the Narragansett and Pequot tribes are interested. There will be undergrad and graduate scholarships available. God, I'm psyched!" Dayton said, letting his flimsy layer of professorial mien slip.

More clapping all around.

"So we are going to celebrate at my place. Celebrate right! And we would be doing it tonight, but we're going to postpone that for a bit. I expect we'll do it next week. I know you can all handle delays. Anyway, turning to the safety issue, Mitchell?"

The hydrologist took to the erratic.

"Attention, everyone. First, things are fine. But we need to take some additional precautions. The Brook Trout Forever group, as you know, is monitoring heavy metal levels in the river. They spiked Friday, after that last storm. We are not sure whether the dam removal has disturbed sediments just upstream of the position of the former dam. It's not unusual in an area that has seen some industrial activity to accumulate toxic materials—and there was a mill here and a dyeing operation here. But the signature of the heavy metals doesn't quite fit."

At that point, the hydrologist began rattling off compound

names, selenium, arsenic, etc. Dayton shook his head, and Mitchell cut short his list. "The upshot—you folks who were scanning and mapping the river bed will need to stay out of the river and away from the bank until we've got reasonable background levels again."

Someone yelled out from the crowd. "Kim Davenport went home in the late morning complaining of a nasty stomach."

"She's on the riverbed crew!" another student yelled out.

Dayton scrambled back up on the boulder. "Ok, folks. Remember! All injuries and sicknesses on the dig need to be reported to me directly. The procedures you all signed off on? I don't want any of you at risk."

After Dayton spoke, the meeting broke up, among a chatter of conjecture.

Asia and Wes left together, driving back to Ponkipaug Village in Wes's green MINI Cooper. "Sure puts a damper on the grant announcement," he said.

"You know more than he told us?" Asia asked.

"I'm thinking they're not sure what's causing it," Wes replied. "But you know, there's some sort of who-haw going on at the quarry—just came into the newsroom today. With the silica dust, I think. I wonder whether there's anything else amiss upstream?"

CHAPTER 15

Saturday, May 26, 2018

In the shower the next morning, it hit Vieve. It usually hit her in the shower, or when she was swimming or walking in a soft rain. What was it with water and movement? There it appeared in her mind under her wet locks—the whole spooling out of the Basset commission piece.

She whooped and dashed out of the shower, grabbed her bathrobe, and ran downstairs to her studio, Jack West hot on her heels. She worked the sketch until she got so hungry she had to do something about breakfast. In the meantime, Jack West hit up Asia for a meal, having given up on getting Vieve's attention.

When Vieve finally got dressed and headed to the breakfast table, she heard her phone ring back in her room. Gordon. Would she be around later in the afternoon? He had some news. She told him she planned to be in the studio most of the day and he could come over anytime, but if he thought he was going to get a sneak peek at the Bassett triptych he had another thing coming!

Gordon laughed. "Maybe I'll send a drone by to snap a picture through the window."

"Remind me to close the curtains," Vieve said.

The household was running late in getting started that Saturday, except for Asia, who'd already made a breakfast quiche.

"Mr. West! I owe you an apology for the lateness of your

breakfast! Thanks for feeding him, Asia." Jack West was napping on his plaid bed, his eyes moving back between Vieve and Asia. She bent over him. "Won't happen again, my friend!" Jack West thumped his short tail against the bed. *All forgiven, Mom!*

Vieve turned to Asia. "I had this aha moment in the shower and had to get it down on paper before it evaporated from my head."

Asia laid a hand-painted plate holding a generous slice of quiche in front of Vieve. "No problem. If you get obsessed again, and I'm here, I'll feed him."

"How did you learn to cook?" Vieve said. "I'm impressed."

Asia laughed. "When I was about twelve, I just got sick of what Dad was making. He doesn't care too much about food if he has to make it himself. Obviously," she said. Quietly, she said to Vieve under her breath, "It's weird, but Marley's always felt more like an older brother than a father to me. Not that he's a bad father; it's just...I don't know. Weird. But I don't know any other way, and he's always there for me so no complaints." Then more loudly, "I learned to cook mostly from YouTube videos."

Catching the end of the conversation as he entered the kitchen, Jud said, "The rest of us are useless in the kitchen." He crossed to the dining room table and propped his newspaper against the coffee carafe. "Except I can make really good coffee and chili. That's it."

Vieve perched on a stool at the counter she'd sat at that night she'd heard about Carl's disappearance. Jud sat at the table and scowled at the first page. "Quarry's back on page one I see."

Vieve ate her quiche, savoring each bite. Her curiosity about the quarry—and Richard's potential involvement in something amiss—put aside as she considered the Basset piece. *Was the contrast enough between the subjects and the background?* Jack West went out for his Frisbee game with Jud after breakfast. He was turning into a communal dog. Marley bought him a bed, Asia feeding him now and then, Jud playing Frisbee with him. Everyone enjoying his company.

Wes dropped in, hauling his backpack, when Vieve was finishing washing the dishes. He called Asia and Vieve into the living room where he opened a thick, black three-ring binder and placed it on the coffee table.

"What's that?" Vieve said.

"Come take a look," Wes said. "You might be interested since you're working on the mural for real now. Asia told me. Congratulations!"

Asia, Wes, and Vieve sat on the sofa in front of the coffee table.

Wes said, "My great-grandfather grew up in this town. He was just sixteen when the hurricane hit in '38. He fancied himself a writer—actually went on to become a reporter for *The Boston Globe* after World War Two."

Wes leaned over the binder. At the front were *Ponkipaug News Post* and *New Haven Register* articles from the fall of 1938 that Wendell had clipped and saved and that Wes had recently placed into plastic sleeves. Below the plastic sleeves in the binder were three spiral notebooks.

"*Ponki News Post* had to do print runs out of Providence for a while after the storm. This stuff is so cool." He handed Asia and Vieve a couple of the plastic sleeves.

"Spoken like a true newshound," said Asia. Wes smiled.

"Anyway, right after the storm, Wendell tromped around through the debris and chaos, interviewing people and trying to get the word out. He wrote a couple of short articles that were published in the *New Haven Register*. Then enough debris got cleared for the hotshot reporters to get to town. He kept clipping hurricane articles until about Christmas that year, when they started to thin out."

Wes returned his attention to the binder and removed the third notebook.

"Then, after he retired in 1988, he started combing back through the articles and his notes, transcribing interviews he'd conducted in the days following the storm and creating vignettes of stories he'd heard about. He never finished writing and editing them unfortunately. He'd been trying to get something together for the sixtieth anniversary in 1998. But..." Wes looked down at his hands on the binder and then cleared his throat. "He died in '94 of a heart attack."

"I'm sorry," said Vieve. "But how great that you found this binder!"

Asia leaned her head against Wes's shoulder and then sat up straight again. "No one knew about it?" she asked.

Wes looked up from the coffee table. "Not till I found it, apparently. His grandson, my father, our family, moved back into his house last summer after a series of aunts and uncles lived there." He laid the spiral notebook open across his lap. In the back of it were about sixty pages of a manuscript typed on onion skin paper using a manual typewriter.

"When did you find this?" Asia asked.

"Just last month. Mom asked me to return a blanket that she'd restitched the binding back onto to the cedar chest in the third-floor bedroom, where we store stuff. When I lifted the lid, I saw the navy blanket that I had in elementary school. So I picked it up to see what else was in the chest and saw the binder underneath, like it had been sleeping there for a couple of decades."

Vieve, intrigued, leaned over toward the notebook on Wes's lap. "Thankfully, he's got readable handwriting, and it looks like he typed a lot of it," she said.

"Hey, look!" Asia said. "Behind Wes." A cedar waxwing peered at them through the window from its perch on a pussy willow bush, the sun highlighting his waxy crimson red wingtips. "Even he's interested."

Vieve peered at the entry the notebook was open to: *September 21, 1938, 16 and 18 Fort Drive, Ponkipaug Point Beach and Little*

Narragansett Bay.

"How great that you stumbled on this before the eightieth anniversary! I'm surprised no one else knew about it," said Asia.

"That trunk has been around for decades. I think it was my grandparents who put it up there. And my mother had just been dealing with the top layer; she never really dug down. When my parents could see I wanted to go into journalism, they mentioned that they thought my great-grandfather had been a journalist, but they didn't know much else about it."

Vieve left the two to the binder to return to the triptych. She'd tell Marley. Reading it might give them some ideas. Although she felt they had nailed the design at this point. But it seemed like every bit of storm witnessing they could absorb would make their work richer, in ways that might not even be conscious.

It was late afternoon when Vieve heard Gordon's knock on the door. Smiling, she locked the studio door—she'd put a lock on when she converted it from Carl's office, he rarely locked anything—and went out to greet Gordon.

"Let's sit on the porch," Vieve said. "Asia and Wes are in the living room—delving into local history. And you're barred from my studio."

Gordon's ears perked up. "What history?"

"Thirty-eight hurricane. Wes found a journal written by his great-grandfather who lived through it *and* wrote about it."

"I'd love to read it. There's going to be a yearlong commemoration starting in September with the mural unveiling, a whole town thing." Gordon noticed Vieve's eyes widen.

"But hey! No pressure," Gordon teased.

"Hah! None at all. Where can I get a drink?" She laughed and leaned close to him. "I think you'll have to wait in line to read it."

Just then Marley sauntered up the walkway. He nodded at Vieve and Gordon, and went through without speaking.

"What's eating him?"

Vieve said, "I really don't know." She noticed mood swings in him that didn't seem there during the first few weeks of her staying at the house.

"What did you want to tell me?" Vieve asked.

There's something I think you should know." Gordon lowered his voice and pointed to the shed. "Let's sit over there."

They moved to the chairs beneath the gray birches. Jack West happily joined them and took up his excavation.

"Remember the day we did the photo shoot and I had a town council meeting?" Gordon's voice was softer than usual and Vieve moved her chair closer.

Vieve nodded.

"This is not to be repeated, but I know I can trust you, Vieve. I think we've established that?"

Vieve nodded again. "I consider you a trusted friend now, Gordon. I want you to know that. With everything you'd done with, for Carl. For this town—"

Gordon looked away.

Vieve stopped and chuckled. "Ok, I see you can't take a compliment or two."

Gordon did not smile. "Two things. Richard's buddy Guinta is up to his eyeballs in shit over the South Coast Granite."

"What kind of shit?"

"Violations of environmental regulations: noise, air, groundwater, polluting the river. The thing that pisses off Richard, though, is that they are not containing granite dust. The granite around here is very hard, very high in silica. That makes it more hazardous to breathe. So, in addition to adults, kids, and pets getting sick, houses, cars, lawns, and gardens within several miles of the quarry are covered with dust after blasting, and it's negatively affecting property values. It's reached the point where the chamber of commerce is riled."

"So that's when Richard starts to care." Vieve assumed most everything came down to money or reputation for Richard. She also wondered how, with his continued unsavoriness, he'd convinced Tilly to stay with him.

"So today one of the council members reported on the permitting process that he was tasked with reviewing. The former owner of the property—East Coast Mineral & Energy—did not get all the proper permits from the Town of Ponkipaug. I mean the permits that give a variance on conducting industrial operations in a residential area. Someone was very cozy with someone else on the zoning board."

"Why not?" asked Vieve.

Gordon sighed. "It's a long convoluted mess of a story."

He looked at the bay, and then at Vieve, as if for moral support. Then he sat up straight, shaking off his disgust.

"Ok. The upshot is, when they talked of restarting mining operations—which shut down in the 1970s, mind you—the locals protested. They were quieted momentarily by word that the lessee— at that point it was Coastal Builders Supply—was going to go out of its way to run a sustainable and locally sensitive business. You see, that part of the town—and the county—has grown very residential since serious mining operations started in the 1930s and 40s there. In fact, someone said it's the only wetlands-based strip-mining operation in the country. But all that is downplayed." Gordon ran a hand through his silver-blond waves.

Three sharp barks erupted from behind the shed. Vieve jumped up to check it out and Gordon followed. Jack West had run his excavation tunnel perpendicular into an active groundhog burrow. The terrier, on his haunches, barked at what looked like the back of a groundhog at about two feet down.

"How did he dig down that far?" asked Gordon.

"Terriers," said Vieve. "They don't give up! He's been working it since I moved in."

"You should rent him out for jobs. Your own canine backhoe." Gordon stood over the hole with his hands on his hips.

Vieve reached down to pull the dog away, but Jack West stiffened his body. Applying more pressure, Vieve managed to yank him away from the hole, frustrated, but not defeated. They settled back again in the chairs after Gordon laid a board and large rock over the hole for the time being. Gordon pointed to a hole near a stone wall a few yards away. "His back door no doubt."

They settled back under the birches.

"Anyway," Gordon said, "the environmental stuff is bad enough—I'm no tree hugger—but the area is not meant for the scale of industrial operations going on. And it's next to a river, a wildlife management area, and a bunch of houses. But I'm getting ahead of myself. So ECME left for greener pastures and South Coast Granite bought the property a few years ago, and *they* were able to renew the un-kosher variance while scaling up operations, blasting granite and crushing stone on a much bigger scale than the last lessee. And spreading granite dust—silica dust—very toxic—throughout hill and dale. Homeowners are getting sick, literally sick from it."

"This all came out at the meeting?" asked Vieve.

Gordon nodded. "Some of it. Some of it we already either knew or suspected. We did learn at the meeting that one of the state environmental inspectors who was supposed to monitor the toxic dust levels? He was found to have taken a skiing trip in Montreal last winter and another trip to Bermuda arranged for gratis by State Rep. Coburn."

"And Richard?"

"Here's where it gets interesting. I've had a hunch—for years—that Richard wants to run for U.S. Senate. He's close buddies with Congressman Guinta and Rep. Coburn, who folks on the council told me that day were in cahoots to pressure the Department of

Environmental Management guy to look the other way about the permit *and* environmental breaches. And also to look the other way about the bribe. Right now the rep is in deep shit, but Guinta's involvement in the permitting debacle is looking really bad, too."

"Jeessh!" Vieve said. "What's Richard going to do?"

Gordon looked out over the bay, and Vieve followed his gaze. The water was an indeterminate color, not really one you could name.

He turned toward Vieve. "My guess is back paddle as fast as he can. Maybe he's got other connections that would help him with a senate race. Of course, I imagine that's not his biggest concern now. And in the meantime, Tilly told me—" From inside Carl's shirt pocket buzzed an angry burst of static.

Vieve jumped. "What the hell is that?!"

"My phone's version of a page, guaranteed you won't ignore it."

"No kidding."

"Yes?" Gordon said into the phone. He moved away from Vieve, walking toward the bay.

Vieve wondered where this quarry thing was headed. If this all were true, much of the town would be affected. *What about the river? What about Asia's dig?*

After a few minutes, Gordon returned, shaking his head.

"Officer Bliven says Oden is refusing to leave the fort after two warnings. He'll be arrested for trespassing if he doesn't leave now. They've told him repeatedly—they claim—that he can't sleep overnight there. It's dicey at this point. Bliven knows me, and Oden asked him to call me. So I'm going to the point to see if I can sort things out."

"I'm coming with you," Vieve said.

She didn't want Oden treated unfairly either; there had to be a reason why her uncle liked and protected him so much. Vieve found herself fascinated by his quirky otherworldliness. This town, her housemates, Marley's art, the quarry debacle unfolding, Richard

Coggeshall, the hurricane memories—still potent after eighty years—this Oden character. Why was she back in this town? Why was she starting to care about this town? Was it only a few months ago that she lived buried in her next commission without a care for anyone else, except her dead husband? Before Jack West, before Ponki Point, before her uncle left her?

CHAPTER 16

They hopped into Gordon's Lexus for the short drive to the point. The ocean sparkled toward the southern horizon, and all the carousel horses sported young riders. With scores of families descending on the town for the holiday weekend, Candy Crush was doing a land-office business.

Vieve asked, "So what did Tilly say?"

"Oh, yeah," said Gordon, cruising past the carousel and swinging into the cabana parking lot. He hesitated for a moment before he spoke. "She said Richard told her that he misread Guinta and he wasn't at all sure that Fitzwilliam isn't in on the quarry mess too."

Gordon put the Lexus in park, and they practically ran the mile and a half down the beach. Vieve was impressed with what good shape Gordon was in. He wasn't at all winded when they got there. She, on the other hand, took more time to recover steady breathing. Uncle Carl would never have moved that fast. He had a comfortable, never rush, never strain manner that belied a sharp and determined business mind, almost as much tenacity as Jack West, and, unfortunately, the inability to comfort himself when faced with his own bodily weaknesses and terrifying illness. But who was she to judge? Could she know how bad any of his pain was?

They heard sharp voices from the corner room where Oden stashed his driftwood. Not a swallow in sight. Vieve expected a tense scene of conflict. What kind of mood would Oden be in? She could imagine coming across him unexpectedly, eyes red-rimmed from drinking. Or stumbling upon his makeshift fort camp on a cold, rainy evening, ghoulish shadows shifting on his face underlit by a fire. Facing a perceived enemy. Wielding a hunk of driftwood like a club. A modern Viking. Who was this man? Oden? *Wait! Wasn't there a Norse god Odin, with raven and wolf companions?* She smiled at the thought of Munin and Frek, familiars, ageless symbols of imagination and memory rather than a rehab raven and tattered German shepherd.

When they entered the room, they saw Frek first. He was lying with his head between his front paws, watching for Oden's next move. As was Dash Bliven.

"Look," Dash said. "I don't want any trouble."

"Who does? There's too much trouble everywhere," said Oden.

"You cannot stay here overnight. And no fires! Those are the rules," Bliven said, hand resting on the handgun at his right hip.

"Hello, fellas!" Gordon said, as if entering a deck party on a Friday night. Vieve smiled at Oden, while trying to catch her breath. His stony face was trained on Bliven, but he actually winked at her.

Dash turned to Gordon. "Look, I could just Taser and handcuff and be done with it. Tell me why I shouldn't? My boss seems to put a lot of store in your opinion. But this man *cannot* live here."

Gordon opened his mouth. "And before you answer me," Bliven continued, "tell me why I found these in this room?" He held up the boat shoes. "Something we've seen Carl wear?"

Gordon's face tweaked with recognition when he saw the shoes. "I don't know, but why don't you ask Oden?" Gordon kept his voice even.

Stepping toward Dash, Vieve said, "Carl Beale's death was ruled a suicide according to the coroner. As his next of kin, I'm very satisfied with that ruling based on input from his closest...friends. You didn't even want to look for him that night he disappeared as I recall."

"Easy, Vieve, let me handle this," Gordon said, laying a hand on Vieve's left arm.

Bliven glanced at Vieve but didn't respond to her, almost as if he were peering right through her to the wall. As if she weren't there in the room, next to Gordon. Pissed.

"I'll take care of Oden," said Gordon.

"I must show you all something before we leave," Oden said, suddenly exiting the bunker-like room, followed closely by Frek and Jack West.

"Wait!" said Bliven, pulling out his Taser.

"Easy, Dash," said Gordon. "I'll vouch for him."

Dash, Gordon, Vieve, Jack West, and Frek followed Oden down the poison ivy-lined path—shiny green leaves shimmering in the sun—to the west and then down the dune trail toward The Kitchen.

When they caught up with him—Oden moved fast on long legs when he was of a mind—he was bent over a depression in the sand.

"Our fine fellow here has unearthed the granite post that separates the Coggeshall property from the Hallowell property," Oden declared. Jack West began digging again around his earlier excavation, but most of the sand he dug out immediately fell back into the hole.

"How do you know that?" Bliven said, removing his police cap and scratching thin blond-brown hair through which his skull showed in several places.

Oden looked pleased with himself. "There's an old map in the Ponki library. Really old. Seventeen forty three. No, four! Framed, behind glass, top of the stairway on the second floor, around from the elevator. I saw it there last winter on a particularly cold day, when I stopped in to get out of the weather and say hello to Mrs. Hinchcliffe in Reference."

Vieve looked out over Little Narragansett Bay, suddenly mindful of the fresh westerly breeze. Jack West, sitting at her feet, nosed the wind, but peered north toward The Kitchen.

"This is right about where the property line was on the map,"

Oden continued. "The names stayed in my mind, obviously, given how *important*," he mocked, "these two names are in town, and that there's only these two weirdly shaped private parcels on the point. Like a squared over yin-yang thing. Probably has to do with the whole catty-corner side of Ponki Point being sheared off in the big blow. And I've seen these exact same granite posts in the woods at the property edges near the cemetery. Two and two together."

Bliven, skeptical but intrigued, peered at Gordon, who smiled back at him.

"Oden," Gordon said jovially. "A word with you in my office." Gordon pointed to a log near where the cobble beach ended and the dune started. Oden smiled and followed Gordon out of hearing distance from Bliven and Vieve.

"Really, Dash, there's nothing nefarious about those shoes," Vieve said.

"Either way, I'm confiscating them. My job."

Vieve's eyes narrowed on Bliven. If he took just one move toward hauling Oden in in connection with Carl's death, she vowed silently that Bliven would never hear the end of it. She knew Gordon felt the same.

The water lazily lapped the western side of the point, and the gulls soared on high. Jack West looked up. *Was that the thief? Was it? That one?*

Gordon and Oden rejoined the group.

"Oden will come with me off the point tonight," Gordon said. "He will not be staying over. However, you may find that his presence here is...helpful."

Bliven rocked back on his heels. "How so is that?"

"Our friend here"—Gordon put a hand on Oden's shoulder—"has been noticing some unusual activity that may interest you."

"All ears," Bliven said, irritated.

"You've been trying to make some sense out of the twilight

boating activity between here and Connecticut?" Gordon said, almost teasing.

Bliven stood up taller at the change of topic. "Yes?"

Oden jumped in. "There's kids here, the ones who goof around in the fort. Harmless lot of wannabe men. Last week, Kent mentioned they were threatened by one of the guys that comes by boat."

"Why would I believe that he'd tell you this?" Bliven asked.

Oden smiled. "They all like me. I don't think they want anyone to hurt me."

"Threatened how?" said Bliven. "I'm going to record this if you don't mind." He pushed a button on his phone.

"Told to clear out," Oden said. He glanced upward as Munim flew over and shat a foot west of Bliven's head. Bliven didn't notice, and Oden smiled at Vieve.

"So you see," Gordon said, "it might be helpful for you to have Oden serve as a sort of...." Gordon paused, selecting his next word with care.

"Informant," said Vieve, turning to Bliven who was now looking at Gordon.

"I can't authorize that," Bliven said. "Got to get certain... permissions. Red tape city."

"You do that then," Gordon said. "Well, we'll be off. We'll just let Mr. Vacca collect a few things from his...err...the fort."

Bliven let them go reluctantly. He headed for the end of the point, which he had been keeping a closer eye on since the unusual boating activity had started.

Vieve, Gordon, and Oden walked back along the eastern beach. Frek and Jack West had struck up an uneasy truce in which Jack West would nudge and nip and bark to stir up something with the old shepherd, and Frek would ignore him and continue to explore for interesting scents, tolerating the company of the terrier who then bounded along ahead. Oden hung back, staring at something on Poki

Dot.

How did you get him to agree to leave the fort?" Vieve asked.

Gordon smiled. "Well, the trust fund money Carl left him?"

Vieve nodded.

"I mentioned that he would not be able to access the money without staying on this side of the law."

"Which of course isn't strictly true."

Gordon considered Vieve's statement in his lawyerly manner. "Well, that's open to interpretation."

Vieve laughed. "You attorneys are all the same. Opaque as milk."

Gordon looked at her for a long moment. "Tilly said something else, too."

Vieve turned to face Gordon as they walked back to his car.

"Again, between you and me?" Gordon said.

"Yes?" Vieve said.

Gordon began to walk again before he spoke.

"Tilly is convinced Richard was having an affair with Theresa at the time of her death. It's a hunch that she just can't shake, although he's denied it several times."

Vieve listened to Gordon, watching her footfalls on the sand. "This has got to be really painful for you to—"

Gordon didn't seem to hear her. He continued speaking, cutting her off. "She also knows that Richard is seeking to change the ordinance to build on the end of the point. He's not sure who the culprit is on the zoning board, so he's treading lightly. Damn it! We've been butting heads over the point development for the last five years. He thinks he can develop an access point to the fort area on his property if he gets a variance to build a new boardwalk where the old fort access dock was. You've seen those rotting posts?"

Vieve nodded. Jack West rushed up to her with a stick, which she grabbed and threw for him. Frek was sniffing after something in the dunes.

"That sound of crickets in the dune grass just makes me feel like time is streaking by," Vieve said.

Gordon stopped and listened, his eyes drawn back to Fort Devlin.

"Frankly, I think we should clean up the overgrowth around the fort—that poison ivy is ridiculous, zap the graffiti and let sleeping dogs lie. I'm a big booster for history and tourist development too, but this is a dam fickle finger of sand that curls and bends, comes and goes as the ocean sees fit. Superstorm Sandy snatched more dune sand from the eastern side back in '12. Personally, I'm in favor of building something of tourist interest on the lighthouse point. You're not going to like this either, but I don't think you should do a mural on the point. The chamber would be crazy to do that because—one, the topography is too changing and two, who the hell would see it without a dock out there? Only about a tenth of the people who visit this beach bother to walk all the way down to the end. Probably not even that many."

Vieve stopped walking and looked back at the point.

"And," Gordon added pulling up even with Vieve, "you'd have to build a road, and that will go over like a lead blimp with our very vocal town land conservancy."

They heard a soft whirring sound to the south. They both turned and watched Oden. He was sitting on the sand communing with a very distinct blue light emanating from behind Poki Dot. It looked like a sparkling helix spinning up to the Little Dipper just starting to appear overhead.

"Ok, so what is that light, my logical, rational lawyer friend?"

Gordon frowned. "Must be something to do with...with...something in the atmosphere."

"Fairly vague answer, counselor," said Vieve. "So is Oden spending the night with you?"

"He'll stay with his girlfriend in the Beach Plum Development." Gordon watched Vieve. "What do you think the blue light is?"

Jack West returned to Vieve's side. Vieve was quiet a very long time. "A forgotten soul, perhaps?"

"Maybe many forgotten souls," Gordon said somberly.

Vieve watched Gordon as the evening sky darkened from the ground up. A pragmatic, successful man with something underneath. Former marine. She could understand Tilly's attraction to him. Was he really looking after Oden solely for Carl's sake? Had he made his own connection with this damaged, delightful soul?

CHAPTER 17

Wednesday, May 30, 2018

Asia confided in Vieve that morning about Jeff Glackins's harassment.

Vieve said, "I can't believe this never changes, never gets better. Why do all the assholes get the status and then abuse it? It reminds me of some of my clients, the really arrogant bastards. I had to cancel two portrait commissions. I really hoped your generation would have less of it. Or, even better, none of it."

"Well," said Asia, "I told him to back off. If it's any consolation, I have recovered my belief that there are decent men."

"Oh, have you?" Vieve laughed. She refilled their mugs with Rooibos tea from the porcelain teapot on the table in front of them next to the ruins of a blueberry coffee cake. They'd fallen into a delightful habit of having breakfast together a few mornings a week, sitting in porch chairs overlooking Little Narragansett Bay. This morning it was chocked with sailboats like a regatta. Summer folks had returned en masse on Friday, and the locals settled back to rake in the cash.

Asia held up a fist and raised fingers one by one. "Marley, Dayton McClintock, and Wes. And Jud, he's not horrible really." Asia smiled her gap-toothed grin. "Gordon seems all right." She'd run out of fingers on that hand but keep going. "Oden is...is amusing. Richard, thumbs down."

"If Glackins tries anything else, tell me."

Asia looked at Vieve's face, feeling another invisible tug bringing them closer together.

"Thank you for saying that. I will," Asia said. Vieve felt protective of Asia, and Asia seemed to savor the confidences they shared.

"This McClintock guy sounds intriguing," said Vieve.

"Well, you'll get to meet him. You are invited to our little grant-getting celebration."

"Why me?" Vieve said, surprised.

"Not just you. McClintock wants to invite Ponki residents to buy into this multiyear dig thing. Business folks, locals. And you and Marley are doing this mural now, so he'd like you to come. 'A big fat civic deal,' he said. Of course, Gordon, Richard, and a bunch of the yacht club folks are invited." Asia pressed a finger into coffeecake crumbs and then licked it.

"Smells like a fundraiser."

"Well, they did just get a humongous grant, so maybe not," Asia said. She gulped the last of her tea. "Well, got to be off for school. Got that chem final coming up. Ughhh!" Asia stood up and reached for her backpack.

"Helpful subject for budding archaeologists though," Vieve teased.

"I can think of more relevant topics. Anyway, it's okay. Wes and I are helping each other bungle through. See ya."

Vieve smiled. She and Jack West, sitting next to Vieve's chair, watched Asia make her heavily laden way down Salt Pond Drive to catch the bus. "Teenagers are pack animals these days," Vieve said to Jack West. The day was breaking sunny and breezy, as if there might be new possibilities to consider just down the street, over the next sand dune, out in the bay. When Vieve looked down in response to shin pressure, Jack West returned the gaze, leash in his jaws.

Asia settled into the dig. She'd arranged to get independent study credit for it, and next fall being the start of her senior year, there was a lot of flexibility in choosing her electives. She felt certain she could get a scholarship to URI—especially now that McClintock was on her side. She hadn't had any other finds in the last few weeks, those first two rare ones spoiling her for what was the more typical long slog of a dig. Days and days with little to show, doubts about the authenticity, meaning, or interpretation of what you had found. Wondering if you're even digging in the right place....

Jeff had transferred his harassment to Julia, who hadn't yet found a way to stop him. Asia planned to tell Dayton if Julia didn't. It was so tiresome, this entitlement belief that some men had, which Asia was beginning to think was way wider spread than just the idiot classmates and self-absorbed wannabe actors she'd experienced up to now.

Asia was really liking the GIS piece of the dig. She'd been marking some of the locations of the finds in her grid when Jeff appeared suddenly.

"Find any burial plots yet?" he asked. She looked at him, but didn't answer, not acknowledging his sarcasm. "I should tell you that there's going to be stiffer competition for those scholarships I mentioned, so you'll—"

"Jeff, you are so full of shit and you don't intimidate me." Asia didn't recognize her own voice.

He looked at her for a long moment. "Well, I know now who I'll be recommending."

"She won't take your crap either. Not for long. Not when McClintock—"

"You lie to McClintock you'll be sorry you're on this dig."

"We'll see," Asia said sweetly, inserting her earbuds and turning back to her laptop.

Those words she said to him, maybe they were from her river friend. Maybe they *were* her river friend. She didn't really feel like she'd controlled her lips when she said them. When Jeff walked away, she pulled the earbuds out.

After another half-hour of GIS work, Asia looked up from her laptop and peered over the river, hoping to slip again through a rent in time, back to the Ceramic-Woodland days. But then Mitchell appeared at the grid.

"Hey all, another meeting. We've got some answers about the water. We're meeting up by the dam."

As Asia headed up toward the meeting spot, she ran into Wes.

"And?" Asia asked, eyebrow raised. "I'm sure you've sleuthed this already."

Wes, breathless, gathered in air before he spoke. His words came out softly enough that only she would hear them. "The quarry has poisoned an underground aquifer that seeps into the Pawcatuck River upstream of here. There were some issues last year with storm water runoff, but hell, they got some kind of toxic dump there now that's just leaching away."

They reached the dam site. McClintock looked both angry and ragged. He was firing off orders to his small group of postdocs. Someday, she thought, for the first time, I'm going to run my own dig. And no men! It was a delicious and wicked thought she savored, but not entirely practical.

"What does a person think," asked Marley, "at that moment when you realize your top floor, or a small chunk of your roof, is going to be your ocean raft?" He poured a thin layer of self-leveling gel over a rock veneer mounted on a board. Marley had suspended his acrylic panel work for the mural creation, which, he told Vieve, was driving up his prices further.

"You read Wendell's notebooks too." Vieve watched the gel spread over the surface, filling in the niches. "Can I ask what the hell you're doing?" she asked mock sweetly.

Ignoring the question, Marley said, "This is the way it is. You struggle for years, put out great stuff that no one buys. Then you stumble on something that's a hit. Well, if you're lucky, this happens. Suddenly, people don't know how they lived without your masterpieces. What an odd racket!"

Vieve tried again. "How are you going to get the wall to lie horizontal so you can pour that stuff on it?"

"You really are literal, aren't you?"

"Argghhh!"

Vieve concentrated on the final mural sketch. "But aren't we constantly doing that? Building new stories on top of messy, sometimes frustrating old ones."

Marley considered Vieve, shrugged and turned back to the rock veneer. He squirted what look like acrylic ink into a small cup.

Vieve watched, approaching the panel. "I didn't know acrylic came that thin."

"Acrylic paint is the master chameleon," Marley said. "That's how I start my intro class at RISD. The key—all these colors, these gels, this runny goop I just spread over the rock—is all made from the same base material. So it's all intermingleable.

"Is that a word?" Vieve smiled.

"Probably not." They looked in each other's face for a beat. Vieve didn't have a clue what was happening to her with this guy.

"But how are we going to draw on it? I need to draw my stuff, in paint, yes, but I need some grip." *Yes, get a grip, Vieve.*

"No fear! I've got goop for that too! Gritty goop." He pulled out another jar from the middle shelf of his taboret. "This magic stuff creates a gripping, gritty texture you can work your magic on right over top of all these other gels."

Marley half-smiled and looked down. "Not that you need any encouragement working your magic," he said to the drying goop on the panel.

Vieve blushed before she could turn away to compose herself. Blame it on her pale skin. She exhaled and stepped away from the force field of Marley's energy.

"Marley, is this going to work?" Vieve said, moving back next to him. They were both looking at the panel as if that were the only safe place to park one's gaze.

"Yes, compatible materials, remember? Made of the same essence. The Essence of Polymer."

"No, I mean us, working together, it's—"

"Excruciating, I know. All artists suffer," he said lightly, daring to look into her face. He squeezed three drops of a brilliant turquoise into another paper cup.

"Maybe I should move out."

Marley switched from flip to serious, like a color change in his paper cup. "That's crazy! It's your house."

He put down the cup. "I know that I don't replace Kyle or even come close. I'm not trying to. Don't worry, I'll behave myself from now on. I won't lurk outside your bedroom waiting for a moment of weakness to pounce."

Did she want him to? *Again*, she thought, *a nice little* large *glass of wine would do wonders right about now.* She turned away from Marley, confused.

Could she just get out of this hurricane commission? Everything seemed a sticky unresolvable mess. *No*, she thought, *all those folks deserved better.* Even the actual mural didn't matter; it was the doing it, the raising of memory. The hearts of those who would attend the commemoration next year. The children who would learn about it for the first time. Asia had mentioned something in Wes's journal about a Raggedy Ann doll surviving the trip from Ponkipaug Point to the Connecticut shoreline and finding its way to another child. Surely her current pain amounted to nothing compared to the pain they were trying, in their small way, to begin to heal. Pain bigger than even their own lives.

She wandered back to the table on which she was mocking up the figures in the mural. *If he can stand it, I can stand it*, she thought.

Things were quiet for two hours, except for one interruption when Jud walked in, surveyed the scene, and opined, "Hell, why don't you just do a tapestry? Stick it behind Plexiglas? Be easier." Neither artist responded, so he left.

At 7:30 pm, a good twenty minutes after sunset, Asia called out from her bedroom, abutting Marley's studio. "Hey guys, come here quick!"

Asia had the mapping software program up on her computer. She had a shapefile of the pinpoint locations of all native village finds or artifacts on the Rhode Island side of the dig showing on her screen. The outline of the town was overlaid; she'd fist pumped the air when she'd figure out how to do that feat for the first time.

Dusk filled the room, erasing its corners, and it was really time to turn on a light. Jack West, paws on the east windowsill, peered out intently toward...*the storage shed!*

Asia, excited, said, "You guys are gonna freak. Watch! When I hover the pin icon over a spot about five meters, sorry, like, twenty feet, north of Carl's shed, there is a faint white light flickering in the woods."

"Coincidence," said Marley, crossing his arms over his chest. "That's the way the last rays of the sun are hitting the ground." He pointed. "There, see? They are probably reflecting off something to the west, like one of those traffic mirrors at the ends of some of the driveways on Salt Pond Drive."

"He sounds like Gordon," said Vieve. "Everything interesting and mysterious is an easily explicable meteorological phenomenon."

Marley glowered at Vieve. Perhaps he resented being compared to Gordon? She didn't care.

"Ok, Professor Kinnell," Asia said. "Then why when I move the pin icon or even close down the whole program does the light disappear? See, I'll show you."

Asia moved the curser, saved the file, and closed the GIS program. The light dimmed slowly, then went out. Jack West barked once.

"And then comes back again when the pin is back in place?" Jack West leaned even farther forward toward the window glass. Vieve laughed. "He wants at that groundhog again."

Asia opened the software program, clicked on the shapefile to open, and placed a pin icon over the spot in the woods north of the shed. A white glow began at about five feet above the ground. Jack West growled, then started shaking.

"A séance!" said Marley. "Cute. Ok, so what did you rig up in the yard?"

"Not a thing," said Asia. "Go check it out if you want."

"Maybe it's Carl," said Vieve. "Come back to see how we...all are." Suddenly, a rush of pain pulsed her chest and throat. She couldn't stop her tears and dashed from the room, Jack West following. She could really use one of Carl's whiskeys. Yes, she would have one. Just one. Now. It wouldn't hurt. Really.

Vieve knew the bottle was on the back of the counter near a bunch of bananas. As she hurried down the stairs, Jack West suddenly dashed in front of her, grabbed his leash from a basket by the front door, ran back to Vieve, and dropped it on her foot.

"You're right, again. A walk is a better idea." She dashed outside with the dog before she changed her mind. *Single-minded dog or guardian angel?* Vieve thought, smiling, watching Jack West's enthusiasm as he rushed to the shed. Just for curiosity sake, she scoped out the area of the white light. There was nothing to suggest a prank. Maybe it was some effect that originated from Asia's computer? Some hologram effect? Maybe something she'd rigged up with Wes? Not really Asia's style though.

Vieve pulled Jack West away from the groundhog hole to which he was attracted like a wave to the shore. She listened for the ocean's edge to the south. Its ever-changing hem, sometimes smooth and rolling, sometimes ragged, or like a claw, like a hand coming to claim whatever it wants. Today the ocean was calm, steady, and pleasantly whooshing in the background.

"What exactly are we doing in this town?" she asked Jack West. He sat down for a second, taking a breather from homeland defense. Vieve glanced behind the shed. The white light glowed brighter.

"Yes," Richard said softly, half his face shaded by the stark light. "We were lovers that summer." He summoned everything he had to look squarely into Tilly's face.

Bear Hill Ltd was mostly dark, except for the one desk lamp burning in the main office area where Tilly had her desk. Richard had named his real estate/estate auction firm after what the first English settlers called the promontory landward of the Sentinel Lighthouse.

Tilly frowned as she peered back at Richard. Strange, it was almost a relief for her that she'd guessed the truth. Still, there was that snow globe on the coffee table she could so easily hurl at his head.

"At least give me a chance to tell you what happened," said Richard. He reached out to touch Tilly on the shoulder, but she jerked it out of reach.

"I don't need a blow by blow. I can imagine what happened," Tilly said, as she began packing up her desk. She wanted to know, but she didn't want to hear the words from him. She stopped moving her hands for a moment and searched his face. "I would like to know why you lied to me."

Richard watched Tilly's fast-moving hands tossing objects from her desk into a cardboard box. It was as if he just realized she was packing up to leave.

"But we need you here. I need—" It was just a thought that blipped through his head along with many others, yet he'd blurted it out.

Tilly snapped back. "Richard, listen to what you just said. "You were *with* Theresa. For I don't know how long." She exhaled loudly and sat down at her desk.

Richard examined the gleaming laminate of the floor. "Stupid, I know. I didn't really mean it. I, I...I'm so sorry, Tilly." He clenched his hands into fists and then released them.

"How much of the time we had together was really...?" asked Tilly, her voiced raised. Then she held up her open palms. "No! I don't want to go there." She swallowed and shut her eyes. Opening them, she cupped her throat with her right hand for a few seconds.

"I'm human after all, too, and I can't bear to be in this office. There's too much...." Tilly looked around, stared for a second at the Bear Hill logo on the wall, and wiped a tear with the back of her left wrist. "Too many memories."

Richard took a seat at the bookkeeper's desk on the opposite wall. It was a big room for two people, but it also included a waiting area for clients. Richard's office was to the left behind Tilly's desk.

"You know, Richard, I have dreams too. *Urges*," she looked at him pointedly. "But we were a team, I thought, working to build up Bear Hill. Working to maybe, just maybe, get you to the Senate one day."

"It's Gordon," Richard said. "You still—"

"Gordon has nothing to do with this. Just get over him for heaven's sake! I've never, in all this time...done what you've done.

None of us is perfect. All of us feel tempted. But, this is, you've..."

Tilly looked at her husband, the desk lamp leaching his skin of its usual high color from weekends spent on the ocean. His sharp cheekbones and nose cast velvet black shadows on his face.

"How do I know you're not seeing someone else now?" Tilly said.

The words fell on Richard like blows to his shoulders. But before he could respond, Tilly continued. "You're changing, Richard. I'm not sure who you are. The mismanagement at the quarry. You know what you have to do."

Richard straightened and stepped back. "Guinta hasn't been exactly straight with me. I've got to extricate myself. I'm going to."

Tilly eyed Richard steadily. "You do that. But I'm not willing to delay my dreams any more to support whatever you're doing. What used to be *our* dream. If we're not in this together, then let's go our own ways."

"Please, Tilly. It's been five years. Don't throw—"

"I'm going to stay with my sister." Tilly's voice, usually softly musical, with a hint of handed down Scottish from long ago, expressed a hard-edged definitiveness she rarely found cause to use.

"No," he said. "I should leave if anyone does."

Tilly looked up, surprised by the offer. "That's actually good of you, Richard. But I don't want to cause turmoil here at the office. I'll be at my sister's place in Port Judith. We'll sort it out from there."

"Tilly, I need to tell you. You can listen or not, but I need to say this."

Tilly stopped tossing objects in the box. She took a deep breath, and let it out. She looked at the dolphin arcing out of the water on the wall calendar.

"It was thirteen months long. Six months after Theresa came back from Maine. When you and I were going through that tough patch."

Tilly stood and faced Richard, who was standing now on the

other side of her desk.

"It just...happened. I don't know why. Who... Then she wanted a bigger cut of the profits and—"

"On top of her already outsized salary."

"She was used to being a part owner," Richard reasoned.

"Poor her." Tilly opened a drawer, scanned the contents, and then slammed it shut.

Richard looked at his wife. "You're right. What good is hashing this stuff out? I made a really stupid mistake, misjudged her. Misjudged our marriage. I still love you, Tilly. Please believe that. I learned that the not-so-pleasant way and harmed you in the process. Just, don't make any quick decisions. We've still got a lot to enjoy together, now that the business...." Richard's words trailed off as he watched his wife considering his fate.

He looked deep into her eyes. "And there hasn't ever been anyone else."

Tilly considered this news, frowning.

Richard continued. "Hey, if you want to do other work, that's great. This business is not as important as your happiness. We'll...adjust. If you can even start to think about forgiving me. I know it's too early to ask that, but...."

Tilly winced and turned away at the word *forgiving*. Richard walked around in front of her. "Til?" he said softly. "Don't go." He touched her hand with this fingertips. "We can heal." When Tilly looked down at his hand, a tear slid off her cheek. She quickly wiped the tear track off her face with the back of her hand and stepped away from him.

"What happened in that boat?" Tilly asked. She lifted her chin and flung back her auburn bob, her eyes defiant.

The office door flew open and in stormed Congressman Tony Guinta. His dress shirt had worked its way out of his size 52 pants, and he staggered toward the sofa along the front wall, said, "We—," and then clutched his chest, fell on the sofa, and lost consciousness.

"Call 911, Til," said Richard, loosening Tony's peach paisley tie.

Just as Richard adjusted Tony's arms and legs to make him more comfortable, David Hallowell appeared in the doorway. "He's been subpoenaed, Richard."

CHAPTER 18

Friday, June 1, 2018

D ayton knew how to celebrate while helping his team let off steam.

He rented an old white farmhouse in the northeastern corner of Ponkipaug Village in an unincorporated hamlet the locals called Baleford. The property had been left to the university by a longtime oceanography professor. Single, Dayton had come close to marriage once, but his fiancée had inexplicably left for Italy having been willed a ragtag villa with a tiny olive tree orchard for which she suddenly developed big plans. Love runs deep, he'd told a fellow professor, but not deeper than the pull of Tuscany. Dayton didn't spend much time wondering whether there was something deeper than that to uncover. *It works or it doesn't* was one of his mottos in life and in archaeology. When it works, give it all you've got. If not, move on.

In the wake of Justina's departure for her olive orchard, Dayton lived with an extremely large tuxedo cat who seemed to have come with the house. He'd named his housemate The Matador for some weird antics he pulled stalking mice. Dayton also occasionally sublet a room to another professor, although now he was lodging exclusively with The Matador. The impressive cat surveyed arriving guests from the porch railing with wide-open gold eyes, while Dayton lit tiki torches. It was a bit cool for this event to be outside, but it would be an indoor-outdoor party. Let the chips fall where they may.

Just turned fifty, Dayton was the tiger of the Archaeology Department at URI. He'd only been on the faculty five years but had quickly revived the department from a decade of relative slumber, after moving over from the University of Connecticut. Attracting grants like a money magnet, he fired up students, prospective students, and administration with his plans. Some of which took off, others of which were unceremoniously killed by their maker if they proved inoperable.

"The key to Dayton from what I can see," Asia said, walking with Vieve and Wes after they emerged from his MINI Cooper, "is he's brilliant *and* can make things happen."

"And he doesn't suffer fools, I hear," said Jud, coming up from behind them.

"Those two don't always go together," said Vieve as they approached the porch. "Brilliance and results. Just take...wow! Look at that cat! Glad we left Jack West at home."

"Meet The Matador!" said Dayton from the top stair. "But call him Mat if he lets you. Is this Genevieve Beale, Asia?"

Vieve looked up at Dayton from eight stairs down. His straight reddish brown hair backlit by tiki torch light glowed like a ring of copper fire.

She climbed the stairs and extended her hand for a shake. "Call me Vieve, please."

Dayton was about four inches shorter than Marley, Vieve guessed. He had lively brown eyes, which she looked into for the first time to find both mischief and soul. He appeared more mortal to Vieve now that his hair wasn't backlit with a fire ring, and he exuded an air of genuine hospitality. Mustache, no beard. Cute, Vieve registered, handsome actually.

"With pleasure," Dayton said.

That first second of eye contact was a warm flush of pleasure to

Vieve, different from the way she'd felt with Marley. The effect of Dayton was more like coming upon a secret spring in the woods that you have all to yourself. *Chill, Vieve,* she ordered herself.

Reluctantly breaking gazes with Dayton, Vieve scanned the yard. She hadn't been to a party like this since the unveiling of the governor's portrait. This looked a much more comfortable bunch, although she was sure that undercurrents of competition and intrigue were also present if one scratched the surface.

"Thanks for inviting me, us. And the whole town it seems." Vieve swung an arm out to indicate the crowd below the deck spread out across the lawn in tight groups and ragged clusters, children chasing each other in the large opening before the woods started in earnest just beyond its ferny fringe.

Dayton laughed. "The more the merrier. The more people interested in the dig, the better."

Vieve turned to Dayton. "Congratulations on your finds! Asia gives me the inventory. And on your funding."

Jud brought drinks to their little group at the top of the stairs.

"Asia, yes. She's your niece?" Dayton asked. He sipped red wine from a plastic cup Jud handed him.

Asia and Vieve made eye contact, Asia smiling as if the idea had appeal.

"No," said Vieve, laughing. "Although you could do way worse, niece-wise."

"And aunt-wise," Asia echoed.

Dayton put a hand lightly on Vieve's arm. "I must excuse myself, Vieve. Sorry to be a brute; there's someone I have to talk to who just arrived. But I'd like to talk more. Hear about your famous mural. I've heard varying accounts of its contents."

"None of them authorized," said Vieve.

"Probably speculation then," said Dayton. "I know all about that in my world. But please, help yourself to food, drink. I've got an army of students cooking food. I tell them this is their party, I'm springing for food, but they keep cooking. It's the life in the dorm, I fear, the no-kitchen frustration." Dayton turned to walk down the stairs and over toward the driveway, introducing himself along the way to folks he didn't know.

Vieve glared at Asia. "Don't look at me. I haven't given anything away."

Asia introduced Vieve to a sampling of her dig mates and pointed out Jeffrey Glackins from afar. "He's our narcissistic grid overseer," said Asia. Julia was there too, watching Jeff from outside a nearby circle of students and steadily sipping from a plastic cup of white wine.

"Yes, Glackins," Vieve said, making a mental note to take his measure at some point in the night. Asia had already turned away to talk with another student she hadn't introduced yet. The conversation noise level rose a notch. The Matador was prowling for any dropped hors d'oeuvres, preferring the seafood kind. Scallops with a dab of some annoying substance he'd rub off with a stroke of the paw.

Richard and Tilly arrived in separate cars. Gordon was there, most of the chamber of commerce bigwigs, Nina and Maeve, a vast swath of the Salt Breeze upper crust. The rest, making up three quarters of the gang, were archaeology and summer school students and faculty with a few overdressed administrators thrown in. Attire ranged from the administrators and upper crust's light-colored summer suits to chinos and dressy jeans and short-sleeve shirts among the faculty and students.

Vieve heard chords plucked by lank-haired boys with guitars, a girl with a mandolin, and Jud on his bouzouki coalescing into a song. Students were already dancing, and their Baby Boomer professors would not be outdone. Asia shimmed off to dance with Wes.

"No Marley," Vieve noticed a half hour later. She cornered Jud, who'd laid his bouzouki aside for a break, by one of the food tables.

"I tried to get him to come. He said he had too much work to do."
Jud did not look up from the large wooden bowl of garden salad he
was tonging onto a plastic plate.

"What's eating him?" Vieve asked. She almost took a proffered
glass of wine from a passing tray carried by a friendly undergrad. She
almost just mindlessly broke her sobriety! See what happens when
she's not with Jack West!

Jud looked at Vieve a long time, oblivious that his salad was
about to slide off the plate. "You really don't know?"

"No. But he has gotten worse the last few weeks." She considered
the pot in front of her but could not make out what it contained.

"It's you, Vieve."

"Me?"

"He's god damn in love with you. And you're just...just...playing
him along."

"Is that what he thinks? Or what you think?"

Jud put down the plate and raised his glass of beer to her.

"What do *you* think?" he asked.

Vieve felt a flush of heat in her chest and cheeks. She turned
away abruptly and bumped into Dayton, trying to dodge her. He
flailed for balance, then was forced to put his arms around her to
prevent the both of them from falling onto a large Navajo pot in his
living room.

"Whoa!" he said. "Easy." He steadied her and then withdrew his
arms, smiling.

"Thanks. Sorry," said Vieve, blushing. She moved away from the
two men, out to the deck for some air—to consider what Jud just said
and what it felt like to be held so close by Dayton right out of the blue.

Vieve fell in with Asia's crowd and enjoyed the rest of her
evening, avoiding both Jud and Dayton. She introduced herself to Jeff
and got him to expound on his recent dissertation before tossing him
her parting shot. "Oh, and back off from Asia or you'll be very sorry,

Dr. Glackins." She enjoyed the astonished look on his face before he moved off quickly to the bonfire. At ten, Vieve felt the urge to leave, although the party was still in full swing. She walked back to where the cars were parked and bumped into Tilly Coggeshall, striding purposefully toward her car.

"Tilly," Vieve said. "Could I get a lift back to Carousel Crossing?" She looked back toward the crowd. "I don't really feel like waiting until my ride is ready to leave."

"Sure, why not? Hop in," Tilly said, pushing the button on the fob to unlock her blue Prius. They rode through dark forest-lined streets back to the coast.

Tilly broke the silence. "Dayton seems like a great find for the Archaeology Department."

"Who?" Vieve said, lost in thoughts of the evening. Of Glackins, for example, and his well-fortified ego.

"You know, the host of tonight's proceedings?" Tilly laughed.

"Sorry. Yes! Interesting guy. Asia considers him someone to model a career on."

Tilly kept her eyes on the road. "Is she really into that? Digging up old stuff."

"Yes." Vieve laughed. "She and my dog."

Vieve watched Tilly's profile. Tilly's ready smile faded into concentration on driving. She turned right on the main coastal road, and now they could see the moon shining on the ocean.

"This place is beautiful," said Vieve. "Such a turbulent past though."

"Such a turbulent present," said Tilly. "I'll take you all the way to 17 Salt Pond if you like, it's only another minute or two."

"Which turbulences?" Vieve asked idly.

Tilly just smiled. In the moonlight, on her face, Tilly reminded Vieve of the look on The Matador's face when she arrived at Dayton's house. Wise, self-possessed. A little wicked.

"Not mine for much longer," Tilly replied. "I'm off to Port Judith. Here we are."

Tilly pulled up at 17 Salt Pond. Vieve thanked her and walked up the clamshell path that cut across the lawn on a diagonal. There were no lights on, so when she stuck her key in the door and felt the sudden presence of someone on her left, she gasped.

Her eyes, accustomed to the moonlight now, identified Marley and an empty bottle of wine on the small table behind him. They stared into each other's mostly shadowed face. An ocean breeze tousled their hair and raised goosebumps on Vieve's arm. She'd taken off her jacket in Tilly's car, which was hot when they first got in. Vieve thought Marley looked very far away while standing too close to her. Salted, moist air hung in the small space between them.

Vieve turned the door handle. When she reached for the porch light switch, Marley said, "Asia was right. There is a ghost by the shed." She felt his breath on her neck.

At the very tip of Ponkipaug Point on the sand bank, Oden crouched low in the trail cut, facing the incoming tide below. The moon hung like a bright linen medallion over Poki Dot. Oden's left hand held Frek by a frayed nylon collar. He had to acknowledge the collar did come in handy on occasion. Carl had made him get the shepherd a rabies shot and a collar to hang the tag from. If not, and he bites someone, you don't want to think about it, Carl had said. Oden missed Carl; he knew Frek did too.

On the short beach in front of him, the boulder that Oden considered the true end of Ponkipaug Point hunkered half-submerged. One gunshot had brought Oden scrambling up to the trail from where he was sitting on the jetty watching the moon and the star smudge of the Milky Way. Now his attention was riveted on a

Bay Boat, slowly approaching the point from the west, and two apparent captives in the path of the tide that Oden knew would peak at midnight.

The captives, Kent Hallowell and the Bixby kid, *Dag, was it?*, were tied back-to-back thirty feet out from the edge of the beach. The ocean was up to the middle of their chests. *They must be on a rock*, Oden thought, *or their heads wouldn't be above water.*

The motorboat approached within a few yards of the teenagers and then veered north, the wake sloshing up to the boys' chins. By the moonlight, Oden could make out the silhouettes of two men in the boat. Oden knew the underwater shelf around the point kept the water depth below three feet for many yards offshore, until high tide, when it would more than double in depth.

"Ok. Cut them loose, Torin," said one of the men in the boat. "We don't need any more complications here." Over the low-idling motor and the calm surf, Oden could clearly hear the authoritative voice in an unfamiliar accent. *South American?*

"We should take 'em," Torin said, emerging from the western side of Ponkipaug Point on the cobbles and wading out to where the boys were tied. "Get serious," he said before a shallow dive and short swim to the rock.

"Make it quick. Let's get going," another voice from the boat said. *American but not from New England*, Oden thought. The motorboat moved off toward the sandier beach near The Kitchen. Oden's right hand tightened around Frek's muzzle. He could feel the dog's muscles quaver against his legs.

Torin lay a knife across Kent's neck for a few agonizing seconds; Oden saw the blade flash in the moonlight from his vantage point on the dune. Oden was ready to spring, but something held him back. *Was Torin serious or toying with the boys?*

Then Torin disappeared under the water. When he reemerged he pulled the boys up, his massive forearms around their slender torsos.

Torin sliced the rope connecting their wrists and then slowly sheathed the knife. He leaned toward the boys, but Oden couldn't hear whether he spoke to them. The boys turned their heads away from him after he removed their gags.

Plunging back into the water, Torin swam the short distance to the beach and slipped quickly around the point where the motorboat waited. Kent Hallowell and Dag Bixby stood, measuring the distance between themselves and the beach. Although they were no longer tied together, their arms were still tied behind their backs. How were they supposed to get to shore without using their arms?

"Shit, Dag! Shit, fuck! We could have been slashed or worse. You see that knife he cut the rope with?!" Kent sputtered.

Oden and Frek dashed down the dune toward the beach. Dag noticed Oden's movement. "Hey!" Dag yelled. "Who's there?!!"

Oden crept forward still holding onto Frek. "It's me! Oden! Stay there. I'm coming!"

"Oden, *Christ!*" Kent said. Excited, he pivoted toward Oden's voice and fell off the boulder. Face down in the sea and unable to right himself.

"Don't move, Dag," Oden yelled. "We're coming!"

Oden let go of Frek, and they hurried through the water. Frek reached Kent first and nuzzled the side of his face. Oden reached him seconds later and turned him over on his back. Kent exhaled loudly. Oden extracted a small Swiss army knife that Munin had pilfered from the wildlife refuge beach and cut Kent's wrists free. Oden pulled Kent to the beach and sat him among the cobbles. Frek sat next to him while Oden went back for Dag.

Oden led the two boys back to the fort and built a driftwood fire on the main floor, open to the skies. *The hell with Bliven!*

"Get dry, lads! Then we'll get you home." Oden began stoking the fire with larger branches from some of the dead bushes that choked the end of the point.

"Are you ok? What did they do? I just stumbled on you right before the guy was about to cut you free. Heard a gunshot."

"Lots of threats," Kent said. "We heard that gunshot, sounded like it was coming from the direction of the boat."

"Was it a signal that the deal was off?" said Oden speculatively.

"We were on the fort top. Heard the shot and saw a guy come out of that stairway near the gun turret and run back down toward The Kitchen."

Dag was shivering despite sitting a foot and a half from the fire. "He held that knife to our throats before they tied us up," Dag said softly.

"If it had been that Torin guy by himself, he'd a thrown us in the ocean off Poki Dot. Like he did with our cell phones," said Kent.

Oden looked back and forth between the boys' faces. Kent looked manic, and Dag appeared subdued, shivering. "You need protection, guys. I'm going to walk you back down the point and then—"

Kent interrupted. "If we rat, we're dead. Torin's parting shot." As Kent's dark bangs dried, they fell forward, covering his eyebrows. Oden felt a sharp longing for the lush hair of his youth.

"I think not," said Oden. "First, don't come out here anymore. Second, I'm going to talk to some folks."

"You can't, Oden. They'll kill us!"

Oden put a hand on Kent's shoulder. "We won't let that happen. Right now, I'm getting you back home. You need to talk to your parents."

Kent said, "You know my dad. He'll probably want to blow up the point once he hears!"

Dag was still shivering, still staring at the fire, and still unceasingly stroking Frek.

PART 4

W es left a photocopy of the typed portion of the hurricane chronicles—as Asia had dubbed Wendell's manuscript—at 17 Salt Pond for her and the housemates to read. Jud turned to a page two-thirds of the way through and read it aloud that morning after breakfast.

September 21, 1938
16 and 18 Fort Drive
Ponkipaug Point Beach and Little Narragansett Bay

Annette White, her sister Ruth, and their young cousin Ivy waited for the Coast Guard cutter on the back porch. In the front yard, the ocean bludgeoned its way through the bay window of the three-story beach house. Annette remained calm. She scanned the channel just off the long spit of sand west of Ponkipaug Point. The cutter would appear any minute. Securing her rain hat under her chin, Annette leaned forward, addressing Ruth crisply. "We'll be evacuated shortly."

Ruth thought otherwise. One step down from Annette, Ruth was praying for all she was worth. In particular, she begged forgiveness for the sin of not stopping a little boy with a clam rake heading down Fort Drive a half-hour ago. Every schoolboy knows clamming is great before storms.

Ivy clung to the porch stairway but could not find a place for her feet above the rising water. She watched in silent horror as the ocean sloshed around the house's outer walls and poured out through the first floor windows.

Next door, the Gages had taken to the third floor. Molly Gage, husband Bradley, handyman Roy Cotrillo, and the children BJ, Roger, Bonnie, and Cammy. Theirs was the largest and most reinforced house on Fort Drive, yet the second floor was about to go. Roy pulled the Gages' Dalmatian, Winchester, to safety on the third floor just before the ocean pushed the stairs through the opening where the back wall had been. Their mother cat Grace had vanished along with her new litter of ginger-colored kittens.

Roy took a deep breath before glancing out the bedroom window toward the White cottage. At the same moment a wave pulled Ruth and Ivy from their back porch. Roy's heart thumped painfully, and he tightened his grip on Winchester's collar.

Bradley busted a hole in the ceiling with a crowbar where a prior leak had loosened the plaster. He was glad he hadn't asked Roy to fix it last week. Then Bradley began boosting family members one-by-one up onto the roof. Roy handed Winchester to Bradley through the opening in the ceiling and then he shoved a bureau beneath the opening. Roy stood on the bureau from which Bradley and BJ hauled him the rest of the way onto the roof.

Suddenly, the roof lurched at a forty-five degree angle and became a raft. Bradley wrapped his leg around an exposed pipe and held Roger and Bonnie. Molly held Cammy close and clung to Bradley's waist, while BJ wrapped his leg snugly around Winchester. Roy lay almost completely on top of Roger and hooked a foot around the same pipe and a hand over the triangle peak of the top of the roof. The yellow sky pressed down angrily just above the seething emerald waves.

If it were only just *waves*, Roy thought. Instead the sea around them was a churning boil of wall chunks, mattresses, appliances, dock pieces, whole and partial boats, and lumber. The wind pressed everyone low to the roof in between waves. BJ called the incoming wave alarm, and everyone held their breath, bracing for the cold deluge. Roger inched up the roof to grab his father's left leg and belt.

Suddenly, a wave deposited Annette White right next to Winchester. She'd lost her rain hat and her companions. Relieved to see Annette, Roy quickly pushed her toward Bradley, now a human anchor for his entire clan. The next wave hurled a dock fragment that smashed against Roy's chest before he could flatten himself again on the roof. And the wave after that peeled him off the roof. When he surfaced for air, a wall still connected to part of a ceiling swept into grabbing range. He pulled himself out of the frigid sea and onto the ceiling. Before the water-air churn obliterated everything, Roy noticed the Gage family still all linked together on their circumstantial raft.

When his view cleared a bit, Roy noticed a dark fin breach the ocean surface and another to his right. For the first time, he wondered if he would make it. The agony in his chest was so acute that he had to concentrate hard to keep his grip on the ceiling tight enough to stay aboard.

But then he saw land, off to his right. It was a vague distinction between storm and rock and soil. A few houses appeared through the foamy mist. *Maybe I'm not heading off*

*the coast? Maybe there will be a landing place that isn't
the bottom of the ocean?*

Another wave slammed something into the back of his
knees. He clenched his teeth and loosened his grip on the
edge of the plaster. While longing to warm his icy fingers
in his armpits, his thoughts turned to his wife. He hoped
she could collect the life insurance. He hoped that they
would find his body in the debris if he hit land in
Connecticut. He hoped that the mirage ahead really was
land.

Roy drew in another breath. Another wave caught him
off guard, wrenching him off the piece of wall.

He surfaced one more time. There was so little left
now. He had wanted to do much more for his son Ben. His
wife was strong and would carry on. As Roy began to slip
under the water's surface, something banged his head and
right shoulder. It felt like a slap in the face from some
benevolent force. A surge of energy flowed through Roy's
torso and arms, and he pushed himself an arm's length away
from the object. It was a bathtub. Looking up, he saw a
Raggedy Ann doll, riding high with legs tangled in the
faucet knobs. Roy laughed and cried together in a short
burst of sound. Then he spat out seawater and yelled,
"Hell, little lady! If you can stand it, so can I!"

Roy grabbed the lip of the bathtub, his energy surging.
He pushed the thought of giving up completely out of his
mind. Five minutes later he saw a treetop and grabbed it.
Then he saw the familiar roof go by with a spotted dog on
top. *A beacon in a tempest*, he thought. The Gages ended
their transit of Little Narragansett Bay at Newell Island,
Connecticut. Roy clung to his treetop as the storm swirled
northwest and the water slowly receded.

CHAPTER 19

Tuesday, June 5, 2018

When Vieve returned from the grocery store, the letter was on top of Marley's massive art supply catalog in the stack of Tuesday's mail on the counter. The upper right corner bore a Providence postmark. The envelope contained another envelope bearing only the handwritten words *Genevieve Clough Beale*. She fumbled a finger under the flap of the inner envelope and opened it, the tearing sound loud in her ears.

She retreated quickly into the living room, trailed closely by Jack West. A gust of wind knocked against the house, sending the maple leaves roiling and flashing their lighter silver-green undersides. From the bay window, she noticed the steel blue ocean, shadowed by clouds, looked solid. As she sat back on the couch, she exhaled a long breath. She'd noticed her breathing a whole lot more since she began her sobriety. How had she not been aware of her own breathing for half a century?

Closed eyes, another deep breath. Her heart thumped as if it were the only heart in the world, then silence. She opened her eyes, and Jack West was on the couch next to her. Front paws on her left thigh. She was not alone. He looked into her face. *You're great, Mom!*

"Thanks, Jack West. My mental health counselor. My sobriety sponsor."

She pulled the sheet of printer paper out of the envelope. She read the computer-typed words with the handwritten signature:

Hello my dear Vieve,

I don't mean to startle you, coming back into your life like this. But I also know that my choice of departure caused you pain, which is so very regrettable. And it was my decision as I'm sure you know by now. Don't let anyone else make up stories about it. So why not tell you definitively in a note left in my cast-off coat, or under our tomato can, or some other such melodramatic thing? Why give Ferdinand, my delightful rainbow hematite ore man, this envelope to send you at this time? By the way, he doesn't know what the contents are, so no hard feelings toward him for not telling you sooner.

Well, there is no reason, except that I wanted you to have a little peace in your soul about me before you read these words because I know I caused you and many others great pain by my final choice. I had advanced brain cancer, a large tumor, actually probably three, but we don't need to go into all the gory details. Only Beryl knew. If for some reason she was unable to tell you, I wanted you to know. To really know the reason. I didn't like what was happening to me. I couldn't accept it. The doctors were happy to lie to me. I was only going to get way, way worse. More helpless. Maybe I lacked courage. Maybe I came up short. Maybe I made the ultimate mistake. But by the time you read this, it won't matter anymore what I thought.

What matters is what I love and that you love and are loved. What do I love? You, Beryl, this crazy town, my new jewelry line, Gordon, Oden and that tattered dog of his. Asia's grown on me too. But you are way, way before any of those others. And of course Bonnie, who will always dwell in her own special chamber in my heart. Maybe this was some clumsy way to bring you back to the town I love. Maybe you can heal your broken heart here (I know it's still broken even though unselfishly you won't speak of it). You will be inspired again by its beauty as you were when you were a girl and rode my shoulders as queen of the summer sunshine. Maybe you can show those with broken hearts and scorching memories that no matter who or what has at them, our imperfect love is still our greatest treasure. That's where your art is going.

And, after you live a ridiculously long and wonderful life, I look forward to seeing you again, with your special person, and all those dogs, when it's time for them to join us. Along with other assorted Beales, even your father, and of course your splendid mother and sister. Ever yours, Carl

What am I supposed to do with this?

Without thinking, she crumpled the paper in her right hand, threw it across the room, and then covered her face with her hands. When she opened her eyes, Jack West had retrieved the letter and placed it in her lap. He was sitting next to her, his eyes on the ball of paper, his tail rapidly thumping the couch. Vieve smiled. Reconsidering, she smoothed the paper as best she could and carefully tucked the letter back into its envelope and slipped it into her back pocket. She grabbed Jack West's leash and a mostly full bottle of wine—Jud's—from the fridge and opened the front door, letting Jack West slip through, and ran out into the front yard. As she looked at the window of Carl's bedroom, now hers, tears streamed down her face.

"Damn you, Carl Beale! Why did you have to be perfect? Your idea of perfect!" she said to the window. Of course, the pain, how could she know or measure his pain?

Jack West, ignoring the shed dig, stayed by Vieve's side.

She twisted the already loosened cork out of the wine and took a long drink. Cells throughout her mouth and throat danced in recognition of the long-withheld elixir. After swallowing she hugged herself, peering up as the sharp silhouettes of chimney swifts skittered high over the house. She exhaled. *Yes,* she thought, *I can still exist. I won't fly apart.* She took another pull on the bottle. And then she rose and hurried back into the house and up to Marley's studio,

Jack West in tow as if he were leashed.

Everyone was out of the house late that Tuesday. The mural preparations covered the work surfaces in the studio, but Vieve was after that acrylic panel, the one that caused her heart to skip—or was it Marley?—that she'd noticed the day she arrived at 17 Salt Pond to meet Uncle Carl for the dinner that was not to be. The day her uncle most likely jumped in the ocean or whatever other wasteful thing he did with himself. Rowed himself to oblivion. She took another pull on the opening of the wine bottle. Her body, flushed with alcohol to which it now had little tolerance, reeled with the poison. She shut her eyes and waited for the wave of disorientation to wash over.

The acrylic panels were organized in four vertical stacks, ten-deep each, on the wall abutting Asia's bedroom. "Stock! Inventory!" Marley had teased, as he organized them to make more room for the mural work—to which he seemed to be increasingly pulled. To her they were Marley's Magic Panels, something she still hadn't processed. *You can't process magic!* There was something in these panels she needed in her art, but she couldn't figure out what it was—certainly nothing that could be easily explained, nothing as simple as switching media, like changing to acrylics, or adjusting techniques or becoming less representational.

She flipped through eight panels in the first stack before she found the one she was looking for and pulled it out, leaning it against the north wall. Orange, gold, green, metallic blue-violet. *Did he find,* she wondered, having slid to the floor in front of it, Jack West in her lap, staring at the shiny, sinewy, multicolored striations—like the veins and other biological tubes of a dissected body—*that the process of discovery and possibility was more compelling than production of something of which you already knew its contours?*

She swallowed another mouthful of wine and stared at the dark green wine bottle. The level had gone down steadily as outside the studio the sun set in the thickening clouds.

Even in her worst drinking days, Vieve had never drunk straight from the bottle. Then, only then, when she placed the bottle to her left, did it dawn on her that she'd broken her sobriety. She swatted the thought away. *Now is now and I'm flying apart!* She felt as if she were parachuting without a parachute.

As she reached for the bottle again, a leg kick of Jack West, propelled by a doggy dream or perhaps disapproval, knocked it over and most of the rest of the wine—about three-quarters of a cup— spilled out onto the studio floor.

"No!" she cried, anguished, looking at the bottle. I need that tiny puddle of protection, she told herself without moving her lips.

Then another shallow breath, and all the anguish of losing Kyle and losing Carl flowed back into her again.

"Damn it. Damn it!" The pain rocked her and she leaned over onto Jack West. He sprang off her lap and looked at her quizzically.

It was then that Marley walked in.

After surveying the tableau, he crouched down and whispered kindly into Vieve's left ear, "I thought you didn't drink."

"I don't!" snapped Vieve. "This didn't happen. None of this happened. You don't attract me. And many other assorted lies." She tried to turn away from Marley's gaze, but her head and body seemed to be moving in different planes. She shut her eyes and held her breath, trying to prevent herself from vomiting on Marley's shin.

Marley offered Vieve his arm. She clasped his forearm, and he pulled her slight body up. Vieve felt a plumb line boring into her head from which she now off center. She fell against Marley's chest, eyes shut, trying to feel the bones and muscles in her legs. "And you don't still want Kyle anymore," he said softly, holding her as she regained balance.

"Of course not," Vieve whispered, feeling drained, leaning on his chest. Then, realizing that was what she was doing, she stepped away from him.

"What happened?" he asked, looking into her eyes, her checks glistening as rain began to pour down the window panes.

She felt another a wave of dislocation in her head, but stood her ground. She moved a hand across her forehead. And then, like an icon portrait, Gainsby's dignified face appeared in the vision of her memory. Her shame returned. She shut her eyes again and rode that wave of pain without trying to disappear. She opened her eyes when she heard Marley speak.

"Vi?" Marley said. "It's okay—"

"I got this from Carl today," Vieve whispered, pulling the grass-stained envelope from her rear pocket and extracting the letter bearing dogtooth holes. Now that she'd smoothed the paper as best she could and handed it to Marley, she knew what she wanted would never happen. Carl's message could never be taken back.

"Erosion has many stories to tell," Dayton proclaimed, wrapping up a short lecture to a group of dig students that included Asia. He was pointing to a soil horizon beneath the most recently exposed facet of the eastern riverbank, on the Rhode Island side of the shell middens. Wes wasn't there. He was trying to get what he could on the story of the teenagers on Ponkipaug Point, but Kent and Dag still weren't talking.

"Ok, troops! I want all the non-river grid teams to look at our most recent GIS layers. It's great for you to see what everyone has uncovered in a big overview. I want you to think as you dig, think as you sift, think as you brush your teeth...beyond what you might expect to see. Always, always...keep fresh eyes. But know what you have. Know what's been espoused. Know the wheat from the chaff."

The group blinked, swallowed, and shuffled their feet nervously.

"Know the bull from the shit," added Dennis Ballou, the dig's new Archaic Narragansett Culture Specialist. "Follow me, gang."

The group headed for the main dig cataloguing and presentation tent in a small meadow. Dennis had set up a laptop and projected onto the side of the tent under an outside awning that added some contrast with the late afternoon light.

"You see," he said. "We've got the star of the show here. The stamped pottery chard."

"So far!" yelled a master's student.

Dayton nodded and smiled. "Right! There's always more under the ground."

"Then we have the finds from Grid 41a." Dennis nodded to Asia and then continued. "The shell bead, the fishing hook fragment. And slightly to the east we've got those projectile points that could be anything from Early Archaic to Ceramic. And a most interesting tidbit here," he indicated an object on the screen with a laser pointer, "a likely pronged hunting club, Early or Late Archaic. We don't know yet."

Moving over to Grid 53f, we've got what is mostly likely a Ceramic war club prong." Dennis nodded to a PhD student who unearthed that treasure yesterday, the final piece of data he needed to wrap up the premise for his own study. "Yes," Dennis added, smiling, "Vincent is still reveling in the realization that *now* he has enough for the discussion section of his dissertation."

Smattered nervous laughter erupted from the master's students, while the PhD students responded with subdued smiles of recognition and shared pain.

"Friends, this is the only site we know of in New England that has this breadth of artifacts located so closely together. We are talking potentially *8,000 years* separating the fishing hook and the ceramic pot."

"Plus," Dayton added, "we've got the overlap of hunting and warfare clubs. So, who can tell me what the hell's going on here?"

The group laughed, fueled by nerves. Asia smiled. She looked over at Jeff, who was standing to Dayton's left. Asia assumed he was still working his way through the female students trying to find the most vulnerable. He no longer bothered her.

"And what I *really* want to know is, did the Niantics just 'melt away' as is claimed by lazy scholars et al., *or* do we have an enclave that existed under the protection of the Narragansetts farther east and closer in time to the ramping up of colonial settlement in this area?" Dayton asked.

The question hung in the air while a few bits of pine cone dropped down onto the group, and they heard a tiny splash of water from the river. Asia looked up, expecting to see Munin mocking them, but the foliage was too thick to identify the culprit. *Maybe a squirrel,* she thought. *And the splashing water? A fish jumping or my Niantic friend?*

"Hard to tell from a few pot chips and clubs," declared a student in the front row, eliciting nods here and there in the crowd.

"Touché," said Dayton. "But! What other data can we bring in here?" He waved his arms at the screen. "I mean, has anyone looked that closely at the written documents in this part of the county from the founding of Ponkipaug Village onward? Remember, the early settlers had better relationships with the Narragansetts than the later ones starting in the late 1600s."

"He's just getting warmed up," another student joked to Asia. "Just thinking out loud." Asia loved hearing how Dayton thought these questions through. Yes, this is her path. She hadn't told anyone other than Vieve about the woman over the water. She didn't trust anyone on the dig enough yet. Wes could be an option, but she felt her Niantic friend had something to say only to her.

Dayton continued, rolling along with obvious enjoyment. "We want to look for other ground anomalies. We're going to be pulling in ground-penetrating radar after the second shot of grant money hits in January. But what can we learn from the overlap with English colonial settlement?"

"You mean, the folks that got kicked out of Massachusetts for not being Puritan enough?" someone yelled, followed by another smattering of laughter.

"That was Providence," someone else yelled. "William Rogers."

"No!" Dayton said. "I mean from the actual building sites! Physical evidence, my friends! And town records, primary documents! Ok, enough rant! Back to work."

Asia approached Dayton after the talk. "That early colonial contact connection you mentioned? I'd like to help with that if there's anything I can do."

"There certainly is," said Dayton. "I'm glad you're interested. I'll have an open postdoc position focusing on this, probably in late in 2019, but there's so much ground work to do to prepare. Arggh! Pardon the pun!"

They both laughed and then Dayton continued.

"You could spend as much time as you want scouring what's out there already. I can see to it that you get undergrad credit. We'll have to jump through a few hoops. But hey, what's academic life without hoops? Especially the high flaming ones." Dayton's eyes sparkled. "Game?"

Asia nodded. She almost thought of telling him about the river woman but held her close instead.

"What's going on at the quarry?" she asked.

Dayton's expression lost some wattage. "All new excavation operations are closed as of yesterday. They are trying to contain the hazardous runoff first, especially the main one going into the aquifer. Who knows how they're going to remediate—line the aquifer like a landfill? Idiots! Then come the lawsuits." Dayton shook his head. "We're not going back into the water for a bit."

It was the night after this conversation with Dayton, after Asia retreated to her bedroom to see what was on Open Access regarding colonial settlement documentation, that she first witnessed, with the GIS program closed, the river woman hovering above the ferns in the woods behind the storage shed.

CHAPTER 20

Tuesday, June 12, 2018

R ichard got there first and sat at Tilly's desk, where he'd convinced himself that some of her scent still lingered. He'd told Tilly that morning what happened on the boat. Now he was determined to get her back somehow.

Her scent was there, probably in the cloth of the chair. Very faint. Lily of the valley and sun-warmed fern. She was probably the best decision he'd ever made. Planning a life with her. Destroying it with mindlessness. His headlong dive into Theresa. His clear-eyed blindness.

He was still haunted by that day.

They were a half mile off Poki Dot when the waves got choppy and she'd said those words, that he must leave Tilly for her. She tried to make him promise; she'd been building to it for weeks. No, he couldn't. This couldn't continue—them. Richard and Theresa couldn't be *anything* into the future. It had already gone too far. Theresa's eyes flashed a look he had never seen before, of self-confidence shot with anger.

Richard was aware that the storm was worsening, the sea much choppier than even twenty minutes ago, but his attention was focused on calming Theresa down. She said that she would tell Gordon and the client about those emerald estate jewelry pieces that seemed to have "gone missing" in the transfer of the Weymouth estate lots. The insurance fraud. Was she so desperate that trumped up blackmail was all she had to keep him?

"My name was cleared, Theresa. That was a misunderstanding by the staff," he'd told her, levelly, belying his concern about the boat, them, and everything in his life poised to collide with the truth.

"Yes, after you bribed Weymouth's lawyer? Or something worse," Theresa said, pommeling his chest with her fists. He'd grabbed her wrists just before the boat lurched starboard toward Poki Dot. He knew the ocean was shallow here. And crowded with tiny little Poki Dots that never broke the ocean surface, waiting there through millennia just to gash a hole in the bottom of a pleasure boat.

Then the boat rocked steeply to port, the waves grown by half again as large. Richard fought to right himself, but he lost his balance and released Theresa's wrists. She fell and banged her head sharply on the corner of small sink behind the steering seat. Richard lunged for the steering wheel, angling the boat northeast toward Sentinel Point and away from the masses of submerged islets. When he moved to help Theresa up, she wasn't breathing. There was no defibrillator onboard. He'd meant to take care of that the week before.

Richard tried pumping her chest, tried to get breath down into her, pumping, breath, pumping, breath, pumping, breath, pumping, breath.

"Theresa, breathe!" he yelled. Pumping, breath, pumping, breath. Pumping, pumping, pumping, pumping.... He fell onto her chest. Nothing.

Richard sped back to the marina, radioing for an ambulance. She couldn't be revived at the hospital despite more rounds of heart stimulation and CPR.

His worst fear materialized: Theresa was dead.

The coroner reported Theresa's death as heart attack, with a high level of cocaine and alcohol in the system. They'd had one glass of wine at lunch with Gil Weymouth. Richard had a lot of explaining to do that day. Police, state and local (no, he didn't know she was using, a hit now and then but not an addict), Oden (who was beside himself with grief, anger, blame, enough for a restraining order for Richard's protection), David Hallowell, his marina employees (the horror when he came into port with Theresa's newly lifeless body). And the one with the most stake, the one who wouldn't buy his story, Tilly.

He didn't knock, just banged through the door. Bag and a six-pack tucked under an arm.

"What the fuck happened at the quarry? And more important, who's threatening my kid?" David Hallowell kicked the door shut behind him. He stopped at the sight of Richard sitting at Tilly's desk, frozen like a Rodin statue, head titled forward in his hands.

"You ok?" David asked.

Richard raised his head slowly and opened his eyes. Resurfacing from reliving the whole horror, like a film loop, of that boat ride and how that day—and the run-up to it—had ruined so many, many things. Even his son, Mason, stopped saying much to him. Now, just the scent of lily of the valley and sun-warmed fern in his nose. Or was it only a memory of that scent? A desperate longing for that scent? Theresa's life on his hands, if not in law than in soul trust. He stared down at his hands, noticing for the first time that his 18k rose gold wedding ring now sunk into the rising flesh of his left ring finger.

Richard took a deep breath and leaned back in the chair and ran ten fingers through his hair. Then he let his breath out and reentered the room in body. "We're looking into it. I didn't know the extent—"

"How could you not know?" David asked. "Monkeying with the permit through the zoning board? Is that true?"

"I thought we were going to talk about our joint interests in the point." Richard spoke slowly almost as if he were trying to keep his son focused on the conversation at hand.

"We are," David said. "You ok, man? You look like shit."

Richard nodded and peered out the window at the jetty, but he couldn't see it. The bay had misted over.

"Look, I brought takeout. Grinders. Beer. Just like high school." David placed the bag on Tilly's desk and pulled the six pack of microbrew out from under his arm. He tossed aside his windbreaker onto a coffee table in the waiting area.

Richard reached for a beer, while David produced a bottle opener from a multifunction Swiss army knife he extracted from a hip pocket. "Comes in handy in a marina."

"I thought you just pushed paper at this point, or should I say, pushed touch screens?" said Richard.

David laughed. "I wish. I've got to fill in for anyone who doesn't show. Fuel deliverer to labor negotiator to head marketer to dock washer." He pulled up the chair from the bookkeeper's desk and put his feet on Tilly's desk.

Richard scowled at David's shoes.

"What's with you?"

"Do you mind?" Richard indicated David's feet. "Have some respect."

"What's eating you?" David said, unwrapping his grinder. "I'm the one with the kid in trouble." He lifted his feet off the desk and sat up.

Richard met David's gaze. "They arrest anyone?"

"No. They disappeared in the night toward Connecticut, dumped the kids' cell phones in the sea."

"I know your kid was one of the ones who tagged the fort. Tagging 4.0 probably."

David sniffed. "He paid for that. More than paid. You know—"

"Don't get your hackles up. Look. Let's civilize the point. I've been saying this for years. Since the nineties, for chrissake! We need to get a dock put in and make the fort presentable. Lights. No gun runners, no drug dealers. Whatever the hell they are. Make it a tourist magnet. Good for you, good for me. Good for the town."

"Yes, that's the question. Who are they? What do they want?"

They both attacked their grinders. The fog lifted and Richard could see the jetty on Ponkipaug Point. Something happened there with Genevieve Beale years ago that he still didn't quite understand, but he blamed it on some old threat or attraction or did she—

David interrupted the memory. "If you're really Senate material, you should be able to finagle the chamber to finance the whole thing at the fort. Aren't they planning to do something in advance of that mural thing later this year?"

"The Senate," Richard let out a harsh nasal cackle and shook his head.

"You haven't given up on that. You—"

"A few things to sort out before I can even *dream* of that."

"Richard, I'm with you when it's time. If you can explain how I can explain to my people about what's up at the quarry, then—"

"I can, but let's not hash that out now. Let's get back to the point.

"Yes, Ponkipaug Point. Capital P." David smiled crookedly.

Richard nodded. "Yes. Let's move on."

Richard went into his office and retrieved a detailed, brightly colored GIS map of the site with a blowup of the end of the point, clearly showing the town land just onshore from the dock, the fort and its gun emplacements, and the Coggeshall and Hallowell properties.

They leaned over the map. Richard said, "If we install the new dock slightly to the north—"

"Yes, slightly closer to *your* slice of property, I see," countered David.

Ignoring the dig, Richard explained, "There's a slight dip in the ocean floor there, meaning that it would be usable for more time during the day given the tidal heights. If, ehh, *when* we get the dock by the town council, we will just have to slightly improve the trail over to my property and open up the access point between our properties. We'd have to be careful in contouring around that dune." He pointed to the map.

"What are we putting there? We can't really build anything."

"So we clear out the poison ivy around the fort. That's going to make it a thousand percent better. The dock will access a walkway— which we'll most likely have to make permeable or raised—that will lead to an interpretive kiosk about the history of the hurricane and the fort. Maybe make it into a green infrastructure demonstration site to get it past the conservation commission."

"So the chamber will want to put the mural there? I thought they we're going to do it between the jetty and the rocky end of the point."

"Too exposed. They still haven't gotten a permit. They'll never get approval."

"Speaking of?" David pointed to the area of the map showing the beach south of The Kitchen.

"I know. We have to get permission to build on a barrier beach, which you basically can't get under the current regime. Old Rhody doesn't like folks improving its sandy beaches. I can get Guinta to get Coburn to fast track it at DEM. Park and public access improvement. Money pot for the town."

"Yeah, before he gets arrested too. He must owe you something big."

Richard looked thoughtful. "I think he'll see why it's important. Anyway, Guinta's been subpoenaed, not arrested. I'm sure his lawyer will straighten it out."

David grunted. "Maybe. But what about the thugs?" He looked back at the map.

"That's the next question, isn't it?" Richard grabbed another beer.

"What are you doing in here?" Asia padded into the living room with a mug of Rooibos tea. Vieve was sitting in the dark, an empty water glass in front of her on the coffee table. Jack West lay stretched out diagonally across Vieve's lap, napping with his head between his front legs.

Vieve looked up but said nothing.

Steam rose from Asia's mug and she blew on it. "Ah, brooding, I see. A fine night for that, what with the fog. It's starting to break up though."

Vieve laughed. "You really are honing your observational skills now that you're a bona fide field archaeologist."

"Hardly," Asia said. "I just like to dig."

Jack West's head jerked up and tilted in Asia's direction.

"God!" said Vieve. "He even knows the English word for it. D I G!"

Jack West looked between Vieve and Asia, wagging his stubby tail.

"Any news today?" Vieve asked.

Jud walked into the room. "Did they cut off our electricity? Or are we just being eccentric?"

"We're resting," said Vieve. "Ready for the big opening night?"

Jud snorted. "Hardly! I'm a wreck and my scene painters are behind. Two costume designers walked out in a huff. We're sold out though, so the show goes on!"

"Good for you," said Asia. They exchanged glances.

"I coulda made you a star, kid!" Jud said.

"Spare me."

"Asia is making herself a star. Digging in the dirt," Vieve said.

Jack West growled.

"See! He knows the word 'dirt,' too. Or the gerund of dig. Maybe *he* should be getting credit at URI."

Jack West stood up, placing his front paws on the sofa back, which looked out over the side yard to the shed.

"I've got calls to make. Good night, ladies!" Jud left the room humming the tune "Good Night Ladies."

"'Night," Asia and Vieve called after him.

"Is Dayton really going to make good on this scholarship thing?" Vieve asked.

"He's working on it. I'm really excited about getting closer to my dream. I know there's a Niantic village I'm supposed to find and— Hey, look! Look where Jack West is trained!"

Vieve turned around. "What, where?"

"Oh, it's gone now! I'm going out to see." Asia ran from the room, Jack West following.

Vieve watched them under the bright half-moon, the fog having burned off in the last quarter hour with the southerly breeze. The teenager and the terrier walked past the shed. Jack West barked twice. Ahead of them was a tiny white helix, a small version of the blue one that Oden watched at the point. Spiraling, then a flash lasting two seconds. Then nothing. They stood on the spot where Asia pointed out the light on her computer program.

Vieve opened the window behind the sofa. Suddenly, a burst of noise from above Asia. Munin. Leaving his roost. Asia laughed. Vieve could hear the delightful tinkle of sound through the open window. Something shone in Munin's bill, a prism for the moonlight piercing the fog, as he flapped back toward the cabanas.

Regardless of recent events and current theories, Jack West started digging at the spot.

r.

CHAPTER 21

Tuesday, June 19, 2018

The ocean, its gentle chop, foamed dirty cream and, underneath that, hunter green, turquoise, baby blue-lavender, steel gray. Vieve stood on the top of Fort Devlin and let the wind blow her hair to the west. She was glad that two weeks had passed since that drunken episode—or whatever it was—in Marley's studio. She knew now that that was it. For the drinking. She would not proclaim this far and wide, or even at "home" with her housemates, but they would see by her actions that she was back in the world of sobriety again. For good.

And even then, she didn't regret what she'd done. When she was on the studio floor that day, looking at the orange, gold, green, metallic blue-violet, something struck in her gut—through the pain, through the loss, through the just plain terror. There was something there in the quality of the colors and the story they told together. That wasn't the sum of it, but it is all she had managed to put into words so far. And the way her soul vibrated when her eye took in the metallic blue-violet after first dwelling in that particular gold. An odd way to find the path toward solace, but she would take even the faintest of pathways back to sanity.

But underneath that she realized, as she watched Marley throwing a Frisbee to Jack West just north of the jetty, was something heavy and tangled. When the drink wore off and she decided not to wallow in shame about her lapse, she felt the most profound aching pain around her heart. Kyle. Still.

Carl. She had an easier time leaving him to rest in peace without judgment even though she'd felt such anger at his last choice. How did he know there wasn't going to be something even better for his soul that he would only experience because of what was happening to his brain? But she couldn't judge his life, ultimately. She could only know that his life had made hers more delightful. The fact that he wouldn't get to feel everyone's growing love for him made her grieve, a deep ache spreading throughout her chest. Today, it was just bearable. Now. On this fort.

Kyle. Not so. She wanted those lost years and their children, those souls who would never be. She wanted to grow old with him. That wasn't going to happen. No matter how she tried to engineer it.

And Marley? She glanced at him flicking the Frisbee with an agile wrist, and Jack West pounding down the hard wet sand and launching himself to catch it. Their passion was a rapturous distraction but she was harming him by holding her heart separate from his own. *Because?* Because it was not free to give.

East of the point, foam broke off in fingers from the waves. *While you're not looking, spring advances to greet summer,* Vieve thought. Late June. She looked at the jetty, and laid a hand over her heart, knowing that Richard could no longer twist that particular timber of her psyche. Had he even registered how she'd suffered there?

A small waterspout swirled between the jetty and Poki Dot and then suddenly dissipated. She saw the arc of a dark gray back just breaking the surface west of the tiny speck of island.

Vieve turned to full west, her hair flowing around her face. She caught her hair and corralled it into a ponytail. She'd read somewhere—in all the research for the mural—or maybe it was in Wendell's notebook?—that Ponkipaug Point, pre-hurricane, extended for another mile west, a scythe of sand, a ninety-degree angle to the beach that Marley and Jack West played on. That the hurricane had sheared off that whole, unanchored side, pushing it over toward Connecticut where its remnants were now an island. And the sand at the end of the point, enveloping The Kitchen, now curled around itself like a comma. She put a hand over her heart again and shut her eyes.

"Can I let you go?" she whispered.

She opened her eyes, tearing now, hair escaping from the hastily devised ponytail and writhing around her face. The ocean that dwelled in Little Narragansett Bay was calmer than the open ocean side. A bevy of small sailboats dotted the bay, and gulls wheeled above. She looked off to the right where oystercatchers and sandpipers worked the tide line at The Kitchen. *Is that a figure, a man, in the dunes?* No, she thought not, as she blinked and looked again.

A cloud floated overhead, an elongated scoop of vanilla ice cream smeared on the Delft blue sky. Behind her the wind had snatched a bark from Jack West and sent it her way.

"Will you go if I let you?" she tried. She shut her eyes and listened to the cool breeze flow over the point carrying the scent of wet rock and seaweed.

When she heard the click of toenails on cement, she opened her eyes. Jack West stopped in front of her, right paw raised, looking at something toward the left in the direction of the rotting dock posts. Marley settled in close by on her right.

They stood there, silent. After a time, Marley said, "Sometimes, I don't know how we can even begin to deal with the enormity of what happened here."

Vieve turned to look at Marley. "Only fools would ever even try."

Marley smiled. "No matter what we do, someone will hate it. Someone will feel left out."

"There is no way to shape memory in a universally appealing way," Vieve said. They were quiet again for some time. "The only thing we can do is try to honor their spirit with our meager materials.

Who else would even attempt it?"

More clouds floated over Little Narragansett Bay, mares' tails foretelling a new storm story.

Marley looked at Vieve. "This is the last I'll say of it, Vi. But I must tell you that Kyle was a very lucky man. To have your heart. Your total soul. Even dying so young. I would have traded places in a heartbeat."

Marley turned and walked off down the path to the southern point of the peninsula in the direction of the dock posts. Jack West followed eagerly.

Richard was back at the quarry at dusk. The main gate on Route 12 was locked and guarded.

"No exceptions," said the guard. "No one goes in who's not state or EPA. Total lockdown." He stepped out of the small guard house as if to prevent Richard ramming the gate with the sedan.

Richard had heard speculation, tossed about at the marina bar, that there was hazardous material both leaching to the aquifer and running into the Pawcatuck River after heavy rains. But there also had been lots of lies bandied about, passed off as investigative reporting in the *Ponkipaug News Post* and even making their way into *The Boston Globe,* and Richard was determined to get to the bottom of it. He was backing out away from the gate when Fitzwilliam's text came.

At the high wall. Expect trouble.

Richard groaned. The highwall bench. The height of excavation on the north wall. The only place from which one could surveil the whole quarry and, if you played it right, without detection. *What the hell was Fitzi doing there?* He'd expected to meet him in the trailer office.

A few minutes later, Richard parked on a dirt pullout along the shoulder of Templin Road. There was another gate, but it only blocked car access and could be skirted on foot. After hurrying along a short trail through thin maple trees, Richard emerged onto the high wall and smelled the dry chalky odor of broken rock.

Fitzwilliam stood two feet from the edge, Jack Coburn pushing fleshy palms against his chest. Fitzwilliam stepped away from Coburn. "I didn't know. Lay off, Jack!"

"Gentleman," Richard said. Coburn straightened his suit jacket, glared at Richard, and exited the head wall on the trail toward Templin Road.

"Never meet an angry investor near the edge of a cliff," Fitzwilliam said, brushing dust off the sleeve of his summer-weight suit jacket.

"What do you owe him and what didn't you know?" Richard stepped next to Fitzwilliam and looked over the cliff, which dropped vertically a hundred feet to the quarry floor. "You should install a more serious fence here. Some drunk, some kid, could *easily—*"

"Calm down, Richard," Fitzwilliam said. "And step away from that edge. We're in telescope sights I'm sure."

"Because we're trespassing on our own property?" Richard stepped back. Why *exactly* had he trusted this man?

"Look," said Fitzwilliam, moving a hand down over half of his left eye and temple, but not before Richard noticed the eye tic, something he hadn't picked up on before. Fitzwilliam turned slightly away from Richard and lowered his arm. "I've had a hunch, but now I'm sure"—Fitzwilliam continued—"Groves isn't clean either. Groves has some connection to people bringing drugs in at Ponki Point using Fort Devlin. I haven't figured it all out. You think he might be trading construction materials to some drug cartel?"

Fitzwilliam scanned Richard's face and then wiped perspiration from his own forehead with a paper napkin from his pocket. "He's raking in cash apparently. And the DEM guys are letting him have his way in the trailer. I've seen him coming and going without any hindrance, just half an hour ago actually. He's paying off everyone."

"He beat you to the DEM guys, too, huh?"

"What?!"

"The site inspector? A little on the side if he doesn't look too closely? Send him on his merry way to Montreal?"

Fitzwilliam looked flabbergasted.

"Oh, shit," Richard said. "Was that our friend Guinta's doing?"

Fitzwilliam turned and glanced through binoculars toward the candy green holding ponds. "They're tarping the nearest sand pile."

Richard stood, staring at the remediation workers below, mentally reviewing whether any of the dozens of emails he'd sent to Guinta could implicate him. The Senate was a rapidly fading dream; staying out of prison would be a good goal now. It was time to move on Ponki Point, get his name associated with something for the civic good. As he'd hoped this revived quarry would be. Should he stand with Fitzi to take Groves down? Hell, whom could he trust?

Wednesday, June 20, 2018

Below where Vieve had stood the day before, Torin leaned against the stone block with all his weight. He'd placed the knife between his teeth so he could use both hands.

He told the boss they should wait until it got darker, but the boss was getting nervous and impulsive, and Torin didn't like it. After surveilling the point the whole day, based on the other side of Poki Dot and by sailboat, everyone was getting antsy. There had been no townies or tourists out here that day, and they were behind, delayed by four days what with the two artists messing about on the fort and, before that, a couple guys with surveying equipment south of The Kitchen toward the point's tip.

Torin didn't like all this traffic either. He'd scared off the taggers and was hoping that the only company he'd have to worry about now would be these god damn green birds who flew too low for their own good. The boss insisted they run out the stuff till the end of the year. Then move the operation east where it wasn't so crowded or maybe to the west where there was an unoccupied concealed landing point on the western end of the nature refuge. If he were running things, they'd do the switch now. Better all those damn mosquitos than getting caught. They already had that thing with the kids. The place was too hot. *God damn Grand Central Station!*

No, the boss had said, the fort will calm down again. The artists and the surveyors will likely take a Fourth of July break soon. If not, they'd cook up another scare, or some scheme to get the beach closed for a bit. Got a big shipment to go out in July; ferry it on three or maybe four pleasure boats and a few moldering lobster boats in Little Narragansett Bay. Two, three in the morning. Maybe take two nights. Drugs in, pink and gray granite out. And whatever other stuff the boss had promised. Shitloads of sand. *Hah!* thought Torin. And now someone in the marina promising to rat if they don't get a cut. He needed to be dealt with. If they just moved operations over to the nature refuge they could be happily ignored without all this changing of plans. Or if they finished the last exchange in March as planned none of this—

"Damn this rock!" Torin said, heaving himself against it, but it only moved a quarter inch, still not flush with the wall.

A deep, wet growl filled the dank room as Torin leaned once more against the rock. Startled, he slipped off the dilapidated bench and fell to the floor, the knife clattering from his mouth. The beast, whatever he was, fell upon him. Torin managed to shove him off before his jaws got purchase and flail behind himself for the knife.

That mangy shepherd—*rabid?*—now blocked the only exit. Torin cast about his feet. He needed a shield or a weapon. *The remains of a bench?* He grabbed the seat piece, which broken in half when he ripped it from the ancient hinge that held it to the wall.

When the dog advanced, Torin was able to bash him with the bench piece just hard enough to stun him. Torin fled the room. Advancing up the Stairway to Hell, he collided with Richard Coggeshall coming down. They both tumbled to the bottom of the concrete steps. Torin got up immediately and ran up the steps. Richard, having banged his head smartly, lay for several minutes in a heap at the bottom of the stairs. When he revived, Frek and Oden were standing over him.

"Were you in my room?" Oden asked.

"No," Richard said. "Some idiot smashed into me going up the steps and..." A drop of blood rolled down the side of his face. Richard put a hand to his temple and groaned. Then he sat up.

Oden reached down to help Richard stand up. "Then you might be interested in this." Oden led the way back to his room. "Our interloper has stashed something behind this rock. I just bet! It wasn't at this angle before. Help me move it."

Richard and Oden rearranged the pieces of wood from the broken bench so they could reach the level of the rock. They pulled the rock cube out from the wall after much grunting and heaving. "Nothing," said Richard after feeling around behind it. Oden stepped up on the remains of the bench and reached behind it. "Look, my arm is longer!"

Oden pulled out a plastic bag containing a shiny new Omega watch, a raven feather, a smaller baggy of white powder, and a piece of paper with numbers and letters. And behind those objects, a small drone.

Richard took in the objects, letting out his breath in a huff. He picked up the paper with letters and numbers.

"Dates?" Oden asked.

"Weights?" Richard said. "What the hell is all this?" Water dripped from somewhere inside the wall. *For pink granite? For coke?*

"Grand Central, this place. I told Bliven. No one listens," said Oden. "Hell with 'em!"

"This is not good," Richard said, pulling out his phone. Disgusted, he shut his eyes as he realized all the fingerprints they were leaving on the evidence. None of this fit with his hopes for quieting down the quarry and civilizing the point.

"No reception in here," Oden said. "Better go topside."

CHAPTER 22

Sunday, June 24, 2018

Tilly and Gordon pulled up to the Bear Hill office late Sunday afternoon. She parked the Prius in a spot overlooking the ocean, the spinning carousel off to the left below. They heard teenagers laughing on the boardwalk in front of Candy Crush, their voices carrying far in the soft evening air. Down to the right, families streamed back over the Ponkipaug Beach dunes to shower and change for dinner.

Tilly wanted to retrieve a few things that she'd left in Richard's office and would rather do it when he wasn't there, when no one was there. She peered at the cedar-shingled building and then frowned at the cars in the lot.

"I'll come in with you," Gordon said. Tilly nodded.

Tilly turned the key in the lock but there was no resistance, and she opened the door quietly and they both entered. Richard's office door was closed, but a light shone in the crack below the door.

Tilly paused. Gordon stopped behind her.

They heard Richard say, "We're only talking twenty-five, thirty yards of variance, just a strip of sand."

Another voice they didn't recognize said, "People are very touchy about that point. Guys will jump down my throat if—" The rest of the sentence was spoken too softly to be understood by Tilly and Gordon.

Then another voice, David Hallowell's, said, "Look. There's got to be a way." Again Tilly and Gordon heard him continue, but he must have turned or lowered his voice because the words were inaudible.

Silence. Then paper rattling.

Then someone said, "...access road that's constantly sinking cars in its sandy clutches."

A chair scraped along the floor. "But that inlet keeps flopping around with each blow."

"One property we can still sell."

Suddenly the door opened, Richard emerged with a coffee mug. He started when he saw Tilly and put the mug down on her desk.

Tilly and Richard stared at each other. Gordon stepped forward but remained off to the side.

"Tilly," Richard said. "Tilly...it's...why is he here?" Richard nodded toward Gordon.

Tilly looked at Richard. "I came to get more of my things from the office."

Richard turned and faced Gordon.

"I'm her guest," said Gordon levelly.

"You're trespassing," said Richard.

"Oh, come off it, Richard." Tilly stepped between Richard and Gordon. "I'm not abiding any middle-school fistfights today."

Richard considered Gordon, how he was standing too close to Tilly. How he just put his hand on her shoulder. Richard's voice rose. "He's your lawyer now, too, huh? On top of.... Leave now!"

Gordon smiled. He shifted back on his heels and crossed his arms over his chest.

Tilly stepped closer to her husband. "Richard, I have a right to be here, and he's my guest. We are just going to pick up a few things and—"

"Gordon always outstays his welcome," Richard said, his tone icy.

"What's going on out here? I thought you were getting us coffee." David Hallowell emerged through the office doorway. "Tilly!"

"Richard—" Tilly said.

"No," said Gordon. "Finish what you were going to say, Richard. You know, after thirty odd years we ought to just have it out."

Congressman Guinta walked out of Richard's office and headed for the door without a word.

Gordon, smiling, said, "Great to see you on your feet again, Tony! How's the old ticker?"

As Guinta hurried through the doorway, David called out, "Thanks for your support in dealing with the crime on the point."

Gordon offered another wry smile. "Too late, David, we heard your illicit tidbits. We're not here for that anyway—"

"Then why are you here?" Richard demanded. "Besides eavesdropping?"

"Hey, guys, chill. We—" Tilly put a hand on Richard's upper arm.

"You leave too, David," Richard said. "We're done."

David frowned and glared at Richard, his eyes narrowed. "Call me later then." He left, shutting the door loudly.

Tilly said to Richard, "Gordon is right. Thirty, thirty-five years. What a spectacular waste of time! Clinging to a grudge. I picked the wrong one to begin with. But it's taken this long for me to understand that."

"No, you didn't, Tilly. I'm going to prove that." A lower, softer voice from Richard. He locked his gaze on his wife as if that would keep her with him.

Gordon said, "Can you will someone to forgive your sins?" Richard ignored Gordon but he continued. "It's not too late. It's up to Tilly to pick who she wants to be with. If anyone."

A look passed between Tilly and Richard, a look of shared years. A son. But disappointment and regret. Small illusions of happiness. Tilly broke eye contact first.

"Gordon is not your problem, Richard," she said. "But you don't know that yet."

Tilly grabbed a notebook and a flash drive from the bottom drawer of the bookkeeper's desk and a pile of folders from Richard's office. Returning to the main office waiting area, her gaze fell to the coffee table. It was still there. The snow globe with Santa and his reindeer on the beach. It had been a present to her from Mason the Christmas right before he turned eight. She'd put on the coffee table to amuse the children of Bear Hill's clients. Santa still looked ridiculously out of place surfing in a red bathing suit, his reindeer lounging under a beach umbrella, the sleigh a cooler for drinks.

She shook the snow globe and watched the plastic snow settle a minute before shoving it into her purse, momentarily happy to cling to the idea that Mason was away in the Rockies this summer with friends. At least he didn't have to witness the great unraveling.

Without another word to Richard, Tilly carried her box of possessions out to the Prius. As she opened the trunk, Tilly turned to Gordon and said, "My marriage feels like one of those trees, you know? The ones that look sound from the outside, but then when they are knocked over in a storm, you discover they've been mostly hollow for years."

Monday, June 25, 2018

Vieve folded the triptych portrait and placed it in the back of her car. It was awkward but not so heavy that it couldn't be moved by one person. Jack West sprung into the car as she opened the driver side door. She'd truly enjoyed the whole process of creating it, a new feeling, no, a renewed feeling for her, as in her days of learning her trade. The day was optimistically sunny and warm. Classic summer.

Jack West sniffed the sea air through the passenger side window on the short jaunt to Gordon's driveway where Vieve pulled in next to the Lexus.

The answer from the doorbell was a small pack of Bassets careening down the hall, barking, ears flapping. Through a small window next to the door, she saw Gordon emerge from the rear of the house. He clapped his hands twice and said, "Enough!" Instant silence broke out, with the three dogs awaiting further orders, sitting side by side in the hall.

"Well, we know who's boss," said Vieve when Gordon opened the door.

"I have no time for people whose dogs get the better of them. Running their lives. It's as if people have forgotten that they have to train a dog and instead plead with them as if they're spoiled grandchildren. Enough! Hello! Come in!"

Vieve and Jack West entered. Jack West touching noses all around.

"I've brought your screen, finally!" said Vieve. "It's in the back of the car."

Vieve led him to the rear of her sport utility vehicle, and Gordon insisted on carrying the triptych. Being five-foot-two, Vieve was constantly having people underestimate her strength, which had nothing to do with her height. But she picked her battles.

Gordon brought the screen into his living room, which was appointed in a color scheme similar to his office, with a slightly heavier emphasis on burgundy. Vieve tilted the triptych to vertical and pulled out the side sections, standing it in front of the bay window.

The screen composition and color play had resolved itself during the painting. That's how it usually happened. Vieve had learned through hundreds of paintings that you could intend for it to go a certain way, but your hand could simply not do it that way. It was as if the painting were emerging itself, with the mechanics being resolved by the artist through an unseen master.

The tableau: Gordon sat to the left, at the toe of a dune, the sun high in the sky on the right, casting cool, clear shadows on the sand to the left sides of the figure of the man and the three dogs. Long blades of cinnamon red dune grass arched over Gordon. Vieve had worked off a basic tetrad of blue, orange, violet, and yellow, with a subtle dance of tints, tones, and shades highlighted by short strokes of complements. No black pigment.

Gordon's arm was still in front of him, extended from the Frisbee toss. He was smiling, his rogue curls lifted in the wind. Winston looked ahead and slightly out of the canvas at something in the sea. If Winston turned his head at the exact same angle as his pose, as if to look through the back of the canvas, he would see a tiny U-boat surfacing beyond the point.

Clementine leapt for the toss, ears swung back, heedless that the Frisbee arced too high for her to catch. MacArthur, farther down the beach, prepared to spring to catch it when it neared the dune. The late afternoon sun lent a purple glow to the low-tide water and the sand glowed coral-pink. If one took care to examine it closely, one would see oystercatchers fringing the surf in a tide pool area to MacArthur's right and, under where the Frisbee floated and slightly uphill from Gordon, a ghost crab just emerged from its burrow.

Gordon said nothing as he stepped closer, examining the piece, the painting's subjects milling around his ankles, his joy evident as he examined each dog in the painting. A smile of pleasure spread across his face when he noticed the U-boat far out in the sound.

"I didn't think you'd put me in it," said Gordon, steeping back to take it all in, running a hand through his silver hair, then leaning in close to examine it again as if inch by inch. "I'm speechless," Gordon said finally.

"Speechless in a good way, I hope?" said Vieve.

"It's phenomenal," he said. "I love the way you've captured the personalities of each of the dogs." He examined it some more. "Truly superb."

He inspected her signature. *VC Beale 2018.* It was scripted in medium-thinned paint in a muted burnt orange of the same intensity as the warm navy wash of ocean it was painted on.

"Of course, now my hopes for the mural are even higher than they were before."

"But no pressure," said Vieve.

"Never," said Gordon. "Would you like a drink, err, some coffee, iced tea? It's more iced tea weather today," Gordon said, peering out the grand bay window as if to make sure the day was still spectacular.

"Ah, the weather," Vieve said, "never far from our thoughts here in Ponki, huh? I'll take coffee, please."

Gordon walked through the doorway over to a coffee machine in his kitchen. "What flavor?" he asked through the wall cutout.

"Dark roast, nothing flavored."

"I hear you," he said. "I have to keep these damn silly flavored ones for entertaining clients."

When Gordon returned to the living room, he said. "I didn't think you'd paint me. It's a full-blown portrait really. I should pay you more."

"This trio of Bassets just makes more sense with you in it. You're their sun."

They both looked at the triptych. "Yes. I see that."

They sipped coffee and admired the painting. Gordon spoke next. "How is the mural coming?"

"It's coming. But now the chamber isn't sure they go along with putting it on the point. They vetoed the idea of just up dune from the jetty."

Gordon sipped his coffee and looked out the window. He too had a view of the end of the point from his living room.

"The incident with the Hallowell and Bixby kids got them jittery. And they may have to deal with Richard too?"

"Richard? Why."

Jack West and the Bassets settled onto the cool stone hearth of the gas fireplace. Gordon smiled at the Bassets' total acceptance of the terrier as one of their pack.

"Well, Richard's got his eye on the point. Don't know exactly what, but Tilly and I overheard him plotting some scheme with Congressman Guinta and Hallowell yesterday. Meanwhile, he's in an ocean of hot water about the quarry."

"Asia mentioned that. It's affecting their archaeological dig downstream on the Pawcatuck River."

"Really?" said Gordon.

"The aquifer connects to the river upstream of the dig site."

Gordon nodded. "Ah, yes, I didn't realize that was the same place she was digging. Well, anyway, I'm not sure what Richard's trying to do at the point."

"Richard loves to get what he wants. Whatever it is, it'll be for drumming up business for Bear Hill."

Gordon examined Vieve's face. MacArthur's tail thumped against a hearthstone. "Richard irritates the hell out of you, doesn't he? It isn't just harassing you about the house?"

"No, that's cooled down. He knows he has no case in court for the house. No. It goes back to when we were kids."

Gordon waited, finishing off his coffee.

"He bullied me mercilessly. Tried to half drown me off the jetty. Four times. Always seemed to have something about me, that he had to get me or something."

"No doubt attracted to you," said Gordon.

"Hmmph! That's sick. Anyway, I think it was something else." Vieve glanced at the dogs on the hearth, smiling at the group dog nap. Richard need not foul her mood.

"Well, for my part," Gordon said, "he was stupid about Tilly. And as for the quarry, I don't think he really tried to engineer any of this mess for his own profit. I think the whole thing has taken him by surprise. He does have a civic streak in there somewhere. I have to give him that."

Vieve considered Richard's past, his present. *Who was he? Villain or victim. Or both?*

Clementine sighed and laid her lower jaw on Jack West as if he were a pillow. Vieve looked from her to the screen to Gordon, who was looking out the window, faint smile on his face.

"Any signs of a U-boat?" Vieve teased.

"No, something even better. I've been given a second chance with Tilly."

Thursday, June 28, 2018

Defying Bliven, Oden stayed at the fort the entire night of the next full moon to see what the blue light would do. It was there—after he fell asleep next to his dying bonfire and with an arm thrown over the snoring Frek—that he heard Theresa's voice again.

There is a secret storage area once underwater. Tucked behind rock. There are voices when you visit there, and cool breezes blow on your neck in sealed off passageways. There are voices—some say it's the relationship of air movement to rock and sand when the tide moves out. But I know it is forgotten memory. Their voices. My bones are on Poki Dot, displayed by Neptune on his underwater pedestal. I escaped the cremation urn. They think they have me.

The moment I slipped through the membrane of time, I too heard the souls of those who lived on Fort Drive and breathed ocean in Little Narragansett Bay. Lying near the sink, I heard them through the boat hull. We are the blue light, and we come back to the land when the living leave, the ones who don't believe. Our friend the red fox has joined us too. Sometimes he doesn't leave when you, my brother, return to the fort. He trots blue-white through the paths crisscrossing Ponki Point. In the springtime, he helps himself to swallow eggs and leaves a shell or two to float out on the tide.

CHAPTER 23

V ieve stepped gingerly on the moss-covered bottom step of the Stairway to Hell. Emerging from the fort, its dank odor thick in the heat, she inhaled the fresh sea air greedily, as if she'd been holding her breath. Walking over to the end of the fort, she inspected the flat area abutting the bank covered in poison ivy, sweet pea, and blooming beach rose.

"Forget the fort proper," said Vieve.

"Huh?" said Marley, following behind her.

Vieve spread out her arms. "Look, this is a natural courtyard. Sheltered by the fort and the bank. We don't have to mess with cleaning up the fort and all the safety issues. We can use this space here. Just need to hack back some vines."

Marley stopped, considered. Jack West appeared above them on the top level of the fort, scanning the view over at The Kitchen.

"Perhaps a memorial sculpture or wall with names in the center, and the mural in its kiosk on the western side." Vieve gestured in front of her.

Vieve started for the crumbling staircase leading down to the flat area just to the north of the fort. Twenty feet from the bottom of the stairs, she tripped over a short stake tipped with an orange flag and landed in a heap on the path.

Jack West came running. Marley helped her up.

"What was that?"

"Someone beat you to the spot, I'd say," said Marley.

Vieve frowned. "How much does the town own in this direction?"

Richard crested the hill, up from The Kitchen.

"Richard, what are you up to?" said Vieve.

"Enjoying the point. And you?"

"Tripping over stakes."

"Trespassing, I'd say. On my land. Time I exerted my rights."

"Your land?"

"I own here to that bluff, and David Hallowell owns from there to the edge of that dune. 1.78 acres total." Richard pointed to ambiguous landmarks in an otherwise poison-ivy-topped sandscape.

"How is that? I thought this was a town parcel. The whole point, bought out after the hurricane?"

"Check the parcel records. Two slices remain private, and you're standing on one. I've allowed public access. So far." He shifted his weight onto one hip and glanced at his GPS device.

"Oh, yeah," said Vieve, remembering Oden's run in with Bliven in May. "So Oden mentioned." She glanced around the area that she and Marley had been eyeing. That parcel marker that Jack West uncovered must have been the real thing.

"So you really do own this plot here? I didn't imagine that your property line ran so close to the fort."

Richard nodded, beaming, his arms crossed over his chest.

"So why are you staking it all of a sudden?" Marley asked.

A great black-backed gull screeched above them. Jack West returned from The Kitchen, a small bit of wood in his jaws.

"Improvements in the works." Richard waved to another man, who signaled to him from the top level of the fort.

"Of course, if you'd like to trade these two parcels for 17 Salt Pond Drive, I'm sure that could be arranged. For our little community art project perhaps?" Richard titled his head slightly and smiled.

Vieve narrowed her gaze on Richard's eyes. "You're not getting my house."

A look passed between them that made Vieve wonder whether she still had to worry about holding onto her house. *Nonsense!* Gordon had said she was golden. Deena wailed and moaned about how the place should be hers, but still. You never knew with Richard. Rumors of Beryl wanting the place were patently false.

"Well then, I'm off," said Richard. "Watch your step, Vieve." He looked at her again, with that look of forty years ago. *Or was it something else? Some false bravado?*

Vieve and Marley watched Richard climb the embankment and head with the other man toward the tip of the point.

"You want to smack him? Don't you?" Marley observed.

"You have no idea," Vieve said, her gaze turned to Newell Point. And then she looked down at her feet and picked off the bit of wood that Jack West had deposited on her right sneaker.

That evening in her studio, Vieve considered everything. The mural was at an impasse in terms of location. There wasn't a budget or a timeline to do the kind of Fort Devlin courtyard project she proposed to Marley. Maybe she should run it by Gordon; he knew the kind of movers and shakers who might be able to just push it through. She'd also lost motivation to get new portrait clients. She hadn't really thought about her living expenses, and it was going to be a good nine months to a year before Carl's estate settled.

She reflected back on the night she broke her sobriety and plumbed the depths of that magic panel. There was something in her that wasn't coming out in these pretty-people-and-their-pets pictures that she was now thinking of throwing herself into. What was she doing in this town? Why did Carl want her back here?

And Marley, when they weren't working on the project, ignored her. It was almost like her being in the house, without their passion, drained energy from him. Should she move out? She loved 17 Salt Pond, and she didn't have the heart to kick Asia out.

Quagmire.

Jud was sulking too. After what he thought was a great run of *The Master Builder*, he was annoyed the show wasn't getting the kind of reviews and publicity it deserved.

The only one not in a funk seemingly was Jack West, who remained devoted to two things: Vieve and the excavation by the shed. Well, and Asia—Vieve's thoughts were interrupted by the front doorbell. She was the only one home, so she went to answer it, Jack West following along as security contingent.

It was Dayton McClintock. In field dress. Work pants with mud patches. An ancient canvas shirt jacket. That insouciant moustache.

Jack West wagged his tail and bounded forward. His paws landed on Dayton's shins.

"Hello, little guy!" He patted the top of Jack West's head, which made him wag harder. "Trying to win over a cat person, are we?"

"Come in," Vieve said, surprised. She scooped up Jack West. "He's a bit enthusiastic."

"Delightful fellow."

"Please come in."

Dayton shrugged. "I'm a mess. Don't want to get mud on your floor. I'm looking for Asia or her father?"

"Both out."

"Oh," he said, deflated. "Well, just passing through this side of town and I had news to share. Thought I'd do so in person. Frightfully old fashioned of me."

Vieve laughed.

"You have a great laugh, by the way," Dayton remarked. "Just makes a person..." he looked at her for a moment. "Feel happier."

There was silence for a time. *But not an uncomfortable one*, thought Vieve.

"Why don't you come in? I was just brooding about the mural and getting nowhere. Chances are either Asia or Marley will be back soon."

"Ok. But I *am* a mess."

"We're all a mess," said Vieve, turning and leading Dayton to the living room. "It's who can make the best of the messes that matters."

"True," Dayton said.

"Would you like something to drink? Water, coffee? I don't stock anything stronger, I'm afraid."

A look passed between them. That look. "Don't need anything stronger. Water would be great."

They sat in the living room. Vieve on the armchair, Dayton on the couch. Jack West on the couch.

"Friendly guy. What's his name?"

"Jack West."

"Sounds like that cartoon kid from the olden days. Johnny Quest."

"Yes, it does. But it's a reflection of his mixed parentage. Jack Russell and West Highland White Terrier."

"Fits him," Dayton said.

"So," said Vieve.

"So," Dayton said, smiling. He did not break eye contact with Vieve but reached over to stroke Jack West.

"What's the news from the dig?"

"Lots of goodies. And the best thing is we're getting serious interest from some of the Narragansett tribe members. The farther east we have findings, the more interest there is. This could really turn into a big fat regional deal. And a local school curriculum."

The front door opened. Shortly after, Asia appeared in the living room. "Dr. McClin—err, Dayton!" Asia said. "I still have a hard time calling you that." She giggled.

"Asia Kinnell! News! Join us."

Asia took a seat on the couch on the opposite end from Dayton. Jack West's tail wagging began again in earnest as he rushed over to greet her.

"Your full scholarship has been approved, including through the master's level. Of course, that is pending your application and agreement to enroll at URI. What you did on the dig is a major big deal."

Asia squealed and then asked, "Really?"

"The details will be out next week. Again, pending a complete application, you're in. I had to twist a few arms. But hey! All in a day's work."

Asia looked out the window behind the shed. She smiled. "I've got to let Dad know!" She left the room to call him on her cell.

"She's a great kid," said Vieve.

Dayton nodded and then rose. "Yes. Well. I've got to get back to the dig. Thanks for the refreshment. I'd like to hear more about the mural sometime."

"Uggh! Ask me in October when it's over."

Dayton smiled.

"Thanks for dropping by. Glad to hear the news."

Vieve thought Dayton looked like he was going to say something else but changed his mind. She and Jack West accompanied him to the door.

Her funk seemed lighter after Dayton left. She applied herself again to the mural design and felt that her and Marley's approaches would integrate after all. She was ready to get this thing out into the world!

CHAPTER 24

Thursday, August 2, 2018

Reckless as it sounded, Nicholas Tuttle and the other bigwigs at the chamber of commerce decided to put the final mural location to a town vote. They'd been inundated with ideas, opinions, complaints, and fantastical visions through their website, phone, and email inbox and spewed from the booths at JohnnyCakes. It would be duked out in the town hall that Thursday evening.

Marley and Vieve braced themselves for the event.

"This is the time when many fortify themselves for the fray with a stiff drink," joked Vieve.

"I take it that's still out of the question?" said Marley.

"For me it is, but don't let me stop you," Vieve said. "Let's walk over there." *The summer evening air is elixir enough*, she thought.

Vieve saw the entryway first and took on the voice of a local reporter. "The place, as they say, was packed to the gills! Folks were already spilling out into the hallway, passing around ancient photo albums. Ponkipaug's unusual municipal architecture, the Romanesque town hall—"

"—was only outdone by the Greek Revival Post Office," said Wes, coming up from behind them and taking up the narrative.

When they arrived together, Vieve, Marley, and Wes surveyed the hall. Town staff were hurriedly setting up ancient gray metal folding chairs next to the newer padded ones they'd run out of. There were even a few nylon sports-watching chairs set out.

"You'd think there's more here than just input on a picture," said Vieve. "Eighty years of history to rehash?"

Mayor Philip Nester took a spot in the front row. The entire library staff was present as were representatives from churches and businesses all over the town—the florist, the hair salons, the real estate agents, the granite monument cutters, the grocery store employees, the dry cleaners, fisherfolk, a few men from the quarry, the JohnnyCakes crowd. Vieve recognized some of the students from the dig party, and Ponkipaug High School administration and faculty were there in force. There was a clique of elderly residents on the right side in the first three rows.

"Eyewitnesses," said Marley nodding in that direction.

"No pressure," said Vieve.

"None," said Marley, not skipping a beat. They chose seats on the far right, behind the old folks.

"The ol' high school served as a temporary morgue"—the women in front and to the left of Vieve said to her companion with an awed reverence—"so folks could identify bodies."

Nicholas Tuttle, head of the chamber, called the meeting to order.

"Friends and...more friends!" he said. The crowd chuckled. "Come in, folks!" Nicholas waved new arrivals in from the doorways. "We'll get more chairs. Shoulda scheduled this on game night!" More chuckles.

Folks entered and took seats or stood along the back wall.

"We know how excited and involved everyone wants to be on this mural project. Tonight, we are talking location, folks. Not content. Our fine artists here have a splendid design that we are just waiting to put out to you."

"Let's see it tonight!" someone yelled from the middle of the crowd, followed by claps and foot stomping throughout the crowd.

"We're not ready to do that, folks. You'll just have to work with me," Nicholas Tuttle replied, his forehead breaking out in perspiration. The room was heating up, literally, and at over capacity. The new air-conditioning system, usually cooling the room to a subarctic chill, wasn't functioning well tonight with the packed crowd and the front door opening constantly for new arrivals. Nicholas mopped his brow with a paper towel. He'd gotten an earful from the fire marshal about being overcapacity right before he addressed the crowd.

"In fact, before we can finalize the design format, we need a firm grasp on where it will be located. That will affect the size and materials we can use to anchor it to the site. Our original site behind the library has become...unavailable. And we were not able to secure a permit at the jetty site. So we need a new location. As we all know, we want some spot that can withstand a bit of wind."

"No kidding," someone yelled out from the middle of the crowd. Nicholas nodded.

"So we'd like to offer the two suggestions we have." He nodded to a town employee off to the right who dimmed the lights. Another town employee at a laptop in the center aisle threw up a map of Ponkipaug Point on the screen to the left of Nicholas with two areas highlighted.

"One is on Atlantic Avenue, up from where our church ladies lost their lives. You see at the top right of the screen. And two is on the small parcel of land adjacent to the north side of Fort Devlin. With that option, we will be committing to building an access dock and offering pedestrian and handicapped access to that area of the point. Those components will not be going in in time for the eightieth anniversary, more like next spring."

"The fort is a spectacular place to tell the story," said the assistant librarian.

"You're just pushing for a tourist draw, people financially benefiting from the tragedy. Can we make it so the whole town benefits from the point development?" said Melissa White, great-great niece of Annette White.

"It's not really development. It's—" Tuttle was interrupted by the head of the Ponkipaug Land Conservancy.

"We don't need development on the point," Belinda Wylander stated firmly.

"Wait folks! Simmer down," said Nicholas, regaining control of the room. "Wait until I call on you! Everyone will get a chance to speak. Now, we've set up a microphone, and Phil here will be directing folks up in turn. But first, the town planner would like to say a few words to get us started."

A thin, thoughtful young professional, sporting thick black eyeglass frames, once again stylish, compared the pros and cons in a very value-neutral way in keeping with the source of his paycheck. The crowd grew restless as he spoke. Then they had at it. Back and forth the residents went.

"It'll be great for tourism, the economy!"

"We shouldn't be monetizing their memory!"

"It would be a great thing so that people will remember what happened. The kids coming up. People are forgetting."

"And maybe think ahead for once."

"It would just be great if you finished it before I kick the bucket!" said Elmer Dewey, one of the last three living mattress babies.

The crowd hushed itself after Elmer spoke. Everyone knew he'd already had two strokes but insisted on being transported to the meeting from his assisted-living facility in the van. *Unstoppable old coot*, Nicholas thought. *Elmer is an inspiration to us all.*

After a respectful interval, Gordon Boothroyd rose last and made a case for placing the mural at a heretofore unconsidered location—on Sentinel Point, near the lighthouse. "We could finagle the access issues. That would keep Ponkipaug Point free of development, which would keep many happy, yet offer folks a viewpoint both of the town and the point—and remind folks of those who survived the storm at the lighthouse and life-saving station. And I second Elmer—let's get this thing *done!*"

"Thank you, Mr. Boothroyd. But that will take more research. We'll flag that one."

Then the conversation level in the room rose as if it had taken the crowd a beat to disgust Gordon's idea.

"Add that one to the mix!" someone said. "My great uncle was in the life-saving station at the time, agonizing about not being able to get to Ponki Point to evacuate folks. Town folk and relatives and good friends."

"Ponki Point was devastated," someone else yelled. "Fifteen dead, forty washed over to Connecticut. All houses gone!"

There was a simmering of chatter. Heads nodding.

"Hold it, folks!" interjected Nicholas. "Let me steer you back here. Raise your hands, and when we call you, come up to the mic."

An elderly man stood and walked to the mic to make a case for the Atlantic Avenue site. "My great aunt died in that ladies' church gathering for which we have the stone memorial. Let's put it there and build an educational exhibit around it."

"Let's make a film!" one of the high school students said. Jud sat up straighter in his seat on the aisle opposite Vieve and Marley.

Nicholas held up his hands for silence. "Ok!" he said. "We're going to do a very low-tech show of hands for the now three offerings. One is Atlantic Avenue; two, Ponki Point; and three, Sentinel Point. If the show of hands is close or inconclusive, we'll do this electronically with accommodation for those fine folks who can't find the *on* button on a computer."

"Like you!" Nicholas's son said, from the front row. The resulting laughter of the crowd helped let off some of the growing frustration.

Nicholas orchestrated the voting. It was very close, maybe a few more for Ponkipaug Point.

"Ok!" Nicholas said. "Here's what we're going to do! We're going to offer a voting platform on the chamber of commerce website, and for those of you without computer access, we'll arrange for a non-tech way for you to weigh in. That's it for tonight, folks. Enjoy the rest of your evening."

Folks spilled out into the hallway and began swapping tales. About thirty of them went over to JohnnyCakes, where Nina and Maeve were ready for them with an $8 all-you-can-eat buffet.

"We got out with our heads," said Vieve. Marley nodded. Gordon came up to them in the lobby.

"Vieve," Gordon said, nodding a greeting to them both. "I hear Richard's working on a variance to try to do something on his parcel on the point. Won't that affect your proposal here?"

Vieve replied, "Everywhere I turn Richard's in my face!"

"Town ain't big enough for the two of you." It was Dayton joining the small group. His eyes sparkled mischievously. "I've been hired to do an archaeological survey in the dock area. Scan the joint before there is any benthic...err...ocean floor disturbance."

"There's a chance there's Native American artifacts out there?" asked Vieve.

"Off to the east, there are the remains of native villages way out offshore. It came out when folks were pushing for that wind development project a few years ago. A tribe even sued to stop it."

"How could there be villages that far out?" Jud asked.

"Well, for one thing, sea level was much lower back then. Eight, ten thousand years ago. The shoreline was much farther out. The continental glacier in the 'ice ages' sucked up a lot of seawater."

Dayton warmed to his impromptu lecture. "But really, off Ponki, there's more likely to just be infrastructure bits from the fort. There's actually another piece of the fort that's only seen at very low tide. I don't think Paleo-Indian materials are likely to be found there. It's really shallow and the hurricane did a lot of sand moving already. But you never know."

"Sounds like a mural on the point is a pipe dream, trying to get a dock in. Trying to wheedle Richard into donating the land," Vieve said.

Gordon said, "You've got a huge battle ahead with the conservation folks over a dock, so I'd make a Plan B. Or C."

Vieve and Marley walked home. As they headed down Salt Pond Drive, Vieve turned to Marley and asked, "Why is it that I let you talk me into doing this?"

"So I could be tortured by proximity to you."

"You're a masochist?" The ocean made its next splash against the land to their left.

"No, we're doing it to give memories a peaceful place to abide. To put that damn blue light to rest. Look, there it is again over Poki Dot!" Marley pointed back behind them.

Vieve turned to the southeast and noticed a very faint blue smudge off the point.

"The paranormal takeover of Ponkipaug Village," said Marley. "What with the blue light and whatever is going on in the backyard."

"You don't think it's something to do with moonlight on a traffic mirror?" Vieve teased.

"I don't know what the hell is going on. I'm totally open to ghosts at this point."

"I hope we get this thing up in time for the twenty-first. I think we'll need a bit of a miracle," Vieve said, turning left on Main Street as they headed toward Salt Pond Drive.

When they reached the gate at number 17, Vieve glanced up to the second floor. Jack West was silhouetted in her bedroom window by the light blazing in the hallway, waiting for her to come home.

PART 5

Saturday, August 4, 2018

Vieve noticed that Asia or Wes had left the notebook open on
the coffee table. She settled in to read another entry.

September 21, 1938
Fort Devlin, Ponkipaug Point, Rhode Island

"We've got an hour to kill. Would you like to see the
point?" Fred asked.

"Sure," Evie said.

Fred Harralow steered his father's '36 Ford Cabriolet,
canvas top down, out of the Sentinel Hotel parking lot. He
was determined to enjoy this day despite last year's
lingering recession and his mother's illness. She'd still
been sick on his eighteenth birthday last month and not
much recovered since. But he knew she'd want him to enjoy
this rare sunny day.

Fred had worked diligently all summer at the textile
mill in Baleford, while his father had been promoted to
head of the landscaping crew at the biggest hotel on the
coast, The Sentinel. After finishing his engineering
classes early that Wednesday, Fred had picked up Evie at
the high school. It was her senior year, and Fred was
itching to persuade Evie to join him at URI next year.

Evie's family had just moved to Ponkipaug from the Town

of Narragansett. She hadn't set foot on Ponkipaug Point beach yet but was eager to see it. She'd been too busy helping her mother set up housekeeping. And the rain all summer had kept everyone indoors.

Yet, Evie felt uneasy riding next to Fred that afternoon. The sky over Ponkipaug Point looked strange after the sunny morning. It was a thick paste of sickly yellow cloud batten pressing down on the coast. As they turned onto Fort Drive, she noticed the wind frothing the bay. The water grew choppier as they headed south toward the fort.

Fred drove on while Evie noticed three-foot waves crashing against the low seawall just east of the road. Evie shuddered and pulled her cardigan more tightly around her shoulders. She glanced at Fred's profile as he saluted a boy on the beach with a clam rake. The child waved back before continuing down the beach on foot.

After another quarter mile Evie said, "Sea's getting uppity. Hey, look, there's a boat headed—Heavens! No one's in it!"

While Evie spoke, Fred was admiring the Gages' summer cottage to his right. Wouldn't he love to have one of those someday? Three stories high and cedar-sided, it looked grand. Fred glanced to the left where Evie pointed. At that moment, the first of the waves breached the seawall and rolled halfway up to the road.

"That should be it for high tide," Fred said. He slowed the car and scanned the southern horizon. "I've never seen it come up all the way to the road, so we should be fine."

"I think we should turn around." Evie glanced at Fred's profile and then back toward the Sentinel Hotel on the mainland.

"We'll be fine. Really." Fred drove a scant quarter mile more before his smile diminished. He tightened his grip on the steering wheel.

They noticed a car a half mile farther ahead on the road, close to the rock jetty. As they watched, two men hopped out and ran toward the dune beyond where the houses ended. A wave crested and collapsed ten feet from the men's '27 Chevrolet. Its churn reached the windows. The same wave reached the top of the tires of the Cabriolet.

"Get out, Evie!" Fred yelled. "Now! Run toward those houses!"

Evie pushed the passenger side door open and scrambled onto the running board. As she lifted her right foot to jump off, her shoe heel caught on the edge. Evie fell hard onto the packed sand. Fred, following close behind her, lifted her to her feet. He hugged her close as a wave broke directly over the top of the car. It hurled Fred and Evie against the front right tire as it pounded the sand. The seawater's shocking cold startled Fred like a fist punch to the jaw. He pulled Evie away from the Roadster. They ran shoeless toward the row of houses. High ground there was only the height of a man, six feet higher than the rapidly rising ocean.

Fred scanned the beach as the waves advanced, watching the ocean engulf the seawall.

"Let's head to town! Stay close to the houses! We'll go in one if it comes up that high." Evie, shivering, nodded.

The full brunt of the storm swept down over Ponkipaug Point as the couple turned toward the mainland. The waves advanced up the beach, over the road, and down the cottage driveways as if invited for a visit. As Fred and Evie passed by, the wind ripped a sign for *Summer Swell Cottage* off its pole, leaving it angled to the northwest in the packed sand.

Behind them, the old Hallowell place broke in two. The upper part launched into Little Narragansett Bay. Fred and Evie could make little headway on the dunes, even with their waists bent ninety degrees from the vertical. Horizontal rain stung their arms and faces. Evie's long, narrow skirt hindered her progress while the wind stole their shouts of reassurance before the other could hear them.

Fred's arm curled tightly around Evie's waist. He would not let the storm take this best thing—his only love and their future. He pulled her toward the Larkins' small cottage, now the last house before the end of the point. They had to get purchase somewhere. That's when it hit Fred. *Of course, the fort!* He'd played there ten years before.

"Turn around!" he yelled into Evie's ear. "The fort at the end of the point! These houses aren't holding!"

Evie could not speak. To Fred, the terror in her eyes was worse than the storm. He pulled her toward the end of the point. It seemed beyond reason to head south where there was no visible shelter, where the ocean tore off chunks of land for its own amusement.

But Fred knew there was a solid cement bunker underneath the tangle of bushes and briars up ahead. He still carried with him the thrill of its discovery when he was eight years old. Where the narrow trail through sweet pea and poison ivy spilled onto the beach, the couple converged with the two men who'd abandoned their car by the jetty. Both the Chevrolet and the Roadster now rocked in the shallow sea just offshore.

It was clear the two men were also headed to the fort. They too had tried their luck in Hallowell's house, making it out of a second-floor window just in time.

Fred led the way, followed by Evie and the two men. A wave rammed into Cal and shoved his legs out from under him. He fell into Bruce, sending them both sprawling to the ground. Ahead, oblivious, Fred and Evie kept walking. They crested a short rise and stood on the top of Fort Devlin. Cal and Bruce soon caught up with them.

"You boys are soaked!" yelled Evie.

"Ocean got a lick of us!" yelled Bruce, scanning the top level of the fort.

Fred didn't remember the layout as he looked out across the top of the fort. Bruce pushed ahead of Fred on the trail. "Follow me! This tide is still rising, god dammit!"

Bruce turned right, and they all followed him, edging their way down the hill into which the fort had been built. Cal brought up the rear. Before he descended the trail there was a brief break in the wind. He scanned the beach and frowned. "Bruce! The Wilcox boy never showed!" he yelled. "We—" The wind again gathered strength and shoved Cal uphill along the path. He struggled to inhale against its force.

The foursome settled behind the wall near a cement stairway leading down. "Stairway to Hell!" yelled Fred.

"Let's hope not!" said Bruce. "It may be our only escape route."

The waves found them in no time. Over the fort's top the foamy emerald seawater poured, around the back it swirled below them. The wind drove ocean and debris northwest. Fred knew they were on the most exposed land along the entire Weekapaug Coast with the ocean on two sides, bay on the other. And that in 1815 at this place, a storm of historic magnitude had stripped off all the trees and they had never grown back. He stepped closer to Evie.

"We have to get off here!" Cal yelled. "It's coming right over the top!"

Bruce led the way down the darkened stone stairway. Evie searched Fred's face. He nodded and motioned for her to go ahead of him. A wave poured over them just as Fred and Cal were exiting the stairs, hurling them against the wall across from the base of the stairs. Cal bit his lip, and Fred banged his temple.

Evie and Bruce helped Fred and Cal stand up, and they all hurried down the short hallway. At its intersection with a larger hallway, the foursome turned right and walked thirty feet until they reached an interior room. There was nothing in the room except a few large rocks and an old wooden bench along the south wall. Its left end had collapsed long ago.

The waves pursued them through the passageways and into the room. Evie was the first to step onto the bench. Above her head was a four-inch-diameter iron ring drilled into the wall and its rusty stain, which bled to the joining of the ceiling and the ten-foot-high wall.

The ocean now poured through the doorless doorway, filling the room three feet deep, fourteen minutes later four feet, and then, in short order, six feet. Fred lifted Evie and held her up when the waves came within two feet of the ceiling. It took longer and longer for the fort to drain between waves. With each wave Fred feared the ocean would fill the fort completely.

Bruce took over from Fred, lifting Evie to give him a

break. Cal did his turn too. Evie unzipped and stepped out of her skirt in between two waves. She grabbed the iron ring to lighten the load on Bruce when the next wave pushed her within a foot and a half of the ceiling. With her other hand, she grabbed the lip of a break in the cement where there was a line of rectangular rocks just below the ceiling. One was loose, and she shoved it back an inch so she could get a better grip at the edge.

"We should go back up," Bruce said. "There's so little head room left!"

"We'll be swept into the bay!" Fred said. The cold water distracted him from his throbbing head.

Cal looked at Bruce, Bruce glanced at Fred. Bruce nodded to Cal. Eve mumbled something to herself.

"We're going up," Bruce said.

Bruce led Cal out of the room. Fred had second thoughts about his decision to say in the fort. A few minutes later, he led Evie out into the hall, but another wave immediately drove them into a smaller room by the stairway. There was no bench there, but there was a rectangular window opening that allowed water to spread out among the rooms. With each wave, darkness deepened. Fred wondered what the next moment would bring. The storm compacted the breadth of life down to whether they would *be* another moment.

The next wave sloshed within six inches of the ceiling. They held their breaths and titled their heads back so their mouths were as close as possible to the ceiling. Braced against the cold, they hooked their arms over the window opening.

That's when time stopped for Evie. Had she weathered ten waves or fifty? She didn't see Fred after the largest wave pushed them almost to the ceiling. And then the water drained enough so that she could open her mouth. She screamed his name, but there was no response.

Then, something clung to Evie's left ankle. She held her breath and went under. After pulling Fred up, she hooked his two arms through the open window space. Evie smacked Fred on the back six times. He wretched seawater. A wave rolled past the fort and the room drained once again.

Evie clutched Fred's shoulders as he hung in the window, which kept them both out of the water. The waves slowly diminished. Each one crested a bit lower than the one before. An hour passed before the keening gusts stopped completely.

Evie and Fred trudged up the Stairway to Hell and out into the night. Fred laid his jacket over Evie's shivering shoulders. Achingly bright stars glittered overhead, with all the dust blown from the atmosphere. They looked north toward town. No houses. Two figures emerged from the nearest disappearing-gun emplacement a few dozen yards away.

Together again, the foursome headed back to town, fording two thigh-deep breaches of the peninsula until they reached one too deep to cross. The new inlet cut off Ponkipaug Point just south of the start of Fort Drive. Their cries for help brought Ron Pelphear with his rowboat, ferrying Glenn Wilcox across the breach to search for his son.

"I didn't think there'd be anyone to save," said Ron, landing on the south side of the breach. His features readjusted as he examined the space where houses should have been.

"Was your son carrying a clam rake?" Evie asked Glenn

Wilcox, when he stepped onto the Ponkipaug Point side of the breach.

Eyes widened in panic, Glenn stared at the peninsula to the south. Evie put a hand on his forearm just before he took off running toward the bayside of the point. The one missing boy as great to his father as the whole humanity of Fort Drive, now lost, drowned, or stranded somewhere unseen under the sharp stars.

CHAPTER 25

Sunday, August 12, 2018

Vieve, accompanied by Jack West, walked out to the point that afternoon. Jack West was always raring to run the beach and, perhaps, finally retrieve his pilfered stew bone. Marley and Asia were dug in at the kitchen table working on her URI scholarship paperwork.

The point had been selected in the town vote as the mural location. Several volunteers had pledged their time to clear the site of brambles so the installation could go ahead next month. The dock was still an issue. But the chamber gave them the nod. Nicholas was ready to strike a deal with Richard and David, he assured them. Things would be sorted out. Vieve wanted to do some measurements and start a scaled layout.

Vieve stood in the future spot of the mural and envisioned the whole finished piece. The day was unseasonably cool, and a brisk onshore breeze blew steadily so Vieve zipped up her light windbreaker. As she stepped toward the edge of the fort, she heard a scream to the south. *Was it south? At the end of the point? Or maybe just a gull at The Kitchen to the northwest?*

Jack West tore off down the trail that ended in the swallow nest bluff. Vieve followed. Another scream, louder, reached her at the top of the swallow bank.

"Here! Over here! *Please!*"

She peered over the boulder garden at the ragged end of the point. There was the source of the sound—a man, near the old posts.

She ran down the embankment and into the shallow surf. The tide had just turned from its lowest point a half an hour ago. A splash next to Vieve was Jack West launching himself into the water.

Vieve gasped. The man was *tied* to the posts? *What kind of sick....* She ran forward two more steps and saw those cheekbones, that turning colorless hair.

It was Richard Coggeshall.

Well, Vieve considered, *a change of circumstances.* There was no choice really, but in some other moral universe, there was the delicious option of...*revenge.* No, that wasn't who she was. She lunged through the water the last few paces to him.

Richard could barely keep his head above the water.

"Help me! I think my...." Richard clenched his jaw as the next wave swirled around them.

"Where are you tied below the water?" Vieve said, glancing at a cord from his waist secured to the middle of the dock post.

"I'm tied *and* chained," Richard said, exhausted.

"Ok! Richard! This is Vieve. Hold on. We'll get you out of this."

"My leg—" Richard said, his head falling against Vieve's stomach. *Shock most likely,* Vieve thought, *first stage of hypothermia.* Her mind raced.

Damn it, why didn't I bring my phone? Then she remembered she left it charging in her bedroom and forgot to collect it after Marley had asked her to look at the mockup in his studio. *Where the heck was Oden?* She could either hold Richard up or go get help. The tide advanced methodically, the water level rising after each wave chilled them on its way to shore.

Vieve felt around the chain under water. They'd tied his hands behind his back with something like a bungee cord and chained his two ankles in a contraption that felt to Vieve like a modified leg-hold trap connected by chain to the base of one of the posts. After much struggle and cursing at the water-tightened knots, she untied his hands. What could she use to free his legs? She glanced around at the rocks in the water around her. Cobbles, all sizes. All annoyingly round. *Wait!* Didn't she have a friggin' pen knife back with her drafting equipment?

"Richard, can you keep your head up? I'm going to get a knife back at the fort."

He was still out, his lips bluing. *No*, she thought, *he can't hold up his head.*

She considered her options. A gull shrieked to the east, startling her. She looked at Jack West. He stood on a rock to her right, above the water.

"Jack West! I need you to stretch out on this post and hold Richard's collar." She patted the post, he jumped into the water. She put him on the rock closest to Richard and tried to get him to grab Richard's shirt. He was eager but had no clue what she was asking. She took a breath, acknowledging how impractical that approach was. Then she realized she could secure Richard's shoulders to the post with the bungee cord she'd loosened from his wrists to keep his head out of the water.

After securing Richard's torso above water, Vieve dashed back up the dune to retrieve the knife. From the top of the fort she scanned Ponkipaug Beach and The Kitchen. There was often someone on either side, poking around on the beach or in the dunes. She called and her voice faded away, first in echoes through the fort and then erased by wind on the beach. No answer, empty beaches. No time to waste.

She ran back down the pathway to the dock, Jack West following. The water was a hand higher on Richard's chest. She caught her breath and waded back out to him.

How long had he been tied here? How long until hypothermia would start? She readjusted his torso so as to keep his head up as he'd slumped somewhat while she was gone. She bent over to get access to the contraption that ensnared his ankles. It felt strange to be so close to this body, this person she'd avoided most of her life. The one who seemed to delight in keeping her down.

Vieve knew she was bigger than all of this, than that rancor, than the fact that Richard thought himself so much more important than everyone. Shit, all of it was an illusion. Her vulnerability when he'd held her underwater, she was looking at that again. In him. We're really no different. None of us. We all struggle against the odds in front of us, or the obstacles we put there.

Richard came to and murmured, "They said they would come back and let me go if.... My cell...my ankle!" He passed out again.

Who? Vieve wondered. *The drug people, Big Shark, the quarry people? Some private—or public—enemy of Richard's?* While these thoughts flitted through Vieve's mind, she tried to devise an approach to defeating the ankle handcuff contraption. It was hard to get a hold of the thing.

Another incoming tide wave washed past. Jack West barked at the gulls who'd gathered around some of the larger boulders in the direction of The Kitchen, wondering, perhaps, whether this small gathering of souls near the dock posts were going to produce something in the way of food. The gulls began closing in, hopping rock to rock. Jack West let out another volley of barks. *Stay back!*

Vieve found a key slot or release mechanism on the foothold trap and tried shoving the pen knife into the opening. Nothing clicked. She tried seven more times to spring it open. On the ninth try the thin knife blade broke inside the mechanism. *Damn!* The water was now up to Vieve's waist and Richard's chest. Another group of gulls arrived from the direction of the jetty, and Jack West ran down Ponkipaug Beach, barking louder, shooing them back.

Oden, walking under Munin's nest platform on the jetty side of the point, turned when he heard the sound. He recognized Jack West, smiling at the determined staccato bark, and thought to pop in to greet Vieve at the fort. He liked Carl's niece. *How fortunate for all of them that she had come to town!* he thought.

When Oden reached the terrier on the path leading toward The Kitchen, Jack West leapt at Oden's knees and barked louder. Then he tore off toward the end of the point, with Oden following.

Vieve was looking in the direction of Jack West's barks when she saw Oden. She called and waved her right arm. "Oden! He's chained! Do you have a phone?"

It was only just out of her mouth when she knew he didn't. Oden wouldn't have anything technologically practical like a cell phone. Oden splashed into the water heading toward to Vieve. "It's Richard," Oden said, as he pushed against the incoming tide.

"I know!" There was a suspension of time when their gazes locked, and Vieve saw in Oden's face that same contemplation of revenge that she'd entertained and rejected immediately.

"Look! We've got about a half hour, forty-five minutes before it will get really difficult to keep his head above water."

Oden's face was grim. "I know who did this."

Vieve yelled against a newly rising wind, "I'm going back down the point for help. Can you hold him till I return? Or I'll hold him and you go. We've got to act now!"

"You go," Oden said, settling into a support position. "You should get out of the water."

Vieve pushed through the rising ocean toward the swallow bank, ignoring the cold wind pressing her soaked jacket and pants against her body. She tore back down the beach with Jack West close at heel. She pushed herself to run faster, thankful she was in decent shape with all the walking this summer. In a blur of short legs, Jack West accelerated, keeping up with Vieve.

She burst into Dash Bliven's office twenty minutes after leaving Oden supporting Richard.

After catching her breath, Vieve said, "Richard's chained at the dock posts! Take the Coast Guard boat. And the dune buggy. He's probably got a broken leg! And God knows what else!"

Startled from a sleepy Sunday reverie of catchup paperwork, Dash jumped on the phone.

Vieve returned via the dune buggy with a young police officer. As they rounded the point on foot, they saw a Bay-Boat powerboat closing in from Poki Dot. A bullet whizzed by and ricocheted off a boulder behind Oden. Oden crouched over Richard, Vieve scooped up Jack West, holding him against her chest.

"Shit," Vieve said. "They're back!"

The young police officer, half Bliven's age, fired warning shots over the Bay Boat. Then he radioed Bliven that the police boat was approaching the victim on The Kitchen side of the point. The Bay Boat veered southwest toward Fisher's Island after the warning shots.

At least it's two to one, thought Vieve.

"Don't pursue," the officer spoke urgently into the radio. "Victim needs immediate rescue. Contacting Coast Guard to pursue perp. Over."

As soon as the police boat neared the dock posts, a man in a wet suit holding a pneumatic chainsaw plunged into the chest-high water near where Oden now struggled to keep Richard's head above the incoming tide. Twenty tense minutes passed for Vieve before the boat team pulled Richard, still connected to a length of chain, into the boat. Oden was taken aboard also. Vieve knew he'd been in the water long enough to possibly become hypothermic himself, the wind now blowing steady 30 knots from the west. And Richard, *would he make it?*

Vieve saw the police boat turn and speed back toward the Ponkipaug Village municipal dock on the Little Narragansett Bay side of the point. Jack West shivered in her lap. She'd been holding him tightly to herself since the first shot was fired at Richard and Oden; she just now realized that. As the officer turned the dune buggy around, a loud *croank* pulled Vieve's attention about a hundred feet above Poki Dot. Munin. He flapped steadily, following the police boat to shore.

CHAPTER 26

Thursday, August 30, 2018

On the last Thursday night in August, Vieve drove home from a meeting with Maeve Pelletier, who wanted a portrait of her golden mink Tonkinese and her dark calico former barn cat. It hadn't taken Vieve long to talk her into doing a group portrait of Maeve, Nina, and the two cats. Vieve smiled as she turned onto Salt Pond Drive. She really hadn't escaped the human portrait biz, but somehow the quality of her clients, accessed through the initial interest in their pets, was making the whole thing click. Clients loved the thought of their whole family, pawed and nonpawed, captured in oil as forever friends.

The portrait work was actually making a nice reprieve from the race to finish the hurricane art work. Installation would begin September 8. After that horror story on Ponkipaug Point, Richard talked to the chamber of commerce and had decided to donate a piece of this land to the town for the hurricane commemoration art installation. On which, no doubt, the Coggeshall name would be prominently featured.

Vieve was working up a few sketches in her studio when Asia popped in.

"Storm's coming, big blow," she said. "We spent the whole dig time today battening everything down.

Vieve looked up and toward the bay window. "What storm?"

She'd been lost, absorbed in a mass of woodless pencil sketches and possibilities for Maeve's family.

"Nor'easter and a regular storm from the south, crashing together over us. Bordering high blocking from the north."

"You should get a job at The Weather Channel."

"Not me," said Asia. "I'm a digger!"

"That's a great thing. To be sure so early what you want to do. Save you a lot of grief and turmoil."

Vieve considered her subjects on the drafting table. The key is simplifying—but not *too* much—in an intriguing way.

"What are you working on?"

"Maeve and Nina and the royal highnesses. Look!" She showed Asia the reference photos of the four of them, only a few of which showed everyone peering at the camera.

"Cool!" Asia looked carefully at the photographs. "They seem like genuinely happy people."

Vieve looked at Asia. "Half the things you say surprise me."

"What do you mean?" Asia smiled.

"You seem wise beyond your years."

"I just have a really fine-tuned bullshit detector, and I don't care what people say about me," Asia said, waving a hand like it was nothing.

"You'll go far!" said Vieve. "How's your friend?"

"You mean Wes?" Asia actually blushed. "We're really not—"

"No, the woman. The one you've seen behind the shed."

They exchanged glances. Vieve smiled.

"You actually believe there's something there? Dad's now decided he doesn't think it's a ghost."

"Except when he's had too much California red." Vieve chuckled. "Well, I've found it's not helpful to just dismiss things for purely rational reasons. How do I know there isn't something there? Have I really investigated it? No. It's like people insisting that animals don't think or plan or cooperate or communicate in multiple ways. Or feel. Just because we haven't perceived it. That's bugged me for a long time."

Asia sat in a chair. Jack West napped on the bed. The wind gusted against the house. Green maple leaves tore by the window as if fleeing the shore. And then larger twigs and small branches sailed past.

"Yikes! Whatever it is has started!" said Vieve.

All night, wind battered Ponkipaug Village, alternating from the northeast and the south. The low areas of Atlantic Avenue and Main Street near the Flying Horse Carousel flooded. Candy Crush took on water, and the cabanas lost dozens of windowpanes. There was a half foot of water in Richard's real estate satellite office on Main Street. By morning, inland flooding near rivers and creeks was widespread. Bridges were closed, and rumors flew about runoff from the quarry. Three houses adjacent to the quarry were evacuated. The ocean ran freely between the cabanas and the rest of Ponkipaug Point for another thirty-six hours before behaving itself again. There was urgent talk of moving the mural location again to somewhere closer to the village on more fortified ground.

Friday, August 31, 2018

Vieve went to bed late the night after the megastorm. She was exhausted, from the storm, Richard's rescue, and some lingering funky, unspoken tensions with Marley. By mid-day Friday, the chamber had acted quickly to move the mural location to the near side of the cabanas so it would not be cut off from access by any future storm.

Marley and Jud, in a late-night bull session, came up with a way to modify their current design into a contained space. When Vieve woke in the night hankering for a snack, she was startled to find them at the kitchen table at 3 am. She found their roughly sketched out modification idea brilliant and looked forward to seeing the town's reaction on unveiling day.

By 4:30 am, she found herself back at the Flying Horse Carousel, but the light was odd. There was a sparkling darkness within a deep twilight. A pause. A prelude.

Before her, the theatre troupe prepares to depart Ponkipaug Village. In their red or yellow tunics or orange-and-black flowing robes they appear a different species from the villagers in their somber vests and trousers or ankle-length dresses. The troupe delighted the town with the Flying Horse Carousel they have erected, and Vieve has enjoyed the panto they just staged for the town's amusement.

As Vieve watches, the carousel begins to spin on its own. Suddenly, a man grabs her wrist with an urgent tug. She turns to him, and he turns away from her face but not before she catches a glimpse of a high-chiseled cheekbone that jolts her with its familiarity. No. No!

He pulls her along Ponkipaug Beach. She staggers in the sand to keep up. His leggings are burnt orange and his tunic yellow, with some kind of black symbols on it. Uncoiling lizards? She smells salt and semen in his wake. He pulls her toward the ocean.

Then he slows, letting her regain her balance, loosening his grip on her wrist. She realizes he was the lead character in that evening's panto.

His hands are calloused, yet warm. He puts an arm around her waist. He played both hero and villain. Which is he now?

She struggles against him, but is unable to free herself. His eyes stare at the ocean. She watches his profile as he pulls her along toward the fort. But there is no fort. There is no jetty. There is no time.

Vieve feels pounding on the sand before she hears the stampede. Brightly painted horses—red, blue, and gold—gallop past her, their fluid strides belying their wooden limbs. Black-backed gulls, thousands, lift in a black-and-white cloud and are pitched northwest. The man stops pulling Vieve. They are standing now, his arm still around her waist. High on the osprey perch, a raven stands facing southeast, gripping an iron cross in his bill, buffeted by the first of the onshore breezes. And then by belligerent gusts. Then the wind keens its advancing terror.

Vieve and the man turn east and see it simultaneously—a wall of alien emerald green, angling toward the beach. As it rushes closer, the ocean is jade green cake batter and black liquid marble. The tuniced man dissolves into sand, which cascades down Vieve's body. She is back on Fort Drive, alone under a yellow-battened sky. Time has turned.

The toe of the wave rams the shallow ledge of ocean floor just off the beach, curling over itself. She glimpses Oden, surfing on the top of it. A pack of dogs, including Frek, grab the edge of Ponkipaug Beach, on The Kitchen side, with their jaws, as if tugging on the edge of a rug. But they are not fast enough to save her, so they retreat to the top of Bear Hill. The wave snatches Vieve off the beach and hurls her into Little Narragansett Bay.

Her lungs fill with water as she flails for purchase somewhere. Anywhere. There is nothing to hold onto. She breathes in Atlantic Ocean. There is only wave, driving wind, unplanetary cold. She is surrounded by bright painted hunks of wood, a flank, a leg. Then she loses consciousness. Time slips through a rent in the fabric of memory.

Vieve is deposited breathless among the debris from a battered summer residential street. Iceboxes, trunks, bits of boats, walls, *smashed lobsterpots, and hunks of roof.*

In the early evening light, in the marsh ashore, she lies on a roof, waiting to be taken to the next place. Overhead, black, as if a raven wing the size of the heaven slid in and blocked out the sky over her patch of peace. To her right, the torso of a red wooden horse and a sign for Summer Swell Cottage. Fragments of glass, a car tire, a child's beach pail, a Raggedy Ann doll. An alarm clock.

"Ugggh!" A weight on her chest, and Vieve's eyes opened abruptly. Carl's room. Jack West on her chest. Barking!

Vieve smelled smoke, pouring under the bedroom door from the hall. She tossed off the covers, threw on the jeans and sweatshirt from her chair, and then grabbed the door handle. She yelped and pulled back, her hand scalded by the searing metal.

Jack West barked at the door. Vieve tried the door handle again with a covering of one of her shirts, but it wouldn't move. And it was still searing hot to the touch. She flashed on the fire extinguisher in Marley's studio. But little good it would do to her there. *Where was Marley? Where was Asia?*

Vieve went to the window and yanked it open.

"Jack West, we're going out this way!" She ripped open the closet door to find something she could use as a sling. An old nylon messenger type bag would have to do, a freebie from the art supply place. It would fit most of him in, maybe all if she could get him to scrunch down. She scooped him up and shoved him in, tightening it as much as she could with the buckle. He seemed to trust her completely during these emergencies and settled into the bag. Vieve lashed her dog more securely to her with a thin leather dress belt.

While flames writhed around and under the door frame, Vieve hoisted herself up on the window sill and surveyed her options. A crowd filled the yard, waving their arms and yelling to Vieve. She couldn't make out the words. A fire siren wailed toward the town center. Her nostrils filling with acrid smoke, Vieve edged herself over to the left on the steeply slanted roof line. She was then able to put a foot on the ledge of the high bay window on the front of the house. As she weighted that foot, the bay window smashed below it and a flame leaped out over her shoe.

Below her, Marley dove out through the window, his pants flaming around his shins. He rolled in the grass and mud on the lawn. When he got up, he raced to the window where Vieve was perched.

A neighbor arrived with an extension ladder. "Where's the damn fire department!?" Lou Cullen yelled, leaning the ladder against the house over the bay window. Vieve was able to step onto it and down to the front lawn.

"Asia and Jud?!" Vieve said before she took the last step to the ground.

Marley's voice was steady. "Asia's ok. I sent her next door to get away from the smoke. I saw Jud running by the side yard before I busted through the window, so he must be out. I'm so glad you're safe, Vi."

They hugged, Marley reluctant to let Vieve go. "What happened?" Vieve said. "Was it something in the studio?"

"I don't know. I think something on the first floor."

A fire truck, siren wailing, finally careened up Salt Pond. Lettering on its side read *Tunn's Corners Fire Department.*

"Is anyone still in there?" asked a firefighter who jumped out of the truck after parking it in the mud on the lawn.

"No," said Marley.

"What the hell took you guys so long?!" Lou demanded.

"Move, folks! We got work to do. Show's over." The firefighter yelled to the crowd that now spilled over into the yard of 19 Salt Pond, a classic New England saltbox with a twenty-first-century addition. "Disperse! Watch for flying sparks!" He turned to direct the hose crew. When they were in place, he turned to address the small circle of residents gathered around him. "God damn inferno at the quarry!

Half the state's fire crews are there. And several crews of us from Connecticut."

The crowd watched the hoses thoroughly douse 17 Salt Pond Drive.

Jack West pushed against his restraint, and Vieve unbundled him. He hurried over to a lilac bush to relieve himself. Vieve saw Gordon running up Salt Pond Drive. The fire department let him through the road blockade they'd established.

"Are you ok?" he asked. "Everyone else? Jack West?" Gordon added with a smile, as she nodded for the first two.

"Yes! We're all here. Jack West is fine, too. He's right over...." Vieve looked over to the bush where he'd been relieving himself.

"He was here a minute ago." She ran back to the shed, the terrier's excavation, now flooded out, and then back to where Gordon was standing.

"Jack West is gone!"

CHAPTER 27

Vieve searched for Jack West until the sky began to lighten. At dawn, Gordon found her wandering, dazed, down Atlantic Avenue heading west out of town and drove her back to his place.

Heading toward Sentinel Point, she remembered the day she'd found Jack West at the three-day equestrian event. Had she taken him from another devoted owner? She'd never allowed herself to think that before. If he were ok, would he hook up with someone else and never think of her again? She was getting maudlin after little sleep and too much smoke.

"You've got to sleep," Gordon said. "So do I," he said, with a chuckle. "The town council's been hands on with hazard containment and emergency evacuation in the neighborhoods around the quarry. Nonstop night."

Vieve didn't answer. She stared ahead through the windshield.

"I'm sure he's just misplaced himself for a bit in all the commotion," Gordon said, pulling up his clamshell driveway.

Vieve, exhausted and sooty, let herself be led inside. She called Marley's cell to see how the housemates were getting on. Marley and Jud had crashed at 19 Salt Pond; Asia was going to stay with the Tetlows for now. Vieve thought Marley must be feeling awful if he'd lost all his magic panels, but the curious artist in her wondered: *Did they burn or did they melt?*

"Look," Gordon said. "Stay here till you sort out the house. I've got a guest suite that never gets used. I'm a perfect gentleman, and I could lend you a Basset or two. Three even! Whenever you need one."

A tiny smile appeared on Vieve's drained face.

"You will find Mr. West," said Gordon. "Get some rest, and we'll continue searching."

Vieve went back to 17 Salt Pond later that day to assess the damage, but the fire department inspector, still assessing the smoldering house, wouldn't let her in. The first floor was gutted, and the stairway to the second floor wasn't safe. She checked the yard again for paw prints. There were many since the yard was so muddy— Jack West's, a couple of larger dogs, and a groundhog.

Most of all, Vieve just wanted her dog back. She flashed on her art supplies and the reference materials for her work in progress. All replaceable. Jack West, though.... There would never be another.

She closed her eyes, grateful that everyone had made it out. *Why, though, had there even been a fire?* Had she—or Marley—left something flammable in their studios? They were both very clean and organized artists. She scoffed at depictions of artists in movies who live in disorganized messes creating masterpieces, leaving out palettes of dried paint and unwashed brushes. Stray bottles of flammable solvents easily knocked over. All a myth. Art supplies aren't cheap, and you didn't leave brushes clogged with paint lying around or leave the top off containers of medium or solvent. *Containers?* Would *that* be a clue?

She doubted it was something from the studios. *The kitchen maybe?* Asia liked to bake. Could there have been something faulty with the oven? How good was the electrical wiring? Had Carl had it done up to code? No doubt he intended that, unless something slipped by. But it was, at its heart, an old house, although recently glamourized.

Then she stopped. Her breath caught in her throat. Could it have been on purpose? *Arson?* Did she—or anyone in the house—have that kind of enemy? Vieve scrutinized the exterior of the charred and damaged house. It was—and would be again—a gorgeous place set on prime real estate. Her uncle's pride and joy, and her home now, she finally acknowledged. Was this Deena's revenge or somehow the work of the quarry guys or the drug guys who were after Richard and knew that she rescued him? Or just faulty wiring? These questions reminded Vieve of the ones she asked herself in the wake of Carl's disappearance.

After posting lost-dog signs around town and at the animal shelter and putting out an alert on her dormant Facebook page, she returned to the house in the afternoon. She needed to meet the insurance agent.

"Why are you still here?" she asked one of the fire department crew.

It was the Ponkipaug Fire Chief who spoke, a stocky man ten years younger than Vieve. "Mr. Boothroyd suggested that this might be an arson case."

Vieve was jolted. She'd already talked herself out of that possibility. "What?"

"Recent crime on the point. Your association with Richard Coggeshall and his unfortunate...eh *incident.* The quarry mess, a fire on the same night? I don't know, people are flailing around for answers. But we haven't had arson, or a house burn down, in this town *for years.* And then on one night, this well-built, electrically sound house *and* the office and one warehouse at the quarry burn. Coincidence?" He checked something on a tablet and peered at the broken bay window.

Vieve looked at the chief and asked, "You seen a terrier mix running around? All white, black ear, caramel tail tip. Collar with tag?"

"Jack West," he said. "Boothroyd's got us searching for him too. We've set up a rotation when guys go off shift. They go dog searching.

If he's anywhere on the Weekapaug Coast, he's as good as found."

The chief's gray eyes were kind, and Vieve drew a ray of hope from his confidence. She called Marley and arranged to meet him at JohnnyCakes.

Marley looked, if possible, even thinner. He was there when she arrived, nursing a glass of house red.

"How are you? Where are you going to stay?"

Marley looked up. "With Jud and some of his friends, really patrons. It'll work for a while. Until we talk you into rebuilding?"

"Too early to think about. Or maybe you all would like to buy it from me. Fire sale price."

Marley held up his empty glass.

Vieve shut her eyes. She still wanted one. *God dammit!* Would the craving ever go away? Would she ever find the answer to her life? Would—She looked out at the carousel. She felt that calloused palm closing on her wrist and drew in a breath.

"What?" Marley asked. "You look—"

"It's nothing," said Vieve, waving her hand to shoo away the dregs of her dream. "Just the usual self-indulgent pity. How's Asia?"

"The fire hasn't suppressed her sightings of the Woman of the Shed. In fact, she was back there today."

CHAPTER 28

Sunday, September 2, 2018

Vieve had searched throughout the town and called the animal shelter three times. No one had seen Jack West. She'd scoured all the beaches. Asia enlisted some of her dig buddies and joined the fire department folks, combing the area around the beach from 17 Salt Pond, the Weekapaug National Wildlife Refuge, and back toward the cemetery. Nothing. Not a paw print.

Vieve felt like a piece of her side was ripped out. She leveled with God, kneeling in the muddy side yard of her recently burned house. *I could almost take, God, all this loss, this heartache, all the stupid ass things I've done—but* please *don't take this little guy just yet.* Her mind flooded with memories of loved ones no longer in her life. Kyle, Gainsby, Carl, and her little buddy Jack West. *No!* Not Jack West! He's got to be somewhere!

She stood up, ignoring her muddy knees, and left the yard to head back to Gordon's place. Doubt served no purpose. She would find her best buddy. Her heart skipped a beat when a blue jay scream erupted from the top of a maple tree next to her car. She felt a surge of determination as she opened the driver side door.

Gordon volunteered to help Vieve with the house cleanup and rebuilding as she worked to finish the hurricane commemoration project. Jud got the Ponkipaug High School to loan space for Marley and Vieve to finish the artwork. "Just like during the hurricane,"

Gordon remarked, when Vieve told him the news. "The high school comes through again." Faculty, staff, and students were sworn to secrecy on anything they saw of the mural content, with the threat of sequester if they didn't comply.

On the drive to the high school that afternoon, after another sweep of the beaches, Vieve got a text from an unexpected source. Big Shark! Would she do him the favor of meeting him at JohnnyCakes that evening at seven? His treat. Remembering Beryl's assessment of Big Shark as harmless, Vieve texted her willingness to meet. She might learn something about Carl. He still continued to amaze her, even after death.

She met Marley at the high school art studio. "It's just about show time!" Marley said. "The engravers are all done. We just have to assemble the thing. Well, and do number four."

Vieve tried to smile. "Yes, four. The cleanup." She suddenly seemed so very tired as if she were single-handedly facing the massive coastal cleanup of eighty years ago.

"Look," said Marley, watching Vieve slumped down against the wall near one of the panels. "He'll turn up. I have a feeling. A strong feeling."

"Thanks, Marley. I'm living on that hope now."

They worked quietly and surprisingly amicably the rest of the afternoon—Vieve's transcendent drawing and design and Marley's magic with the colored glue.

As they wrapped up the afternoon's work, Vieve said, "Well, at least we were able to defuse that sexual energy thing over these last three months."

"Speak for yourself," said Marley. He smiled broadly.

Vieve turned to him. "It's ok, though," said Marley. "Gives me juice at any rate."

Vieve had just finished one of the figures on the panel and stopped to stretch her back. Marley stood next to her. "You are a fantastic designer/draftsperson. You ever thought of branching out?"

"Branch out? Like how?"

"I don't know. You've got a lucrative career with the portraits. But I sense there's something more inside you. Design, public design?"

Vieve considered. How did he know these things? He always seemed like he had ex-ray vision with her. Even from day one. Yet there wasn't the kind of heart warmth she had tasted with Kyle—and knew she could never replicate. But being with Marley had pushed her to honor the things her heart spoke that her mind could not translate. He would be a great and magical friend, but not a life partner. Vieve didn't think there would be another chance for that. All this loss in the last year just left her stunned. It made her long to stand on Ponkipaug Beach when the tide turns and let the ocean pull that great cold stinging weight from her.

And it was then she would usually turn to Jack West like a salve applied to a wound. A bright spot for life's inevitable disappointments, which had accumulated alarmingly over the last three decades. Where was her best friend?

"You could be right," Vieve said. "Look, I've got to meet someone at JohnnyCakes."

"Gordon?" Marley said.

Vieve smiled. He'd tried to keep it light, but his real feeling leaked out.

"Spoken like a true jealous lover. How can you seriously be jealous of Gordon Boothroyd? He's simply a friend, who, by the way, has been in love with Tilly for about thirty-five years."

Marley smiled. "I thought maybe they...." He considered. "I don't think anyone moves beyond you, Vieve. I've tried valiantly to behave myself this summer. Now, it looks like we'll be done with this project soon. It probably would be best for me and Asia to move out permanently."

"Don't make a decision now. What with the fire and... Look, I've got to meet a business colleague of Carl's. I may not be staying in the area after...if...."

"That damn dog, huh?! Carl and now him. Kyle..." Marley said slowly, as if something just dawned on him. "We're going to find him, Vieve. The whole town is looking. The whole town loves Jack West. He's left paw prints on everyone's heart. They all—"

Marley stopped abruptly and drained his wine glass.

Vieve frowned and peered out the window. A couple of students Asia's age walked by, leaning together and laughing.

Marley asked, "Does running from the places you experience pain work for you? Over the long haul? It never did for me."

As she walked into JohnnyCakes, Vieve knew Big Shark even before they were introduced. He was at the corner table nearest the carousel, the table she sat at that first night she met Marley. It wasn't difficult to pick him out—lush head of black hair, full, dark mustache, red silk shirt. And he was sitting with...Beryl Martin!

"So!" he said as she approached the table. "This is the artist Vievah!"

Beryl winked at her, as if acknowledging Ferdinand as her precocious son.

"Great to see you both," Vieve said, taking a seat. "What occasion are we celebrating?

"New partnerships perhaps! Later. First we order. Then we eat! I have heard raves about the food along this coast."

Oh? thought Vieve. *New partnerships?*

Nina came to take their orders. Before she left, she touched Vieve on the shoulder and said, "We will find him. We're not amateurs, and we don't give up."

Vieve put her hand over Nina's and squeezed. Tears started, which she wiped with her cloth napkin. She'd struggled to hold them back all day.

"Whom have we lost?" asked Ferdinand, concerned.

"The incomparable Jack West," said Beryl. "Short, wiry white hair."

"He is an elderly gentleman?" asked Ferdinand. His right hand, with a magnificent cabochon ruby ring set in thick gleaming gold, cupped the belly of his wine glass.

"How did you know, Beryl?" asked Vieve.

"Posters everywhere in town. One must be blind to not know."

Ferdinand looked perplexed.

"He's a terrier, my pet. Un perro," Beryl purred. Her pleasing oval face and long, rather narrow nose reminded Vieve of a Modigliani portrait. "A dog!"

My pet? wondered Vieve. *Are they* together? *Well, obviously!*

Vieve ordered a chardonnay when Nina brought them their hors d'oeuvres—a small bright yellow plate of Narragansett oysters. Ferdinand and Beryl leaned together sharing a few words and giggling, something about the effect of raw oysters, apparently, was all Vieve could gather from the Spanish/English mix.

Vieve lifted her wine glass for the first sip. Looking down into it, she felt Jack West as if he were there, leaning, paw against her shin. She put down her glass. What was she doing? She didn't drink!

When Nina returned to the table, Vieve said, "I ordered this by mistake. I..."

Nina reached over to remove the drink, smiling. "No problem, Miss Vieve."

"No mind," said Beryl. "I'll drink it."

Vieve knew for sure then that Jack West was somewhere still. She would never give up the search.

Ferdinand said, "I was very sorry to hear when your uncle died.

He was a grand man." He lifted his wine glass and held it out as if toasting her uncle.

Vieve, chastened by herself and her invisible dog, lifted her water glass in response.

"Yes, a grand man." She looked into Ferdinand's eyes, dark and lively. "How exactly did you two meet? I was never really clear. Frankly, I didn't know for a good while whether you were friend or foe."

"Ahh! Friend. Amigo! Most assuredly," said Ferdinand. "We met through a mutual acquaintance, a gem trader in Providence. You see, I am the owner of the only hematite mine anywhere on this globe that has a serious seam of rainbow hematite running through it. My partners, they were dismissive of its potential. But I had a...what is the word...er...hunch, yes hunch! that the rainbow hematite might be a bigger deal than the one we were brokering for the iron ore. So I bought out that pocket from the co-owners, who were happy for the fall of wind, and when I met Carl—it opened a new world to transform it into the elegance it deserves!"

Vieve looked confused.

"Windfall," said Beryl, winking at Vieve, "but one of his former partners turned out to be...." Beryl and Ferdinand exchanged glances.

"Not so nice," said Ferdinand. He stroked his moustache thoughtfully. "It was around the time Carl...died, and they started pressuring me about Carl's doings and whether he knew Señor Guinta, who'd inquired about investment opportunities in the mine and about the quarry. My former colleagues angled for a piece of whatever they could wheedle or push their way into and cut-rate or pay-nothing building supplies. They especially covet your pink granite."

"In exchange for?" Vieve asked.

"First, it was drugs," Ferdinand said, meeting Beryl's gaze. "Then, perhaps, their lives." He took another sip of house red and glanced at

Vieve. "A Señor Groves eagerly arranged under-the-table deliveries of rare pink granite and sand for almost two years."

Beryl said, "Carl told Gordon—and me, two weeks before he died—that there was some conglomerate that did not wish to see a new Beale jewelry line come to market. They'd heard about the value of the rainbow hematite and wanted more money for the gemstone seam or a cut of the jewelry line. Both Carl and my amigo here," she patted Ferdinand's thigh, "eh, disabused them of their intentions."

Ferdinand smiled.

Vieve ate an oyster and wiped her hands on her napkin. She peeked out the window and saw Asia walk by with Wes. Wes was talking animatedly and gesturing. Asia was smiling. Vieve was so happy Asia found a decent boy. No easy task for a teenager; no easy task for a fifty-something.

"Does this have anything the heck to do with thugs beating up Richard Coggeshall and tying him to a dock post in the path of high tide?"

"Of this I have not heard," Ferdinand put down the last oyster shell. Beryl's smooth forehead tensed as she put a hand on his forearm.

Nina arrived with a platter and plates of entrees.

Fernando occupied himself with his lobster, and Beryl and Vieve tucked into crab cakes. While they were eating, a young girl with curly black hair presented Vieve with a crayon drawing of a dog. Vieve assumed it was supposed to be Jack West. Endearing in its primitive style, Jack West's ears and tail twice as long as in reality. His eyes glittering. His jaws gaping wide in an oversized dog smile.

"Thanks so much," she said to the girl. "Jack West will come back to visit his friends here as soon as he returns from his latest...adventure." Vieve worked to produce a smile for the little girl, who pivoted and ran back to her parents' table.

Vieve filled Beryl and Ferdinand in on the house fire, the assault on the point, and the excitement building around the hurricane art unveiling. Ferdinand seemed very interested in hurricane commemoration. "I would like to donate to this project!"

"Donate to the high school art department," Vieve said. "Get them to sponsor more real-live artists-in-residence. The kids love it."

Dessert was pumpkin cheesecake with a scoop of caramel ice cream topped with a sprinkling of golden raisins. Beryl passed on dessert, joking that she had to stay in fighting weight for an exhibition match coming up to benefit her tennis charity. Ferdinand ate with gusto. Vieve toyed with her cheesecake, her mind, as always since the fire, drifting back to Jack West. *Where else could they look?*

Over coffee, Ferdinand looked to Beryl. She nodded.

"And to honor our hombre grandé, we wish to carry on Carl's legacy!" Ferdinand announced, laying down his fork.

Vieve had been looking out the window at the red and gold carousel horses when Ferdinand spoke. She turned to him.

"Excuse me. I was somewhere else."

"Where?" asked Ferdinand. "You can transport yourself through telepathy?" He laughed.

"Never mind," Vieve said. "You were about to say?"

"We—my lovely friend here and myself—propose to buy the rights, name, and designs of *Rainbow Elite* from you to carry on the Beale legacy. We will be honored to continue using the Beale name!"

Vieve took another sip of coffee. She knew she needed to do something with the line, but she didn't want to do all the work involved in launching the line herself. A silent minute passed.

"No sale," Vieve said firmly and then waited a beat or two. Ferdinand frowned, his mustache visibly drooping at the corners. Beryl's smile flattened into a straight line. She tilted her head at Vieve and waited.

Vieve leaned forward over the table, smiling broadly. "Instead, we launch *Rainbow Elite* together!"

There was a quick intake of breath from the other side of the table. A ray of setting sun projected a tiny rainbow from Vieve's water glass onto the table.

"An omen?" Ferdinand said, smiling.

"I'll keep half the profits; you all get half. I get final say on design, materials, pricing, markets, and promotion with your key input and operations management. Don't worry. I won't mess with things too much," Vieve said, realizing suddenly this would be the best way to honor Carl. He would be happy she'd keep it in the family. She'd been thinking about it on and off since spring, and this was a great way, dropped in her lap, to do it without running the show. She vowed that half of her half would go to philanthropic needs in Ponkipaug Village, which Carl loved.

"Is deal!" said Ferdinand, visibly relieved. He leaned close to Beryl and rested a hand on her long muscular thigh.

Vieve smiled and then turned to Ferdinand. "By the way, there was a phone message from you on Carl's phone the day after he disappeared—*Lay off Hamilton!* What was that about?"

Ferdinand nodded, smiling again. "I found Beryl first, and Carl poached her from me. I was only retrieving what was rightfully mine."

Beryl nudged Ferdinand's shoulder playfully. "I wasn't anybody's. I was enjoying the both of you."

Glasses were refilled and raised.

On her walk home Vieve's reverie at the new venture was disturbed by a buzz of her phone. A text message. Asia was the only one who texted her these days, updates on the dig usually, so she pulled out the phone.

It wasn't Asia.

Will we KILL the dog or not?

CHAPTER 29

Monday, September 3, 2018
Labor Day

"*Croank! Crooaannk!!!*"

Munin spent Sunday night circling Oden's girlfriend's house and perching on the chimney. He had *never* perched on the chimney before, and he just wouldn't shut up.

"There he goes again," Raylee said, attaching a price sticker to a pair of driftwood salad tongs. "Creeps me out."

"*CROAAANK!*"

Raylee was a good decade younger than Oden, although twelve years of hardscrabble living in Providence made up for that. She had moved to Ponkipaug four years ago to care for an aging aunt who died a month after she arrived. Raylee inherited the weathered gray house at the end of the only row of elderly clapboard houses that had not been supersized by the Beach Plum Estate developers. Their neighbor to the west was the national wildlife refuge. Raylee often saw great blue herons posing like elegant statues in her side yard when she got up in mornings to feed Frek and get the household started. Quite a change from the gritty street she moved from in Providence where her west-side neighbor was a bankrupted Seven-Eleven with a booted clunker in the parking lot.

Raylee first met Oden on Ponkipaug Beach on Memorial Day 2014, and he moved in with her a couple of weeks later. She appreciated his poetic grit and large heart. In these last four years, they'd fashioned an unconventional conviviality together as outsiders. Raylee painted houses, marketed Oden wares, and kept them both going, body and soul. Oden found comfort in Raylee's loyalty and trust and appreciated a roof over his head in the winter.

"Shall I get the earbuds, or will you tame the beast?"

Only half-listening to Raylee, Oden said, "Hey, get a load of this!" He read out loud from the morning's *Ponkipaug News Post,* page one, below the fold.

One Arrested after Assault at Fort Devlin
—Wesley Tetlow, Staff Reporter

One man was arrested last evening two weeks after longtime resident, local businessman, and Realtor® Richard Coggeshall, IV, was assaulted and tied to a dock post at low tide at old Fort Devlin on Ponkipaug Point. It is unknown at this time whether the suspect arrested yesterday was connected to the assault of Mr. Coggeshall. Two additional persons of interest were questioned and taken into custody in New Haven after Coast Guard pursuit of them in their 24-foot Nauticstar Bay Boat.

Ponkipaug Police were alerted to suspicious activity by a Ponkipaug resident in the area known locally as The Kitchen on the western side of Ponkipaug Peninsula. There has been suspicion of drug activity on Ponkipaug Point but no arrests until yesterday. Residents have been asked to call in tips of unusual activity or suspicious persons. The resident, who wished to remain anonymous, was photographing the northwest gun emplacement of Fort Devlin when he saw a "suspicious-looking man" landing an inflatable raft at the end of

Ponkipaug Point. The resident reported that the man carried a bulky daypack from the beach up to the top of Fort Devlin. Once on the fort, the man appeared to carry on a cell phone conversation while watching boat traffic at the Hallowell Marina through binoculars. Five minutes later a Nauticstar Bay Boat approached the point from west of the islet called Poki Dot.

Receiving a cell phone call from the resident, the police sped to the scene by dune buggy and also alerted the Coast Guard at Port Judith, which dispatched its 27-foot Utility Boat to the scene. The Bay Boat sped to the west, its two-person crew refusing orders to stay in place. After a half-hour chase, the suspects were captured in a cove of Wiscasissett Island and escorted to the New London Coast Guard Station. They were taken from there to New Haven for questioning.

The man with the backpack was pursued by police and captured at the end of the point in a pocket of sandy beach after he apparently tripped over a horseshoe crab while trying to escape. His backpack contained 2 kilograms of cocaine, 10 tiny drones with cameras, and other equipment that may be for surveillance or communications that the police have yet to identify. The police request that the public stay away from Fort Devlin until further notice and report any sightings of boat landings they may see from the water.

The identities of those taken into custody are being withheld at this time and are expected to be released in a press conference later today.

"Branislau!" said Oden. "Earned his keep for the year!"

"Who?" asked Raylee, stacking salad bowls.

"Horseshoe crab, friend of Marley Kinnell's. I thought the man was daft talking to that moving hunk of shell."

"Not anymore daft than having a raven tail you," Raylee quipped. "You know you really are crazy."

"Then you're crazy for having me." Oden winked at her.

Raylee picked up a coffee-table sculpture of a gull, running, wings spread, about to lift off. "True," she said, scrutinizing the finishing work around the gull's bill. "Where's Frek? Shouldn't he be back by now?"

Oden shrugged. "Maybe he found something interesting in the refuge. Sometimes he—"

"*Croank! Croaannkk!!*"

Raylee glared at Oden. "Ok! Ok! I'll go see what the ol' fella wants." Oden stood up, wood chips cascading off his chest. He was carving a replica of Fort Devlin out of a log.

It was early, and Oden decided to follow Munin, who lifted off from the chimney in the direction of Ponkipaug Point when he saw Oden walk out the front door. Oden thought he'd head out to the fort again before the Labor Day beach crowd descended en masse in a few hours. Maybe Theresa would visit with him again. Or maybe Carl would talk to him and tell him why the hell he jumped in the ocean. Or how else did he end up at Newell Point? Oden considered the arrests at the point. He had told Bliven about seeing that Nauticstar Bay Boat last week at dusk on Tuesday, but he suspected Bliven didn't believe him. Oden smiled.

And no one seemed to have noticed that he saved the lives of two teenage boys and helped save Richard. You would think that would count for something.... Oh, except the Bixby kid's mother. Amanda. She was nice. She gave him a loaf of homemade raisin bread and bought three sculptures from him. Maybe Amanda would buy Fort Devlin when he finished it. It was going to be his masterpiece!

Oden approached Ponkipaug Point from the eastern side. The sun was bright this morning but the air cool. A few clouds blew in blithely from the east, like long horses' tails. The sky and sea merged to a pinky whiteness where Oden scrutinized the western horizon just above Fisher's Island. He entered the path up from the beach, treading, although he didn't know it, the same trail Fred and Evie took eighty years ago to escape the high teeth of the hurricane.

But Oden was not pondering the storm. He was still hoping that maybe Carl would talk to him, maybe that's why he left his shoes on the point. Maybe there was a message in them that he had overlooked? Under the footbed? Or in one of the swallow nests? It couldn't be that he had just chosen oblivion without saying goodbye. A tear leaked out of Oden's right eye and rolled off his face through a sluiceway of crow's feet.

Looking up, Oden saw Munin, who had landed on the fort. Suddenly, Oden heard another sound. *A bang? Is someone in the fort? Is someone in my room!* He hurried up the trail. Maybe it wasn't a bang after all, he considered, as the wind buffeted the point, doing its sound-distorting work again. *A scream?*

On top of the fort, the police had cordoned off access. Although anyone with a half ounce of initiative could breach the yellow tape. And so Oden did, relishing in crossing Bliven's orders. He heard the noise again. It was a bark, not a bang. Definitely. *A bark! Frek?*

Oden raced down the Stairway to Hell, and turned the three corners to his room. No Frek. Another bark. It sounded like it was coming from inside the fort, up some and toward the back. Oden left his room, hurried down the corridor and up another dark stairway.

The barking grew louder, and now he heard some kind of scratching. He knew that foxes sometimes holed up in the fort, right before storms if there was no time to make it back to dens.

The sound was even louder as he turned a corner and stepped behind an area with a high cement bench next to the wall. The barking was definitely coming from in the wall. Had a fox crawled in and gotten stuck, by a rock fall or something? He remembered there had been a tunnel in this alcove, where he had stored smaller pieces of driftwood near a fox skeleton, but they'd been removed or stolen. He thought it was in this area, but maybe not, because there was now a large rock where the tunnel should be.

Oden leaned forward to listen at the wall where the large rock was emplaced. "Hello!" he yelled. "Anybody home?" A fury of barking came from the other side of the rock and the sound of toenails scratching cement.

"Hold on!" Oden said, eyeing the size of the rock. He gripped the edges as best he could but only moved the massive thing a quarter inch. He needed some leverage.

The barking swelled again.

"Hold on! We'll get you!" Was it Frek? It sounded higher pitched than Frek, but Oden knew the acoustics in this pile could do strange things with sound. He would have to get his crowbar. Oden ran back down the point, straight into Raylee's garage, grabbed the crowbar he used in his boatyard days, and ran back to the fort.

"Hello, my friend, I'm back!" Oden said to the wall when he returned to the spot. There was a renewed burst of barking. Staccato barking.

Oden worked the crowbar as fast as he could, wedging it in, pulling the rock forward. Repeating it multiple times until he saw a white paw digging and daubing blood on the cement. He levered the rock out the rest of the way hastily. It was too heavy. He lost control and jumped out of the way so it wouldn't land on his foot.

"Jack West! Who put you in there?!"

Jack West jumped down out of the tunnel, beyond the jumble of bones that had been a recognizable fox skeleton. His front paws were bleeding, he had a gash on his back, but he was eager to be off. When he dashed from the room, Oden followed. Jack West led Oden down the trail to the point, where Frek lay on cobbles, high-tide advancing.

Oden rushed to his friend.

"Frek, they've hurt you!" He felt the dog for injuries but wasn't sure what was wrong. Oden lifted Frek gently and carried him as horizontally as he could around the eastern side of the point and laid him in the soft sand at the base of a dune.

Oden turned to run down the beach when he saw two young women approaching the jetty. He dashed straight at them. Alarmed at the site of the raggedy clothed figure that seemed to appear out of nowhere, the women turned and walked hurriedly back toward the town.

"Stop! Wait! I need your phone!" he yelled. "My dogs are hurt!" He motioned back toward them. Jack West now standing over Frek, nudging him with his nose.

The women considered Oden. He could see they were in their twenties. One of them moved toward Oden, holding out a phone. Oden smiled and took it. He called his vet's office. She was known to respond to emergencies even on a holiday. In fact, she barely took a day off during the busy tourist season, which would end soon.

Oden finished giving directions to his location and pressed End call. He thanked the young woman and handed back the phone, and the two women left to explore The Kitchen.

Oden sat in the sand facing Sentinel Point, cradling Frek's head in his lap. Tears spilled freely down Oden's cheeks, and he wiped them on his dirt-smeared forearm. He said to Jack West, who looked just as concerned as himself:

> *There came a day*
> *of yellow sky*
> *and emerald sea*
> *when shearing winds*
> *and frigid cold*
> *met solid lives*

and liquid souls.
On rising swells
of Neptune's wrath
some were gone
and some hung on.
Who decided
who would stay
and who had lived
their last day?
Now paint the world
with liquid souls
in the calm
between the swells.
So in eighty years
we'll see a trace
of that day of
hell and grace.

Oden adjusted his position and checked Frek's breathing. It was steady. Oden was so grateful he had come to the fort when he did. He examined Jack West's back wound and bloodied paws; the bleeding had slowed. He pulled out bits of leaves from the gashes. He wanted to rinse Jack West's wounds with seawater but did not want to disturb Frek.

Oden considered the importance of everything we do, all the decisions, big and small, that we make. Then he addressed Jack West again:

"*Time stalls in pockets and backwaters, ticks in seconds and epochs, sweeps past us with indifference, pulls us into its irresistible current, hooks back on itself, sucks us through portals that connect all points of time with eternity, spills on.*"

Jack West looked up at Oden and cocked his head quizzically. Then he turned his head to the south from whence a Jeep sped toward them on the beach. The terrier barked and wagged his tail at the arrival of a volunteer animal transporter from the Ponkipaug Society for the Prevention of Cruelty to Animals.

Vieve prepared to search more for Jack West that Labor Day morning. She'd been frantic the night before, called Dash Bliven, called everyone she knew, asking if there was anything they could possibly tell her that might lead to a clue. She even called Richard's house and left a message, told him she was at Gordon's and if he knew anything, please call her. She didn't know his cell number.

She was going to go inch by inch over the whole town if she had to. Look for clues everywhere. As she reached for the doorknob to leave, the doorbell rang.

"Got it," she called back to Gordon, who was still in the kitchen. He had set aside the whole day to dog search too.

Vieve opened the door to Richard Coggeshall. He leaned against the stair railing, easing the weight off his injured leg. It had been a nasty mess two weeks ago.

"Ah, ah.... Come in," Vieve said, startled. "I didn't think you'd—"

"I came to see you. I was actually going to come over today even before I got your message. Not this early, but—"

"Look. I'm going out to find my dog."

"Then you will want to hear what I have to say." Vieve was startled that Richard had actually responded to her phone message.

"Well, then, come in. We'll sit in here." Vieve indicated the living room where the Bassett triptych was proudly displayed.

Gordon looked in, holding a coffee pot. "Vieve, you want the last bit of....?" Gordon stopped talking when he saw Richard.

"Last place I thought I'd find you," Gordon said.

"Don't start, guys! I—" Vieve said.

"Excuse me." Gordon turned and walked back toward the kitchen.

"Genny," Richard said. "First, I'm fairly sure your dog is being held for ransom in connection with your uncle's estate. Or because you rescued me, and I'm in a...bit of a jam with some thugs associated with the quarry."

Vieve frowned. "How would you know who has my dog?" *Is this another Richard prank?* They hadn't spoken to each other since she rescued him. When she'd called him about Jack West, she'd been desperate. Now her previous suspicions about Richard's motives fueled her only shallowly buried anger toward him.

They stared into each other's face for several minutes without speaking. That cocksure veneer Richard usually wore was tempered, *but by what? Memory and regret?* Richard looked down at his hands and then out the window over the bay toward the point.

"Why did you save my life?" he asked.

Vieve stood up and walked to the window. Having a larger space between them allowed her to breathe.

"Why did you try to drown me?" Vieve asked.

Richard examined Vieve's face. "I thought you needed testing, at the time. You thought you were invincible." Richard paused. "I wanted to feel that."

That was not the answer Vieve expected. "Well, I wasn't. No one is."

Richard's gaze went to his lap and then back to Vieve's face. "Yes, when Tilly moved out—things, my whole...."

Richard stopped talking and stretched his leg out along the couch. He turned his gaze to the Gordon and Basset triptych on the right, sniffed, and eyed the sailing magazine on the coffee table.

Vieve said, "Your whole what? It's always all about you, isn't it? Why do you covet my house? And why are you jeopardizing this town for profit at the quarry?" She took a breath and threw out one more. "How do you ever expect to be elected to the Senate? Look, it doesn't matter. I haven't got time to waste with Jack West being—"

Richard sat there, still, as she'd upped her accusations and then suddenly interrupted. "You have no idea who I am."

"Then tell me." Vieve sat up straight, crossed her arms over her chest. Then she sprung up from the chair and started pacing. She wondered that for years but wouldn't give him the satisfaction of knowing that.

"Why did you save my life?" Richard asked.

"Because as much as I dislike what you've done to me and that all you seem out for is yourself, you're still a human being. You were going to drown out there. Any decent person would have done anything they could to stop it. I don't need to twist what happened on the point into a power trip. Any decent—"

"Thank you, Genny. Vieve? They call you Vieve, right? Your friends do." He peered at his leg and then back into her face. "I was going to visit you sooner to thank you, but..."

He stopped talking and made eye contact with Vieve. Thirty seconds passed in silence.

"Look," he said. "You probably won't believe this but what's been happening this past year at the quarry is as much of a surprise to me as to you. I think it was my bringing things up that got me in trouble. Guinta's doing something. Whether he's got the screws on him or not, I don't know. And the point, there's something extracurricular going on out there that I stumbled on when I went to reclaim my private property. I'm still not sure what is going down there, but I'm convinced those are the thugs who've got your dog."

Vieve sat back down on the couch. She realized that, thanks to Ferdinand, she knew more of the quarry backstory than Richard did.

"So what do I need to do to get him back?"

"I'm trying to figure that out. If I could help you—"

The doorbell rang. Again. "Grand Central," Gordon grumbled

and headed for the door. He wore a tee shirt and shorts to go dog tracking.

Oden stepped in carrying something with inverted triangular ears sticking out from a blanket. Vieve brightened as she hurried over to the door to see what Oden had brought. Jack West, raising his head, caught sight of Vieve. He leapt from Oden's arms and crashed down on the hardwood flooring. He sprung back up immediately and scrambled toward Vieve, trying to get purchase with his bandaged paws.

"Jack West!!!" Vieve's scooped up her terrier. He licked her face all over and wagged his tail into a blur. She shut her eyes while her heart surged with joy. One big jolt of love.

"Best buddy, you're back!" She opened her eyes and held a bandaged paw gently. "What's this?"

"Scraped them raw," said Oden. "He's been at the fort! Trying to dig his way out of a cement prison with a big rock blocking the entrance. Frek is in worse shape. Broken hind leg."

"Oh, Oden! Where's Frek now?" asked Vieve.

"He's at the vet's. They were going to call you, but I wanted to deliver the news along with your buddy."

"How did you find Jack West?" She sunk into the couch, still holding on to the terrier, who finally relaxed in her arms, exhausted.

"I was looking for Frek. I hadn't been back to the fort for a couple days." Oden smiled. "Actually Munin insisted I start there. I heard a noise from somewhere inside the walls, which turned out to be our buddy here. He was barking and scratching. When I got him out, he took off to lead me to Frek near where you found Richard."

Oden seemed to suddenly notice Richard on the couch. Richard was staring at the triptych. Oden turned back to Vieve, his eyes holding some secret that raised his lips in a subtle smile.

"Will you sit down?" Gordon asked. "Do you need anything?"

"No, I want to go back to the vet's. They're setting Frek's leg,"

Oden said.

"How did you get here?" Gordon asked.

"Raylee dropped me off on the way to deliver one of my pieces. I'll walk back." Oden smiled at Vieve. "I wanted to bring him to you myself."

Vieve's heart surged with gratitude when she laid a hand on Oden's arm. "Thank you so much, Oden. I can't thank you enough."

"I'll take you back to the vet's," said Gordon.

"Well—" Vieve said to Richard after Oden and Gordon left. "I'm going to see if he's hungry."

Jack West wasn't hungry. He stuck like a burr to Vieve when she returned to the living room. Vieve was so happy that her animosity toward Richard had floated off somewhere.

"I didn't realize you'd done this screen. Very lifelike," Richard said.

"Thank you," said Vieve. "I'm surprised you praise it, given the subject matter."

"The guy who stole my wife. Yeah, well...that's my problem." He shut his eyes and let out a deep breath. "Ok, dog found. There must be something else I can do to repay my debt to you."

"It's not a debt, Richard."

Vieve considered him. Her enemy. The illusion of her enemy. He had no power that she didn't give him. She smiled. "But if you insist. Consider yourself whitemailed."

"Whitemailed?" he asked. He adjusted the position of his leg and grimaced.

"Instead of blackmailed. Do something good with whatever influence you have. I don't know how. Perhaps that was your motivation to run for Senate? You go back a long way in this town, your family a really long way. There's got to be tons of good you can do with your business, your influence, your...new motivation. Rather than just getting ahead. You could also mend fences with Oden. He played a big part in saving your life too."

"Maybe this is why I held you underwater until you could barely breathe. Otherwise, you would have ignored me."

"That's a sick theory. I can't say why you did it. But we can always reframe our lives, even if we're not getting what we think we want. Like juicy real estate."

"Or losing what we thought we couldn't live without," said Richard, his mouth turned down.

"Yeah, well, join the club," Vieve said, a tinge of self-pity creeping in. *No*, she thought, *you have a lot right here, now.*

"If it's right, she'll come back," said Vieve.

"She won't," Richard said. He looked out the window at the bay and then back at Vieve.

"Of course, you've got a bit of work to do to get out of your legal messes," she said. "I'm not sure you know their extent. I have a friend who may be able to open your eyes to what really happened at the quarry. Then you can help get those drug guys. That would really help reclaim that part of our town, the part that has so much significance for everyone. And I for one would like to see that graffiti cleaned up."

Richard shifted the position of his injured leg and peered into Vieve's face. "I think it's time Guinta was fully exposed. That would clean up most of our mysteries."

"Ah! An even better idea," Vieve said. She looked down at Jack West, sleeping now, and watched his side rise and fall.

Thank you, God, she said without speaking.

PART 6

CHAPTER 30

Friday, September 21, 2018
Ponkipaug Village, Rhode Island

B y 4 pm, the group in the parking lot had swelled beyond capacity. It snaked onto the Atlantic Avenue sidewalk and the docks of the Hallowell Marina. Vieve hadn't seen this kind of gathering since Carl's memorial service, but this looked to be twice that turnout. Almost all the local businesses posted CLOSED signs and shut up shop for the hurricane memorial unveiling.

It warmed Vieve to see so many people she now considered friends that she had not known at this time last year. Walking Jack West by his leash, she waved to Maeve and Nina as she made her way through the crowd to the installation. Ponkipaug high school, middle school, and elementary school students had been bused to the site. The students jostled each other or peered toward the large white tarp-covered structure. Phone cameras were poised throughout the crowd of locals and tourists swept up in the festivities.

A work crew hired by the chamber of commerce began pulling off the staked tarp from a large object hunkering between the edge of the cabana parking lot and the start of the nature preserve on Ponkipaug Point. Clapping broke out among the crowd.

"A gazebo!" said Wes, as the tarp was folded down around the structure. He had already sleuthed this out, of course, but was playing along with the suspenseful game that the chamber encouraged.

The crowd surged around the structure as the last side of the tarp was removed to reveal an octagonal resin gazebo, thirty-five feet across. The openings between the pillars holding up the roof were emplaced with slabs of pink granite, etched on the inside with the white outlines of quahog shells that enclosed the name of a townsperson lost in the hurricane. Some contained Christian crosses or Stars of Bethlehem. Vertical openings on the pillar posts and skylights let light stream into the interior where four panels encased in Plexiglas straddled the center of the interior, attached to ceiling and floor.

Nicholas Tuttle began his speech at a raised podium with a mic set up before the gazebo stairs. "It's not going to be a long one, folks, although this beautiful memorial was long in coming! Overdue. Artists Marley Kinnell and Vieve Clough Beale have done an exquisite job designing the granite memorial panels of our fellow townspeople who lost their lives in the storm and creating acrylic panel scenes that remind us, and future generations, of the terrible impact of that storm."

He glanced at a panel, then continued, "Also, if I may, of our imperfectly beautiful redemption. We thank them for their work—which was way beyond what we first envisioned."

Nicholas nodded to Marley and Vieve and turned a page of his notes. The crowd clapped enthusiastically. "Let us in!" yelled a high school student from the front row.

"Yes, indeed. Soon, my friend! This unveiling ceremony is the kickoff for a yearlong memory project during which we will be bringing together the oral histories and writings that were done during the fiftieth anniversary covered by the *Ponkipaug New Post,* the nationally released PBS documentary *American Experience* that covered the storm and those whose lives it touched, and by private diaries and archives at the Ponkipaug Public Library and the University of Rhode Island." Nicholas glanced into the crowd and nodded.

"And, speaking of private accounts, I'm here to announce, a surprise from the great-grandfather of our own ace reporter, Wesley Tetlow! Come on up, Wes!"

Smiling, Wes made his way to the gazebo amid shoulder slapping and photo snapping.

"Hey, everybody!" Wes said, pulling the mic up four inches and flicking his lank bangs off his eyebrows. The crowd cheered again, most loudly from the high school contingent.

"My great-grandfather, Wendell Tetlow, a veteran of World War Two, was also a reporter. But not when the storm hit the town and his own house eighty years ago. Starting on the morning after it hit, he interviewed town folks and asked a lot of questions up and down the coast." Wes paused, stunned at how big the crowd was.

"I didn't know this until April of this year when I discovered a stash of notebooks in an old cedar chest in which he wrote stories of those who survived and those who didn't. He started working on it seriously when he retired in 1988, adding his still-vivid memories and tons of research to his extensive notes and sketches. But the project was never finished."

Wes paused again and Nicholas handed him a bottle of water from which he drank. The crowd was hushed, waiting to hear more, as if forgetting for a minute how curious they were about the mural panels.

Wes continued. "Wendell's notes indicate he was trying to rewrite and publish the stories in time for the sixtieth anniversary in 1998. He died of a heart attack in 1994."

Some of the older folks near the podium nodded their heads. The crowd was still hushed.

"But now, we're making these notebooks part of the hurricane memory project. I'm working overtime to get a polished manuscript published by December of this year. In honor of his memory and the memory of all those who lost their lives here. And those who lived on. Eh, well, thank you, everybody!"

Wes stepped back from the podium and waved. The crowd cheered lustily. Jud's tiny band, the Rip Tides, set up just a couple yards from the gazebo, struck up the state song, "Rhode Island's It for Me."

Suddenly, Oden appeared near the podium. Nicholas Tuttle tried to wave him away. Wes stepped forward and asked Oden something, placing a friendly hand on his shoulder. Oden pulled out a raggedly piece of paper and showed it to Wes. After Wes read it, he beamed and indicated Oden should take the mic. Nicholas looked at Wes, alarmed. Wes smiled.

Oden recited his poem "Yellow Sky, Emerald Sea" and then stepped away from the podium to take a sneak peek at the gazebo's interior. The crowd murmured and then clapped loudly. Someone tooted a French horn. High school students surged forward to snap selfies with Oden.

Wes returned to the podium. "Thank you, Oden Vacca, for your contribution to the day! We'll stick that poem in the front of Wendell's book!" The crowd cheered and Wes nodded to Nicholas.

"And now, please line up to view the interior!" Nicholas announced into the mic.

The near portion of the crowd formed a fat, loose line, and a small group entered the interior. Nicholas stood at the entrance to prevent overcrowding. The Rip Tides segued into "No Body Knows the Trouble I've Seen," a tune poplar in 1938. An old woman, the second one in, placed her hand on the etched name on the first panel to the right of the entrance. When Asia approached her, she said, "I was one of those mattress-strapped babies, but I lost my brother." She patted the stone and stood in silence for a half hour while people streamed around her.

Vieve and Marley stood to the sides of the panels. Panel one was a giant wave of dark green, and there was a dark form of a person sliding below the sea surface, but with a stout arm and fist pulling the drowning figure back up to safety. Panel two was a wide angle view of the agitated ocean and furious wind, the Sentinel Lighthouse burning bright. A beacon of orange-yellow in a swirl of greens, blues, and blacks. Panel three showed a survivor on Newell Point being found by a rescuer as the sun rose.

Panel four was the cleanup, showing the coast from the end of the national wildlife refuge to the town line on the east crisscrossed with downed trees and powerlines, with scores of folks carrying, chopping, hauling, and mending. Restoring order. The faces of those near the front of the panel infused with determination. Roads and wires being reconnected. Boats hauled back to their berths and mended. Houses being built.

Above the pink granite panels, in the highest section of wall before the ceiling started, the artists had painted a scene of Ponkipaug Beach today, showing a glorious afternoon in the summer. A child digging in the sand with a shovel and pail in front of where Fort Drive once lay. In the background, the start of a stunning sunset.

Vieve watched the crowd make slow progress through the gazebo and heard the Rip Tides hit the opening notes of "Amazing Grace." Some, like the old woman, touching a particular name and closing their eyes. Some standing for a long time in front of one of the panels. Some shaking her hand. Many crying. Vieve wasn't prepared for the crying, although she should have been. Marley did not speak with her, but he did speak with a lot of folks as they came through the gazebo.

She overheard Wes telling Asia, "Some of the notebooks are a bit of a snarl. I haven't showed you those yet. Third person, first person. Snippets of observations and weather forecasts. There's even a part where the rookie weatherman in Washington, DC, predicts the exact path of the storm. Exact! And he's ignored. It's all there. All jumbled together!"

"You'll straighten it out, Wes. And in time. I'll help," Asia said. She reached out and took Wes's left hand in hers, and they walked around the interior of the gazebo reading the names from the etched shells. They looked for the names of those mentioned in Wendell's notebooks.

Vieve noticed Asia and Wes lean their heads together. She imagined them trying to understand what it must have felt like to be on this spot eighty years ago. When Dayton McClintock entered the gazebo, Vieve had turned in the other direction. He scanned the etched quahog shells with their names, watched the faces of those who spent time reading the names, and carefully examined the panels, as if they were part of one of his excavations. An uncovered wall of an unknown city in an unfamiliar culture. Vieve noticed him leaving the gazebo after she ended a conversation with the daughter of the woman who touched the shell that enclosed the name of her long dead big brother. She felt a strange pang when Dayton left. She'd like to know what he thought. And what he felt.

CHAPTER 31

Friday, September 28, 2018

"One more, Wes," said Asia. "Oden told me something about the folks who landed on Newell Island from Ponki Point, the same area where Gordon found Carl. The Gages and their handyman and Mrs. White. Oden's related somehow to one of the rescuers, but the story was kind of jumbled coming out. Did your great-grandpa write about him?"

"Sam Bray!" said Wes. His gray eyes sparkled in the afternoon light. They sat on the dune just up from the jetty, facing the Sentinel Lighthouse to the east. The sky was full of the whitest of clouds, some of which resembled the swipes of a bristle brush dragged through white oil paint.

"Yes, he wrote about Sam."

Asia handed Wes the black spiral notebook. And so Wes read one more entry as the evening tide turned and the sharp mineral scent of ocean played once again over the cooling sand.

Wednesday, September 21, 1938
Newell Island, Connecticut

Sam Bray's half-tailed gray cat dove under Sam's cot an hour ago and would not be persuaded to emerge. The keening wind set Sam on edge too, so he took refuge in the last of the rum. As he reverently prepared his pipe for service, the one he tied with string to precisely fit the gap in his front teeth, a loud bang on the door startled his evening reverie.

When Sam opened his front door, a man, shirtless and shoeless, fell into the one-room cabin.

"What happened to you?!" Sam said, pulling his pipe back out of his mouth.

"I traveled on a bathtub and a roof across the bay from Ponkipaug Point. There's—" It was all the stranger could say as he tried to stand up and fell over again.

"Here! Come in and get warm!" Sam gently dragged the man by his shoulders over to his cot next to the wood-burning stove.

"What's yer name?" Sam asked as he lifted the man into a sitting position.

"Roy."

"Mine's Sam. Take your pants off, Roy," Sam said, settling his overcoat around Roy's shoulders. "We'll hang 'em up to dry! Beastly out there! Get some ginger tea in ya." Sam poured water into his one beat-up aluminum pot.

"But there's more—" Roy said. Sam interrupted before he could finish.

"Won't help you much now to be gabbing away. Gimme them pants! Wish I had decent food to offer," Sam said, scanning the food cupboard. It consisted of a board nailed above a tiny wooden table holding a bag of cornmeal and a can of salt. He'd planned to head into town with his boss, the farm owner, tomorrow to get food and supplies.

"Wasn't planning on company. Got a pan of day-old gingerbread." He rubbed his gray beard with thumb and forefinger as if devising a new way to conjure up food.

Roy fell back on the cot. As he began to warm up, the pain from his ribs was colossal, but he wouldn't tell Sam. Other people needed Sam now.

"There's more people out there. Lots more! The bay is full of houses and part of houses and docks and bathtubs. And people, kids too! All those cottages on Ponkipaug Point. One by one the ocean pushed them into the bay." Roy stopped, it was too much to bear. Tears streamed down his cheeks.

"What?!!" Sam said. He scratched his scraggly beard more fiercely.

"I'm telling you: There are more people out there!"

"Why didn't you tell me, my friend! You stay here."

Sam grabbed his kerosene lantern and dashed out in his bib overalls and coarse cotton shirt, leaving his coat around Roy Cotrillo's shoulders. Roy wiped his tears on a sleeve.

As the wind lessened, Roy shut his eyes against the memories that would stay within his body and soul and appear vivid behind closed eyelids. The cold, the fear. How the ocean underneath you and swirling around you metes out mercy to only a few. Its buoyancy only a deceptive gesture of benign neglect until there's no more air for your lungs and its iodine depth hangs its anvil on your ankles.

Back outside, the worst had passed, although there was still a nasty gusting wind. Sam walked through neighboring fields, his nostrils filling with the scent of smashed pumpkins. He navigated easily through copes of flattened bushes that had been waist high that morning. Not more than a hundred yards in the direction of the Pawcatuck River he encountered jumbled debris piled over his head: the upside-down Vs of chunks of roofs, doors, floors, pieces of chairs, iceboxes, whole trunks and chests of drawers. And Annette White, who lay on the narrow beach.

Sam bent over her. She was staring up at the stars, but her breathing was steady. As if she were waiting for him to find her. She'd sustained a shallow gash above her left temple.

"Where's Ivy?" she whispered. "I don't think I locked the back door. I—"

"Don't try to talk a lot, ma'am," Sam said gently. "Are you hurt bad?"

"I don't know," she whispered.

"Okay," Sam said. "I'm going to bring you inside. To my house." Sam put an arm around her and pulled her to her feet. Her legs gave out and she fell down. He positioned her so she could walk with Sam bearing half her weight. As they moved along the beach, Sam called to others to follow him and his lantern light.

He led Annette and two others back to the cabin, settled them in around the stove or on the cot, poured tea, and went back out. He traveled along the shore of the Pawcatuck River below the Black River Dam, his lantern bright along a dark coast. His was the only light burning for miles. The whole coast had lost electricity a couple hours before. Sam hadn't noticed the power outage. His household needs were fueled by wood and kerosene.

As Sam gathered in eleven storm refugees, he marveled at the brightness of the moon and stars. The brightest he'd ever seen.

A man from the fourth house on Ponkipaug Point, now perched on Sam's cane-bottom chair, found the pan of

y

gingerbread. He passed it around the crowded cabin.

"I love these raisins," Roy said, after swallowing his first bite.

Another man in the corner, from a couple houses over on Ponkipaug Point, examined his hunk of gingerbread. He grunted and then said, "I'd say they're flies."

Roy's laughter hurt his aching ribs. But he murmured thanks for bathtubs, rag dolls, gingerbread with flies, dry land, Sam, and his wife and son Ben.

Friday, September 28, 2018
Ponkipaug Point, Rhode Island

Vieve was still curious about where they'd imprisoned Jack West, for ransom as Richard had guessed. Was it that same tunnel that Marley and she had crouched near and overheard some nefarious meeting? Oden showed her the spot. It was the same place; there were even still a few spots of dried blood in the entrance to the tunnel.

Oden and Vieve emerged out of the Stairway to Hell just after Munin landed with his next find, another flat piece of metal. Oden laughed.

"After that stash Richard and I found in my room, it occurred to me that Munin has been catching and dismembering drones," Oden said, holding out his forearm. "Aerial dog fights!" Munin rose from the cement slab where he'd dropped the drone fragment and alighted on Oden's arm.

Vieve was astonished to get such a close-up view of a raven. The impressive bill and intelligent gaze. The black sculptural perfection of wing and body line. And *what?* Did the raven actually just *wink* at her? She thoroughly understood now why Carl had had such affection for this strange man and his raggedy companions.

Vieve thanked Oden for showing her Jack West's prison and then walked out to the end of the point. Jack West, who'd declined to go down the Stairway to Hell, joined Vieve as she moved down the trail away from the fort.

Low tide. Dayton was there marking out a grid with thin poles. Vieve sat just a bit down from the swallow nest bank before the start of the rocks and cobbles and watched the sun slide lower. Glancing up, she saw Dayton now standing next to her. He was admiring the late afternoon glory in the sky as if he owned it.

"What are you gridding out?" She pointed to the spot and shivered when she looked at the dock posts. "That's where they tied up Richard."

"The chamber of commerce and the marina want to explore removing these dock posts now, apparently. After the...eh...incident with Richard. Ghastly! Since I'm doing survey work out here already, they hired me to make sure there are no, as they called them, native artifacts that would be disturbed. Most of the older native villages were farther out. But you never know. Plus there could be something interesting here related to the fort. Between you and me, though, I don't think they're going to get town or state permission to remove the dock posts given they are really an offshore historical artifact. Anyway, I can think of much better ways to spend the money."

"Maybe it's Richard pushing for the docks to be removed," said Vieve. "I was surprised by Richard's response after his ordeal."

"How so?" Dayton sat down beside Vieve. She felt a peaceful calm descend around her. Jack West returned from a jaunt around the west side of the point and settled on the other side of Vieve. Something deep inside her settled too.

"You really want to hear?" Vieve asked.

"Yes," said Dayton. "Tell me."

"Well," Vieve said. "I don't really talk about this much, but

Richard used to basically torture me when we were kids."

"Oh?" Dayton, genuinely curious.

"Yes, innocently at first, I guess. Chasing me with long strands of that green demonic-looking seaweed the tide hurls up around here."

Dayton nodded and bent a knee on which he rested his arms, continuing to listen.

"Then it turned into torture. He tried to hold me underwater near that jetty over there. Several times."

"Really!" Dayton said. "What—?!"

"Well, the whole thing is a very long story. I don't want to bore you."

"Actually, Vieve, I'm interested. But perhaps you just wanted to enjoy the sunset in peace."

Vieve smiled. "Peace. Sunset. Could things be so simple?" She stroked Jack West and frowned.

"What? You can't disapprove"—he swept his hand forward—"of this sunset I've so painstakingly arranged for your pleasure."

She smiled at him. Peace, sunset, Dayton. Could things be this simple? It was both too obvious and too much to ask for.

"No, it's beautiful. Grand actually. I was just thinking of the murals. The gazebo. I don't know whether it really was successful. I think we could have simplified and made the whole thing more healing for folks."

Dayton looked into Vieve's face. "Are you kidding? I think otherwise, and I'm not alone. I've heard people talk, at the dig, in JohnnyCakes, on Main Street. You showed those with broken hearts and scorching memories that no matter who or what has at them, our imperfect love for ourselves and our neighbors is still our greatest treasure. We can transform disaster with our memories and our deeds."

Vieve was surprised by Dayton's words. She hadn't realized he was so touched by the memorial. She felt a warm rush of pleasure. That's what she had been going for in her paintings—her work—but only briefly touched on. Or only one to one, not from a whole community.

Dayton hesitated, looking at the rock-strewn sand and then back at Vieve. "I happen to know, from Asia, who talked of you so glowingly at one of our dig get-togethers, that you had two wrenching marriage situations. I can only imagine how painful that must be. To try to heal from. Move on."

Dayton faced the sunset. "I have a different sort of pain in the heart. A fiancée leaving me for no really good reason. It's really put me off, well, women, relationships. There's so much stimulation with the dig that I hadn't really missed it until...."

He looked out over the dock posts, losing their distinguishing forms in the dusk. Then he turned to Vieve, who was already peering at his face.

"Until you walked up the steps of my deck," he said.

Vieve stroked Jack West and then rested her arm along his side, enjoying his solid warmth.

"There is often someone for you," said Dayton. "When you stop looking for her, she appears. I'm told."

Vieve, still watching Dayton's face, said, "I felt something that night too. But I thought it was just, 'Oh, here's a handsome guy.'"

Dayton actually blushed.

"But yet, you seemed different than anyone I've met."

Dayton picked up a half-dozen small stones from the beach and then let them slide off his palm one by one.

"But then Marley and I were in this weird limbo thing. I don't know if you knew, but he wanted to keep on and I wanted to keep it just friends. I just wanted peace."

"That doesn't work, does it?" Dayton said turning toward Vieve, smiling.

"I'm not sure. It might. From my end, it does. Did. Well, not really. Hah!"

They watched a gull wheel in to land at The Kitchen.

"I'm also, like you, on the sober path." Dayton looked down at the sand and closed his eyes briefly, as if remembering, perhaps, some sharp thing that put him on the sober path.

"A rocky path indeed." Vieve twisted her mouth. She thought of Carl. Tears poised themselves on her lower eyelids.

Dayton put a hand over Vieve's. "You can never really hide ever again on this path. No place to escape to. But you're never alone." Dayton squeezed her hand and said, "I should get back to the grid."

"And I should get back. I've got to—" Suddenly, Vieve wasn't sure what would be more important than this sunset with Dayton.

Dayton leaned in and kissed Vieve. When Dayton pulled away from her, Vieve touched his cheek with her fingertips.

"Wow. I didn't...well, anyway," Dayton said, and then he cleared his throat. "Vieve, would you like to...have dinner with me this weekend?"

"Yes. I would. Very much."

"Good," Dayton said. "I'll call you. Well...good. Actually great!" Dayton smiled at her and walked away to put one more pole in his grid.

Vieve felt her heart again within her chest. Glowing. What he had said about the memorial, it reminded her of when she slid to the floor, wine fueled, and pondered the magic of Marley's panels. She knew she was getting close to that place in her own art. A form and expression beyond what she'd mastered, pulling her forward to a new place of expression. To some new connection with the people around her. What Carl wrote in his last letter.

"The blue light is in our hearts," Vieve whispered to Jack West.

Vieve stood up and felt Kyle's presence lighten. Her sea glass watch slid a few inches down her arm. She noticed how the setting sun caught the cool green glass and transformed it into a magical crystal flashing gold. How wonderful it was to be loved by Uncle Carl, with a heart as big as the ocean. He was still with her.

And her own heart felt possibility again. Dayton found a place she'd hid from everyone. And now—

Vieve looked down in response to an urgent nudge against her shin. Jack West stood, a bandaged paw raised, onyx eyes gleaming. *Where to?*

ACKNOWLEDGEMENTS

Thank you to my beta readers: Cindy Meise, Mary Ann Campbell, and Joe Ludwig. Your time, insights, and critical eyes are much appreciated.

Many thanks to the reference staff at the Westerly Public Library in Rhode Island for helping me access the microfiche of the *Westerly Sun* from September 21, 1938 to the end of December 1938 and for their help in tracking down other resources related to the storm. I greatly appreciate the library's stewardship of the many hurricane stories and images.

Most of all, many thanks to my husband, James W. Supplee, for his steady encouragement, belief in my work wherever it leads, and joy in our life together.

ABOUT THE AUTHOR

Sally Ann Sims is a writer and conservation scientist. Sally's fiction combines literary, suspense, thriller, and romance elements. Her first novel, *Halt at X, A North of Boston Novel*, explores the quirky, ambition-laced world of philanthropic fundraising, the joys and challenges of ex-racehorse rehab, and how to survive when your world comes unraveled...and someone's out for you. Sally's literary influences include M.L. Stedman, Alexander McCall Smith, Anne Tyler, Jane Urquhart, and Rita Mae Brown. Literature, art, history, and nature—human nature and the outdoor kind—are her passions.

    She holds a BA in English and an MS in conservation biology. Before earning her Master's degree, Sally worked as a technical editor and philanthropic fundraiser. She also has published personal essays in the *Christian Science Monitor*. Living on the East Coast, she now splits her time between writing novels and consulting on wildlife conservation and climate change adaptation.

    If you enjoyed reading this book, please spread the word! Leave a review on Amazon.com and Goodreads.com.

    To hear about new releases and other updates, join the Sally Ann Sims Readers' Group at www.sallyannsims.com.

Explore the Hurricane of 1938

To learn more about this powerful storm, explore the Hurricane of 1938 in New England through:

Sudden Sea—The Great Hurricane of 1938 by R.A. Scott (paperback)
American Experience: The Hurricane of '38 (video at youtube.com)

Made in the USA
Middletown, DE
15 October 2018